The Weight of Cloth

A Novel

The Weight of Cloth

A Novel

Dee Mallon

Copyright© 2024 by Dee Mallon
All rights reserved.

This is a work of fiction. All incidents, dialogue, and characters with the exception of some well-known historical figures and some lesser known figures found in Eliza Lucas Pinckney's letters, are products of the author's imagination. Where real-life historical figures show up, their circumstances, words, and personalities are entirely made up and not meant to depict actual events or to lessen this novel's entirely fictional nature. In all other ways, any resemblance to persons living or dead is entirely coincidental.

ISBN: 979-8-9906426-0-7 (ebook)
ISBN: 979-8-9906426-1-4 (paperback)
ISBN: 979-8-9906426-2-1 (IngramSpark paperback)
Library of Congress Control Number: 2024912723

Selections of Eliza Lucas Pinckney's published letters from *The Letterbook of Eliza Lucas Pinckney, 1739 – 1762*, edited by Elise Pinckney (Chapel Hill: University of North Carolina Press, 1972). Based on original documents from the South Carolina Historical Society.
Courtesy of the South Carolina Historical Society, Charleston.

Book design by Ken Potochnik
Cover design by Jonathan Sainsbury
Cover photograph © Dee Mallon

*Dedicated to the American enslaved
and their descendants,
in gratitude*

Contents

List of Characters

Part I
December 1737 – December 1738

Part II
January 1739 – September 1739

Part III
September 1739 – December 1739

Part IV
December 1740

Part V
May 1743 – May 1744

Epilogue
July 1758

Author's Note
Acknowledgements
About the Author

List of Characters

Lucas Family

George Lucas, British soldier/slaveowner, settled first on Antigua, later in Charles Town. Returns to Antigua, becomes Lt. Governor.

Millie (Mildrum), his wife.

Eliza, their older daughter, born 1722 on Antigua, schooled in England from age 11 to 14.

George, Tommy, and Polly, the other three Lucas children.

Grandparents of Lucas children live in Charles Town at Cross Winds.

Men employed at Wappoo Plantation

Craig MacIntyre, overseer, a Scotsman who's worked off his contract.

Nicholas Cromwell, white West Indian indigo expert hired by George Lucas.

Ambrose, black West Indian indigo expert hired later by George Lucas.

Pinckney Family

Charles Pinckney, born in South Carolina, educated in England, prominent lawyer, served many terms as Speaker of the Assembly.

Elizabeth, his first wife. They are childless.

Mary Bartlett, Elizabeth's niece on a long-term visit from England.

Bondwomen, mostly at Wappoo Plantation

July, born in Yoruba, middled aged, highly skilled seamstress and cook. Lost track of her three sons after being kidnapped.

Melody, born on Barbados, purchased by Lucas when pregnant with Moses. Neither man knows she's pregnant. About the same age as Eliza, beautiful, sings like an angel.

Saffron, born in Yoruba, just made the Middle Passage. Her gifts as a poet help her make sense of her brutal circumstances.

Maggie, Saffron's daughter, eight at auction, raped during Middle Passage.

Old Sarah, elder field hand with healing skills.

Phoebe, Polly's tag-along.

Binah, Mo's wife.

Nana Lucy, Cudjoe's mother, free by courtesy, owns property on peninsula, makes a living selling pastries.

Nell, house slave at Cross Winds.

Eubeline, house slave of Jackson's.

Bondmen on Wappoo Plantation

Cudjoe, key slave (entrusted to conduct plantation business), Wappoo's best river navigator, occasional blacksmith, literate. His wife (unnamed in novel) lives on another plantation.

Mo, Cudjoe's son.

Titus, crosses Atlantic with Saffron and Maggie. His twin brother kills himself during Middle Passage. He is a babalawo.

Caesar, young field hand, hobbled due to frequent attempts at running.

Indian Pete, field hand, a mustee of Pee Dee and African descent, plantation's most skilled hunter.

Abraham, field hand who shares patroller-deterrence tricks with Saffron.

Hercules, field hand, the most efficient collector of news on the street.

Quashee, field hand, literate, mixed race (white father), highly skilled carpenter sometimes loaned out to other slaveowners. After building Charles and Eliza a mansion on East Bay, he is freed by Charles and goes on to amass property and slaves of his own. Baptized as John Williams.

Noah, Melody's first son, fathered by a sailor who raped her on Barbados.

Moses, Melody's second son, fathered by first owner, James Whittaker. Can pass for white.

Benji and James, young orphaned brothers.

Neighbors and Acquaintances

Willard Tilton, bachelor with acreage abutting Wappoo Plantation.

Mrs. Woodward, close friend, lives on Wappoo Creek.

Mary Chardon, Mrs. Woodward's widowed daughter, later marries Pastor Huston.

Henri Dutarque, a Huguenot merchant trading in deer skins.

Sarah Rutledge born *Hext*, widow who marries *Andrew Rutledge,* Irish lawyer.

Sarah Hext, her daughter, marries Andrew's brother, *John Rutledge,* a doctor.

Colonel Hext, Sarah the elder's brother-in-law; wife and daughter killed by Stono rebels.

Mr. Deveaux, neighbor.

John Drayton, son of Thomas from Barbados, both with homes on the Ashley River.

Suzanne, John Drayton's first wife, dies of smallpox along with their two children.

Charlotte, John Drayton's second wife, daughter of Lt. Governor William Bull.

Doctor and Mrs. Jackson, neighbors.

James Whittaker, cane grower/slave owner on Barbados, Melody's first owner, father of her second child, Moses.

Rebecca Whittaker, wife of James.

Mrs. Boddicott, Eliza's guardian in England, later guardian to her brothers, and then her sons.

Insurrection Characters

Cato, literate, born in South Carolina, famous for forging passes for others.

Jema or Jemmy, Angolan saltwater, practices Catholicism, speaks Portuguese.

Thomas Gibbs, Highway Commissioner hired to supervise canal crew.

Robert Bathhurst, clerk at Hutchinson's Depot.

Epilogue Characters

Mrs. Crokus, caregiver for stroke-ridden Charles Pinckney

Charles Pinckney, surviving nephew of Eliza's husband.

Charles Cotesworth, Thomas, and Harriott, Eliza and Charles's three children

Nanka, Mo and Binah's daughter.

Jacob, free black deliveryman in Philadelphia.

Anthony Benezet, Huguenot abolitionist in Philadelphia.

Bellfast, runaway from Thomas Wright's plantation.

Cinnamon, runaway, love interest of Maggie.

Saffron and Indian Pete's son, unnamed.

To see notes about the history behind the novel, go to The Weight of Cloth page on deemallon.com and click on the link "History Notes."

Part I

December 1737 – December 1738

December 1737

Stamped Spine
Sally aka Melody, Barbados

Keepers carry no esteem for birthdays. Teeth and brawn, yes, cooking and cutting skills, yes. They wonder, "What can she do for me?" They wonder, "How compliant is this one?" A white ladder of scars on the shin doesn't matter since every cutter's machete slips now and again, but an ugly net of scars on the back? "Watch out," they think. "Might be a runner." Women better be broad in the hip, dropping babies like mares birthing foals in the barn. And they better breed apace, since everyone knows that a season or two in the brakes makes a woman barren. Another five years and a body tends to go cold. All told, seven years from block to grave counts as a pretty good run on a sugar plantation.

But birthdays? Never mind – a rough age suffices. That's why I don't know if I was sixteen or seventeen when I was sold, one Keeper to the next. But I did know something important for certain: I was carrying another baby. And this: men were fools.

Before Mama stopped talking, she told me about her last look of home: river rocks covered in indigo-dyed cloth. Two children crying in alarm. After the long walk to the sea and the long sick wait in a barracoon, she was shoved onto a ship called the *Sally*. The captain was tall and Dutch and my father. Master Whittaker laughed when he came to find Mama was with child, as if it made him shrewd. "Two for one! Two for one," he'd honked. When I was born, First Owner thought himself mighty smart naming me Sally. But how many others were called Sally after that Guinea ship, that Dutch sea captain as father?

When the wind came off the sea a certain way, you could smell a slaver, long before you can even see a chip of sail out yonder. That part of Mama's story I didn't need to wonder on, since I'd been hit hard with that stink. Imagining my father came easy too. My heart-shaped face. My narrow nose, wavy hair. And since Mama was tiny and I'm tall, my long legs too.

Imagining what nasty Slave Trader-Captain-Father did to Mama didn't take any real thinking either since I been roughed. Twice. The first time gave me Noah. He got his name after hearing Bible reading with Mistress Rebecca and Daughter. The ark and the animals, marching two by two. A better kind of sailor than a slave-trading captain.

Noah will always know his birthday: December 27, 1735. He's coming up on two.

When my bloods came, my voice turned from spring water to honey. I thought this only happened to boys, but it happened to me. I didn't keep my singing to myself, but I didn't let it rise up in any old place either. Out in the brakes, I sang with the others, and after Noah came, I sang him to sleep. Once Master pulled me into the house, I wouldn't let my voice rise up if any buckra was lingering about.

For harbor runs, Master sent Big Joe and me together. It was "Keep an eye on her" this and "Don't let her out of your sight" that. But one blustery day when Big Joe had an errand with the cooper, I begged him to let me wait outside. Before I could even lean back and take light to my face, a sailor dropped like a monkey off a near mast and slunk over to the wharf. It looked like he was coming to meet someone. He was.

"Over fast" was one way to think on it. Another way to think on it was "It went on and on." He tore me up good, but I knew the harsh stinging was nothing next to what would haunt me ever after. He walked off, straightening his hat. Jaunty. I stumbled toward the water, where the slap-slapping small waves sounded like flesh meeting flesh. I threw up. The sky swirled. I could've sworn the harbor called out, "Jump, Sally, jump!"

Oh, think on it! My frock heavy with seawater, going under, the ocean's mercy taking blood and sticky man-stuff off me. Sinking into sweet forgetting. Surrender. Instead, I picked up my head cloth, squatted, and wiped up quick. That fouled rag went into the sea. I watched it hump up a bubble of air, float in sorry, bloody swags, and finally sink.

What part of me went down with that rag?

Next time was in the pantry. Wasn't I just minding Master's business chopping onions for supper? I thought he'd traveled to the harbor with Mistress, so I was mid-song when he came in, sweaty and silent. I wiped my hands and waited — for what? He turned and locked the door. Then I knew for what. Something roared in my ears, making the pantry go a-fog. Through it, he hard-whispered, "Oh God! Oh God! Dear Jesus, I resisted!" Like that tar in town, he finished fast, but unlike him, Master pulled out real careful, making sure not a drop of him stained my frock.

Later on, pain snuck into my hips. Got me sore and slow-walking, especially when it rained. That rough morning gave me something else too — a deep and wide mean streak. I swear it glittered. Before the pantry morning, I might sulk and idle out of spite, drop a piece of porcelain here and there, but now anger clung to my side like a needy twin. Anger sharpened things, cleared my mind of dross. My wrath pounded like surf, and if I was to stay alive, I'd have to learn to ride it. Or dress it up in silk.

Did he really say, "Dear Jesus, I resisted" as if God gave credit for holding off on sin? And claiming I tempted him with song just showed how deep his foolishness go. He was a sinner, plain and simple — busy trying to pinch down his taint and cast himself an innocent subject to bewitchment. There was no spell-casting. Only defiling sin.

His hands took to shaking — just a little, but I saw. Did Mistress? Now when I came in a room, he studied her, which was plenty odd, since before he used to ignore her and shoot looks at me. Was he trying to be a better man? Maybe he just needed a good drink of ugly before looking on me again. I told you meanness found a home.

Before even a week passed, Master came back into the pantry. At the sound of his steps I grabbed the knife and held it firm. He carried something about the size of a fat slice of bread. A book! Gold lettering stamped the spine. He held it out, but I didn't take it and I didn't set that knife down either. The door was open and the breech buttons closed, but still my breath went ragged.

It wasn't courage making me refuse, or anger, I just couldn't move. I felt like a tree or a stalled thunder cloud. He kept holding out that book.

"Take it. Take it!" But I would not. Finally, I pointed at the floor with the knife.

"Lay it down and I'm obliged."

Master took a sharp breath. It looked like he was going to strike me with the book, but then, glaring hard, he complied. When he rose, he ragged on about how I best beg the Lord for forgiveness, my salvation being at stake and so on. A sinning fool preaching hollow words. But I knew nothing was gonna turn that skinny cane grower into a decent man.

He left. My knees sagged. I set the knife down, red stripes showing on my palm from gripping so hard. I squinted at the book. A Bible? Was he aiming to please his god with a little bribe? Or did he think he was actually aiding my salvation? Like a machete flashing in the sun, I suddenly understood that he was gonna sell me right quick. Put me in his pocket. With Mistress sniffing about, it wouldn't be enough to send me back into the brakes. Best be rid of me. Never mind the man up-island who dressed his favorite in jewels or all the mixed children running about in rags. Master Whittaker styled himself a preacher and that mattered to Mistress who took a mighty pride in his knowledge of Scripture. To hear her tell it at one of her all-lady teas, that knowledge helped Mistress's father overlook the low-class speech, the humble roots in England and wasn't it grand what was possible in the colonies?

The gold lettering on the spine caught the light. I waited until Master left the house to pick it up. The brown leather felt so smooth, the pages like butterfly wings. Holding the book, a hurting ambition rose up: I would learn to read. It wasn't enough to speak good English. It wasn't enough to learn French sitting by Daughter and her tutor. I would learn to read, and I would teach my children to read. I rubbed my apron with that promise.

That morning, anger partnered up with hunger, and without my knowing how, together they flung down a path to freedom. I didn't know where or when or whose, but I knew that someday a road to freedom would course by near enough to matter. I closed the Bible and held it between my two palms and thought, "So this is how it feels to own something."

Master Whittaker did put me in his pocket and quicker than I would've thought. Just three days after giving me that book, I heard him talking about me to a traveler on the porch, trying so hard to tamp down his soggy vowels. I crept near. The traveler spoke clippety-cloppety English, the kind buckra esteem. But he was lying. Even if I hadn't known with his first sentence, I'd have known with the second. We all knew how to listen to white speech like a doctor with his ear on a sick man's chest so as to scout out the lies. We learned to tell a spoon-sized lie from one as wide as a cane brake. There were the stand-alone lies and those that clustered like grapes on the vine. We knew how a single lie might mean one thing in a silky whisper and another thing growled at the point of a knife.

"What about that young mulatto singing in the alfalfa fields yesterday," he asked. "She'd make a fine tag-along for my daughter." Something about moving to South Carolina. Me being the right age and all. Man didn't even know I was for sale! I couldn't see Master Whittaker's face right then, but I swear I could feel his grin. He was upping his price for sure and he wasn't throwing Noah in to sweeten any deal. He'd charge for my boy, too.

They were two fools striking a deal.

Somebody else's lies were gonna matter now.

January 1738

Pearls and a Song
Eliza, Antigua

Father came home from Barbados a changed man. The waves of wheat-colored hair were the same, his shoulders recognizably broad, and his wit flashed sharp as ever. But he was different. For some time, the ebullience of his return masked the transformation, and I later suspected he fostered that as a ruse.

The young ones, Polly and Tommy, tripped over the ecstatic hounds to be embraced first. George inserted himself right after. The dogs waggled such a greeting they seemed near to shrugging off their skins. One wet the floor.

"Bettany! Bettany," chimed out Mother, "bring a rag!" Not a trace of irritation.

Even before the puddle was wiped away, Father began pulling gifts out of his pockets: a caramel sweet for my five-year-old sister, two lead balls for my brothers; a handkerchief with tatted edges for me.

"Those have seen action, men! Get to the battlements!" The boys dashed out to the terrace, where many a military maneuver had already been acted out. For Mother's gift, Father ushered us into the parlor. Polly curled under Mother's arm. My sister had a way of amplifying others' joy.

"It must be from the sea," she gurgled, one cheek bulging with the caramel. Like all five-year-olds, Polly was given to silly exaggerations, non sequiturs, and many a misguided conclusion. But unlike most, she also sometimes uttered statements marked by preternatural accuracy. It never paid to dismiss her out of hand.

Mother opened the small green leather box, her face lighting up in pleasure, her mouth forming a small "o." "Why, it *is* from the sea!" she said. A string of pearls. Father beamed, but his forehead creased in some unspoken query or worry. Polly clapped, not because she was right, but because the gift offered adornment to her beloved mother. A very special necklace, indeed.

"But George! The extravagance!"

Polly stood on the couch to attempt the clasp, and when she couldn't manage, I performed the honors. My sister jumped up and down on the cushion, prompting Father to grab her and in a series of well-practiced maneuvers, turn her upside-down to dangle her by the ankles as if to make stolen coins rain down out of her pockets. Mother worried about head clobbers and knickers showing, but in her current mood, all she said was, "George, please, she's getting a little old for that." Polly very nearly lost her caramel. Father righted her quickly, sat her on his lap, and issued an overdone exhalation, as if worn out.

Several slaves delivered parcels into the hallway. Behind them came a mulatto about my age and a small boy, both of them looking bewildered. Mother raised an eyebrow. I too was confused. I thought Father had gone to Barbados to purchase two hale men. Before departing, he'd talked about how two more male heads in the stable would allow favorable terms of credit from banks in Newport or Boston, in turn allowing the purchase of more land. Most sugar farmers hereabouts were enlarging their operations or leaving the business altogether.

Father said nothing, instead grabbing Polly's braids and snapping them a time or two. "Giddyup, horsey!" An old game. Without looking at Bettany, he directed her to show the new arrivals to the cabins and find a pallet for them to share. "Giddyup, horsey!" My sister laughed so hard she nearly choked, prompting a round of back pats. Was Father avoiding Mother's face? Mother, in the meantime, waited in an uncharacteristic silence. Father set Polly down and told her to run outside, "in case the troops need a nurse." He strode to the buffet and poured himself a glass of Madeira. I couldn't tell if this was the act of a satisfied man returned to his castle or that of a nervous husband in need of courage. I might not think this way, but I'd just spent four years in England where my guardian, Mrs. Boddicott, had been a little careless in her disclosures about my parents.

"Care for a glass, my dear?" After a silent pause, "Millie – would you rather some tea?"

I answered for both of us, "Tea would be nice." Father sat and swirled the wine, taking thoughtful sips and then holding the glass up to the light. By then, it was clear he had news and that perhaps it was unpleasant. Tea came, slave went, and he finally launched into what seemed a prepared speech.

We were to move to Carolina at last! It was decided – and why ever had it taken him so long to make up his mind? He'd had an epiphany of sorts on Barbados, all the pieces falling into place. A slave song had brought clarity –

imagine! Like a lawyer before the bench, he marched out his reasons. Yes, the balance of power among European nations seemed more or less stable, with treaties in place and black markets thriving and largely ignored, but armed conflict was inevitable.

"We're one intercepted shipment of molasses away from war." We'd heard this before, so the argument merely served to highlight that it was not circumstance that had changed but he himself. "The Spanish navy far surpasses ours, and now they aim to build ships in the only deepwater harbor in the West Indies."

Mother interrupted, "Cuba?"

"Indeed." Father leaned forward, elbows on knees, intent and slightly flushed and rattled on about Havana.

Mother grunted. "Maybe I'll take that glass of sherry, after all."

"You'd think after what the Negroes nearly pulled off last year –" Mother took a sip of her drink. "What are we now, five to one?"

"Six," Father answered. "Six slaves to every one of us."

Being only recently returned to Antigua it hadn't occurred to me to ask for details about the plot that had been uncovered while I was away. Maybe I should have listened to more of the political conversations at my fifteenth birthday party a few weeks ago, but I'd been flush with giddiness at being home and Bettany had made my favorite cake. The time hardly seemed right now. Besides, the West Indies were rife with stories about treachery at the hands of slaves, particularly by poison and arson, meaning the risks were clear enough.

Mother snapped, "You can't trust a one of them!"

Father stood and looked out at his three younger children playing on the sundrenched terrace. Mother's concurrence seemed more reflexive habit than indicative of a readiness to hear whatever was to follow. In a near plea, he said, "I could not square myself with God should harm come to you because of my reluctance or indecision." He sat back down. I kicked off my shoes and tucked my feet under my gown, knowing full well that the intensity of the moment precluded a scolding.

"There's financial promise in Carolina," Father continued. "Everyone knows the small sugar farms are doomed, not just here but on Barbados too. I know my father can stretch facts in service of a good story, but on the issue of rice, I think he's sound enough." According to Grandpapa, South Carolina was "a land of gentility where fortunes were waiting to be made." Every one of his letters from Charles Town asked in essence, "What are you waiting for?"

We'd heard it repeatedly: it took far fewer slaves to bring rice to market than sugar; processing rice was less dangerous than processing cane; Africans were arriving by the cargo-hold to Charles Town with rice-specific skills; British trade restrictions exempted South Carolina, letting Lowcountry planters avail themselves of favorable Dutch terms of credit and also to bypass the costly requirement of sailing first to England before heading to Spain and France, where the vibrant rice markets lay. Demand was high, price fluctuations minimal. Why mess about with cane?

Furthermore, the recent innovation of sluices and canals was extending viable rice land farther and farther inland, compensating for the riverways' tidal ebb and flow. Such innovation dovetailed with the fairly recent conversion of the South Carolina territory from proprietary land grants to royal colony, meaning acreage could be acquired with minimal or no outlay. The new colony offered settlers parcels based on how many heads were in their household (including a reduced count for slaves). Once a planter surveyed a property and filed the survey at the courthouse, memorializing his claim, it was official. He owned the land. It was that simple. With slaves as collateral and no taxes owed for two years, often no initial outlay was required. A colony that had been owned by nine men broke up into parcels owned by many.

"There's a harpsichord waiting for you, Daughter," Father said. To Mother he added, "Seventeen hands, cleared fields, a furnished house, and a reliable Scotsman in charge. It's simply a matter of transporting ourselves there."

"I've read the letters too remember," Mother said sourly.

Father kept on, extolling Charles Town as a place of "culture, society, where life is lived in the English manner." Shopkeepers were very nearly keeping up with Continental trends. "And look who's leaving the West Indies – the Royalls are packing up as we speak and the Draytons left Barbados years ago." Father downed his sherry, and Mother shuddered.

"Would you bring me my wrap?" Mother might be chilled, but I was just confused. If this decision was so very rational, why did it cast such a pall? What was Father not saying, and why wasn't Mother asking more probing questions? I expected her to object, not so much to inform the outcome (could she inform the outcome?), but rather to expose some inconsistency or vanity on Father's part.

Father returned with her wool challis shawl and draped it about her shoulders. She cleared her throat and raised the matter of the boys' upcoming travel to England for schooling.

"I thought we agreed to spare them double voyages." Mother pulled the wrap close, the new pearls now hidden from view. "Or rather, I thought we had yet to agree on anything." She looked smaller somehow, more like a person trying to protect herself from harm than one hoping to avoid a draft. "Safety before convenience I understand, Husband, but this isn't a trifling concern. So do tell, were you feigning concern for your sons' well-being before or was your consideration of my opinion mere frippery? I am to be soothed but not heard? If so, what a shocking demotion I've undergone."

Here were the barbs at last! I fully expected battle to ensue, but Mother slumped back into the sofa. A barbudo warbled from the nearest lime tree. "Wake up, wake up!" it seemed to call, even though warm afternoon light slanted into the parlor. Just then Bettany returned with the new girl. Father waved them in.

"I knew we'd need a tag-along for the children. I've named her Melody. Were you to make her one of your linen frocks, Millie, she'd do us proud. House training's somewhat limited, but I was given to understand she's a quick study."

Mother gave the slave a dull once-over.

"A fine-looking specimen, don't you think?" Father asked. He drummed his fingers on his knee, and I found myself wishing he'd clap that jittery hand on his mouth. Mother's quietude nearly shimmered, reminding me of the taut restraint that predatory animals exhibit just before attack. She shifted her gaze from mulatto to husband.

Father continued to look at the slave, though, and praised her. "Good provenance. Actually, better than good. Father was a Dutch sea captain. Never hurts to bring in a strain of intelligence!" He gave Melody a half-smile. Since it was common knowledge that a few years working the cane brakes often rendered female cutters barren, Father mentioned the two-year-old.

"Of course, sellers can lie to suit their purpose, but our man on Barbados, while decidedly odd, gave me no reason to doubt his veracity. That the boy is hers, I mean. A quadroon, by the by." Mother blanched. Father now tested the limits of decorum by stating the obvious advantages of breeding and selling quadroons. I untucked my legs and slid my shoes back on. It was all I could do not to ask Father whether he'd left his manners on Barbados as well as his indecision.

"But why buy the boy?" Mother asked softly.

"Just part of the deal," Father replied dismissively. "Oh, and wait until you hear her sing – voice like an angel! Hence the name, Melody. Suits, wouldn't you say? Well, how could you – you've yet to hear her sing." To my astonishment, Father demanded that the slave give us a song right then and there. Melody hung in the hallway in awkward delay. Meanwhile, Mother's shawl had fallen off her shoulders, and instead of reaching to pull it back up, she placed two fingers on the new string of pearls as if in reconsideration of the gift. She glanced about in the disoriented manner of a child just woken. She continued to avoid looking at Melody.

"Bettany!" Father barked, as if the slave weren't ten feet away. "A pot of tea and a few savories. Hip-hip!" Bettany disappeared and Melody watched her, perhaps wishing she could follow. Father crossed the room and with brisk efficiency began unpacking items into the secretary from one of his bags. The slave tentatively began a ditty. "Oh now," Father interjected. "With more feeling! Pretend you're in the alfalfa fields, like the day we met."

The day we met?

At that moment, Tommy burst in, sweaty and rouged in exertion or fever. He climbed up onto Mother in panicky appeal and collapsed, head on her lap. Tommy's need jarred Mother out of her reactive dismay as perhaps nothing else could. She placed a solicitous palm on his forehead.

"Oh dear! He's hot. Eliza, pet, show her to the well and bring us cool water and a cloth."

Her.

George, Polly, and the two hounds sped past us on our way out. They were not fazed in the least by their brother's crumping and why should they be? He exhibited one vague symptom after another and had as yet survived every one. I showed Melody where the well was, and together we returned with a full pail and a cloth. Not for the first time, it struck me that the timing of Tommy's malaise served some hidden purpose. There he was, limp and mewling at the very height of Mother's wounding – the slave song deferred. Meanwhile, Father put quills here, ink bottle there. To my astonishment, he continued his narrative, distractedly explaining how hearing Melody sing that day on Barbados had changed everything. What a weight had been lifted! What clarity imparted! I looked Melody over as if to scout out the source of her power.

Even if the mulatto had been homely, her mere association with Father's clarity and release from indecision would've been insulting to Mother, but she was fine-looking indeed. She had perfectly aligned features, with large, deep-set eyes, liquid in their darkness and at once keen, mysterious, and feminine. Her nose did not flatten into the broad, animalistic shape of so many Negroes, a fact no doubt attributable to her Dutch father. Even her ear lobes, showing at head scarf's edge, had the appearance of jewels. Furthermore, the slave was graced with the kind of curves that many gentlemen find appealing, or so I'm told – what did I know of these things? Not only was I untested in matters of love, at the moment my lens was complicated by empathy. There I sat, straining to see the slave through the eyes of my mother, who sat next to me, trying not to see the slave through her husband's eyes. I drank my tea in swift gulps.

Rifling through his bag, Father nattered on. I attempted to excuse him on account of his distraction – for surely, had he glanced at Mother, he would have stopped himself. But with his back to the room, out spooled the damaging monologue. One moment he described a near-religious experience (the sea! the song!), the next he expressed pride in a shrewd purchase. Was it a transformational encounter or a serviceable errand of acquisition? I struggled to understand how it could be both.

Once, when Mother visibly flinched and Father saw, instead of silencing himself, he defended his commentary. "Oh, Millie! You ought hear these words as you would remarks about a well-made escritoire," he scolded. "Or a particularly handsome horse."

"I can't recall the last time I expected a handsome horse to serve my tea," Mother retorted.

"Dear Wife, have you lost all practical sense? Don't forget the head rights," Father lectured. "Both she and the boy will count when it comes time to acquire more land."

As awful as all this was, I had no reason to believe Father was faithless. I assumed that a man with something to hide would take more care with his speech. His casual tone was marked by inconsideration, but it didn't seem designed to hide an indiscretion. Even absent untoward congress, however, the slave's capacity to move my father, even if unwittingly and involuntarily, had to be deeply offensive to my mother. It didn't matter one whit that Mother had consistently avoided discussions about South Carolina, allowing the grip of her homesickness for England to render her passive and coolly disinterested. It also didn't matter that moving to South Carolina might be the right decision, long overdue.

Of course, it was too early to know. I knew not to display even the slightest hint of excitement about Charles Town because Mother would feel it as betrayal. Her stubborn misery often distorted perception, causing her to see slights where none existed. At the moment, however, I found it easy to align myself with her, for I hardly recognized the man in our midst. Where was the gracious figure formerly known as my father? He sat down, clasped his hands at his chest, looking like a philosopher about to opine. And oh Lord, opine he did!

Mother held her sherry in one hand and used the other to stroke Tommy's damp hair. She peered down into the mahogany liquid, as if wondering where its soothing powers had gone. My brother's eyes closed, his breathing evened out, sleep at hand. If only the rest of us could relax, but there was Father, referring yet again to Melody's provenance – her Dutch father!

Clearly, it was Father who needed convincing of the transaction's wisdom, not us. Mother could've pressed harder on the obvious folly of buying the mulatto's son, pointing out that proof of fertility in no way imposed purchase, head rights notwithstanding. The fact that she was not making plain the precise measure of my father's foolishness suggested that Mother was laid low indeed.

Melody kept glancing over at Tommy. Eventually she seemed to screw up her courage to ask if there was any bark in the storeroom. Mother looked up at her angrily, as if being useful and kind could only add to the slave's egregiously exalted status. But since this was Tommy, she set aside her enmity and had me show the slave where we kept the Peruvian.

In the next week, my mother maintained a steely silence, showing her unhappiness with mewling sighs, obstinate refusals to look at the Negress, and a complete avoidance in training the girl. Mother should have been a font of domestic energy as we prepared to leave the island, but she languished and sulked. She made the mulatto serve her meals but managed never to refer to her by name. It was "you," or "New One" if Melody was present, and if she wasn't, "Jezebel."

One night after Mother slid upstairs in a pained silence, Father requested a recital. Melody came into the parlor hesitantly, looking around as if to say, "Why am I here?" or maybe, "Why isn't Mistress?" She didn't know where to stand, so I gestured toward the harpsichord. Haloed by the setting sun, she clasped her hands at her waist and looked for all the world like an accomplished soprano awaiting a tardy accompanist.

"Sing! Sing!" Father leaned into the hearth to light a narrow taper and then lit his postprandial pipe. Melody stood, unable or unwilling to begin. Father waved the taper out in her direction like a conductor before the orchestra. "Don't be shy!" He puffed his pipe. She began.

With the pipe clamped between his teeth, Father said, "Come now! With more feeling!" After a few false starts, she gave us her song. Or perhaps it would be more precise to say that she gave herself to the song and we happened to be near. Father closed his eyes in reverie, half-hidden behind clouds of tobacco smoke. Even as dismayed as I was on Mother's behalf, I too entered a fugue of appreciation. I tried to pinpoint what her voice was more like – silk, honey, a clarion call, or a cool running brook. I'd never heard anything like it.

The next night was the same, but with Mother present. Father lit up. The slave stood nervously by, until again Father's impatience made him bark, "Sing! Come now, girl!" And again, she sang. Even beginning with what I now recognized as reluctant hostility, Melody drew down heaven with her voice. How could one not be moved? And if I, a young woman uncomplicated by masculine attractions, found her music transporting, I couldn't begin to imagine how it must be for a man captivated by her beauty. Mother closed her eyes, perhaps hoping her expression passed for appreciation, but the muscle flexing along her jaw in tiny pulses suggested otherwise. If Father had bothered to look, he would have seen that his wife appeared to be bravely, but barely, enduring physical torture.

When Father did crack open his eyes, it was not to look at Mother, but rather to take in the slave. Did he think the miasma of tobacco smoke hid his interest? *Please, please, Mother, keep your eyes closed.* During what must have been song four or five, Mother opened her eyes and without so much as a glance in the direction of either Father or Melody picked a bobbin of thread and pin cushion out of the sewing basket and swiftly threaded three needles. Suddenly, there was linen on her lap. She plied her needle with a tense concentration, the light not being great. I watched her with brittle worry. She was making me a travel frock.

March 1738

Our Oak
Saffron, Wappoo Plantation, South Carolina

Auction men couldn't say Ifelayo so they called me Saffron. Ifelayo means "love is peace," but where was love? Where was peace? What does Saffron mean? Daughter Ewa, they named Maggie. Her Yoruban name means "beauty of God." What was the meaning of Maggie? Renaming came as casual violence, but what did they know? That cool spring morning, it struck me how keeping our real names hidden was good. Secret love. Hidden beauty.

The street's got six cabins, three and three facing. At supper, the cabins near the creek lay down blocky shadows while the cabins on my side lit up gold.

Behind the creekside cabins, water ribboned through grasses. Lovely grasses! They waved lively with wind some days. Beauty in plain sight. Behind us lay a small garden surrounded by a fence, rows stretching north. It was ours, that one. At the end of the street going toward Porch House, a road snaked past.

Two live oaks rose up like giants on Wappoo Plantation, mighty trunks with branches spreading wide in gestures of majesty. One oak grew on the cabin side of the road, the other on buckra side. Right off, I claimed the close oak as ours, and why not? It stood like a guardian, protecting, shielding. Let buckra keep yonder oak, along with everything else – the land, the dock, the barn, Igbo bones, Mende destinies, our mother tongues. They didn't need our oak too.

Ewa – I mean Maggie – sat between my knees dragging a finger along the old scar lining my jaw, reminding me of the North Cross River people back home who read carved calabashes. What tale does that scar tell? *Mama will never forsake you. Mama is still here.* No matter what they named me, I am still and always Mama and, for now anyhow, I'm still here.

Maggie needed that reassurance for not long ago on board that vile slaver, even before the home coast sank into the sea, we'd found out about the Captain's "dessert." How it was served every day after lunch, sometimes after supper too. How he liked blood and a little torture. How he took them in pairs – one he entered and groaned over, the other he strapped to the bedpost as unwilling witness. Male, female, young, old, but mostly female. He worked his way through our number. Had anything been made plain? *Fetch me a boy* or *Make it a child this time?* I was spared. Eight-year-old Maggie was not.

She was a daughter and a sister. That she would never see her father or her brother again was one kind of suffering. This was another.

Captain Flower was his name. "Flower" was one of the first English words I learned. Later, "deflower." My unstoppable attention to sound and meaning took a twisted path on the Atlantic where words gathered in elegy rather than celebration or wonder. Words tainted by theft and worse crimes. My daughter, so young, so little, and never innocent again.

Our live oak tree was so old it must've grown before the boats came and spread misery every which way. I can dream the way-back time as clear as I can see that dog lounging next to the men yonder. Before the first ship spit up black bodies, that tree hollered to the sun, took drinks of rain. Before the rice fields were cleared and bermed, it sprinkled light on the ground through its leaves, offering peeks of heaven through its canopy. Think on it – those very branches stretched to the sky before slave times. That was something. That was something worth holding on to. When our oak wasn't offering evidence of a time-before, it fluttered pretty shadows along the edges of my broken heart.

I had to tell someone about Titus – Taiiwa in our mother tongue. Don't ask why that seller made Taiiwa Titus, but he did. Titus had a twin on the slaver. His brother had climbed up on the ship's rail during exercise and flung himself in one swift gesture to the sharks below. A final grace. Always, sharks trailed alongside the Guinea, hoping for flesh. We women heard the thrashing from below and then the chaos breaking out up on deck. The Captain's dessert interrupted! Inventory losses not to be abided! He screamed for an hour. The sailors erected nets.

I picked Hercules to tell, because we shared our mother tongue.

"How is Titus still alive?" he wanted to know. I had no answer. Twins share a soul, so it was a mystery.

Hercules told the big one, Cudjoe, and Cudjoe told the light one, Quashee, and Quashee got right to carving an *ibeji,* a substitute twin statue. Quashee whittled a thick hickory branch, curl after curl of wood shucked off in sure strokes. A sharp blade. A good eye. How on earth did the quick cuts turn a fat branch into a little man? But they did. He's got gifts, Quash. Would I ever learn enough words to say how skill was part of genius, but not all of it?

Carving that stick, Quash looked like he went somewhere else. No, I'll take that back. He looked like he came fully here. We saw his real face, not the studied face he put on around Overseer Mac. I was gonna have to learn how to make a slave face too.

Ewa – would I ever get used to calling her Maggie? – watched, keen. Hard to tell if her quickening came from seeing Quash turn into an artist right before our eyes, leaving his slave body a husk, or from the pure magic of a stick turning into a man. Titus looked on, curious, perhaps grateful. It wasn't yet clear that he wanted to live. After Quashee smoothed the *ibeji* with sweet-smelling oil, three men and Titus slid the hickory twin all the way to the bottom of Titus's pallet and stuffed moss round to protect it.

Would it be enough? They wouldn't be able to leave wedges of fruit for the *ibeji* or drape its neck with flowers. I began to see how old rituals had to change to survive. And about old rituals – if Titus survived, would he be able to help Maggie? Because by then it was clear he was babalawo.

At first, Titus went silent, the smile from the sick-island pen on Sullivan's Island where he had talked with Maggie and me, gone, gone. My mother used to say, "There's no pushing the river." Grief was a river. But sorrow couldn't mask his power, so the questions from others on the street started coming. *Where's my boy Tom? Will this hurting tooth kill me? What happened to Sister Peggie? Is my gut aching from a curse or from bad fish?*

One day, coming back from task, Titus got a sign. Down in the grasses along the road, he saw a skunk skeleton and found underneath four perfect black walnut shells, split and dried. Eight halves – just the number needed to make an opele. At home the knots of the divining string would have separated cowrie shells. Here, it would have to be nut shells. "That skunk," he whispered to me later, "gave his life to show me those hulls." The gods had spoken, and who was he to refuse?

After that, Magpie July dug into her sack of cloth scraps and sewed up two bags for him. Titus had clung to the ground and scraped the earth during his capture, carrying home soil under his fingernails all the way across the ocean – the act of a holy man, I knew. July gave him a long waxy thread to make the opele as well. With Quashee's knife, he scraped Yoruban dirt out from under his fingernails and carefully stowed it in one bag and put the nut shells and skunk bones in the other. Now, somewhere behind the last cabin, out past the garden fence, Titus could prepare the Sacred Table. Out of sight of buckra, he could toss the opele, read the hulls top to bottom, and make the strike marks in the dirt. Back home, Titus ranked as a beginner, having only recently been led into the Grove of Ifa and undergone the secret ceremonies. But even so, he had emerged not just a man, but a man with power. Everyone knew it. Who would hear from the gods first?

Fretful

Eliza's Diary, Antigua

I fear that I'm insufficiently equipped with patience and fortitude for what lies ahead. I condemn my father for, among other things, forcing a diminished esteem. He's told the story ad nauseum: the ride along the sea, that arresting voice, the surf, breeze, etc. To his credit, he never directly attributes his awakening to the slave herself, but still... And the boy? Father justifies the purchase in terms of head rights and land acquisition, but it is ill-timed, for we're at the moment land-rich, sterling-tight, and about to move. I considered a less moral alternative – that he bought the boy to seek the mulatto's favor. If so, the seaside experience had deranged him in more ways than one, for no master needs the good will of his slaves, even the beautiful ones, to exact favor. And his blindness to Mother? It confounded me how a heart expanded by sun and song exhibited less kindness and courtesy instead of more.

Worry about Mother had to remain private, for no possible circumstance would permit such shameful speculations being uttered out loud. Imagine my asking, "Do you think Father has lost his mind?" or more to the point, "Has Father forsaken you?"

Polly, Phoebe, and George are jumping rope outside. Snap. Snap. What a bittersweet nostalgia is triggered by the sound. Snap. Snap. Sadness rapidly fills my chest, like spilled ink blooming on rag paper. Life is passing, passing, says the sound. Whoever forgets that a deep loneliness stamps our early years forgets what it means to be a child.

Time to stop – Mother calls. I only hope I'm not being summoned for another of her ramblings about young men in the Lowcountry. There's the Huguenot, the Ulster Irish doctor, and the neighbor Tilton, whose property abuts Wappoo's. I wasn't so shallow as to ask what if these men were hideous to behold, but I did wonder if there was any tar of character sticky enough to render a man unsuitable in her eyes. She calls me smug and withholding, stinging characterizations. Surely she can't expect me to rant and moan alongside her and partake in her loud miseries. But she does seem to expect me to abandon my own sensibilities and go along with her machinations.

Out of Mother's earshot, Bettany keeps counseling me. "No sense pushing back" or "let her be." For the sake of peace in the household, etc. Easy for a slave to say when she's not being criticized every other minute.

Dressmaking
Eliza, Antigua

With their heads almost touching, Tommy and Noah squatted next to a flipped-over rock and examined an ant colony. It turned out that two-year-old Noah served as more than evidence of Melody's childbearing capacities – he proved to be a welcome companion for Tommy. The little quadroon followed my brother everywhere. Before Noah's arrival, Tommy had no choice but to eternally occupy the role of younger brother to George (somehow being Polly's elder not counting in this hierarchy). Not anymore! Tommy offered the tyke advice with both feigned and real authority, and soon, with naked adoration.

Being excluded might've bothered George were he not shadowing Father everywhere. Afternoons, they surveyed the plantation on horseback, and evenings, they pored over maps at the dining room table. George was flush with the privilege. The arrangements therefore suited most in the household, and a precarious balance prevailed.

Now and then I caught Melody watching her son as he toddled beside Tommy. Her mien sometimes showed nervous maternal worry and other times evinced an affectionate amusement. To see gladness warm her features made me realize how much the slave generally shielded from view. Indeed, if ever Melody caught me regarding her at such an undefended moment, she shuttered her expression as suddenly as a door slamming in a gale.

In the meantime, preparations for departure turned Cabbage Tree Plantation upside-down. Mother often retired to her room, but rallied now and then to make critical decisions: which set of China to bring (the gilt-edged white porcelain), which draperies to leave behind (the gold brocades), how the pantry ought to be left (immaculate). One important task languished, however, and that was the construction of Melody's travel frock. The bolt of grey linen lay untouched in the back room like a rebuke or a broken promise. Given my mother's considerable delight in sartorial tasks, it must have strained her to hold back. It occurred to me that she hoped to vex Father with her delinquency. Unless there were other reasons to delay.

Father avoided the topic. Whether he sought to safeguard Mother's fragile health or to preserve his own peace of mind was hard to tell. He must have realized, though, that an overt interest in upgrading the slave's appearance might've been misconstrued. I perhaps naively took his silence as a sign that his more considerate demeanor of old was returning. In easier times, a fluid context of nagging and forgiving would've prevailed. He'd have pestered, and she'd have responded in mock irritation, "Tell me, dear Husband, when you last made a frock." And so on.

Mother's bouts of malarial fever increased in frequency, and it was hard not to conclude that some causes of her withdrawals were not, in fact, physical. I couldn't blame her if she used fever as a strategy to avoid the mulatto's after-dinner "concerts" – and more to the point, to avoid Father's thinly veiled admiration for the slave. Hard to know, but as for the frock, Mother's plying a needle after supper seemed a thing of the past.

Not long before our departure, I realized that of course there were other reasons to delay. A whole host of intimate interactions was required to fit a dress. Imagine the so-called fine specimen stepping out of her tunic to reveal herself in a near naked condition. Then imagine Mother wrapping the tape measure around Melody's hips and then around the fulsome bosom, practically hugging the slave. For a day-to-day house slave tunic, such attentions were unnecessary, but to make a travel frock that signaled something about our station required finesse and precision.

Mother's focus when sewing was epic, the stuff of family legend. Imagine an alarmed Tommy yelling, "Mother! There's a snake in the parlor!" and Mother replying, "Let me just finish this hem!" Tailoring, in other words, would force Mother out of a studious disregard for the slave into a state of unyielding observation. Melody's shoulders. Her hips and waist. Mother would have to attend to the mulatto's every curve.

One morning near the ides, I sat alone with a volume of John Donne, hoping for some distraction. How bereft I felt when the very first verse struck at the heart of our household tension: *"As love without esteem is capricious and volatile; esteem without love is languid and cold."* Were Mother and Father troubled by a lack of esteem or by the failure of love? At fifteen, what could I possibly know of these matters? As if to answer, Mother swept into the room, sewing basket on her arm.

"What is it, pet?"

"Poetry isn't the hoped-for tonic, I'm afraid."

She took the volume out of my hands and snorted, but with affection, not contempt. "You and your books. John Donne! Not exactly a pocketful of glee."

"I'm not given to pretense, Mother," I said out of habit. "Sometimes I really do enjoy elevated works."

"Who said anything about pretense? We should all be so burdened by a sharp mind and a good education." She gently stroked the nape of my neck. "Ambition is not a cursed thing, my dear. In this way, among many laudable others, you are your father's daughter."

"Dullness seems my fare of late, and to be frank, at this juncture, I'm not sure I want to be my father's daughter." I sucked in my breath with immediate regret. I hadn't meant to give Mother entrée to her own complaints or to pit one parent against the other. She ignored the remark and instead launched into a monologue.

Oh, how I would make friends in South Carolina ("You always do!"). There were so many worthy ladies there – Mrs. Cleland, Mrs. Pinckney and her niece,

Mary Bartlett, and very fine neighbors along Wappoo Creek. There would be music – the harpsichord already in the parlor, concerts on the peninsula. She extolled my appearance and predicted that I would make a fair number of gentlemen's heads turn! All of this I had heard before.

My mother the oracle. Though skeptical, of course I welcomed her sentiments, glowing with compliment and promise as they did. I was taken aback by how accurately she had gauged my attitude. The parent made distant and mute by harassing events had just addressed so many of my unspoken concerns that I could not help but warm to her.

"I predict," she concluded, "that you'll not only charm a cohort of genteel females but find yourself spoken for within fourteen months of our arrival." Fourteen months seemed strangely specific. "Don't you raise your eyebrow at me, Missy! You're quick-witted, well-traveled, educated. And there's this hair!" As if to emphasize my final alluring asset, she pulled out a few pins, making my brown locks spill down in waves. She picked up the notions basket and leaned in for a final conspiratorial comment. "Don't forget – between the pox, yellow fever, and too few English arrivals where we're going, there are nowhere near enough suitable ladies. Apparently, widowers mourn for mere weeks in the Lowcountry!"

"What a comfort, Mother." I pinned my hair back in place while she stood and nodded toward the rear of the house.

"Time to measure her up. You'll wrap the tape. I'll make notations."

And so, at last, Mother would make my tag-along's frock. Perhaps stepping out from under her gloom to minister to my need had granted her access to her considerable domestic energies. But no, of course not. The exact reverse. She'd come into the parlor with the sewing basket already on her arm.

We entered the pantry and found Melody there, looking spooked. She took a step back. Mother looked her up and down, already employing her dispassionate dressmaker's eye, but Melody crossed her arms and scanned the counter. That struck me as odd, but then I realized that the slave might have her own set of reasons to dread this moment.

"Allons-y," Mother chirped with a wave of her hand. "Nous allons commencer la robe enfin!" I'd forgotten how Mother's dressmaking brought out her passion for all things Parisian, a pretense she swore was critical to her outstanding results. If Mother was speaking French, it meant that my tag-along would be fitted with a tailored frock and not a frumpy one.

"Certainement, Maîtresse," Melody said.

My eyes widened in surprise, but Mother took it in stride, or maybe even took it as a point of commonality. Who knew the slave spoke French? Who knew how my mother operated? The questions were about on a par.

Collections
Saffron, Wappoo Plantation

We were like a stump of ants tidying Porch House. Family coming any day. Magpie July pointed, saying words. Fry pan, rice, snake, kitchen. Maggie clung close. Benjie and James, boys too young for much laboring, whirled in and out, stomping upstairs, hollering down at the creek, pawing through the slop bucket before we flung it to the pigs. They walked wide circles around Maggie.

We were supposed to "settle," Magpie July said. What kind of word was that? "Settle" carried the metal taste of blood. Maggie's shoulders lived up near her ears, her back a stiff plank. The smallest squeak made her jump like a rabbit. She barely ate. She barely spoke. Was she trying to disappear out this world sideways? And if she was, could I blame her?

I wasn't saying much neither, but no matter what I put my hands to, I listened. Some new words you kick and find bones lying under, like "settle" or "seasoned." Others you hold up like a mirror or sip like wine. Take "marsh" or "stallion." Some flecked my cheeks like rain: "sweet potato" or "particular." Sometimes a word glowed in mystery like a chunk of amber with a bug inside. Take "Choctaw." Now, that's a word full of haunting!

Never could figure if I was given to poetry or poetry given to me. At home, words flowing through like a river didn't worry me none. But here doubts waffled me hard. I wasn't sure I wanted to soak up words and speak them out when so many were spoken in aid of thieving and worse crimes. Already, it was mighty clear that hereabouts speaking out sparked danger. It confused me. Still, English was the tongue of buckra and I had to understand it. Heads got to spinning when they hear how quick I picked it up.

"Magpie July?" I pointed at the bowls, wanting the word. I meant to call her only "July" like most others do, but I forgot.

"Who you talking to?" She put her hands on her hips.

"I –"

"Is that what they call me?" July grunted, turned away. "Just wait and see what you gather up – feathers, pinecones, maybe. Least my thread and cloth go to use! Call *me* Magpie!"

July didn't know, but I was already hard at it. Words, I was collecting words.

At night, sleep ran scant. Spanish moss crackling on account of Maggie thrashing and huffing and sometimes, like tonight, rising up. She headed to the door, eyes shiny with waking dream. Was it a full moon? Being tired didn't help none with remembering. I grabbed the small wooden bowl filled with pitch that Abraham done gave us and followed. Passing Abraham's cabin, I nodded thanks. We padded along a good long while.

Near the Deep Woods, something cried out harsh and loud. A neighbor baby dying of belly rot? A panther? Was it mating time for big cats? If so, maybe they'd pay us no mind – just two skinny humans out walking in the night. I startled but Maggie didn't. She walked in a dream.

I crept behind quiet because waking her could scare her bad. Duck-walking, I scooped out sticky pitch and dabbed her ankles. Pitch, to fool the dogs. The moon showed a little fingernail up above the cypress tops. Not full, then. The woods'd be extra dark. My turn for pitch. I rubbed it on neck and wrists and dropped the bowl, looking back to see where it landed so I could find it later.

I remembered what Indian Pete called patroller's dogs. The word was "savage." To me "savage" sounded like a dish made with hot red peppers and greens, but Indian Pete told us those dogs was stretched to hunger on purpose.

"Hard to tell what they want more," he said, "filling their bellies or pleasing their masters." Leave it to him to wonder what a dog wants. Seemed like maybe he likes dogs better than people.

The first time Maggie took to sleepwalking, Abraham was sitting by the garden fence.

"Don't forget the rope," he whispered that night. "Pull it high and tight!" By "high" he meant high as a horse's chest. To aid night walkers, a rope lay hidden, coiled up in the scrub near a pine tree – the one with two cut marks in the bark. "About a bowshot into the woods," he said. We found it and I shimmied the rope up the trunk, pulled it across the road and then tied it to another tree. After, I had to trot. Maggie didn't slow for nothing.

Once covered by the dark woods, my heart go sudden glad. The sliver moon showing nothing. Maybe with only the dim shine of stars, patrollers and savage dogs would stay home. The ground sagged a little, giving off a piny scent. I tried not to think how tired tomorrow was gonna find me. I tried not to think on how a patroller toppled by a rope might go from a casual killing mood to a killing mood filled with fury.

Maggie stopped and talked to a branch — soft, fast nonsense — then rushed on. After a while, the path curved down a little slope. Maggie slowed and an owl called, sounding near and sad. From somewhere farther off a panther screamed. This time I was sure. Was it the same one, trailing along? My arms pimpled.

The path ended at Hell Hole Swamp. Abraham told as much, also what "hell" means. You couldn't see much, but you could feel how big and deep the spooky waters went. Maggie clapped. The air got warmer here with a clammy stink that slapped you like a warning. The stars shone like pricks of metal ready to wound while swollen cypress trunks looked as if something in the black waters bloated them out of spite.

What lived here? A wild pig with a raccoon head wouldn't surprise me none. Nor would a crow-headed turtle. They'd cackle and spit out bones and then shape-shift right before our eyes. Water moccasins fatter than logs! Alligators the size of small wagons! I turned the swamp's name over and over and felt it in my mouth: Hell Hole, Hell Hole. For once, a buckra name made sense. This was a terrible place, a good place for sinners. It made Maggie giddy.

She sang a little tune, reminding me of the sailors on the slaver. A shudder passed through me with my own remembering and then with wondering what Maggie remembers. I wished I could hold it all for her. As it was, I could see the Captain's pasty grey balls slapping my daughter's tender, bleeding opening. I could hear them, too — slap, slap, slapping — along with the bed joints creaking in misery. I saw every detail — my daughter's little feet, tipped out, toes curling in pain, him rolling over with a foul groan and sigh, his limp manhood glistening with Maggie's blood as if I'd been the one tied to the bedpost forced to watch and not the woman from Benin.

I put my arm around Maggie. "Ssh!" Just in case men and dogs were about. We listened to the swamp: things plopping into black pools, chiggering insects, snapping reeds, and that owl again. How much suffering can a place hold? Or a person? Maybe once full up, a person's got no choice but to go crazy or die. I already know there are lots of ways to die in the Lowcountry. Going numb is one way. Striking a white is another. Filling your apron with bricks and walking into the creek. Eating poison roots. I made it my business to find out where trumpet vine grew, which parts to use, and how long it took.

Maggie's full up with suffering. Maybe there's no more room. But here in the face of bottomless rot she finds glory. The swamp holds her misery better than I can.

Soon I'd ask Titus to toss the opele for Maggie. Maybe it was selfish to want her back and maybe she couldn't come back. Maybe even a powerful babalawo couldn't lift a curse laid down by a white man with a soul as foul as this swamp.

I pressed my cheek into Maggie's head, wanting the sweetness of her smell. Maggie began sucking on her cheeks and held her elbows in her hands as if she was both mother and child. She was waking up. I felt the heavy tea-dark waters tugging at us as if they hungered for our bones. And I was tempted. Just ten steps. Just ten steps and we could let the swamp take us. Maggie's head would wet before mine, her ears filling with slime. Her crown would go under just as the swamp licked at my collarbones. Soon, we'd both be swallowed by muck. Gone. No trace of having been here.

Just as the dark began its dawn wobble, we returned to Wappoo. Not "home." I wasn't ever gonna call that place "home." Ever. That was one of the words buckra turned inside out, like a dirty sock. "Kindness" was another.

I knew we'd be back to Hell Hole. Over and over we'd be back, finding peace somehow in the dank mystery. Just then, a tiny blade of hope, or something like it, slid near my heart. I thanked the slimy ground and rotten air for it. Not much made sense anymore.

Arrival
Eliza, Cross Winds, Charles Town

The trade winds that powered our sloop into Charles Town Harbor stole my lace cap, causing it to puff full of air and drift lazily upward before collapsing and dropping out of view like a bird diving for fish. The sight made me giggle, something my mother might have enjoyed had she not been sick down below with my sister and Tommy. Father placed an arm around me as if I too might fly off – a not completely ridiculous notion, as I weighed just over seven stone.

The wind snapped the canvas sails in great slapping jerks and whipped one tress after another out of my exposed coif. By the time the salty breeze had stirred my hair to a wild Medusa-like mess, I was downright giddy. Who wouldn't be with her new home coming into view – her new home in the American colonies, no less? A place where – what had Mother said? – I'd "blossom" and assume an "exalted place."

Foamy crescents dimpled the harbor under a flat pewter sky. As our full-bellied sails drew the peninsula near, we passed a veritable forest of other ships. Dozens upon dozens of tall masts tick-tocked in the same gusty air that stole my cap. They looked like misbehaving clock hands stuck at midnight, forever jerking to get past the hour but unable to do so. I giggled again. Father squeezed my shoulder. He too seemed glad. When we spied our pilot's skiff approaching, some passengers waved heartily with cheer and pride in returning home. All along the gunwales, they shouted out the names of landmarks, the wind tossing their words about like so many leaves in a hurricane.

"That's the Main Guard House," a young man hollered.

"There's St. Philips," called out a lady. "And over there – Smith's Bridge." What we called a wharf in the West Indies, they called a bridge here.

"There's Sullivan's Island! We summer there!"

Another hand waved to the right, "There! See the current change? That's where the Cooper River runs in."

Normally, such a tribal exercise wouldn't charm me, but this was a day like no other. Such excitement! So much to learn! Soon my ten-year-old brother, who had stationed himself near the quarterdeck as if poised to take orders from the Captain, joined us, jumping up and down for a better view. Father picked him up and held him tight about the thighs, making their two heads level. George's enthusiasm almost made up for Mother's sulky reluctance.

The Ashley River's on the other side," a man near Father said, pointing to the left of the peninsula. Apparently, he'd learned some of our particulars, for he continued, "Wappoo Creek is a little cut off the Ashley. If you paddle straight across from Mill Pond on the southwest side of the peninsula, you reach the creek in no time. Wappoo connects up to the Stono River to the southwest." He then explained that the eastern bank of "our" creek was actually James Island and that another island called Johns Island butted up to James like a puzzle piece.

"Off to the north, if you squint, you'll just make out where Colonel Rhett brought Blackbeard's protégé to justice – that scurrilous knave known as Bonnet. Heard of him? They named the wharf after the Colonel." George's face lit up. Pirate executions! Here!

We knew a lot about the geography from Grandpapa's letters. Situated at the confluence of the Ashley and Cooper Rivers, the big basin of Charles Town Harbor provided easy entrance for trading ships, most notably the slave Guineas from Africa, Newport, and the West Indies. These vessels came and went at such a phenomenal clip, in fact, that at the time of our arrival settlers were the minority. Two to one, verging on three to one, black to white.

The Lowcountry undulated between rivers, never rising high above sea level, stretching for about 100 miles inland before rising into rolling hills and then climbing a ridge some 3,000 feet high. Flooding worried all, especially in spring when inland snow melt or torrential rainstorms produced what was called "the freshet" – a dramatic rise in the rivers sometimes measuring as high as fifteen feet. When not rendered treacherous by currents and submerged deadfall during the freshet, the Lowcountry's rivers made for convenient transport. Case in point – the distance from Charles Town to Wappoo Plantation was seventeen miles by land and only six by water. Why travel north by carriage to reach a ferry, make a river crossing, and then travel back south, for instance, when a flat-bottomed boat called a pettiauger could take you there in half the time?

The wind continued in intermittent blasts, making frocks cling in revealing closeness one minute and puff outward in air-filled bells the next. Holding the last of my curls in place with one hand and clutching the folds of my frock with the other, I cautiously stepped over to the hatch to see how the rest of the family fared. In the murkiness, I could make out Tommy curled into the crook of Mother's shoulder, Polly sitting erect next to him but probably asleep. Polly's tag-along, Phoebe, slept by her side. Melody occupied the other end of the bench, holding a bucket at the ready. Noah crouched on the floor near his mother's feet. A wave of fetid air rose out of the hatch, but it wasn't as bad as the smell outside. How the harbor stank! The atmosphere swirled with the rank odor of fish and animal droppings as well as the smell of exposed tidal mud.

When they all emerged in a tentative clump, they blinked and held their mid-sections. Mother's nostrils flared, and Polly fanned her face rapidly, as if she could prevent the harbor smells from entering her nose. Tommy upstretched his arms to Mother in that universal gesture. She obliged by picking him up and then satisfied one of her own needs by burying her nose in his hair, which, while sweaty and in need of washing, likely smelled better than low tide.

Melody and Noah climbed out of the hold last. She moved slowly, carrying our on-board travel bags, one in each hand, while her nervous boy clung to her hem. She had another bag slung across her chest, one of unadorned, faded cloth. It dawned on me that all of her worldly goods were in that sack. And right on the heels of that: "What on earth could she possibly possess?"

Once we were aboard the skiff and heading to the wharf, Polly blinked, giving the appearance of a fairy tale heroine emerging from a hundred-year sleep. My sister often exhibited an uncertain allegiance to the physical world. She smiled her agreeable smile, in her agreeable face. Phoebe was five years older than my sister and skinny, with the whitest teeth I've ever seen. She was a good match for Polly temperamentally, obliging and kind and attentive. Almost always cheerful. My mother looked grim.

At the wharf, such a lively clatter! Chains clanking, boxes bumping, ropes and pulleys squeaking, humans whistling, grunting, and cursing. Sailors rolled hogsheads down planks with a repetitive thudding while sails added their own loud commentary, flapping in hard whacks. I heard Dutch, Portuguese, English, and tongues I didn't recognize.

All manner of people crowded about, some in uniforms and finery, others in the plain garb of slaves or indentured servants. Gulls called out their hunger, and a half a block away, a parade of vultures walked in slow steps, looking as if they owned the place.

A bell tolled midday and hawkers called out their wares. I counted as many black faces as white moving about freely, intent on business. At makeshift tables and crates set up along the street, black women sold pastries and platters of sorrel and radishes. I watched a young Negro proudly present a string of fish to a passerby, while an older black man lowered a basket of oysters from his shoulder and counted out two dozen for one white customer, three dozen for another. Some Negroes wore livery, clearly conducting business for their masters, but the status of others was unclear; they were seemingly possessed of an authority at odds with their dark skin. How unlike any other marketplace I'd ever seen!

Father scanned the street and soon found Grandpapa. None of us children had ever met our grandfather and were eager to do so. Mother tucked stray hairs away and smiled broadly.

"Come, Mildrum. Come, children!" Father hollered over the bedlam. How happy a greeting ensued! Grandpapa seemed unaffected by the noise and glowed with welcome. He wore standard Lowcountry casual garb: fine linen breeches buttoned at the knee, white socks with clocking slipped into unadorned black shoes, a lightweight jacquard waistcoat. No wig. Hair tied back loosely.

"Your journey – how was it?" He led the way down a cobbled street and did not wait for a response. "You're here! That's what matters!" The boys pulled at Mother, nearly wild in their curiosity, peppering her with all manner of questions. Mother remained impervious, mouth clamped in a thin line.

Paralleling the water, we progressed along East Bay Street. My grandfather took inordinate pride in our surroundings, explaining that Charles Town now competed with Philadelphia, Newport, and Liverpool. One had the sense that he felt partially responsible for Charles Town's success.

"They can't get 'em here quickly enough, that's how fast land's being cleared," he exclaimed. "The more heads you own, the more credit you can acquire, the more land you can survey and then memorialize. Wealth is yours for the losing!" Then he took to crowing about how refined society was: the theatre, houses of worship, a new library. "Shop after shop aglitter with baubles of Empire! You won't want for Flanders lace, French cambric, Hyson tea, or the finest Madeira!" Had he practiced this list? Mother's smile looked a little forced.

Three-story mansions lined the streets, artfully shuttered and adorned with frilly ironwork. Palms rattled in the gusty air. Most planters owned properties both in town and along the rivers, Grandpapa wanted us to know, and these homes were modest compared to their country seats.

Grandpapa probably stood five foot six, but his spirit and confidence made him seem larger. Like many gentleman settlers in the Lowcountry, he was not the firstborn son. Also, like many South Carolinians, he had come to the colony by way of the West Indies, where he still owned land on both Barbados and Antigua. He met life with a persistence that was a little rough around the edges and might have been considered aggressive were he not so good-humored.

We headed down a narrow street where a large crowd of people had gathered. A plain red flag snapped in the wind, fiercer now because of the closeness of the buildings. As we neared the flag, it was plain to see that the crowd was comprised of people of consequence, dressed in the same quality linens and jacquards as Grandpapa. I was so captivated by the finery that it took a heartbeat to notice the Negroes lined up along the back of the lot. They must have been elevated on blocks for they were visible across the crowd. They hunched their shoulders, whether in response to the invasive wind or in shame at being so scantily clad and on display, I could not tell.

The auctioneer clucked and hollered, "Sold to the gentleman in blue!" As the buyer left, the throng opened momentarily, affording a clearer view of the wares. The Negroes were tied to each other with rope at the waist and connected by iron manacles and chains at the wrist. The two largest men were further restrained by spiked iron collars clamped upon their necks. The women were rendered decent by cloths wrapped and tied under the armpit, save one who had lost her top cloth, leaving her bosom exposed. She wept.

I had never before witnessed an auction. I hurried my sister along, not wanting to inspire her broad and indiscriminate sensitivities. Cats, fish, pigs, blacks, turtles, young, old, Irish, snakes – all could trigger her compassionate excess.

"Angolans mostly – or Kongolese, I can never keep them straight," Grandpapa was saying. "Some Gambians and Yorubans. We avoid the island slaves. We're not fools, after all!" He looked at Mother, as if to win her approval and explained. "The West Indians sell off the insolent ones. Doesn't do to purchase treachery!" He grinned and patted Father's shoulder with affection.

"You'll find it takes far fewer hands to work a rice field than to bring sugar to market. Have I said?" Yes, he had, many times in his letters. I wasn't sure what bothered me more – Grandpapa repeating himself or the implicit reference to Father's unprofitable sugar plantation.

"Profit!" Mother harrumphed with a surprising venom. Did she find Grandpapa's claims of easy wealth implausible, or was she expressing a negative judgment about Father's business acumen? Either way, Mother maintained a vague attitude toward what was being earned or how. Such ignorance never silenced her adamant opinions about financial matters, nor did it stop her from acting as though what she valued – style or love or allegiance to the Mother Country – was all somehow removed from profit.

"Why are they wearing rust?" Polly pointed to the Negroes. The boys kept turning and staring too, presumably for different reasons. I was surprised that Mother hadn't shielded the sight of a half-naked woman from them.

"Look away, Daughter!" Mother barked.

I pulled Phoebe round so that she walked between the auction and Polly. "Let's catch up with Father," I said.

Just then, Mother gasped. I turned to see Melody bent over the curb, vomiting once, then again. She swayed slightly as she unhinged herself to a stand, holding one hand on her belly, the other gripping her son's hand.

"Mama!" cried Noah in alarm. Mother eyed our two satchels, perhaps to confirm that Melody's sick spray had missed the fine leather. "Mama!" Noah repeated. Another mistress might have gone to the slave's side and offered a steadying arm, but the enmity that lay between the two precluded such a simple gesture. I stood frozen, knowing that any assistance I proffered would be problematic.

Three or four of the auction-goers turned at the sound of Melody's distress, one of them commenting loudly, "I wish that Negress was for sale!"

Another: "Oh Lord, yes! That's a fine-looking filly for sure!" Mother looked about to vomit herself. Melody leaned down to Noah, who continued to look fearful. Proceeding forward at last, she contrived to carry our two bags in a single hand so as to hold Noah's with the other.

As we passed a leafy square crowded with people, Grandpapa instructed us on rice growing. "Sluices are critical," he said. "You'll need a good trunk minder." The trunk minder was the slave in charge of the flow of river water onto the rice fields through sluices constructed of tree trunks. He then talked about the current slump in rice prices and the wisdom of planting an alternate crop – indigo, perhaps. What slump? I surely hoped that Grandpapa's reports about the Lowcountry economy had not been exaggerated.

Father frowned. "But tell me about all the dark-skinned peddlers on the waterfront. A spectacle, that!"

"The Assembly's on it, don't you worry! At this very moment, they're debating how to limit the number of Negro hawkers and petty chapmen. Too much competition!"

We turned down a quieter, smaller lane. Grandpapa changed the subject. "I've got seventeen or eighteen heads already at Wappoo. A handful Carolina-born, the rest saltwater – Yoruban, the Windward Coast. One mustee – half black, half Pee Dee. His Indian father died in the Yamasee War according to your overseer, Mac – Craig MacIntyre. Mac came across more than a dozen years ago and might be the only Celt I know who's managed to work off his contract. Taciturn, but reliably knows more than he lets on. Seems rather charmed by the mustee, who'll be your tracker if one 'em runs, by the by. And also you should know that breeding natives with the Africans helps build tolerance for our winters."

Grandpapa went on to highlight the overseer's skills. "Stays away from Angolans, says they're runners. And the Kongolese, too. Too many of them know Portuguese and weaponry – not a good combination, least of all here, where we're sorely outnumbered. And if that all weren't bad enough, some of the Portuguese-speaking Negroes are Catholic." In a lowered voice he predicted that the Taylors and Middletons were in for a heap of trouble for overbuying Angolan and Kongolese stock. "Oh, and Colonel Hext, too."

We passed an enticing shop, causing Grandpapa to chirp, "Baubles of empire! Baubles of empire! There's a little depot down on the Stono River you'll want to visit too, Hutchinson's, practically in the middle of the marshes, but packed to the rafters. Porcelain, velvet, silk, novels, buttons, ribbons – you name it!" Just how much of my mother's homesickness Father had disclosed? I hoped the spritely grandmother I'd heard so much about would cheer us all up.

We arrived at an iron gate, and Grandpapa waved us through. "Welcome to Cross Winds!"

The Weekend
Melody, Cross Winds, Charles Town

In the hall, sudden dark turned me blind. I blinked and blinked. Soon enough, I saw a woman hugging and smiling. Grandmother, her gown silver-grey like her hair. Looked like she aimed to blend with the shadows until she smiled. That lit up the dark some! The boys made her laugh. I gripped Noah's hand tight. None of that grinning and tousling was for him, and maybe he didn't know that yet.

Next to Grandmother stood a woman so tiny she seem more boy than woman, maybe more bird than boy. She had nervous ways. Her frock was darker than her owner's, going toward brown, but even so, she seemed to shimmer. Back and forth she looked from Grandmother to Mistress like she was watching a ball toss and Lord, she better be ready when it came at her. Was she eager to please or close to panic? She took the wraps as if she served the royals. Nell was her name.

Once the family disappeared on up to the parlor, Nell waved me and Noah down a long hall. Phoebe went up with Polly. Nell kept clucking her tongue, as if calling chickens. All that clucking and quivering made it seem as if she might fly off. Light blinded us again in the long rectangular yard out back which was littered with crushed shells. The wind had died away some, leaving the sky innocent, calm. I squinted hard and lifted Noah onto my hip to spare his feet.

And then I had a bitter thought: if Nell could fly away, she would've done. She turned to check on me, even though the shell chips crunched loud enough to say. When she turned round again, I saw it wasn't me she was checking on, but Noah.

A four-foot iron fence lined one side, each iron rail twisting into flowers at their tip. *Fleur-de-lis.* Along the opposite side, short palmettos. At the back was a small structure sunk a few feet below ground. It had no windows, and for the third time since coming to Cross Winds, the change of light blinded me, only orange embers at the far end of the room visible.

Nell moved around. Soon enough, I could make out two women with big baskets in their laps on either side of the hearth. They nodded and then talked in low voices. I put Noah down and scanned the floor, half-expecting to see puddles, but it was dry. Noah grabbed my frock, keeping his thumb in his mouth. A large worktable took up the middle of the room. Nell stepped up onto a low stool and started peeling potatoes. She nodded at another paring knife, so I began to peel too. Nell was so fast I kept stopping to look at her. She cradled each tuber in her palm and after a quick knife pull tossed it up with a slight spin. Peel. Toss with a spin. Catch. Peel. Toss with a spin. Catch. Peel. Done, done. Nothing nervous here! No need to ask why.

In the gloom her face was hard to see but when a sudden sorrow came to me, I knew it was hers, not mine. Sometimes sorrow grows so broad and heavy you can't tell who it belongs to, and if you're a slave, sorrow doesn't really belong to anybody because it's all of ours. I looked at my hands, not wanting to intrude on her sadness, but it was so alive it seemed near to pulsing.

She said nothing but kept glancing over at Noah.

Some silences wear a crab shell saying Keep Out. Others wave you in. This one throbbed so soft it came over the table like an invitation. I glanced up to say something but clamped down on my tongue when I noticed that Nell was missing her left ear. How had I not seen? The blinding dark. The blinding light. The blinding dark again. I dropped my knife in surprise. Seemed Nell took it as signal to talk.

"Like 'bout a hundred year ago, it seem, on Antigua my Master Lucas, not you Master Lucas, he done buy me. But Mimba, my girl, he left at the block." Nell stopped. She didn't need to say more. The two words, "my girl," carried the full weight of misery. "Them buyers bid and waved and shouted out like we was rice or molasses. I think I broke one of Mimba's fingers, I gripped she hand so tight, but they pulled her from me anyway. Don't remember what happen after that." She nodded at Noah. Her girl was about his age at the time. Noah trundled over to some shelves and began pulling wooden bowls onto the floor. None of us stopped him.

"If she alive still, she be thirteen." Nell sighed. "I try'n picture her. Did she get my mama's full hips or my bony ones? She had a crooked little smile as a knee baby, and I wonder is it crooked still? Does she still smile?"

One of the women near the hearth got up and stirred a pot, blocking the light but Nell kept right on working. "I asked Master who done buy my Mimba, but he didn't know or wouldn't tell, so I run off to find her." She ran east one time, west one time, and south the last time. "We sailed here afore I could run north. Never did find her. For all I know, she dead or here in the Lowcountry, living up the Ashley River – imagine that!"

She finished by telling about the punishments. When speaking on Mimba, her voice had been honey spiked with cayenne. Now it was a hollowed-out cane filled with spiders. One time they sliced off an ear, another time they branded her face. She pulled up her head cloth to show the lumpy scar. Even in the half-light

I could see it. It looked like a dead sea star stuck to her forehead about to slide off. It was meant to be the letter R for "Runaway."

"The last time I run, Overseer tapped a machete at my heel, but Master Lucas done stop him seeing as how Missus keen on me laboring in the house." I silently thanked whatever gods that be for my first owner selling me and my baby together. Together.

We turned the dusty brown potatoes into milky white wedges in a pot of water. Nell swept the peelings into her slinged-up apron and dumped them into a second pot by the fire. A broth for our supper.

That night we served Lucases butter-soaked mashed potatoes flecked with herbs, oysters dusted in cornmeal and fried in pig lard, nettle salad, and early peas. For dessert, creamy syllabub. Even the boys and Polly got syllabub, wine and all. What an occasion, they said. After clearing up and supping on our broth and fried greens, we had a treat, a tall glass of buttermilk split five ways. We let Noah lick out the syllabub glasses before setting them to rinse.

Later on Mistress Millie told me to sleep in the house across from Nell, Noah to go in an outbuilding behind the kitchen. When I lay down on a proper bed for the very first time, I couldn't enjoy it because it was the first night without my Noah near. I lay still for a long while. The house went quiet. Moonlight hit the floor, and I could see the grain of the planks, swirls so pretty, no two the same. Like children. No two the same. Rubbing my belly in soft circles, I wondered who the next one was going to be.

The Weekend
Eliza, Cross Winds and Wappoo Plantation

Built in the unique and fine style of Charles Town, Cross Winds stood three stories with the narrow end facing the street. Long porches flanked the southern façade, with beautifully wrought iron railings running between columns and chairs clustered to take advantage of the view of the harbor.

My grandmother stood in the grand foyer aglow with greeting. She turned to my sister first. "Look at you, in the pink of health." She patted Polly's crown, spun her round, and stroked her two plaints admiringly. The boys read the gesture otherwise and simultaneously clucked their tongues, squealing, "Giddyup!"

"Two little jokers, have we?" Grandmama was a slight figure but seemed imperturbable. She gave the boys a beaming once-over before turning to me.

"My, my, my! A young lady. Another beauty," she said, looking at Mother as if my appearance were solely her doing. "Beautiful" was not an adjective oft applied to me – "handsome," more like. The bits were arranged in a pleasing enough manner, but my nose ran a little long and my eyes were too small. Father always said my smile was "my ticket," and Mother repeatedly commended my "glorious head of hair." What they omitted was telling.

As we climbed an elegant staircase, Grandpapa told us that the mahogany wainscotting was from Domingo. "Nearly cheap as pine! And the carver's one of yours – Quashee. He'll be worth his weight in sterling with proper loan-outs."

In the finely-appointed parlor, Grandmama gestured for us to sit on a divan covered in black and ivory toile. She opened the bottom drawer of an escritoire behind us, pulled out a felted bag, and flung it halfway across the room to George. He caught it easily and grinned.

"Now run along until tea, boys!" To Mother's raised eyebrow, she explained, "Pawpaw. The rules are as arcane as the rituals of the Masons, but children are masters of invention." Polly climbed into Mother's lap, and within moments her eyelids fell to half-mast. Her capacity to drift away into the deepest of repose at all hours and in almost any setting was one of my sister's most enviable gifts. Mother nodded at Phoebe, who slid noiselessly out of the room.

Grandpapa, still in a didactic mood, opened an upper section of the escritoire and pulled out one of his prized maps. He and Father disappeared into the dining room to pore over it. Female intercourse turned to fashion, a topic near and dear to Mother's heart. If her face was mildly masculine, her outfits were anything but. She knew how to drape herself in the height of style, in colors and cuts that expertly flattered her overly thin shape. We touched on where to source linen and silk, how to adapt patterns, and the names of a few good local dressmakers.

After a while, Grandmama turned to me. Maybe she sensed my restlessness. Maybe she recognized that not everyone in the room was so enthused about clothing. She wanted to hear all about my studies in England and quickly discerned my love of horticulture. I happily rattled on, even going so far as to describe some of the scientific experiments we'd performed in the greenhouse fortuitously located next to my boarding school.

Grandmama then brought up the topic of young men. Eligible young men. My mother wore her casually gracious face, but I knew her keen recall for detail would later reveal itself. There was Mr. Dutarque, a widower, or was it a dead fiancée? Not a planter and also a Frenchman, but a merchant of means with properties in both Charles Town and on the Ashley, and so a prospect nonetheless. There was Mr. Tilton, whose acreage abutted Wappoo, second-generation Lowcountry resident with no brothers competing for his father's fortune. Then there was an Ulster Irishman, John Rutledge, a doctor and quite the bon vivant, but probably spoken for.

"As handsome as the day is long." Grandmama said, giving me a sly smile. She tugged at her bodice as if the mere thought of the man required a decorous rearrangement. "His older brother, Andrew, came to the Lowcountry a few years prior, trained in the law. Now Andrew's nearly as well-to-do as the Manigaults. How, you might ask? The widow Sarah Hext said yes, that's how." We should meet them, she said, and Sarah's brother-in-law, Colonel Hext, too.

"I've heard that the unmarried brother, John, has eyes for Sarah's daughter, also called Sarah, an only child and heir to that great fortune. She's thirteen and not quite ready for the marriage bed, though I'd wager she'd say otherwise." To her credit, Mother did not so much as glance my way.

My head was spinning. Two Sarah Hexts, both somehow involved with Rutledge brothers, one officially, one potentially? I wondered what the brother-in-law, Colonel Hext, thought of these arrangements.

The mantel clock chimed four, causing Grandmama to chirp, "Oh, but it's time for a quick lie-down before tea!" She showed us our rooms.

Map in the Dust
Eliza, Wappoo Plantation

The next morning dawned crisp and clear, with a washed-out sky. After crossing the Ashley River, three Negroes paddled our pettiauger into the mouth of Wappoo Creek, where our route meandered through fields of golden and green grasses. Here and there, a clump of cypress trees or a solitary live oak rose tall, but otherwise, the flat expanse stretched as far as the eye could see. Each dip of the oars refracted the midday light in shiny crescents and Father held a hand to his brow to shield his eyes. The boys threw off their vests in what seemed a declaration of freedom, while Mother laid the garments on her lap with a distracted air. She did not care for water travel. A wide-eyed Polly watched her brothers drag their hands in the water. George first, then Tommy copying. Phoebe tipped her head back, eyes closed, enjoying the sun.

After some tranquil moments, the tall Negro called Cudjoe spoke. "Snakes mighty good swimmers." The boys snatched their hands out of the water and started scanning the surface. Cudjoe kept on. "Sure, they got no legs, no arms, but they get along, barely breakin' the water. Sometimes all you see's a biddy head."

As Wappoo's key slave, Cudjoe transacted much of the plantation's business, entrusted to carry coins, bills, and letters of credit. He also kept a full set of keys. He was the plantation's most experienced river navigator and its resident smithy.

"You want to know why we's out here in the middle?" Cudjoe asked. Both boys nodded. The key slave pointed with an oar to a tangle of branches overhanging the water. "They like napping in them bushes. Been known to drop into boats and make mischief." I couldn't tell if the slave was teasing the boys or educating them.

"Best be listenin' to my father," said a younger paddler with a broad grin. His name was Mo.

As we rounded a bend, I closed my eyes to better feel a slight breeze but snapped them open a moment later when Polly bounded off the bench. Father cautioned her against tipping the boat, even though it was flat-bottomed and not easily o'erturned. I twisted to look where my sister pointed and saw the white siding of our new home telegraphed in flashes of light through fluttering foliage. I nearly stood too.

We were greeted by two male Negroes, one of them very young, seven or eight, the other a little younger than I, maybe fourteen. Next to them stood a man of medium height holding a big straw hat. Overseer MacIntyre. The overseer hollered hello and then barked, "Caesar! Bags!" At the command, Father gave Mother a troubled look. What was that about? Caesar propelled his knobby knees in a most inefficient manner, bobbing up and down like a broken toy on a string. He managed to help tie up the boat. The younger slave, called Benjie, chattered like a magpie.

"I know the best fishing spots!" he announced.

The overseer, known to all except the slaves as Mac, seemed to glow with warmth, but perhaps that impression had more to do with how the sun lit up his frizzy red hair than with his actual demeanor. The hair, though thick, was receding, and the broad forehead speckled with freckles. His smile was wide but close-lipped, and it wouldn't be until later, when I saw his yellowed denture and missing front incisors, that I understood why. He wore dark breeches and an ill-fitting grey linen tunic under a formless vest. He spun his hat between his fingers, nervous hands making a commentary at odds with his projection of confidence.

Tommy and George dashed toward the large barn to our left, presumably to find the source of a yelping cacophony. Polly dashed off too, but toward the house, looking like a lacy and exotic bird. Just as she pattered up the stairs, two female slaves emerged. They positioned themselves on either side of the door and clasped their hands behind their backs. Polly barreled past.

A small white flower landed on my shoulder. I plucked it off, surprised at its resemblance to an orchid. Up above: the canopy of a tall tree with leaves the size of dinner plates.

"Catawba," Mac said. "Come the morrow, the path'll be so littered with flowers, lass, you'll feel like a Queen to walk upon it." At forty years of age, our overseer was older than most, many of whom died before attaining the age of thirty-five. Untimely overseer deaths were due not so much to the strain of their station as to the dangerous afflictions that made all Lowcountry residents vulnerable – heatstroke, yellow fever, a canker gone bad, snakebite, the pox.

"You mean catalpa," Father interjected.

"No, sir, Catawba, after the Indian Nation. You misspeak something long enough, it sticks like a burr."

The path from the dock led up a slight rise to the house, pounded dirt for its first half and the rest a surface known as tabby, a mixture of sand, water, ash, and crushed shells that hardened like stone. The path had two offshoots, the left veering off toward Mac's cottage and the slave quarters, the right paralleling the creek back in the direction we'd come.

The two-story house seemed higher, as it was perched upon square brick pillars roughly three feet in height. Long windows flanked by black shutters graced the first floor, while two dormers on the second level accommodated smaller unadorned windows. A deep gallery furnished with wooden rockers ran along the entire front, with a wide set of stairs set in the middle. The house was not as grand as those in Charles Town, and by English standards it was downright humble, but it looked commodious enough and well-suited to the location.

Two giant live oaks graced the property, one to the immediate left of our new home and the other on the far side of the road near the first of the slave cabins. Spanish moss hung like expensive cut velvet, giving the massive trees a delicate and almost feminine cast. Two trees could not, of course, afford the grandeur of a mature alleé but their stature and beauty nonetheless impressed.

Mother swept a few stray tresses from her forehead. She looked wan and immune to the excitement that our arrival had produced in the rest of us. The boys' vests hung lifelessly off one arm. I took them from her as if relieving some significant burden.

"You'll see the place on the morrow," Mac said, "but let me give ya a quick lay of the land. The eave pokin' up near the water yonder, 'tis the smokehouse. The spinning shed beside." He pointed the other way, to the left side of our house. "Past the slave quarters, you'll find alfalfa fields and then, 'bout half a league yonder, a stand of gums and loblolly pines we call the Deep Woods though it ain't nothin' of the sort. After that, the path splits in three, the right goin' to the Ashley, the left to the Upper Fields and straight ahead ends in Hell Hole Swamp, if you're fool enough to follow it."

Mother raised an eyebrow as if to say, "Is such language necessary?"

"Oh, it's a right apt name, Ma'am. The soupy land offers treachery at every turn: black cricks, water prairies, bogs, cypress bays, brackish ponds, moving islands. Nothing stayin' the same week to week. Cane Creek's another spot you wanna avoid, but 'tis further on. Was a big Indian settlement once, Cane Creek, but a massacre emptied the place. Now, if rumors be true, a steady flow of runaways keeping camp there."

Mac picked up a knuckled Catawba branch and scratched some lines in the dirt. Apparently, a map was in order. Mother would've been better served by a glass of water, so we two made our way to the verandah. Once seated in one of the gallery's rockers, Mother pointed at the taller female slave.

"Name?"

"July, Mistress. Welcome to Wappoo." I had the sense that the utterance cost the slave, but whether because English was difficult for her or out of a reluctance to offer welcome, I couldn't tell.

"This here, Saffron."

Saffron made an awkward curtsey. Both women wore plain grey frocks with white bibbed aprons and the customary kerchiefs round their crowns. July stood a head taller than Saffron, but her lean and angular frame made her seem taller yet. She was middle-aged, but whether that meant thirty or forty-five, I couldn't begin to guess. Saffron had a moon-shaped face with wide eyes giving the impression of a skittish or mystical nature. Neither wore shoes.

Mac was pointing his stick at Caesar.

"Been hobbled, he has. If he runs again, law says you can kill him dead. If you ask me, though, such a practice runs counter to thrift." Mac chuckled.

"Indeed," Father agreed.

The overseer lightly tapped Caesar's backside as he went by and the slave twisted round in a spasm of fright. Mac laughed. "Oh easy, boy, now easy!"

A heron lifted off from the creek's edge and flew directly over our barn, legs extended like tiny eyelashes in the sky. I sighed like someone coming home. Grandpapa's letters had not exaggerated the beauty of the place.

Wardrobe and Words
Saffron, Wappoo Plantation

Master gave me to Miss Eliza, like I was a bracelet or a book. Here, she yours. Melody tagged along with her on the sloop, a pairing based on fraud, it now seem. They switched us up. Melody some kinda problem and I'm telling you right off I know more about buckra's business than I wanna know. Lucky for me, I tend the girl, not the mother.

Today Missy's locks was slipping and sliding and causing torment: how many pins was it gonna take? She was talking on and on. "These live oaks are magnificent, don't you think?"

I nodded but right away I stopped listening cause the word "magnificent" bounced behind my forehead. It was a keeper. I was gonna say it soft and slow to see if it drop like a bead through sun-warm honey. Beautiful words do. Take "azure." Just the sound cause a swoon, never mind the heartbreaking blue of what it means. "Azure" so beautiful, it ain't a bead sinking in honey, it's the honey itself.

Miss Eliza rose up cock-a-crow early. I done seen her a time or two on the road striding past the cabins all chipper – and dressed, by the by, meaning she could do it her own self. Most mornings, July, Melody, and I haul water to Summer Kitchen first thing. Start a fire. Brew up tea. Work up a batch of biscuits or porridge. We each got our own soundin' bell, and when Miss Eliza jangle mine, that's when I go and help her dress.

She was still chattering about trees, beeches now, rows of them, it seemed, two hundred years old. Some place called England. I tied up the corset tight like she say, thinking how it must make breathing a chore. It sure didn't stop her talking none. "Magnificent trunks like elephant legs, but bigger!" She musta thought the word "elephant" was new to me, so she curled one arm in front of her face and blasted out elephant sounds. What'd she know about elephants? Of course I seen 'em back home, but now I got the buckra name.

But wait. Hold on. There was that word again – "magnificent." It was chiming good.

"Tomorrow, I'll be riding out in the morning with a visitor, so have one of the little ones polish my boots." Ugh. Those boots. They took wrestlin' to get on, wrestlin' to get off. Too much close touching.

She raised up her arms and I put the first slip on, then the other. Why two? Finally, the frock, a pretty navy with swirling white flowers. Them swirling flowers was sweet. I set to twisting the buttons into tiny loops. "And make up the guest room. Her uncle is Charles Pinckney – one of the most important men in these parts. We want to make a good impression!"

Last, I lay the lace tucker over Miss Eliza's shoulders, but thank goodness she push it down into the frock by her own hand. I sure didn't want to slide my hand down into her bosom every morning. "Bosom," I can tell you, is a word I don't like. One reason? It sound like one thing, when it mean two.

Back at Summer Kitchen, the word "magnificent" gathered hard and soft in my mind. I swore I was never, ever, gonna sound it out loud near buckra, especially never, ever for their oak. No way. But for ours? Oh, yes. *Our magnificent oak.*

Like I been saying, once I got to seeing how words string along here, they came fast. I tried keeping my ways secret, but how do you hide something as natural and plain as skin or hair? Muttering "azure, azure," or "possum, possum" didn't help and anyway, I learned there wasn't much hiding from Melody or July.

One night early on, family taking tea in the parlor, chitchatting, supper done. There we be, just the other side of the door, rags in hand, wiping silver 'til it shine. We slid 'em piece by piece into a box. I got to nodding at one thing and another, and July got to naming: "biscuit," "rice spoon," "knife," "velvet." Velvet sounded soft, same as the cloth. The box for silver was lined with it. Velvet for buckra forks. Coarse cotton for our backs, or "osnaburg," "Negro cloth."

Now and again, Melody spit on fork or knife. She was shining and grinning at the same time, but not July. She wore a dark look. Melody made it look as if spitting was part of shining and shining require spitting and so why wasn't we at it too? I laughed. Buckra and us live so close and so far – a door and worlds between.

Master was gonna want a song. We dreaded the call. Why couldn't them frogs peeping out with mighty love down by the creek be enough for him?

Captain Calls
Melody, Wappoo Plantation

I stood where he said to. Belly full of butterflies. And a baby. How long before they see? July's so sharp, I'm thinking she knows. But anyone else? When the count of moons comes clear, what're they gonna think?

Master acted like he owned the air. Wasn't it enough owning my body and my son? I closed my eyes and sang to the falling night and to the frogs. Not to him. When I got to the part *"Jesus comin' back / Jesus comin' back,"* I swear the frogs sang with me. Sharing praise! I've never seen Master praise a single thing. Only possess. How do you possess a song? How do you possess beauty?

When I opened my eyes, Mistress was fiddling with cloth. No lantern lit. No thread or needle to hand. A nervous Mistress was never anything good for a Negro. Miss Eliza walked in with the little ones. Seeing Noah and Tommy sharing a secret made my throat close.

"Tommy n' Noah caught frogs!" Polly chirped. "George too." One of the frogs got loose and jumped on the carpet near Mistress. Oh, she got seething mad! Jabbed her finger at the door and screamed.

"Get it out! Out, out – this instant!" The children jerked and obeyed. Master frowned. Miss Eliza's eyes went dark. Mistress yelled again, and anyone with half a gill of sense could tell who she really wanted to banish: *Get that slave out! Get her out! This instant!*

George caught the disobedient frog and flung it out the window. Tommy and Noah took theirs outside and laid them down on the tabby, full of care. The quiet in the parlor turned thick and heavy, like scratchy wool. I watched Tommy pat Noah on the back. When Tommy waved "so long" to the frog, Noah did too. "Two peas in a pod," they kept on saying. As if.

The hurting silence would curl stomachs soon if nobody came round to smooth it over. Master nodded at me again. Now? He thought I was the one to ease the stiff and ailing quiet? Good Lord! But I sang because what else could I do? By the time the second verse came up, the little ones had clattered up the stairs, July following on. Saffron came round through the back hall to take Noah over to the street for supper. My heart skipped. Could I ever learn to be in two places at once?

Miss Eliza lit a lantern with a flare and a hiss. The family wasn't rich like my cane-growing owner, so they scrimped on whale oil and paraffin, sometimes even burning stinky tallow. Out of nowhere, Mistress chirped, "Melody, fetch my brush!" Sly and cheery.

That was the first time she ever did say my name. First. Time. The quiet dropped down to a new place, a spike of terror poking up. Captain stared at the embers, a pulse in his jaw. He wasn't going to be any help.

"On my vanity." She waved a hand. When I came back, my stomach a-churn, Miss Eliza played something slow and gooey on the keys. Full dark now. Peepers gone quiet. One lantern flickered big shadows about. Orange embers died down.

Mistress pointed behind the sofa. "Stand there. Do my hundred strokes – mind, I like it hard." The dim light made finding hairpins hard. Mistress Millie slapped my hand away and tugged them out lickety-split herself. The hair fell down in heavy clumps, and I started brushing.

"Harder!"

Master got busy with his pipe, but he wasn't fooling nobody. It was mighty tense. Foul play twisted and snickered in the room. It curved and slunk, sometimes hiding a minute before springing back with bared teeth. What ugly foolery! Miss Eliza's hands dropped into her lap. No more tunes. A strange idea came over me in that wounding quiet: maybe being taken bloody and rash-hard between the legs was easier than this. Easier than hidden barbs, hidden pleasures, broken alliances. At least brute force left no doubt about who was doing what and to whom.

I'm certain Mistress and Master been going sideways at each other long before he bought me, but somehow they got to making it my fault. White people extra good at that – turning their own sins into the fault of others. Here was Captain stealing my voice. Here was Mistress coating me with angry sighs. Here was Captain side-eyeing me. Here was Mistress flaunting my touch, trying to win something back or to vex. What a viper's nest!

Just when I thought the mood would snap like a frayed harpsichord string, Mistress started conversating about decorations – what she wanted and all. Like she was sitting round the tea table with white ladies on a Tuesday. She pointed to the wall at my side.

"A mirror there'd catch the light off the creek. Not just sunlight." Mistress turned to look, causing the brush to pull. "Ow! Careful!" Then to him, "After dark, it'd be lovely too, doubling the light of the lantern and the warmth of the fire." Mistress was laying on a rally – but why when it seemed she got everything she wanted around here? Everything except happiness.

I couldn't count past twenty, so who knows how many strokes were left, but I'll tell you this — the thought of a big mirror shuddered fear between my ribs. Think on it: Master with two places to look me over, one a little sneakier than the other. Was anybody counting?

Mistress started in about carved flowers. In a frame. Their voices grew dim. The brown hair snapped with sparks now and again. Was Noah sleeping yet? Was July singing in my place? How long could one hundred strokes last?

Effective Parry
Eliza's Diary, Wappoo Plantation

How foolish the husband who underestimates his wife (or the daughter her mother, for that matter). After weeks of sullen quiet, Mother made her strike and did so stealthily, without any appearance of attack. In fact, her coup consisted of just four words: "Bring me my brush." Had she planned it, or did it come as sudden inspiration? In either case, what an effective parry! Commandeering Melody for her own intimate use and in Father's face! She gave him a taste of her own discomfort.

Thank goodness her strategy worked, for the tense evenings had become unendurable. On what turned out to be the final night of singing, I'd set the lantern next to Mother's elbow, sending a hulking shadow of the slave onto the wall. Melody's shadow was bigger than the escritoire, menacing and spooky, offering up a more accurate depiction of the scale of her presence than her actual form.

With a stab of discomfort, it occurs to me that the charged triangle might be resolving itself in my parents' bedchamber, and further, maybe that was what Mother'd been angling for all along. Did it matter to her that their conjugal joining might be fueled by her husband's desire for someone else? Such salacious musings for a fifteen-year-old.

April 1738

Campaign for a Mirror
Eliza, Wappoo Plantation

If we had moved to an English manor with room after room to appoint instead of the somewhat humble Wappoo house, my family's domestic peace might have fared better. Mother liked decorating, and when it came to such matters, she was invested, opinionated, and talented. She knew when to be bold, when to be subtle, and unlike most genteel women, understood that light was an important design consideration. Soon after our arrival Mother determined that the dark parlor would not be complete until a large mirror occupied the interior wall.

I suspected Father worried that his folly regarding the mulatto would be further exposed once the house was "done" and so granted one request after another with magnanimous flexibility. By the time the mirror came up, his resistance seemed a matter of form only. He may have called it "an extravagance" a time or two, but Mother's assertions that Domingo mahogany could be purchased for a trifle won the day. The glass would be ordered. Quashee would carve the frame.

After the wood arrived and Quashee set to his work, Mother crowed about the slave's artistic talent, while Father lauded his intelligence. "Always good to have superior blood in the line," Father would say, referring to Quashee's white father.

"The deft hand of vision," Mother would reply.

I surely hoped this wasn't about to slide into one of their tiresome debates over the relative virtues of logic and creativity, a dispute they hashed out in sour repetition over the seasons. The arguments weren't strictly about the purported topic, but I hardly knew their unvarnished content. Part of me thought that the conflicts arose out of Mother's bitter resolve to be considered an equal – a status she could attain only by undermining Father.

In Mother's view, logic, engineering, and mathematics were the stuff of dullards, whereas creative intelligence flourished in bold, intuitive strokes. The artist added value to the world, whereas the bookkeepers merely tracked it and the engineers shored up the soggy banks. Her position was as simplistic as it was self-serving, but since Father controlled the purse strings and this rankled her, from time to time she took up her thesis with relentless fervor. I'm certain that he sometimes gave her what she wanted merely to silence her.

Once he said yes to the mirror, a pleasant quiet filled the parlor. These days such quiet was suspect.

A New Tongue
Saffron, Wappoo Plantation

As clocks tick-tocked and weeks churned past, Porch House life started coming clear. My fast learning of English set heads to turning. Soon I carried more words than July, and she's been here many years – I don't know the number. I was as bad at keeping numbers as I was good at catching words.

Something else I was bad at was guessing Mistress Millie's moods. She was changeable, like the moon. One minute she sank like a stone in the creek and the next flew off like a leaf in a hurricane. They say it's malaria, but I think she might just have a sour heart. By now my English ranges even with Melody's, but unlike me, she could spot Mistress's foul misery from two rooms away, even before one harsh word sliced the air.

Luckily, I tended Miss Eliza. Miss gave little trouble – no harsh words or flashing fatigue. And unlike her mother, Miss Eliza was easy to figure, so easy in fact it'd blush her scarlet to know.

Today's words: soufflé, neighbor, windowsill, fickle. Yesterday's words: gloomy, rascal, quinine, and one keeper: bubble. Wasn't that a sound to love? Bubble, bubble.

Back home in Yoruba, stirring the pot of words came natural and pure. When people asked for me, I might stand by the wedding couple or the baby at his naming and open to verse and it would stream out to fit the occasion. One time I'd speak like a cool breeze in summer, another time like a fire crackling against blackest night. Moods high or low, but every time capturing a necessary piece of the world and handing it over. A gift.

Here, all that go sideways. For one thing, no matter what music English rings out, it comes stained with corruption, plain and simple. Buckra speech. No way round it.

Certain words spit nasty poison, transacting bodies or shaming and smearing what's true. One word makes my head stretch and pop, and that word is "owner." Two sounds – "oh-ner" – but a mire of evil. I can't make it make sense. I whispered it to the laundry line, to the wood pile, and to my own feet: owner, owner, owner. Would it ever make sense? I was owned. They owned my daughter. They owned a wood table, a soup tureen, silverware, and all my unborn children. They used papers or coin to buy a donkey, its harness and feed, and my daughter. My daughter.

Listening range different here, too – survival in it. Silence a shield, information a weapon.

Melody and July tolerated my mutterings. Maybe they listened in, I don't know. What I do know – saying new words in curious wonder makes poetry all its own: cloud, pin tuckings, rooster, hoe cakes, bitter love.

Fifteen Hands
Eliza, Wappoo Plantation

When Mary Bartlett leapt off her Arab and handed Mac the reins, the dappled grey danced sideways in willful and skittish resistance. The horse stood easily fifteen hands high – clearly no easy animal to manage, causing Mac to appraise our guest with admiration. Before turning to me, Mary removed two panniers and made sure that our overseer would properly cool the animal. When she finally did turn to me, it was to introduce the horse.

"Meet Theodore."

I laughed. "And I'm Eliza."

"Oh, indeed – I'm Mary! Don't you just love not having to ride sidesaddle? This is not Richmond Park, after all!" Mary had grown up in London, where her mother still resided. I rather indecorously lifted one leg to reveal that I was wearing a voluminous pair of pantaloons.

She clapped. "Oh, may we ever be equestrian sisters!" I smiled and announced that she would soon meet my horse, Sir Raleigh.

Older than I by two years and taller by six inches, Mary was statuesque – large bosomed, big-hipped, broad in the shoulder. Her face went from pretty enough to notably attractive when graced with a grin, and happily, she smiled often. Perhaps the teeth were slightly large, but not so much as to warrant the disparagement "horsey."

We were to ride together later that morning, but first, there was a craft! We settled on the porch, where Mary disgorged the contents of her satchels: paint brushes, bags of lacquer chips, two unfinished wooden trays, and a sheaf of colored paper.

"What do you mean you don't japan? It's so very popular in England." I would soon learn (though perhaps not soon enough) that japanning involved applying layers of lacquer on black-painted wood, often on top of cut paper designs.

Mother poked her head out and chimed hello. Introductions were made, Mary's uncle and aunt, Charles and Elizabeth Pinckney, asked after. Mother quickly determined that Mary's mother was Elizabeth Pinckney's sister and then disappeared back into the house.

"Let me begin again," Mary said. "First, we apply a layer of black paint. Then, we cut −"

I laid a hand on her arm and suggested that we ride while the day was young. "We could gather botanical specimens," I said.

"Oh yes! Flowers make such stylish subjects."

Once astride our horses and heading toward the Upper Field, Mary described life with her aunt and uncle. How kind they were. How they rather spoiled her. They were childless, did I know? During the cooler months, they entertained constantly, and I should come and stay before the miasma gathered, and did I think it would be the pox or yellow fever this time?

"When you come," Mary said, lowering her voice, "pack some cotton balls." To my questioning look, "For your ears. Uncle Charles snores like a rhino! Even with an empty bedchamber between us, he startles me awake some nights." She honked a laugh. "I don't know how Auntie Elizabeth does it − sleep, I mean." Mary looked off into the distance and added somberly, "Sometimes I think all my aunt's physical ailments arise from a lack of sleep. All that raucous snuffling."

I wondered how Mr. and Mrs. Pinckney might like their niece making such revelations, and on a first meeting no less. Raucous snuffling? And what ailments? I changed the subject. We talked about schooling in England − hers in London, mine at Mrs. Pearson's School for Girls in Devonshire.

Mary's sturdy grace impressed me. In between gathering roadside flowers, how fluidly she dismounted and mounted Theodore! I was less easy. Plus there was the matter of her temperamental horse. Every time she handed me Theodore's reins, the Arab objected and took to snorting and prancing in place. Placid Sir Raleigh looked on with disinterest or disdain, I couldn't tell which.

When we reached a fragrant clump of jasmine, I barked that it was my turn and leapt to the ground. I was lucky I didn't twist an ankle and wasn't quite sure how I'd recover my saddle, but I didn't want to be responsible for that Arab again. I plucked fistfuls of blossoms and then found a log half-covered with undergrowth, where I was able to remount my horse, if rather ungracefully. For a second I wished I was as tall as Mary. But I didn't allow the self-deceit to last – clearly her superior coordination had little to do with height.

Mary would happily ride for another hour or more, but I was done. I wheeled Sir Raleigh around and suggested we head back.

Upstairs in my bedchamber, I rang for Saffron to remove my boots. After a great deal of tugging, the first boot came off with a pop, sending the slave nearly head over heels. I laughed, but when Saffron sat back up her face was a wooden mask. Well – perhaps if she were more acquainted with civilized garb!

Once Mary and I were refreshed with tea and candied pecans, we convened on the back gallery and set to japanning our trays. By lantern-lighting time, we'd fallen into the kind of friendship one generally has in childhood, one born out of accidental proximity and marked by a certain silliness. This, even though we weren't temperamentally similar and our interests didn't overlap much. Given the overly personal divulgences during our ride, I told myself to be wary in future about self-disclosure, but even so a warm bond formed between us. I began to have the satisfying notion that life in South Carolina might be populated with friends.

Devotion Stronger than Hunger
Saffron, Wappoo Plantation

Caesar plopped the string of fish down next to the bucket – splat! Stood proud. "Is they alive?" James wanted to know. A silver one flipped, and Benjie jumped back. The boys begged Caesar to let them put the fish in the bucket.

"Hooks out first," Caesar said. Benjie ran off, making a big loop round our oak and then back, but James, even though younger and clumsier, set to it. Caesar squatted by to make sure he didn't stick himself.

Indian Pete would prepare the fish, and it was Melody's turn to cook, so I sat in the door frame with Maggie between my knees, like we do. Hummed a little. The smoke off the fires twisted toward the creek, as if it wanted water more than it wanted air. I heaved a big sigh. Maggie looked up at me, afraid. Oba! Sometimes I forgot to hold everything in tight. To make up for the sigh, I smiled big.

Indian Pete glanced over. Was he tending to my heavin' sigh or the smile rounding on after? My hands hung off my knees like sad cloth. I was tired. Best not think on it or I might get more tired. And angry, too. Then there wouldn't be enough sighs in all creation. I'd be spitting at the rising moon instead. I'd rather listen to Maggie breathe.

Something warm down below my apron told me how the moon and me danced together. Every time it curved new, my bloods let down. Thank Oba I wasn't like my sister with thirty-three days between, making the moon a stranger to her rounds or like my skinny cousin who go dry for no reason and then start back up for no reason.

I stuck my hand in my pocket and fingered the loose nail I found in Summer Kitchen that morning. Looked up at Indian Pete. Even though regular, I planned to make strike marks on the wall. The moon and me, counting together. Though I can't see the future, I know for sure I don't want to give buckra another baby. One idea was presuming, the other asserting. But when one heartache nested inside another heartache, not knowing where one began and the other ended, maybe you planned a little.

As if either was up to me.

Indian Pete held one fish after another in his palm, silver belly up. With his short knife, he slit 'em open and then flicked out the curling grey-pink guts. Still as a statue, Chester the dog sat near. He looked up at Pete, eyes aglitter with hunger, without so much as a peek at the growing pile of innards. What mighty waiting – a devotion stronger than hunger.

The gutting gave me a lesson on words, not just on devotion. It came to me how buckra gutted the word "home" as sure as that knife slitting open fish and flicking out innards. They gutted the idea of home and fed it to the dogs. That's why the word caught in my throat like the slime of sick lungs. Home. Can you hock up evil like phlegm and launch it away? Spit. What was home for us? And while I'm asking questions, how come their dogs eat so well while fielders' ribs get to jutting out?

"Okay," Indian Peter said. Waiting done, Chester scooped up that pile of guts in two snuffles. "Good boy," Indian Pete praised. "What a good, good boy!"

Of course Porch House wasn't home, but the street wasn't either. Oh, we make the cabins homey as best we can, what with jokes and secrets, admiring looks, sometimes spite, the smell of okra sticking to the pan and delicious benne wafers from time to time. But the place was too stripped down, too open, and too run through with sorrow and exhaustion to count. Each day that ended, we were slaves. Each day that started, we were still slaves. We needed a word for "a place we have to call home but isn't home."

And what of the places we came from, we traveling saltwaters, plucked out of our villages? Dragged, coffled, shoved, chained, sickened for weeks at sea? Being torn away tainted memory bad, meaning buckra's destruction didn't just ruin now and the future, it ran back in time too. "Nostalgia" is a word no slave needed to know. When I remember my mother rising up from bed, all soft and dreamy, or when I recall Husband at the river at dusk, humming, my throat burns so hot it seems my bones might melt, leaving me a pile of flesh, smoldering and bitter. You learn not to think on them.

Indian Pete might've been admiring the slant of my collarbones just then, because I caught him looking at me again – all the fish gutted, two in the pan. Maybe he was wanting to know what my breasts look like just below. Maybe he was wishing it was his finger tracing my jaw scar and not Maggie's.

Maggie's finger felt cool and reassuring and the fish smelled good. The sky turned a pale blue, as if it was powdered. It wasn't azure, but heading that way and beautiful.

It came to me that they couldn't take everything.

Buckets of Water
Eliza, Wappoo Plantation

Soon the marsh shrugged off the dank blandness of winter and soft breezes came in off the creek like long-lost friends. By April, grasses hazed the landscape in glorious and variant greens, the sky often wearing a gracious aspect. Naturally I used the mild weeks to install a garden. When it was time, I ordered Phoebe and Maggie to bring water from the creek and then sat in the sun, halfheartedly picking at the dirt under my nails, imagining a new pergola overhead.

Phoebe kept up a lively chatter, while Maggie trudged along in silence, perhaps an attentive, slightly charged silence? I couldn't tell. Maybe Maggie was moved by Phoebe's attentions, maybe she wasn't. In either case, Phoebe's generous outpouring struck me as a display of faith, one based on the assumption of eventual response. Or perhaps she was not the sort of person who required a response.

With her sunny disposition and forgiving nature, Phoebe often seemed more like Polly's sister than I did. When Mother recently insisted that the slave start calling my sister "Miss Polly," I wondered what lay beneath Phoebe's compliance.

Meanwhile, Mother lamented how long it was taking for her silvered glass to arrive, the frame for her large mirror having long since been carved.

Scalded
Saffron, Wappoo Plantation

At dimming-time, sore feet padded to the street. We waited for possum stew and ash cake, maybe clabber, joining a tired circle. Fireflies went sparking and drifting along the creek, going about their business. I sat on the stoop most nights, Maggie between my knees, and I would get to hunting out one face. How would the embers light his nose and chin and where would shadows land on cheek and chest? Would my breath catch? How did desire fit here? His face was a lesson in beauty, making me remember something old and fresh, familiar and alarming. Sometimes, I could feel his quiet quiver cross the circle and meet my quiet, both of us breathing, in and out, out and in, like the marsh, silent and alive.

Not tonight though, because Miss Eliza ordered a bath. Bucket after bucket from the steaming kettle in the laundry shed had to be carried down the slope to the house, up the stairs to the bedchamber, and dumped into the tin tub. July and me, we took weary care so not even one drop of boiled water hit our thighs or feet. How it would burn!

Earlier Mistress made claim to first washing, since Miss Eliza gardened for a smidge today, wearing dirty fingernails just like Titus had all the way on the ship except she was nothing like Titus because this was home for little Miss and she tended garden where she belonged and where she stayed no one was trying to pull her off and drag her away to take her to some other land where she didn't belong and didn't want to stay but had to, homeless and afraid. Sold!

But Mistress Millie was sleeping, and everybody knew to leave her be. Sometimes fever took her to bed, sometimes spite, but whatever it was, it was mighty clear you best not wake her. So second, it was. Poor Melody'd be stuck with Mistress stewing in daughter's dirt, yammering complaint. Earlier Melody had laughed and said, "I don't mind the whining, as long as he's not in the room." We all knew who he was.

Miss Eliza came in and closed the door. Just as it clicked shut, the door across the hall clicked open, then shut. Was Mistress Millie up or Master in? Low voices. No feet clobbering down the stairs, so it was Master in. He sometimes took his chances waking Mistress. Would it be a peaceful welcome or a tongue-lashing? Pretty quiet now.

I unbuttoned the studs running down Miss Eliza's back and she tugged loose one petticoat tie, then another, letting the cotton bells drop into a puddle. I unhooked the clutching bone corset, and she flung it across the room like it was a mean raccoon out to get her.

She stepped right quick into the tub, not testing for heat or asking for my arm. Was the cool air that jiggled the curtains also tickling her, or was she bothered standing there in pale skin and nothing else while I stood in frock and apron, married to the dark? Maybe gleaming nakedness pushed her into an unfamiliar corner. She was undressed and I was clothed, meaning that for a little minute all the claims she lived by wafted in the breeze, unsteady – claims to riches, claims to land and labors, claims to her future as well as mine. Well, the warm water washed all that away in a swoosh. She leaned back and groaned like a queen.

Even with all that pampering care, it came to me sure as the planks under my feet that if the dark had to take sides, it would take mine. Last light disappeared fast off the creek as if one of the orishas tugged it back to Heaven in a jealous fit. Miss Eliza said "ahh" and "ahh" again. I was reaching for the taper to light the lantern when I heard a softer "ahh" from across the hall.

"Just the candle," Miss Eliza hissed. I forgot how she liked the forgiving shadows. I would want covering too with a stranger. Make no mistake: we were strangers. She left on the lacy cap, meaning no hair washing. Suited me fine. The less touching, the better.

I soaked the sponge and squeezed hot water down her back. Her two knees stuck up out of the water like cypress knobs. She relaxed with another "ahh." This right here was the hardest taking of all. Meals and mending, polishing and chopping – all added up to one kind of laboring. But for my own two hands to give her pleasure? She lifted an arm and I soaped underneath. My stomach curled a whine of hunger, and then another "ahh" came from across the hall. This time Miss Eliza heard it too, I think. Why else did she get to humming and splashing about? We both knew how it'd go.

Off came the lace cap! Down under she plunged! Bubbles blown. Up she came humming, down she went, blowing more bubbles. Third time she came up, the sounds across the hall were climbing higher and faster. Something was squeaking – the wall or the bed frame.

Polly flipped over on the bed, tangling her covers but not waking. One arm shot up toward the ceiling as if tugged on a string. How odd. She called out, "Ouch! My arm! My arm!" She still didn't wake.

More hot water was needed, and just in time here came Maggie up the stairs. I could hear how she struggled, her size forcing her to first set the bucket down on a stair above, feet following after. How much water was she toting? How hot? Was she grunting, or was that Master, adding his low notes to the high notes of Mistress?

Mistress yelped of a sudden, sounding like an animal being killed. Next came a crash, a scream, and something thudding down the stairs. Howls of pain! Miss Eliza was underwater blowing bubbles, probably thinking Maggie's scream was her mother. I bolted out and down the stairs. Knelt and grabbed my Maggie up in my arms.

How could they go on up there? But they did. The wall or the bed kept right on creaking – six, seven, eight more times. They were going to finish no matter what! After what seemed like a long while, a flurry of feet scuttled down the stairs – two wet, four dry. I was crying, rocking my daughter. "Miss Eliza! Miss Eliza! What should we do? What should we do?" Maggie wailed, wordless. Mistress tied her robe tight before crouching down.

"Get the honey, George!" Then Master was taking too long, I guess, because she yelled, "On the second shelf up, next to the eggs!" Mistress blew and blew on Maggie's scalded arm, waving Miss Eliza and me to blow too. Maggie looked up, tears dripping off her chin.

Master flipped the wire on the crock and handed it over. Mistress tipped it and let the honey slide out, gold and thick. It puddled all over Maggie's arm. Did it cool the pain or just come as a surprise? Either way, Maggie choked back her tears and looked down in silence. Mistress used the edge of Maggie's frock to keep the honey from flowing off and told Master to light a lantern. Maggie started crying again. I rubbed her back and held in my own tears. Why oh why was howling pain the way I got to hear her voice again?

Melody rushed in, and Mistress asked for the cloth strips, but Melody said it was best to keep it open. "Did you wash her arm before applying the honey?"

Mistress shook her head, and Melody pinched her lips. She took Maggie's arm, tipped it in the lantern light, and started singing a song about peas and rice. Maggie grew quiet.

Seemed Master couldn't abide his rank sunk so low in a cluster of women. He stood and Melody sang stronger, both to please Maggie and to rile him. His face went sour. "So she sings yet, after all," he said and left, telling us to give Maggie a couple days' rest, but what he really meant was, "Get her out of here." Small spirit and hate are hard to hide.

Too bad Master didn't go to Waccamaw this morning instead of tomorrow. Or too bad the galloping finish in bed didn't come sooner. None of this would've happened.

Outside, the sky stretched empty of moon, but stars spangled out in all directions. It hit me hard how those same stars draped over my village. I longed for Mama then, even more than Husband. What would she say – to hold on, be strong? My little girl already scarred up on the inside, now wearing angry burning on the outside. How many ways would Maggie be wounded? What could Mama know of this place?

Very Well Met
Eliza, Wappoo Plantation and Woodward Residence

By the time Mother and I tied our bonnets the next morning, Father was many hours gone. A good day to travel ourselves. Mother preferred the dry route, even if it meant spending a little more time in transit. For some reason, Cudjoe's reliable skill on the riverways could not allay her anxieties. A pair of roans and a serviceable carriage would take us to the Woodwards in a relaxing rhythm, so I wasn't about to complain.

Every other journey to our neighbors had been marked by a breezy affability. Today, however, Mother was peeved. "What's the point of overseers and drivers, and slaves for that matter, if the lot of them can't be relied upon to conduct business?" Father wouldn't return from the newly purchased plantation on the Waccamaw River until Friday. Mother invariably took his absences personally.

"Early stages," I replied vaguely. I wasn't about to mount even a mild defense on Father's behalf, lest Mother redirect her ire from him to me. The ride was fairly brief. Let her ramble on.

"What is it with men and their devices? Must I know every detail?" At tea yesterday, Father had waxed on about the elegance of sluices – how simple their design, how instrumental in increasing yield. Given how obviously I did want to know every detail, perhaps Mother was baiting me. "Whatever happened to sowing seeds and letting Nature do the rest? All this wetting and draining, then more wetting and draining – Good Lord, even saying the words bores me to death, so don't you dare start with your explanations, dear child!"

What she meant was "dear, heartless child," for in this mood my curiosity about running the plantation constituted an offense. Clenching my jaw, I vowed to keep silent. Even a mild suggestion that she misconstrued my motivations could trigger a maelstrom laced with vitriol about the deficits in my character. With a look of challenge, she asked, "You do know he plans to mortgage all three plantations?"

I did not. "To what end?"

"To purchase a better commission, of course." Her ire made more sense now, for if Father succeeded in purchasing a commission, he'd return to Antigua – an absence of a wholly different order. Would he take us with him? If not, it was difficult to imagine how we'd manage without him. Mother fell silent, perhaps reveling in the fact that I'd been left in the dark about so important a matter. Cudjoe slipped off his hat and set it on the bench beside him.

In the silence, I got to thinking. Perhaps accruing grievances constituted Mother's only power. Imagine how different life might be if, for instance, she could sell Melody without consultation – merely because it suited her – or if she'd been able to say to Father, "Send Mac to Waccamaw. Don't go," and have her wishes met. I didn't really want to think about it, but maybe the intimacies in the bedchamber last night represented Mother's attempt to keep Father home or Father's bargain for a peaceful departure. More transaction than love.

What I could not have realized until the blossoming of friendship with Mrs. Woodward's widowed daughter, Mary Chardon (yes, I now had another Mary in my life), was how much strain could be relieved by a sympathetic ear. Mary's sweetly astute nature offered one insight after another. I marveled at her broad sensibility, one enlightened with love, strengthened by truth, and rendered flexible with intelligence.

We were passing the bank of buckleberry bushes that signaled nearness to our neighbors when Mother exclaimed, "And those brothers of yours!" Had she been speaking while I was reflecting on Mary's graces? What now? When Mother complained about the boys to me, they were "your brothers," and if to Father, they were "your sons." She disowned them thoroughly in these moments.

"They've turned into savages. Savages! Your father best not give them muskets. Good Lord! Where'd he get that idea, I wonder. And tell me, must that little Negro go everywhere they go? And where do they go, by the by? Do you know? Does your father? Every absence could mean an encounter with a dangerous creature of these parts – heavens! Fangs and tusks and endless rows of teeth. Poison! Why can they never wait until I can round up a slave to go with them? And I don't mean Noah!"

Mother caught her breath and gave me a look. "I suppose you think your father's idea of supplying them arms is a good one – some essential rite toward manhood? At six and ten! You do remember how old your brothers are, don't you?"

I rolled my eyes.

"And there we have it! Disdain from a child who has yet to attain the ripe age of sixteen." I was pretty sure I could tolerate her for as long as it took to pull into the drive, but nevertheless found myself gripping my silk reticule. Our new friends might afford insurance against a ruined afternoon, but at this distance they couldn't save the delicate ribbon embroidery on my bag.

In a lowered voice, I rattled off what I thought she wanted to hear: how the musket idea was ill-advised and worse, a form of caving to my brothers' wishes; how awful for her to constantly worry about their safety; how primitive life was here in the colony. That last statement was a rather shameless ploy at directing her complaints away from her family and onto Lowcountry living.

"A good attempt, Eliza. But I will say this. Because we live in this – this – place," she sputtered, "this time next year, I shall be lamenting my boys' absences!" Ah! They were "her boys" again. She teared up. "I shall wish for their unruliness then!"

I reached over and grabbed her hand. When my brothers sailed to England next year for schooling, they would be gone for years. It seemed far off now, but we both knew the time would arrive in a heartbeat. After they sailed, uncertainty would govern – letters arriving sporadically and months after being penned, meaning that a son reported to have fever in an April missive could very well be dead by the time we received it in June. Such are the payments exacted for an English education.

We clopped through the arc of the drive in an uneasy silence. Cudjoe didn't make eye contact with either of us as he helped us out of the carriage. Mother shook her head as if to jigger her public visage into place. The corners of her mouth, so tight for the entire ride, now relaxed by a force of will, and her eyes lightened. Some mastery was at work. All I could manage was to brush the wrinkles out of my frock, as if ridding myself of the remnants of our conversation. I wondered if I ever would be as adept as Mother at shape-shifting.

Fortunately, the pleasing vivacity of our friends' company soon dispatched any and all traces of riled mood or resentment. Mrs. Woodward and Mary greeted us as if we were a pair of conquering heroes instead of two ordinary beings weighed down by the miserable complexities of relationship, trying to find our places in a new world.

The Woodwards lived on the north bank of Wappoo Creek as we did, but unlike us, they enjoyed an unobstructed and panoramic view of sky and the broad mouth of the Stono River. Wappoo Creek was no river. It meandered through reeds and grass as if trying to make up its mind whether to be a creek or a marsh. The Stono, on the other hand, asserted a muscular intention to reach the sea.

Mary had married Isaac Chardon one year and been left a childless widow the very next. Though only three years my senior, she had the deportment of a much older woman. Was this from encountering grief at so young an age or from a natural inclination toward sobriety? A deep inner faith and peace suffused her features in a way that turned a fairly unremarkable visage into one of great beauty. Her cheeks were often sculpted by a warm smile, and her dark brown eyes frequently expressed deep sympathy or humor.

She must have inherited her looks from her father, whom I saw little of, for her mother, Mrs. Woodward, could not have been more different. Where Mary was olive-skinned, her mother was light-complected, and pretty in a classically feminine way, with almond-shaped blue eyes and dainty, perfectly shaped lips. Clearly, Mrs. Woodward had been a great beauty in her youth, and even though approaching her fifties, she retained the mannerisms and confidence of a woman who has been an object of admiration her entire life.

Mary Chardon's laugh was a restrained, deep-toned warble while Mrs. Woodward's chimed out like the tinkling of bells. Mary wore dark hues, not drab exactly, but close, while Mrs. Woodward favored pale pinks, silver, and powdery blues. Mary's sober gestures brought to mind a pastor's wife, while her mother's gleeful and exuberant manners might have suited the aristocratic social circles of Paris (or so I imagined).

However silly Mrs. Woodward might appear, she was unmistakably a woman of substance, possessed of sterling social graces and deep intelligence. Her underlying gravitas was likely heightened by having married into the oldest family in South Carolina – Dr. Henry Woodward was her father-in-law. Whatever the differences between mother and daughter, their mutual devotion was obvious. Did I mention that Mary was an only child?

Mary's mother and mine struck a lively chord, instantly finding themselves in agreement on important matters of fashion and politics. Perhaps even more critically, they seemed to share a similar, somewhat sly tolerance for gossip. How nice it was to hear Mother's laughter and animated banter – even if to do so was to notice how tamped down and bleak her moods had been at home.

That visit began with what was already a favorite topic: news about the charismatic but controversial Anglican preacher, George Whitefield. All four of us shared no small amount of alarm at the idea of his spreading the Gospel to any and all comers. Who could possibly think it wise to offer a vision of salvation and freedom to large assemblies of slaves? While my Christian sensibility readily embraced the notion that all beings, even slaves, possessed souls, it did not run to promulgating ideas that could pose dangerous risks to Lowcountry life.

"His sermons are downright incendiary," Mrs. Woodward was saying. "I do hope the petition to defrock him succeeds – you've heard of it?" Yes, we had. The illustrious Reverend Alexander Garden had corresponded with the Bishops in London to demand that they slow the preacher's mission, if not stop it altogether.

On a lighter note, Mary said, "They say Whitefield's sermons inspire acts of charity with such suasion that one should empty one's pockets before taking a seat near his pulpit."

Her mother laughed that musical laugh and added, "I've heard it said that his mere utterance of the syllables *Mesopotamia* will make a grown man weep!"

"Surely, Whitefield would arouse no controversy were his sermons dull and narcoleptic," I said.

"Oh indeed! And there's that unfortunate misaligned gaze to overcome," Mrs. Woodward said, referring to the minister's notoriously crossed eyes. She slyly added, "They call him Dr. Squintum."

"Oh, stop!" I said. "Controversy or no, I should like to hear him before he's run out of the colony." Mother asked for more details about the efforts to defrock the man, in part, I think, because she was interested in the attorney defending him, Andrew Rutledge.

"Who knows what the powers that be in London will make of our squabbles," Mrs. Woodward replied. "In any case, it ought to be clear that Whitefield's purported offense of not following *The Book of Common Prayer* is pure pretense."

The topic was dropped as a trio of slaves came out onto the verandah bearing trays of refreshments. We shuffled over to a table on the other side of the porch, and though it was only two o'clock, we enjoyed an array of savories: oysters dredged in cornmeal and deep-fried, small slices of sausage made from a heavenly combination of pork, turkey, and spices, and a toothsome rice bread speckled with herbs. For the finish: lemon cream, served in cut crystal glasses. The food alone would have cheered the most miserable of souls, but when you added the lively exchanges and warm goodwill, it was impossible to imagine any distress lasting for long in this company.

Talk turned to neighbors. "Mr. Tilton you'll meet soon enough," Mrs. Woodward said, savoring a spoonful of dessert. "His family arrived before the transition from Proprietorship to Royal Colony, which is partly why all he was able to scoop up so much land."

"How much land?" Mother asked.

"Oh, heavens, I haven't a head for such things," Mrs. Woodward laughed, "but it is in the many thousands – four, maybe?"

Then we heard about the illustrious bachelor sons of Arthur Middleton, each more inventive or civic-minded than the last: one studying law, one with a seat in the Assembly, two with land along the Ashley. Then there was Henri Dutarque, descended from a wave of Huguenots who came to the New World seeking religious freedom, some apparently lured by pamphlets drafted by the Lords Proprietors in which the French's considerable skills regarding silk, olive oil, and wine were shamelessly lauded. Mrs. Woodward was vague about him and it struck me that perhaps there was something vague about the man, not that the grapevine had failed our host.

To stave off the need for an afternoon nap, Mrs. Woodward and I took turns at the harpsichord. Mary pulled out her quilt top and plied her needle while Mother hummed along. Once our lunch had settled, Mary and I headed out for a stroll. This routine not only satisfied my botanical curiosities, it afforded both generations some privacy. As we made our way along a well-tamped path through the spartina grasses, the shiny yellows and hazy greens of midday deepened into the flints and pewter of late afternoon. A soft breeze corrugated the creek. It was one of those rare moments when the briny scent of the Atlantic made its way across the barrier islands. We both inhaled appreciatively.

I lifted my arms with one deep breath and Mary followed suit. In unison, we dropped our limbs and puffed out vigorously. This calisthenic was repeated until hysterical laughter o'ertook us. We must've looked ridiculous! "Deranged herons!" I proffered between gasps.

"Umbrellas wrecked by the wind!" Mary countered, snorting.

How lovely that my philosophical new friend could let down her guard!

On the ride home, Mother and I were both so revived that the earlier unpleasantness seemed akin to a bad dream, but then Mother ruined the cheer.

"Mrs. Woodward tells me that Willard Tilton has yet to find himself a sweetheart. She can't for the life of her understand why not."

"Indeed," I said.

"You know his property touches ours." Mother said this casually, but I knew it was the start of one of her campaigns. I was curious about him too, but not nearly enough to overcome the sour bitterness of being confronted with such coercions. Could the horses go any faster?

Apparently, my resistance was plain, for as Wappoo came into view, Mother's mood sank. Cudjoe pulled the horses to a stop and Mother leapt out and bustled into the house without waiting for me. Instead of following and appeasing, I walked round to the back. I'd sit on the gallery for a while, delaying my exposure to the weight of her unhappy judgment.

Indian Pete and the Carolina Dog
Eliza, Wappoo Plantation

The last chords of Bach's Air in D major left an impress in the parlor, like a whisper from an angel. I lifted my hands from the keyboard and placed them in my lap. Mr. Jenkins nodded with a smile. "Well done, well done!"

Father clapped from the gallery, where he'd positioned his rocker to listen. "Brava, Lizzy. Brava!" It was my turn to smile.

"The notes were crisp," I said, "but perhaps overly sad for D major?"

Mr. Jenkins laughed. "Stuff and nonsense! If only all my students did as well. You're ready for the Rondo in D Minor. And rest assured, that's a piece you may invest with all the melancholy you possess!" He laid the new score on the harpsichord and made some fingering notations.

"Next week, then?" Mr. Jenkins packed up his papers and gave a bow, arm extended in a dramatic flourish. We were saying our farewells on the verandah just as Overseer Mac and the slave called Indian Pete approached.

Mac's bearing told me that he had no urgent business. His casual visits during these early weeks may or may not've been calculated, but they generally provided instructional anecdotes or barely disguised boasting. He wanted to make a good impression.

"Have you time to meet Wappoo's best hunter, then?" Mac began. "Good with live animals too! This chap can sweet-talk a mean-tempered mule into a yoke in a heartbeat!" After a nod hello, the slave turned to look at the barn, where he'd no doubt prefer to be. A bump on his nose called to mind the Chickasaw traders we'd seen in town. He was average height, with a large head, deep-set eyes, and a chin squared-off as if by a sculptor. His body was sculpted too, unlike the thin frames of most of the field hands. He wore his hair long and tied at the nape and his skin shone like cherrywood. A nervous dog sat at his side.

He wore the standard breeches and tunic of other field hands, but his calves were sheathed in leather boots that laced to the knee. About his waist looped a strap from which hung two sheaths, each six to eight inches long.

"And weather?" Mac continued, sticking a forefinger into his mouth and popping his cheek in comic gesture. "Forget studyin' stars or sunsets or the brine of breezes. Ask Indian Pete!" He elbowed the slave.

"Animals tell moren' the sky, Overseer, sir," Indian Pete said, turning slightly toward Mac. "You wanna tell the freshet comin'? Listen to the pigs. Watch 'em. They get busy building dams with their snouts when high waters coming."

The subject changed to crops, in particular, cassavas and ginger. The fawn-colored dog at Indian Pete's side whined. With a simple flash of his palm, the slave quieted the dog, and the results were so immediate that I recognized his power for myself. I'd later learn the short-haired dog was a Carolina, believed to be the only indigenous breed on the continent.

When the topic turned to hunting, my brothers appeared as if by magic. Both Tommy and George had been begging Father to teach them to hunt for months before we left Antigua, and Father's vague promises about "when we get to the Lowcountry" were now being held up like notes come due. In particular, the boys wanted muskets.

Tommy made a move toward the dog and the slave stepped decisively between them. The dog's hackles stiffened. He growled. Indian Pete issued a sharp "No" to my brother and turned toward the dog. The canine's glare at Tommy was nothing compared to the ones my parents now directed at the slave. Speaking to the master's son in such a manner! And then turning one's back!

In just another minute, Indian Pete leaned down toward my brother and said, this time deferentially, "Never come at a dog you don't know. Dogs want to please their person. Protect them too." I noticed that he didn't use the word "owner," and indeed the question of who owned the dog formed itself in my mind. He was Father's, surely, like everything else? But then, perhaps not.

Indian Pete said to Tommy, "He's ready to meet you now." The encounter between my brother and the dog, whose name was Chester, then went without incident.

"Pay heed, boys!" Mac said and then dismissed them. Slave and Chester headed toward the barn, and the boys followed.

We heard Tommy ask Indian Pete in all seriousness, "So pigs talk in these parts?"

We all laughed, except Indian Pete, who nodded. "If you know how to listen."

Mac gave Father a look. "'Tis great, you being up on a bluff here," he said with pride, as if he himself had sited the house. "No freshet's yet come close." And with that, the visit was over. Mac made a slight bow and headed up the road toward the fields, placing his straw hat back upon that wild crown of red hair.

Cloud with Wings
Mo, Wappoo Plantation

Clouds blew in, turning day to dark in the shake of a stick. Most storms give warning, sometimes as much as two-three tasks. "Task" what we call a part of laboring. I'm grown, so I work three tasks, more during harvest. Old Sarah bent in age, so she work half a task nowadays. Other signs a storming comin' might be the smell of dank ground, prickles in the air, pigs shoving mud about in piles. But today the dark came up sudden. No signs.

I looked up and saw a cloud that weren't no cloud. It went one way, then the other, fast and inky. Squinted and made out wings. It was a flock of birds! A flock so big it blot out the sun. It flowed this way and that way like a rag on a stick, wheeling round faster than a man could drop his hoe and clap. Looked like those birds shared one mind. No one leading, all following.

'Course I seen maybirds swarming and swooping, greedy for rice shoots. They'd gobble acres in a blink if you wasn't paying attention. Trunk minder better be minding then! Opening the sluices letting in creek waters. Bird minders too. Soon enough Overseer Mac'd be telling the little ones to make a racket and they'd come round banging on pots, waving brooms, and snapping cowhides.

But 'twas April and too early for maybirds or bobolinks. Abraham whistled low and looked high. Quash glanced up but turned back to task – he was helping Old Sarah finish hers. Everybody else stared yonder. So many birds! I looked up too, but then my eyes drifted down and settled on Binah, two rows over.

Binah so new and raw to Wappoo she hardly yet talking or eating. Her small bones and long neck made her like a bird too, 'cepting she was strong, bound to earth. She had a hard body, one that looked like it could run all night. Spidery scars fanned out over one shoulder – I'd seen 'em when she bent and her shift slid over to one side. Maybe she already done run once. Why did Master buy her?

Them marks wasn't fresh, so if she was saltwater, she wasn't lately off the slaver. We knowed how them traders punish on the sly, making pain without leaving marks what with scars chipping off value. She looked twelve, maybe thirteen. Narrow shoulders, that long, beautiful neck.

Just like scars was telling a story, so was her missing front tooth. Was that buckra's work too? Maybe her old Master yanked it out instead of branding her. A missing tooth a catchy item for a runaway notice.

What tongue do she dream in?

When the birds moved north a little, the sun hit her head scarf and neck, like someone was shining a light just for the pleasure of my looking. I'm guessin' she was just-sold-quiet right now, not forever-quiet. I wanted to hear her voice. I wanted to see her smile. If ever I could kiss her, I wanted to put my tongue into that gap between her teeth. Would she like it?

The birds swooped and swooped again. Was they flying just for fun, showing off, or maybe looking for something and all that turning and swooping was meant to find it?

Quashee's heel struck the ground, making seed holes in time with Old Sarah's heel. They dropped the seeds that was muddied ahead of time so they wouldn't blow in any wind and then slid the dirt back with they toes. Old Sarah didn't glance up at all. Maybe she lived long enough to see flocks this big so early in the year.

The flock sailed east toward seven tall chestnuts growing like a picket fence along the field's edge. The birds swung round and over the biggest chestnut and roosted, all landing in that one tree only. That was some sturdy chestnut, but sure didn't look sturdy enough for all them pigeons. Looked like having one mind gave grace to flying but folly to roosting.

The chestnut groaned. Branches sagged, even the mighty ones. They sagged some more. Then: kak-kak-kak – three branches snapped off and crashed down so loud it sounded like musket fire. I felt them landin' all the way over here in my feet. It was like a piece of sky broke loose.

Binah jerked and crouched, hands over head. Abraham squatted by, talking soft like a father, taking care not to touch her in case that scare her too. I wished it was me doing the talking. I'd know what to say, wouldn't I? I'd know how to hold back touch, wouldn't I?

"Branches broke," Abraham said. "Look." Binah stood slowly.

Everybody knowed Overseer was on Johns Island training a new horse, otherwise we coulda only seen the spectacle over our shoulders, working all the while. But now there was dinner bounty and no one to stop us. Quash nodded at four men to finish the planting alongside Old Sarah, waved the rest of us away, and whistled sharp for Benjie and James. Even little hands could carry pigeons.

We all dashed off to the edge of the field. Like birds of one mind.

Walnut Shells and Skunk Bones
Saffron, Wappoo Plantation

Something shatter air with bang-bang-bang, loud like that. Benjie and James scrabbled to the door and stood there, half in and half out, all of us wondering who got kilt. I gave July a look. Where was Maggie? Where was Noah? We all looked out toward the rice fields. Silence. But then, sharp as a hawk scream, it came: Quashee's whistle. Off the boys flew.

Seemed like they were back in no time at all. Like a man home from war, little James raised up his hands, one dead pigeon hanging off each. "Fry up!" he yelped.

"Quashee say bring the dirty lard," Benjie added, two birds dangling from his fists.

Dirty lard was the fat we set by, the stuff too dotted with food bits for Porch House, but not gone over. Tasty enough. When supper cleaning was near done, July pulled the lard crock out and she and Melody headed off, but I stayed back. It was my turn to get the dishes done and feed the pigs.

By the time I got to the cabins, heat rose up off two kettles, wrinkling the air above. The plucked pigeons was piled in heaps taller than Noah and that's a fact, cause there the boy was, looking on, curious, hungry, and shorter than those two piles of birds.

"Step back!" July said, waving her wooden spoon at him. She dropped in six birds to a pot, setting off a crackle. Oh, that smell!

I found Maggie in the vegetable garden, alone. Frying fowl hadn't brung her round? She was eating peas right off the vine, guilty-like. I plucked a pod or two and ate 'em, smiling wide, showing how it was fine and not thieving. When we went back round, we sat in our usual way, in the cabin doorway, me leaning against the frame, she between my knees. She sniffed the air and gave my ankle a little squeeze.

Usually, Indian Pete filled the pots with meat: wild boar, possum, squab, deer, fat crows, and coon or squirrel, depending on season. Or so they told me. What buckra gave out each week, one of this and a quarter of that, was never enough by half: corn, molasses, fatback, salt now and again, sometimes clabber. Already, Indian Pete was going on about turkeys even though they were two seasons off. How plumped up they got by the time of the Panther Moon, how tasty they came off a spit, the skin crunchy and ever so good.

Of course we ate fish: chubb sucker, jackfish, bowfins, catfish, plus shrimp and oysters. Even Benjie and James knew where to pick oysters, and like as not they'd be showing Noah soon enough. Now and then, Cudjoe and Abraham paddled to market on the cypress raft they hide in the reeds to sell some catch. Mostly Overseer ignored the runs, but now and again he demanded a cut – ten or twelve oysters, a couple of chubb suckers, some coin. That made him a cheat – coins were supposed to go Master – but we'd heard the harm other overseers dished out after finding secret fish traps and rafts and counted ourselves lucky.

Once the fried birds were handed round, talking pretty much stopped. July loaded up the pots again – a happy sizzle. Pigeon was slim pickings but good all the same. We learned which tiny bones to crunch down on and which to spit out and how to suck out the brains, but no one had to show us how to lick our fingers. Leave it to Mo to moan out his pleasure. Binah glanced over a time or two, and maybe that was why he did it.

I looked over at the live oak by Porch House, then back at ours, the sameness and unlikeness striking me hard. One tree delivered a burned-out feeling and the other filled me with wonder. These days, before task, Titus hid his medicine bag in our tree, five feet up. I'm betting our oak and those skunk bones traded secrets all the day long. Maybe the opele soaked up the power running up and down that tree. Maybe Olorun sent greetings from the gods through those big branches right into Titus's medicine sack. When I tipped my head back, took no stretch to think the oak leaves were rattling praise to the sky.

Titus wore the medicine bag round his neck while eating. After dinner, he sometimes took it off and tossed it up and down, like a gambler warming his cowries for a game of mancala. Every time the bag landed in his palm, the bones and hulls clinked. That sound was as near to home as anything yet. It also called out the sound of our hunger, soul hunger.

Ever since Titus scooped up those skunk bones and walnut hulls from the roadside weeds, I'd pestered July for words: "skeleton," "walnut," "medicine." SKEL–E–TON sounds bony, don't it? Any word sounding like its meaning gave me a happy jolt. Those tiny curls of skunk spine looked more like tiger teeth than backbone. BACK–BONE. A stiff and sturdy sound.

Maggie watched Titus or studied his medicine bag, I couldn't tell. She wasn't like the other little ones, hopping near the pots, hoping for another bird, dancing away from July's swinging spoon. I watched Titus too. How bad I wanted babalowo's wisdom! What was Daughter's oddun? What was her remedy? When was it right to ask? What offering could I give here in the land of scantiness?

Twilight came in soft and sweet. Soon one then another star pricked out and a breeze rattled along the creek, swaying the grasses. Air as lover. Ancestor sky. Even the murk of evening was pretty, royal even, more purple than gray. Crickets chirruped and oak toads called out. We were in the doorway, Maggie and me, just about to go lie down, when Titus started talking.

Hercules translated for the others. Maggie fell sound asleep before Titus even finished one whole thought – as sure a sign of babalawo's power as anything else. And the little boys? Even though they hate to miss a thing, Benjie and James fell stone cold asleep too, curled up on swept dirt near Mo's feet, each boy holding on to an ankle. Where was those boys' mother? What happened to her? Nobody said. Maybe no one knew. Around here, fear always takes a seat at the table like an uninvited guest.

"Our Ancestors are here with us!" Titus started. "No ocean can keep them from us, nor can wickedness! Our guardians have traveled here too, swiftly, painlessly." He paused. It seemed like the whole of our street breathed in and out of his lungs. A silence fell. It wasn't the silence of grief or fear, but the alive-quiet that truth-telling calls up.

Titus looked round at us, one by one. When he came to me, I felt his blessing as sure as I felt timber against my spine. Soul to soul. For the first time since being rowed away from the barracoon and shoved aboard the slaver at the coast, peace filled me up. That's another kind of silence, maybe the holiest of all. Peace-silence nested inside truth-silence, like it belonged. Even the smudging dark felt like a consecration. Did sleeping Maggie feel it, too?

The electric air and shifting hearts spoke to the beauty and strength of our people. Look at us! Beauty and strength even in a life of abuses.

Titus started tossing the cloth bag up and down again. With eyes closed, he started singing. "A hot season coming – a sick season. But nothing stops Olorun from his mighty work." He opened his eyes and looked round again, quickly this time. Hercules kept up with his words.

"They thieve our bodies. They thieve our labors. They split our families. Over time, their thievery will take more than you can imagine. But they cannot take everything. Our meanings will bend. Our ways will shimmer and hold, right under their noses."

The babalawo's words moved everyone, both the binyas born in these parts, and the comyas from all over, the Windward Coast, Sierra Leone, the Kongo. Titus waved at Porch House, where lantern light glowed in the windows. I knew how that light glinted off crystal and how the crystal like as not held a warming dark liquid, rum or sherry.

"Cruelty and hate are sicknesses, and like many a disease, they spread. For buckra, the cure is a very long way off. We will dwell in the shadow of their disease for twelve generations. Twelve generations, maybe fourteen. All those years with them coming for us hard."

Firelight showed tears on Abraham's cheeks. He wasn't even wiping 'em off. Melody stared at the ground, one of her pretty hands on top of Noah's head, the other resting on her apron, near the belly button. Something jiggled my mind seeing her hand like that – but why?

To close, Titus called forth the Ancestors. Chills ran up and down my spine. The top of my head opened up, just like a teapot, letting starlight pour in and something else. Titus seemed on the verge of changing himself up, into a thundercloud, maybe, or a lion. The sleepy ones round the circle felt the change and woke, even the children.

The Ancestors gathered round and surrounded us with an even bigger silence, a velvet silence so wide and open and deep that time melted away. I only felt this way one other time and that was when my babies needed pushing into the world. Our oak shuddered in holy accord. Titus got up and went to bed.

Seemed like all the widening left a crack where sorrow could come charging back in, cause before I even stood, sadness tugged at me like a riptide. Do the opposites of peace and love demand a turn? Maybe. Even so, for the first time since thieves grabbed me and Maggie and coffled us up, I knew help was to hand. Some kind of help.

Easter
Saffron, Wappoo Plantation

The day was cool, so we cooked Easter supper in Porch House pantry 'stead of Summer Kitchen. Easter's a Praise Day, they say, but not much praise going on. The family done stay put. Mistress and Miss reading by the fire. The big book. Looked like a regular day to me.

The parlor hearth sits on an outside wall, but the pantry hearth is on an inside wall, the one between pantry and parlor. That wall holds strong magic. How else could it keep us separate? The door swings in. The door swings out. It's just a door. But oh my, what a difference, one side to the other!

They don't come back here but now and again, but we go out there every other breath. Back and forth. Fetch and serve. Prep and deliver. The journey through that door pains us. We wear one kind of look out there, different looks in here. One kind of words spoken there, another kind here. Slavery takes nothing out of them. Where they sat was where they belonged. But bondage forced us to be two or three people all day long, most all of them pressed down, silent. We belong nowhere.

The sun threw down glad rays. Summer's coming! I didn't know what summer'd be like here, but a soft happiness rose up knowing that sunlight didn't give a hoot about what side of a door it shone on. Shadows didn't care where they fall neither. If buckra could claim the sun and boss the dark, they would, you know they would, making the world both gloomier and more full of glare for us and shinier and more comfortable for them.

Shelling peas, I could see the corner of the barn out the window and a silver piece of the creek and the closest cabin. Their live oak. I should've been learning words while shelling, but today I just stared, quiet.

In here, shelves run all the way up to the ceiling. Naming all that's stowed will take time, especially seeing as how July likes to cook quiet. She doesn't mind when I stare, but soon enough I'm asking for more names: peach preserves, vinegar, marrow spoons and fish forks, baking plates, honey crock, lizard for the fire, silver, flannel, salt and cinnamon, bowl, eggs, potatoes.

Under one counter you got your sugar cabinet with its bright cones inside, a hogshead of rice, a bucket for the pigs. They lock up the sugar cabinet, "to keep you out," Mistress said. They lock the liquor cabinet too, but that's in the parlor. Master keeps the keys. Even dumb-fresh, I could tell it pained Mistress, his hanging onto the keys. In the liquor cabinet, bottles wore shiny necklaces stamped with letters. Bottles on a plantation are dressed better than even the house slaves! Sherry from Spain, two kinds of rum, cognac, and claret. Those words would come later.

July turned the spit, butt sticking out to avoid spatter. Melody poured hot water into a pot, the steam rising up and clouding her face. Like she did before, she gobbed up a marble of spit, but this time she didn't hawk it into the pot. With a tight little nod, she swallowed it back and stirred the tea. Maybe she got to feeling they don't deserve that little piece of her.

What passes for usual round here ran so far afoul of nature, you'd think nature might pick up and go, like a poor loser at pawpaw. In a huff. Clouds might decide buckra doesn't deserve rain and the rest can't shelter from it, so goodbye! A barren sky would match what lay below – acres barren of justice. Comfort allotted by skin.

That Easter day, my body craved fresh peas from the garden and I felt curious in my bones to know the next Lowcountry season. But tomorrow I might ask the Ancestors to come take me and Daughter home. Made no sense, I know. What was keeping me alive? My dreaming, Maggie's breath? A hunger for life that abided in spite of everything? Soon enough frost will glitter on the ground, bringing us round to a solid year as chattel. I don't want to mark time this way – one full cycle of seasons surviving, a second spring owned? A few months passing for buckra go like ten years to a slave.

I passed the shelled peas to July. She turned away from the two pork tenderloins, shining with grease in a wire basket hanging off a spit. Melody hitched a yellow bowl on her hip and stirred batter.

"Spoonbread," she said to my look. It was yellow, but not from sweet potatoes or cassava. Corn, she told me. The spoon clap-clapped, bringing two boys in. July raised one eyebrow but then with a small smile nodded at the pig barrel, meaning, "Have at it."

Melody set down the bowl and helped them tug the slop barrel out. Now I understood why they sometimes peeled apples and cukes like clods instead of cooks. Just today, July pulled one ribbon off a cucumber after another in thick strips, bringing white flesh along with each one. Apple cores went in with fruit-meat clinging on, now and then a pea pod full of peas. They kept sticky stuff like coffee grounds, lard, and tea leaves apart. Believe it or not, there's a few things pigs'll eat but near-to-starvin' boys won't.

They were almost done digging in the slop barrel when Melody scooped a dollop of cornbread batter with a finger and offered it up – first to James, then another to Benjie. Both boys jumped up and down in place, happy, but quiet-like, begging for more. Hardly a sound. The way they looked like Yoruban dancers made me suck in my breath.

Melody mixed the batter with a final clackety-clack, then tipped the bowl to fill the iron molds. The boys knew what that meant! A bowl to lick. A spoon.

"How you boys gonna make this fair?" Melody asked, holding spoon and bowl up over her head.

James piped up in his knee-baby voice, "Miss Melody! Benjie got the bowl last time."

Benjie nodded, disappointed but fair-minded. They grabbed spoon and bowl and disappeared up the slope to the Summer Kitchen. No sense risking Missus coming in and seeing them boys licking batter.

Figs, Oranges, and Seeds
Eliza, Wappoo Plantation

By mid-April, the Lowcountry unfurled her beauty all about us. The majestic pine put on a fresher green, the young myrtle joined its fragrance to that of the golden jasmine, and a riot of color from honeysuckles, daisies, and a thousand more beauties lined the banks of the river. One day, I shall know all their names!

I was donning my bonnet for a walk when I heard the rumble and clink of a horse-drawn vehicle. A cloud of dust appeared at the road's crest, followed by two shining roans and a new-looking carriage. Shutters slapped open from the second floor, meaning Mother too had heard. Not such a terrible headache, then.

"W'all halloo up there," a man hollered.

I did not recognize him but could tell that he was a gentleman, in spite of his plain garb and casual speech. After handing his gloves over to his Negro, he hopped down to the ground, skipping the step, demonstrating the agility of a much younger man. Whether he did this by habit or for effect, I had no way of knowing. The slave handed him a dark green haversack.

His face was both plain and handsome, if such a thing is possible. I guessed his age to be early to late thirties. With the facial weathering that distinguishes colonialists from their English cousins, it was often difficult to tell. And anyway, quite frankly, anybody past the age of twenty-five just seemed old to me.

Mother burst out of the front door in a clatter of welcome. "Why, Mr. Speaker of the Assembly! Whatever are you doing in these parts?"

This was Charles Pinckney?

"Come up! Come up!" she nearly sang.

From halfway up the stairs, such that their heads were at the same level, he leant to kiss Mother's knuckles, saying, "Charles, please. No need to stand on ceremony."

Mother turned to ring the bell for July while Charles attempted to brush off some of the dust from his breeches. "Would you permit me to direct the care of my horses before our introduction?" he asked, looking at me.

"Yes! Yes, of course," Mother replied. "Your slave will find everything in the barn."

Our guest nodded to the young driver, who led the horses and carriage down to the barn. Mother waited a polite interval and then said with airy pleasure, "Attorney Charles Pinckney, may I present my daughter, Miss Eliza Lucas." He climbed the final two stairs, standing easily two heads taller than I. My hand received the same glancing kiss as Mother's. Mother turned to me and asked where Father was, unabashed, apparently, to reveal her ignorance of his whereabouts.

"Up with the overseer quite a ways past the alfalfa fields, probably until late afternoon."

Charles apologized for not having arranged the visit in advance, but as he had business on Johns Island, he hoped we wouldn't mind.

"Oh heavens," Mother gushed, "you're welcome anytime. But it sounds as though you'll have to see Husband another time. He'll be so very disappointed to've missed you." When had my parents met Mr. Pinckney and where was I at the time?

As we arranged ourselves in the gallery rockers, Mr. Pinckney pulled the first of his welcome gifts out of his haversack. There was dignity in his profile, in his small, well-formed ears, and in that healthy ruddiness as well. A cleft in his chin imparted a slightly boyish look. As he produced a small sack of figs, I was struck by how large and warm his eyes were – lustrous brown, nicely framed by eyebrows arching above. I supposed had he been in possession of any hair on his crown, it too would have been dark brown. But in its absence, his forehead stretched into a bald dome that was slightly startling.

"Figs! How delightful!" Mother exclaimed.

After speaking about the provenance of the figs, Charles seamlessly turned to the topic of his wife, Elizabeth.

"She sends her apologies." He explained that she'd stayed in town that morning on account of a slight stomach malaise. "It's nothing to worry about," he assured us, "but it does recur with some regularity. Perhaps we ought to ban sausages in our home!" Charles laughed, but then added that Elizabeth ailed a little more during the sick season, so if it was some time before we met her, we weren't to take offense. Sick season would soon be upon us.

He produced two more gifts. The first was a wrapper full of bright curls of candied orange peels. "Next year, I shall bring you fresh oranges too," he promised. For long minutes we were silent, sampling the lovely mix of sweet and tart flavors. I helped myself to another, while Charles handed us recipes – one for shrimp and one for bluegill.

"The orange peels add a wonderful piquancy," he explained. Such warmth and civility! Was his wife of equal refinement? I glanced at the recipes, wondering if they were written in his hand or hers; the script had a decidedly feminine look to it.

The final gift he handed to me with a slight flourish. "I've heard quite a bit about you already, young lady," he began, "in particular, about your love of the garden." I may have started for he quickly added, "From my niece, Mary Bartlett, of course." There was that slightly teasing smile again. The charming dimple below.

I opened a small cloth envelope to find more than a half a dozen seed packets. Apparently, as a side venture, Charles purchased seeds from England, grew them, and then gathered and sold the seeds locally by way of advertisements in the *Gazette*.

With giddy pleasure, I spread the packets out in a fan. Each was labeled with that same elegant cursive. His, then. I read off the varieties. "Sweet alyssum, cornflower, daisy, foxglove, periwinkle, snapdragon, stock, thrift, and violet – oh how truly wonderful!" Mother must have sensed that I might very well launch into planting ideas, for she placed a hand on my forearm.

"A more appropriate gift for our Eliza could not have been devised."

After another brief spurt of pleasant small talk, the visit was over. When Charles stood, he put two pinkies between his lips and blew out a piercing two-tone whistle. Would the man ever lack for surprises? His driver quickly appeared out of the barn, giving a big sweep of his arm.

Mother laughed merrily, though I'm pretty sure that if virtually anyone else had employed such a startling country call, she'd have deemed it uncouth. I guess we were both of us a little smitten. He was magnetic, intelligent, and gracious. He had a pleasant face and a sturdy frame that were attractive even at his age, whatever that was.

"Give my best to your husband, Mrs. Lucas," Charles said, bowing, uttering all manner of invitations to his home on the Cooper River. After donning his hat, he launched his bulk into the carriage with surprising agility and was gone.

As if by cue, the boys came scrambling up to the verandah moments later, disheveled and smudged with pluff mud. Mother let out an exasperated sigh and rang for July. It seemed that the excitement of our visitor had tuckered her out. She'd likely return to her room – perhaps with a genuine headache this time – and when she did, I'd take up my quill and plot out where to plant my new seeds. Eight for sun and one for shade. What pleasure!

News of a Neighbor
Eliza, Drayton Hall site

We climbed aboard the pettiauger on a crisp and beautifully clear April morning, light of heart, heading out on one of our first social visits as a family – except for Polly, she was staying back with July and Phoebe. Although it was slightly out of order for us to be received by the young John Drayton prior to being introduced to his father and mother, we were not about to pass up the invitation. There would be a picnic lunch at his newly memorialized property on the Ashley River. I could almost hear Mother thinking, "Such is the way of the colonies," but even she seemed eager.

Like many other early settlers, John's father, Thomas, had come from Barbados, arriving at the propitious time of the colony's shift from proprietorship to land grants. Because he brought a large number of hands with him, using the head count system, Thomas was able to acquire a huge tract of land along the Ashley River. He built a lovely estate in the Caribbean style, converted much of his land to pasture, and continued to make a fortune in beef. As Providence would have it, just as he cleared out of the West Indies, lands formerly devoted to raising cattle and food crops on the islands were given over to cane production, forcing the islands to import their meat. Since most Lowcountry planters cultivated rice, he suffered little competition.

John, meanwhile, acquired a 350-acre plot of land south of his father's estate, also with frontage on the Ashley River. Ground had yet to be broken.

A slight wind met us at the mouth of Wappoo Creek. None of us spoke. Between the rhythmic splashing of the oars and the riotous chorus of birds, there seemed no need. After a spell of heading upriver, we heard him, our host.

"Hallooo! Welcome!" A young man waving. Mother tensed, perhaps wondering what we were in for, and indeed, it looked as if John could barely restrain the impulse to wade into the river and pull our vessel ashore himself. But never mind, Cudjoe and Abraham had the task well in hand.

John was patrician, with thick, burnished hair pulled back in the style of the day. His angular features might've been called handsome were it not for the prominent eyebrows that slashed across his forehead. He wore unbleached linen breeches and a dark blue jacket that flapped about with his overly broad gesticulations. Were the sleeves a tad too short?

Young Drayton's wife, Suzanne, and their two young sons had stayed back at his father's place, so the business of welcome fell squarely on John.

"She's not inclined to muck about in any case," John said with a sonorous laugh. "Well, welcome! Behold!" John swept his arm in an arc indicating the land behind him. "Soon to be erected – Drayton Hall!" His words seemed to be a declaration to the heavens as much as to us.

We headed away from the river, passing a ditch filled with sweaty slaves.

"They're digging our ha-ha," John informed us.

"Ha-ha?" I inquired, and then immediately felt foolish, as if I had just forced a laugh. I needn't have worried, for John appreciated the opportunity to explain anything and everything about his new property. We learned that a ha-ha is a ditch designed to keep cattle from coming near the house without the view-blocking height of a fence. We approached a magnificent live oak, under which sat a rustic pine table with a lone book on its surface.

"The Hall will not face the Ashley as is the custom," John announced. "Instead, a reflecting pond will be installed just beyond its front entry, there." He pointed toward what would eventually be the front of his manse. His long strides forced me to trot a little. I dragged Mother along by the elbow. We paused next to the table. I looked around for chairs or picnic hampers and saw none.

John reached into his waistcoat, pulled out a pair of thin cotton gloves, and reverently lifted the tome off the table. He barely missed a beat as he continued to stride away from the river. "William Middleton lent me this! Charming fellow!" I guess he directed this to Father, who was keeping up. "In possession of a marvelous library! His place is up near the Taylors – Crowfield Plantation. Have you met them yet?" A tendency to let his enthusiasms run rather unchecked meant that the occasional spray of saliva landed on the person nearest by. In the morning sun, I saw an arc of moisture between our host and my father. If Father felt it, he was too courteous to show it.

By now we were a distance from the river. "This will be the back entrance," John said, sweeping his free arm wide, narrowly missing my father's head. He trotted another distance and turned to face the river. "Here will be another entrance, opening onto a loggia. There must be a loggia! Up half a story, the entry will allow the first floor to capture both views and breezes." Indeed the river at that moment looked idyllic with the spring light gleaming off its flat expanse. "A large staircase will be built on either side of this entry, creating symmetry and dare I say, grandeur?"

My father stepped forward briskly and asked to see the book. It was Palladio's *Four Books of Architecture*.

"I'll lend you gloves, if you have none." John pulled a thin pair from another inside pocket, revealing as he did about an inch more wrist than was customary. Perhaps he was still growing?

Father leafed through the tome while John spoke of Palladio's principles with a slightly reverent air, which meant that the volume of his voice diminished to about normal levels of discourse. While he talked symmetry and air circulation, a slave approached seemingly out of nowhere and with a practiced snap laid a large damask tablecloth on the ground near the oak.

"It is near enough midday for some refreshment," John said by way of invitation. We returned to the tree's shadow and sat in a rough circle. What a delicious array of savories came out of that wicker hamper – pear slices, figs, a soft tangy cheese, and rice bread – all washed down with pale ale. The book, I noticed, was kept safely away from the acids and fats of our meal, but quickly brought back out after we finished and the slave had tidied up.

Father took great interest in John's plans, perhaps enjoying his bold and youthful vision, but Mother seemed a little bored. Or perhaps I was. Redonning the gloves, Father carefully flipped through the book while John described carved friezes, fluted pilasters, and mahogany-carved lotus and squash blossoms. Mother perked up at the idea of carved floral motifs, given that she was so proud of her recently carved mahogany mirror frame.

The rules of Palladio were to be applied in the main, we learned, but departed from when Lowcountry climate dictated. "With the Carolina heat" – John's dark eyes engaged my father's intently – "I'll not decrease ceiling height with each successive floor as Palladio suggests, but the opposite. For cooling, my good man!" Mother frowned, the tone too informal for her taste, no doubt. "It's all about air circulation!" Two flankers would be connected to the main house by curved colonnades, one flanker housing the summer kitchen.

The slave produced a second hamper, and conversation turned to other topics. How quickly the time passed, with delectable sweet cakes and candied pecans and stories about Winters, John's crazy Scottish herdsman, who had taken to inviting cows into his cabin for dinner. Despite Mother's avid interest in human oddities, she steered the conversation in a different direction, the better to take the measure of John Drayton. She drew forth a wealth of detail about his wife, his two older brothers, his parents, and their ties to England. Eventually, John shot to a stand and told his slave to pack up. I squinted toward the river to see Tommy and George exploring the ditch-in-progress, walking its length up and back, hooting, "Ha-ha!" as they went.

The declining sun lengthened the oak tree's shadow such that it stretched long across the grasses. John grabbed a small brazier from under the pine table and after lighting its charcoal with a striker led us toward the water, presumably to our boat. But no, there was more to show us! He swung the brazier in and around us so as to distribute the bug-deterring smoke, all the while, regaling us with horticultural plans.

Mother glanced at the boat, rather longingly, I thought. The marshy areas along the river would make for marvelous rice cultivation, John informed us. Alas, these areas were also the preferred home to all manner of flying pests. Despite the waving brazier, we were all of us bitten.

"Right here" – John swept his arm broadly in what now seemed one of his signature gestures – "I will situate an orange grove." We murmured our approval. He had well considered his land's features. I admired that.

"The pamphlets say that we're on the same latitude as the Holy Lands. I suppose that's why figs thrive in this clime?" I asked.

"Ha! Those pamphlets!" John's scorn was evident. Grandpapa had condemned them as well for being full of "damned lies." But then, it wouldn't do for prospective settlers to read about how steamy South Carolina was, how buggy, and how often pocked by disease.

I wasn't easily deterred from the topic of botany, however. "One cannot believe everything one reads, naturally, but as to climate?"

John rattled off a list with ease, "Figs, peaches, pecans, rice, cassavas, alfalfa, cotton, tobacco, magnolia, catalpa, oak, all thrive here. For the introduced strains, it might take a year or two. Consider rice." And now I was the recipient of John's intensity. I found I could tolerate his gaze reasonably well because the topic compelled me, but wasn't sure how I'd fare otherwise. "We are just a bit beyond the tidal ebb and flow here, so we'll have to find lower patches of ground and employ canals and sluices. Have you walked your plantation's perimeter yet?" Rambling on without waiting for a reply, I was beginning to see, was also characteristic of him. "Rice will be well-suited here, I hope!"

The afternoon was now gone. John walked us back to the pettiauger, discoursing along the way about river conditions: windfall clogs, dangerous currents brought on by river rise. "The freshet's not good for business!" His father, apparently, was crafting legislation about the construction of drainage canals to help direct run-off during the high-water weeks. It was soon to be filed, the new law, perhaps this fall.

We set off at last. Mother dragged a hand in the water, her mind elsewhere. Tommy and George chucked pieces of crushed shells that they had packed into their pockets across the water's surface.

Soon enough, the boys sat and an abiding peacefulness took hold. The reeds rattled here and there and the sky darkened to sapphire along the treetops. Light flashing off riverside shrubs seemed to speak of promise. I, for one, was dreaming about a fig grove. Mother was perhaps drawing up a guest list for our first gathering or guessing when our new tea set would arrive. Father's contemplation might be focused on rumors of war with Spain. I had a hunch that only the boys fully occupied the moment, with nothing on their minds but the possible sighting of reptiles, until Tommy curled up on Mother's lap and fell soundly asleep

May 1738

Letter to Mary Bartlett re: Pox
Eliza, Wappoo Plantation

Dear Mary,

Deep apologies for delayed thanks, etc. A very busy household here! One slave says Tommy & George are "busier than a stump of ants." Who knows what they get up to? New curtains for the dining room arrived – bold and bright russet brocade. A pergola's being built over the back terrace. I sit out there afternoons to observe its progress and to pick at Ovid – the love poems, of course. Trying to keep my Latin up.

So, many thanks for japanning – my tray sits in parlor, pride of place, etc.

Your uncle visited recently, bringing nine packets of seeds. If you "seeded" Mr. Pinckney with the notion, additional thanks! Soon enough, my perennials will be "elegant subjects," as you say, for future japanning. I shall, of course, write M/M Pinckney a separate note of thanks, but if this missive arrives first, please convey my deepest gratitude.

Sad news: have you heard? One of the Middleton children died of the pox Saturday last. One can almost feel the miasma creeping along the waterways. Will you be leaving Belmont for the duration? And if so, to where? Perhaps home to London to see your mother?

Re: inoculation – my parents leave it up to me. I find arguments that such measures "interfere with God's will" easily dismissed. Is milling grain for flour an "abhorrent interference"? Is weaving cloth an affront to His pleasure? I think not. Grandpapa cautions against being swept up by the death of baby Mary Roche. Both doctors Kilpatrick and Dale are employing the practice for developing immunity, but as competitors they're not above using the baby's death as a tool of ambition. Despicable!

Risks aside, I shall venture it. I understand there won't be time to correspond w/your mother about the matter, but you're welcome to join. If so, quarantine would be more easily borne! Remember to wear a worn frock if you come, as all exposed cloth will be offered up to the purgative power of fire.

This morning's Scripture was interrupted by a troop of boys and men, white and dark, shaking sticks at our catalpa tree. The caterpillars rained down! Excellent fishing bait, apparently. Five little boys – three slaves, plus Tommy and George – took turns atop some field hands' shoulders. Held aloft, the boys looked like jousting medieval knights.

One caterpillar made its way down Tommy's shirt. He stripped out of it in a trice! When I picked up his shirt, the creature crawled onto my arm, its black and green striping shining in the sun. For fishing, they'll be slit up the middle and turned inside out before being slipped onto a hook. Such violence to put dinner on the table! I cannot for the life of me understand why the lowest beings in this chain of consumption should be clothed in such dramatic hues, can you?

Yours, etc.

Tongue Clucking
Cudjoe, Wappoo Plantation

Overseer handed out sticks yesterday and cheered the boys and men swatting on the Bait Worm Tree. After all the trouble Overseer gone to maybe I should've tole true where best fishin' be at? Nah. I lied to his face.

Just looking at them worms got my mouth watering. The white perch love 'em. The channel catfish love 'em. The bluegills. But you gotta know where to go. Overseer smart to ask me, what with all the paddling and conversating I do on the riverways. I see rings where fish rise and I remember. And naturally we mens talk – where's good this season, what's running in numbers. We lie to each other too – probably 'bout a third of the time. Abraham and me, we got secrets.

Take that big bend in Wappoo Creek heading Stono way. The water lay flat and still there along the outer bank. Deep enough for perch and blue gills. Why would I give it out? Harbor-way, you gotta go further – do Overseer know that? Abraham and me leave at dawn on a Sunday now and then and go round to the ocean side of Johns and James Islands.

Overseer never gonna know them places. As it go now, we gotta share what we trap in the reeds nearby or he go tell Master. Those traps a mighty boon. Good thing Overseer don't know about the raft – built out of cypress deadfall, hidden in the grasses past the smokehouse. If he did know, he'd hold it over us, demand a share, but probably not go frothy with rage, like Doc Jackson did, yelling about slaves not deserving fish and axing a raft to sorry bits.

I tole Overseer, "Try opposite the Taylor place." Never did fish that part of the Ashley. Could be fine as fine can be, but maybe it's poor. I happen to know from one of Drayton's men midges swarm bad there right now. Ha! Makes me laugh thinking on Overseer's freckled face dotted with bites! Scratching, scratching, new red dots dancing with old.

Problem is, Overseer cabin close enough by to smell a fry-up on the street, meaning if we net of pile of bluegill, say, the pan's gonna give up a powerful appetizing smoke. But I got a plan. If ever Overseer come back empty-handed, I'm gonna dodge and cloud. "How you splitting them worms?" No matter the answer, I'll cluck my tongue, tell him to do the opposite. Then I'll ask, "You casting in sun or shade?" Whatever he say, I'll cluck my tongue and say it's s'posed to be the other. If he get suspicious, I'll tell him where Mo goes gigging for sturgeon – I don't like sturgeon. Not one bit. And gigging ain't for me neither. Overseer can have all of that freak fish he can spear for what I care.

Overseer get plenty of food, by the by. What he get in a day'd feed a whole cabin for two – that's five men hard at task. If he wasn't a few bricks shy of a wall, I might worry more about lying to his face, but I don't. Worry, I mean. He drink, too. He know plenty about planting, harvesting, and horses, but fishing? Hunting? No. That's how come he think Indian Pete walks on water, even though he's mustee – half African, half Indian, a type most often doused with hate. All us admire Indian Pete, course we do, look how fast he calm that nasty mule two weeks back, plus Indian Pete say more with a grunt than Hercules do spooling out a tale. But us admiring him don't have no strangeness to it like Overseer admiring him.

The first Sunday in June, Overseer handed me a basket full of slats. Kindling? No, not that. "Master Lucas, being gracious n'all, is providing you sh'ites with shoes." He pulled a slat out, dropped it, stepped on it, and struck a pencil line at the toe. "Everyone over thirteen. Write the darky's name on the back." Overseer paused. "You don't need any help writing now do ya, boy?" I shook my head quick and looked down. It's bothersome, Overseer intimatin' I can read and write. Maybe it was a lucky guess. "Only them's over thirteen," he said again, and walked away. He must not've caught anything good for the fry pan, cause he cranky.

Smokehouse Quarantine
Eliza, Wappoo Plantation

A scuffling sound and a stiff neck. The smothering darkness pinpricked with light. What was this place? A confinement infused with a musky, smoky odor, thoroughly animal in its depth. I sat up and patted my cheeks, as if to confirm that bones underlay. Cheeks had structure, but did thoughts? As my pupils enlarged to accommodate the velvety gloom, I discerned rough-humped shapes some yards away and remembered: the pox variolation. Those sheets clung to Mary Bartlett and Polly, my sisters in quarantine. Were they sleeping? I hoped so.

To recall the doctor's scalpel, its quick slice to the shoulder, was to flinch. And soon it would be time to see about the result. Mother had been against the measure, asserting that the procedure was a gamble. "Pawpaw with terrible odds." Father thought it wise. I'd deemed the benefit worth the risks. So the doctor was called and the insertion of a minuscule splotch of the pox secretion done. Fever followed, for I know not how many days. There'd been unsettling dreams and the jagged uncertainty about skin and survival.

I sat up and leaned against the planks of the smokehouse. On the crate next to my cot lay my silver-backed mirror. Even in the half-light, I could see the scrolled monogram etched in its center. I felt a bleary sense of possession. The silver accessory, so incongruous in the rough hewn shack, seemed nearly magical, like the bauble that glitters on the forest floor in fairy tales and leads the heroine to her destiny. Whether I liked it or not, my face would inform my fate, perhaps to a greater degree than I cared to admit.

As a relatively plain woman, my appeal lay in possession of a certain expressive vitality, if my parents were to be believed, that is. My forehead stretched a little too much heavenward, while my jaw carried on just a little too long in the other direction. I lacked both the large doe eyes of the beautiful woman and the feminine stillness of spirit of the accommodating woman. I was neither overly receptive nor equipped with dainty deference. My voice often lacked sweetness, and my mien ran to determination, occasionally frowning with intent. That these expressions almost always arose from concentration rather than ill-temper was a distinction not apparent to others. Mother told me so at irritating intervals. "Smile, Eliza! It won't kill you." According to her I had good hair and Father made much of my smile when it was in evidence. I had long ago decided that was enough.

Half-dreaming, I thought again of the magic trinket in children's stories, how its power to do good or ill was never revealed until it was too late to turn back. At that moment, I had no idea if my mirror was ally or foe. When Mother presented it to me as a gift along with a matching brush and comb, we were saying our farewells on the West Indian wharf in St. Johns. I was eleven. Before handing over the mirror, Mother had traced a finger along the engraved initials as if naming me for a second time. I'd been holding the items to my heart when we embraced, and the crush had caused the comb tines to dig into my chest. Even at eleven, I understood how well this jabbing sensation represented the bittersweet nature of my departure. Now, at fifteen, I saw how well it also represented the mixed nature of our relationship.

I had to find out if my cheeks were pocked and my forehead disfigured!

Leaning into one of the thin bands of light coming through the horizontal planks, I grabbed the silver handle and in a sudden burst of courage flipped the mirror. In the dim air, my image was slightly blurred, but nevertheless, not a single red spot or divot was in evidence. My cheeks and neck showed smooth, nose and chin appeared normal. At least from the neck up, which was what mattered for a woman of marrying age, I was unmarred. Relief flooded me.

I spun the handle of the mirror between my palms as if it were a toy. An oblong flash of light appeared and disappeared on the ceiling. Where was everybody? What day was it?

My span of fever, the tumbled and heated sleep, slave entrances and retreats, days melding into nights and each other, seemed to be over. I wondered what had happened during my quarantine – how bad the pox toll, for instance, among the Cherokee or Catawba. According to Mary, Mr. Pinckney said that one more pox epidemic might wipe those tribes off the face of the earth. Had we lost any slaves? Even one, never mind two or three, would constitute a financial catastrophe. Many settlers believed the Negroes carried some sort of "jungle immunity," but I remained unconvinced.

I stood with a wobble. Judging by the light along the tree line visible through a crack, it was still early. Just as I was about to investigate how Mary and Polly were faring, July approached with a basin on her hip. When she stooped to pass through the low-framed smokehouse door, her eyes widened in surprise and I realized that I must have looked like a ghost standing there with the sun shining through my white sleeping gown.

Why July was assigned to the role of nurse mystified me. Mother should've selected a field hand – someone more expendable in the event of contagion. July was our most experienced house slave, her silent competence the most seasoned. She was needed for the ongoing training of Saffron and Melody. And several of her dishes were among the household's favorites – peach compote and lemon pound cake, to name just two. She possessed the greatest skill turning out dough for berry pies. She knew how to render beef lard for tallow and how to smock a bodice with precision. I'd heard, too, that she and Old Sarah had woven every single sweetgrass fanner basket on the premises.

Perhaps the fact that Mary Bartlett shared our quarantine had driven Mother's choice. A question of appearances. Imagine a field hand grunting in here and waving her hands about trying to make herself understood. In a fevered state, the scene might have resembled a nightmare.

After placing the enameled bowl down on an o'erturned wheelbarrow with a plank across its legs, July pulled a cotton rectangle out of her apron, wet it, and wrung it out. The sound of the water cascading back into the basin was both strangely loud and full of content. Perhaps I was still delusional.

Neither of us had uttered a word.

Polly turned herself over in a huff, tossing off the sheet.

"You's looking better," July finally said. "Fine, even." She cocked her head and laid the damp cloth over my forehead even though I was standing. She placed my left hand on the cloth. "Maybe the fever done." The moisture felt good.

"What time is it?"

"A pot's boil before the cock's crow, Miss." She bent over Polly and laid a cool cloth on her forehead. My sister immediately yanked it off. She was still asleep.

"What day is it?"

"Two days past Sunday, Miss." The sharp angles of July's hips poked out of her tunic as she bent to retrieve the washing cloth from the floor. She rinsed it in the enameled bowl and tried again. Polly turned roughly at its touch, this time making the cloth slump near her chin.

"Is she still feverish?"

July gave a noncommittal shrug. She flapped out the cloth and laid it down a third time. It stayed put. July performed the same routine for Mary without incident. Somehow, Mary's quiet worried me more than Polly's restlessness.

"What about Mary? Has she come through?"

"You the first," July said, dodging the question. "Seeing you will make Mistress smile."

"Well and yes! I want to get dressed." I declared this with an energy I didn't quite feel. In fact, as I turned to look for some clothing, I swayed and put a hand to the wall for support. July told me that the clothing I'd worn last had been burned. I looked down at my nightgown remembering that it too would be fed to the fire.

Would we be able to use this shed as a smokehouse again, I suddenly wondered. You might think the slow burn of the smoking-fire would kill any traces of disease, but who would be brave enough to sample a hock of pox-pig? I sat back down in a wave of dizziness.

The rest of that day consisted of making demands and being rebuffed. I was not to go outside yet. No, I could not see Mother. Yes, she had been told of my progress. No, I was not to disturb the other girls. I was forced to drink vile tar water for two more days, with only stewed prunes and milk for supper. I was bored silly, and because I pouted, July finally brought me my red-leather-bound Milton. That I was prepared to sacrifice *Paradise Lost* to the bonfire just for the pleasure of reading it during the interminable wait indicated the tenor of those final days.

Polly and Mary slowly came round, the mirror shared. Relief and fatigue braided together until the days accumulated into an acceptable period of decontamination and we were done. We were blessed.

Not so many of our neighbors. Negroes too had died, and were being struck off ledgers up and down the Ashley with a grievous air. One night not long after I resumed sleeping in the house, a terrible wailing wafted out over the muggy air. We did not know the tongue of the dirge, but knew well enough its import. July came through just fine.

June 1738

An Uneasy Pact
Eliza, Wappoo Plantation

He laid down the newspaper with restraint, not quite disguising his dismay. This was Father's first breakfast home after a week-long visit to one of our newly acquired properties, where malfunctioning sluices had demanded his attention. Mother had things to say. In his absence, her complaints had thickened. I excused myself from the table, saying that I owed Mrs. Boddicott a letter – not only was she the wife of Father's factor in London, she'd been my dear guardian during my stay in England, a stand-in for Mother in all kinds of ways.

Mrs. Boddicott taught me needlepoint and dished up delicious scones, along with a fairly steady stream of gossip, much of it about my parents. By the time I departed England at fourteen, I possessed a more nuanced view of my parents' marriage than was common for a child.

The short story went like this: Mother hadn't married "down," exactly, but by marrying Father she'd forfeited an opportunity to better her social standing significantly. For this sacrifice, she was entitled to regular tributes from Father.

Dear Mrs. B,
I flatter myself into thinking that you would want to know that I like this part of the world. I naturally prefer England to it, but find Carolina preferable to the West Indies by a large measure.

While my mother's stylish presentation and elegant manners spoke to good lineage, I wouldn't have known absent Mrs. Boddicott's narrative that her prospects had included a titled gentleman, Sir John Bluett. He was an Earl possessed of a grand manor in Devonshire. Mrs. Boddicott never tired of heaving big-bosomed sighs on behalf of "Millie's untraveled road." Oh, think on it! Mother a Lady, entertaining Barons, Earls, and even the occasional Marquis!

One weekend – I might've been thirteen – the two of us set out for a picnic that just happened to take us past said gentleman's grand manor. The pretense of seeking out a general pastoral setting fell away: we were here to spy on Mother's unlived life. Settling under a beech tree some distance away, we opened our lunch quietly, as if the residents of the manor house might hear. It was the first time I'd partaken in so illicit an act.

Imagine! Had Mother chosen this man instead of Father, I would not have been sitting there. She might've been spared regular battles with malaria, migraines, and misery.

We've been received with much friendship and civility. Charles Town is a polite and genteel place. People live very much in the English taste.

In conspiratorial tones that day, Mrs. Boddicott told me that my parents' match had been approved by all parties, if slightly more so by Father's family. "Sir John Bluett, even with his pedigreed wealth, didn't stand a chance!" How spoiled my mother was in a family of boys, Mrs. Boddicott said, her father helpless to his Sunshine's will, etc. My mother made her preference known early and emphatically. "Oh, she enjoyed your father's spirited defense of a political position! So vital, so – dare I say? – manly!"

"Wasn't the Earl equally well-informed?"

"Oh yes, but so wooden on the dance floor!" A downright clod, it seemed. "Not like your father! Such a charmed pair they were and how handsome your father looked in uniform, with his broad shoulders and all." She winked at me as if I were her contemporary and not the thirteen-year-old daughter of the subjects of discussion.

"She used to quip, your mother, 'Nothing boyish there!' Oh, and your father – always one for the prank or well-timed insult!" Mrs. Boddicott chuckled in recollection. To hear Mother tell it, my father's well-rounded education (not his shoulders), his impeccable manners (not his grace on the dance floor), and his strong sense of duty were the sources of her esteem. For his part, Father spoke admiringly of Mother's vivacity and charm, even praising her strong will – as if that feature had not proven over time to be a burden. Did they miss the younger versions of themselves?

I dipped my pen into the well again just as my brothers and Noah ran out of the barn down to the water's edge followed by three hounds.

We sit on a slight bluff rising over the marshes. Our plantation is called Wappoo after the creek that runs by. Mother's impeccable taste works its magic within our two-story home. Guests are often impressed.

At that long-ago picnic, I'd been powerless to interrupt my guardian's provocative monologue, corrosive as it was. Even then I'd recognized that Mrs.

Boddicott might not be the most reliable of narrators. Though I'd been unable to parse out where she strayed from the truth or for what purpose, this much was clear: I could never unhear a single word. Further, there'd be no subsequent confirmations or denials. Can you imagine my asking Mother, "Is it true you were charmed by Father's prankish ways?" Or, more to the point, "Do you ever regret your choice of husband?"

I chose not to mention Mother's poor health to my correspondent. After all, Mrs. Boddicott had once asserted that Mother never quite found her footing as a wife and mother, and I didn't wish to add fuel to the fire of her criticisms.

That day in Devonshire, Mrs. Boddicott produced a packet of Mother's letters. Yes, indeed! She'd packed them in between the sandwiches and the Madeleines. Were I not distracted by the biscuit's buttery sweetness, I might've placed a hand on Mrs. Boddicott's arm and said, "Enough." But I chewed and she scanned, and summarized. When she got to the part about Mother admitting she wasn't sure she could endure a life in the tropics, I flinched. Mrs. Boddicott at last recognized she'd gone too far and tucked the letters away. "Whatever the case," she concluded, "there's no denying that your mother's placid nature seems to've been undone by the move."

Placid nature? I took Mrs. Boddicott to be an uncommonly good judge of character – gossips often are – but this assessment struck me as wildly incorrect. At this very moment, Mother was likely employing a rather acid tone with Father, imposing, if not her will, then at least her misery – all with the tacit and unmistakable implication that he was responsible for whatever was lacking in her life. Even on her sick days, Mother possessed a commanding quality, as if her malaise expressed not just the ills of the body but the disappointments of her spirit. Furthermore, Mother's positive qualities – charm, creativity, and her remarkable powers of observation – all seemed an expression of a restless character, not a placid one.

Even now I have no idea what Mrs. Boddicott was trying to convey, but I came to a single important conclusion: the idea that Mother could have married "better" gathered importance over time, collecting her unhappiness, much as a cuff collected burrs in a weed-laden field.

While my Father's store of patience generally seemed up to the task of enduring the bite of Mother's tongue, he must have wondered if there was any end to it. His wooden air of forbearance made the image of the charming prankster particularly surprising. He had a sense of humor, but it was wry, restrained. Perhaps as Mother's physical health sagged, his humor retired behind an increasingly stoic exterior.

Mid-letter, I realized that Father's disappointment must match my mother's. How oft I'd heard him lament, "If only she were happy …" The hope that his wife might "settle" and create a life of value away from England was surely one Father had abandoned long ago. No wonder a slave with the voice of an angel had gained entrance to his heart.

Wait. Had she?

A loud splashing commotion erupted at the dock. Noah came running up to the house, pointing. There was George, lying belly down on the planks, reaching one arm out to a flailing Tommy. Before I even attained the foyer, Father stood at the water's edge with a soaking wet Tommy in his arms. Mother's skirt belled out as she ran ahead of me. Poor Noah started to cry. This time it was George who placed a brotherly arm about the little Negro's shoulders.

Melody greeted us on the gallery and was directed to fetch some sheeting. Mother entered the pantry. "July? July?" The slave appeared at the back door. "Some tea."

"Never mind that," Father called from the parlor. "The boy needs a hot toddy." He unlocked the liquor cabinet and handed July a bottle of rum. "Half a gill of this heated with honey and lemon juice."

"There's at least one cinnamon stick left next to the egg bowl," Mother added. Once Melody returned with the sheeting, Mother requested biscuits for the rest of us. Noah left the room with his mother.

In short order, Tommy was sitting on Mother's lap sipping his very adult drink with a measure of satisfaction. Once again, he acted as savior, defusing a tense moment between my parents. Peace would likely now prevail until Mother was certain of Tommy's well-being.

Out of nowhere, she started harping on me.

"You know, Eliza, your Father and I hope that you will oblige the gentlemen we meet with a modicum of courtesy." Already, she had taken up the causes of Mr. Dutarque and Mr. Tilton. I reached for a biscuit with what I hoped was a casual air.

Mr. Dutarque
Eliza, on the Ashley River

Mother fanned herself to no avail. The dollop of shade provided by my parasol proved equally useless. Cicadas thrummed to a pitch, then quieted. The rise and fall of their cries struck me as the breath of the Lowcountry – the intake, the out breath. It was as if we inhabited the interior of some creature's lungs cupped above us with a smothering closeness, trying to gain air and on the verge of failing.

The carriage left a dusty trail as we headed off. At the mouth of Wappoo Creek, we angled northwest where we would track the Ashley River for the four-mile distance to Mr. Henri Dutarque's. He had invited us for lunch. Cudjoe's neck beaded with perspiration, his head bare. The sun must have been terrible bearing down on his face.

"It's possible we should have deferred until September," Mother murmured. Cudjoe clicked the horses to a trot, and their long tails swiped repeatedly at all manner of insect. Bugs and heat. Heat and bugs. No respite from either. The fine cotton lawn handkerchief in my hand grew moist, thoughts turned sticky, and my face burned. What a terrible state for a first visit!

We'd heard some about Mr. Dutarque already. How his father immigrated in one of the middle waves of Huguenots, how a warrant under the seal of one of the Lord Proprietors granted him acreage along the Santee River. Our host had three – or was it four? – brothers, all of whom remained up north, making their fortunes in rice and lumber. Our neighbor had broken ranks to try his hand at the import/export business and since proximity to the port of Charles Town was essential for a merchant, he'd moved here. Of his more personal attachments, we knew virtually nothing.

Not for want of trying! On several occasions, Mother had attempted in that disarming manner of hers to ferret out details, but each time had come away with nothing more than a vague rumor about heartbreak and the pox. She concluded, with what I thought was rather too much certainty, that he was unlikely to have invited us for a luncheon so early in our stay had he been promised. I, on the other hand, considered the possibility that a betrothed might be included in today's number.

"It could be worse," Mother said, apropos of nothing. "It could be raining." I tried to form a response, but none came. Instead, I looked around at the flat, marshy fields stretching off to one side, each demarcated by ditches and berms.

This time of year, rice seedlings dotted fields flooded with dull water, tending toward black because of the silt suspended therein. This, I was told, was the stretch flow or long water. Nary a slave in sight. Even their tempos changed under the merciless Carolina sun. They could be constructing fanner baskets under a live oak, say, or working a turpentine site in the woods.

At last a two-story clapboard structure came into view and even though the house faced the river, we could see that one of the verandah rockers was occupied. "Why, he's out awaiting our arrival," Mother said, as if this small gesture raised him in her esteem.

"Indeed." My voice croaked. The figure rose, lifted an arm in greeting, and approached. Cudjoe helped us down off the carriage, careful to avoid the unbecoming patches of damp under our arms. I tucked my moist hankie into my waistband and extended a hand.

"Welcome! Welcome!" Mr. Dutarque's hand, so large in comparison to mine, was remarkably dry. His kiss to the back of my hand was also dry. "So pleased you oblige me a visit even during a heat such as this!" Perhaps he expressed himself more fluidly in French? "Come, come. Let us sip a beverage and discuss the heat or whatever else might interest two such lovely ladies." He gave me a quick sidelong look, mildly appraising. Seeing no one else on the gallery, I had to concede that Mother had correctly guessed his status – unattached.

Mother apologized for Father's absence. "He's off to one of our recently acquired plantations. Today, on the Waccamaw River." She said this with pride, in spite of the fact that Father's mission this week was in service of obtaining a mortgage.

Mr. Dutarque smiled, nodded, and followed up with commentary about the falling prices of rice and the probable rise of indigo as a commodity. His was a broad and pleasing face, with an unremarkable nose and narrow lips – almost no upper lip at all, in fact. His chin-length brown hair was oiled, swept off the forehead, and tucked securely behind each ear.

He wore the standard garb of a planter entertaining in the afternoon at his country seat: linen breeches; white tunic of hollands; jacket of broadcloth. Only the shoes were unusual. Rather than the polished and buckled shoes of city fashion or the utilitarian boots favored by planters in a rural setting, he wore flat leather slides with rawhide laces. I could not place their design. When he wriggled his toes in a pronounced manner, I quickly looked up.

"Moccasins, Mademoiselle. Cherokee. Best shoes ever to meet my feet!" Mr. Dutarque held up both feet, flexed and pointed his toes. I was relieved he had taken no offense. "Every season, they grow more supple, the leather meeting my feet better and better." He let his feet fall. "It will be a most terrible shame if we force the Indians away completely. Or kill them off with our pox." I glanced at Mother, who hated to dwell on disease and pestilence, even concerning a people she deemed dispensable. She was doing her neutral best to look interested.

Mr. Dutarque informed us that the Cherokee were a proud people and suffered not just the immediate effects of the pox but also lingering distress over scarred skin. "Many survivors kill themselves, such is the shame of a ruined face."

Our host traded primarily in deer skins and therefore traveled along the native routes and became acquainted with many tribal customs. Business dictated that he attend to the various political tensions, too. We learned that one hundred acres on the north branch of the Edisto River had just been set aside as a reserve for the Pee Dee Indians and that the Notchees would settle there as well. "People forget this, but during the Yamasee War, natives killed almost ten percent of white settlers. Sobering, *n'est-ce pas?*" Two decades struck me as such a long time ago that the dreadful carnage seemed irrelevant, but not so Mother. She blanched.

Luckily, tea time came and we removed to a table at the end of the verandah. First came a shrimp bisque and then a perfectly prepared herbed soufflé. A rich coffee cream capped the meal. Servings were small, on account of the heat, but delicious and satisfying. Somewhere between the soufflé and the cream, Mother plied her charm. How surprising that such an accomplished and handsome man was without a wife, etc. Her manner was a little cloying, if not downright flirtatious. Mr. Dutarque's responses seemed genuine enough, though perhaps a little practiced. There had been the fiancée who died suddenly a month before the nuptials. Several years had passed, but alas, his heart had not quite recovered. In other words, we learned nothing new.

Perhaps to shift the subject, Mr. Dutarque brought up Spain, specifically their attempt to lure slaves to St. Augustine, Florida with promises of freedom, a topic much discussed that summer. "Governor Manuel de Montiano of Florida issued the order himself, meaning the divisive strategy is an official act of the Spanish crown." He waved at one of the two slaves fanning us for more coffee all round.

"Are any runaways actually making it?" I asked. Yes, since January, apparently, some fifty-five had been rumored to reach Florida. Fifty-five slaves traversing the entire coast from here to St. Augustine, a trek of some 278 miles, much of it nasty, snake-infested swamp or nearly impenetrable scrub.

Mr. Dutarque rattled off names. Planter Benjamin Godin lost Harry, Cyrus, and Chatham. Thomas Wright, who branded his initials into the chest of every new Angolan purchased, had lost three slaves, including one called Bellfast, a mere boy who'd disappeared astride one of Wright's horses.

Our host laughed. "Imagine, the slave boy with TW seared into his chest atop a dappled grey with TW branded into its hindquarters!"

When at last it was time to leave, farewells were warm enough, but didn't include overtures for a subsequent visit. It was hard to tell if it was the fatigue of smothering heat or a lack of interest, and if the latter, on whose part. After we were situated back on the carriage, Mr. Dutarque's face lit up, asking if we'd yet met our neighbor, Mr. Willard Tilton.

"He's an equestrian of some repute," he said with enthusiasm, rather more enthusiasm than had been on display during our entire visit. "And his hams are among the Lowcountry's finest!" Looking directly at me, he ended by saying, "I'm sure you would enjoy his company, *Mademoiselle*."

Later, over dinner, Mother ticked off Dutarque's real property – 800 acres along the Ashley and a three-story home in the city, on East Bay, no less – and then prompted me for my impressions.

I stalled, knowing full well what she was after. "He's old," I said finally, making a face, "but I liked him well enough." How far would Mother take this lukewarm assessment as an endorsement? In truth, I had liked Mr. Dutarque, a charming gentleman possessed of a demeanor both generous and kind. But there was something about him that rankled, and I wasn't quite sure what to make of that oiled hair.

"Yes?" Mother clearly wanted more.

"Well, he wore interesting shoes." Mother glared at me, so I quickly added that his manners were fine, the repast worthy.

"How's his English?" Father interjected.

"Good enough, but I did sometimes think – maybe you did as well, Mother – that he was translating French to English as he spoke. Certain awkward turns of phrase."

Mother pointed out that he was born in the colony and demanded to know what was wrong with a Frenchman, if he was the right sort. As she rallied her ideas about soufflés and pomades, she nearly forgot to eat the crab cake sitting in a lukewarm lump on her plate.

July cleared the table with her usual demure grace, but I sensed something was dampening her mood. Why should I think so, given that her implacable mien was impossible to read? Meanwhile, Mother kept up her energetic flourishes about moccasins and riverfront acreage. I had the unpleasant sense that her vigorous promotion of Mr. Henri Dutarque expressed feelings of her own dressed up as advocacy on my behalf.

"He rather pepped up at departure, didn't you find? Endorsing our neighbor Mr. Tilton? Fine equestrian, famous hams, and all that."

"Indeed," was all Mother would say.

"He'll find a lovely bride," I declared with a nerve I didn't really feel. It would not be dark for another few hours, but it seemed that the day was suddenly and irreversibly over. A band of tension crossed my forehead. A headache? Perhaps the coming of menses? I excused myself to worried looks.

Halfway up the stairs, I found myself longing for a pair of moccasins. How quietly they would tread, how softly! At the top stair, I felt a slight gush of wet down below. At least now I had reason for my malaise.

Supper Under the Oak
July, Wappoo Plantation

June come on blazing. Clammy. Sundown: no relief. Back full-on ache. Laundry day left knuckles raw, elbows ashy. Never mind. Hominy hit the spot. Sprinkled with benne from last year.

Things astir since Eubeline done showed up two nights back. She run from Doc Jackson's and made her way 'long the creek, bleeding, crying, one eye gouged out. Way before Eubeline got to here, we knowed that Doc Jackson was as cruel a planter as ever did live. But this time it weren't him, but his wife.

Don't be fooled by aprons, hankies, bonnets, and whatnot. Some mistresses mean as rattlesnakes. Oh, not all of 'em. Some just run dishonest, turning round and looking away when the lash strikes, as if not looking kept the blood off 'em. Others egg mens on with sly hints and whines. And then there's the really rotten ones like Mistress Jackson, not content to sit back or nudge, she craved blood.

When Eubeline come, it weren't just the hole where her eye s'posed to be, her back was tore up good too and still sticky with tar and salt. Can't you just see a devil in a lace tucker wiping tar and salt on a bloody back? I bet she done it just like she was buttering a biscuit.

Eubie trying to eat now. When she look about, she have to turn her head round. Melody took off her apron and give Eubeline a little pillow, got her to lie down. Maybe that'd help, maybe it wouldn't, but it'd keep her out of sight. Won't do to get caught harboring a runaway. More backs cut up then for sure.

Saffron crossed the grass from Summer Kitchen, carrying a big bowl of chitlins, piping hot. Overseer Mac done butcher a hog this mornin' and since they wasn't gonna butcher another 'til December when it's Hog Butchering Time, Mistress give out the bits they don't like. James and Benjie ran behind Saffron like as if steam tugged them by the nose.

The mens come from the fields, rounding onto the street in two clumps, one of them clumps laughing. That always get me, how they come back with anything but dull rage or flat-out weariness. Cudjoe come over from the barn, where he smithy from time to time, working iron, mending leather, and there come Mo. Abe nudged Indian Pete, sharing some joke. Pretty soon we was fifteen or so, sitting enjoying chitlins, but also nervous and sad on account of poor Eubeline.

Benjie squatted right next to the girl and patted her head above the bandage just as gentle as you'd pat a newborn calf. James sat next to me, one hand on my knee, eyes wide. Eubeline scared him.

We all knew the story by now.

Two nights ago at supper, Mistress Jackson jumped up like a demon and poked Eubeline with a fork, right in the eye. Just like that. Eubeline wasn't dawdling. She wasn't sulking, spilling, or sassing. She didn't drop nothing. Apron on straight. She done nothing wrong, nothing a-tall, but when you got a she-devil for a Mistress, it don't matter how you do.

And that wasn't the end of it. After gouging Eubie, Mistress Jackson force the girl down on her knees and read Bible at her. Eubeline was a breadth from fainting dead away and made to listen to lecturing words about sin – how she deserved what she got, how she better shape up. How strong you gotta be to kneel through Bible jaw-smacking and then sneak away and walk the long way here?

Now she asked Melody for help sitting up. Did it all seem like a bad dream? Was she happy to be alive or wishing she was dead? Maybe that hole in her head gonna heal, maybe it's not.

My elbow took to hurting on laundry days, but today it was especially sore on account of working hard at getting bloodstains out of Eubeline's yellow calico frock. I got most gone. It ain't right for a girl to have to wear her own blood around, especially below a face ruined by hate.

Not Dead Enough
Saffron, Wappoo Plantation

Early Sunday: Eubeline gone. Like as not walking back up the creek to die. I hate to think it, but I did. Something going clunk-clunk now. What? The hidden raft? No, too far away. Thump-thump. Early light, hard to see, sun not even cracking above low scrub.

The sound full on woke me, so I crept over to the barn to peek round. There was Indian Pete, tying the raft to a cypress tree and then tugging another rope off the raft's end. Did the man ever sleep? His back muscles flexed hard, arm muscles pulling strong too, all but making my knees go out from under.

What was he doing? I was close enough to hear him grunt. Soon enough, I see a gator snout sliding up on the back of the raft. Dead, I hoped! A mighty big one. Did Indian Pete think he was going to pull it out of the water on his lonesome? That's when four others came along, startling me. When Pete turned to see them, he saw me too, and a smile broke through his stern face. You'd have thought it a pass to freedom the way that smile made me feel.

Now all of them tugged and grunted, but quiet-like since it was Sunday and early and all. After some wrangling, that giant beast came up and out of the water. It was longer than the raft by a lot. Was it the one Indian'd been tracking all these years? A man's body long and another half a one. Crafty too, to hear Pete tell it.

They struggled – five men! – and slid that thing all the way over to the smokehouse and let it drop down on the grass. They were still huffing and puffing when Mac showed up. Lucky for them, the raft was already hid away. Overseer set to pacing alongside the dead gator, slow and steady, heel toe, heel toe. He grinned, his rusty hair afire. Where was his hat?

"Seven hundred pounds if it's a stone!" he crowed. You'd think he hunted it. He'd take the story up for sure.

Once Benjie and James woke up, they dashed on over but stopped a bowshot short. They weren't taking any chances. We watched the men stretch out the limbs and begin. The cutting and hacking took up one hour after another. What work! First Indian Pete sawed away the skin with just the right slice and tug, saying how it wasn't like deer skin that you pulled free in one go. No sir, gator skin had to be cut off inch by inch. Then he curved his blade round a front leg and pulled it off in a big hunk. By then, Tommy, George, and Noah were squatting and watching too. Seeing that shoulder torn off convinced the little ones the gator really was dead, so they scooched closer. After the other shoulder was carved off, Pete cut down the back along the ribs.

Miss Eliza and Master came out of the house. The sun was clearing the trees by then, making meat and knives flash and glisten. The squishy sound of cutting through fat and muscle turned my stomach. There was another sound, too – the scritch-scritch of knife sharpening. Turns out that butchering a gator is a two-knife business. All the time Indian Pete was cutting, Caesar was swiping the other blade on the stone. Every now and again, they swapped blades.

Indian Pete was sure-handed, sliding the knife in right where it needed to go, finding joints no trouble. All the meat was taken off and piled high – top loin, or jelly roll, bottom loin, shoulders, ribs, jaw. Indian Pete wasn't about to waste anything. No self-respecting hunter would. Just before taking the carcass off in the pettiauger to dump down the creek a ways, Mac gave a grunt and pointed to the alligator's organs.

"Why don't ya slit the stomach open? It's such a big 'un we might find a pile of bones!" Mac laughed, but he was curious. Indian Pete hesitated, but no slave was going to argue with Overseer, especially when holding onto a portion of his kill was at stake. He laid the stomach out where we all could see and slit it open, holding his head back from any gassy smells.

Caesar had the best view and yelped. I quick told the boys to run down to the dock and haul up some water. I had no need for water, but whatever made Caesar yelp the little ones didn't need to see. Miss Eliza and her father got close.

"Oh, no!" Miss Eliza gasped. Even Master made a face. I had to look.

Twisted in the goo was part of a yellow calico sleeve, the arm still in – Eubeline. Indian Pete looked at me, the dark pools of his eyes a small comfort. I held my stomach and fled. Thank goodness Maggie'd been set to sweeping Summer Kitchen and was nowhere near.

Later, before the day edged into murk, Indian Pete hung the gator skin off a branch of our oak. Tomorrow they'd scrape and salt it, but for now what a fright it gave! The skin danced like a cursed ghost, one that might gather itself up and walk over and loot everything we had, coming first for our clothes and feather collections, next for our teeth and hair and finally, for our souls. At supper, we were quiet and glum. Benjie slung his arm over James's shoulder, and both huddled tight inside the shelter of Mo's legs. Maggie stared and stared, but for her that was nothing new. Nobody told her what we'd seen, but it seemed like she knew anyhow. Once a person knows horror, they can smell it from miles away.

Poor Eubeline. She must not've seen the critter in the grass. I sure hoped it was quick.

It was hard to not to think on that girl's spirit. Unfinished business, for sure. She must be needing to go and damn what killed her. We all knew that alligator didn't kill her. Doc Jackson's murdering wife killed her.

Could dead ever be not dead enough?

Unpacking the Porcelain
Eliza, Wappoo Plantation

Just after midsummer, the porcelain arrived by flatboat. The stupor-inducing heat clogged ambition and slowed all life on the plantation – even my squirrely brothers, even the rugged field hands, even the grasshoppers in the weeds – so the long-awaited order of dishes received a rather muted welcome. Somehow Cudjoe managed to lug the large wooden box up from the dock and lay it carefully down on the dining room floor without keeling over. How it helped for a slave to be fully seasoned!

We realized by way of painful contrast that our Cabbage Tree Plantation in the West Indies had been propitiously sited to take advantage of gracious sea breezes. There had been tropical heat there too, but also refreshing air and the cooling sight of aquamarine seas. Here, the water along our property's edge ran dark and murky, and at certain tidal phases, sank low enough to expose a rank rim of mud. The ocean was no help. The air off the Atlantic passed over the barrier isles and reached Wappoo with clammy stodginess, not refreshing at all.

Knowing how far inland the marshes webbed in all their boggy, swampy variety lent the water in these parts a threatening air, as if a nearly animate foe, in fact. Not just because water hosted multitudes of insects and repugnant reptiles, but because of its treacherous lack of predictability. Pools came and went. Rivers rose and fell. Debris lodged in giant piles causing delays, laborious interventions, and sometimes death. These waters shifted with season and the moon and weather, making them mysterious and unreliable at best, frightening and life-robbing at worst. Yet the creek supplied us with oysters and channel fish. It was our transport to neighbors and town. It refracted light in marvelous variety. And yes, on an otherwise unremarkable morning in June, it delivered a crate of porcelain embellished with the most beautiful roses and ribbons ever to decorate a tea set.

Mother uncrated the delicate cups with an air of satisfaction, holding one then the next up against the dining room window. The new China was thin enough to let the morning light through.

"Well," she said, humming with pleasure. "They work in here." Mother had such unerring judgment in these matters that I was a little surprised that she'd harbored any doubt. At the time of selection, I'd been mystified as to why Mother had opted for a pale orange floral design instead of the more traditional pink or red, but now I understood. The swags of terra-cotta-colored rosebuds and ribbons harmonized with the window's damask, the color of fresh rust.

Mother bent to unearth saucers from beneath the hay and asked, apropos of nothing, "Whom do you think?"

She and I were in accord in many ways, but I could not yet read her mind. Still, I learned to guess accurately.

"The widows Anne – Anne Drayton and Anne Belmont?" I suggested, since they had been the subject of some speculation at last night's dinner. Both women were in possession of substantial properties, and as widows, vested with title. Both had reputations for being outspoken. Certainly, interesting dinner guests? "No good, however," I said, continuing a recent grievance, "unless they bring their sons. Have they sons? Oh, and not just any sons, but preferably the eldest, unpinned ones?" Whether this was a preemptive strike or a retaliatory one, I hardly knew. "Whatever the case," I continued recklessly, "let's not bother to consider whether said men are in possession of reason or charity!" I stacked saucers carefully, then found myself wishing I'd applied a similar caution to my speech.

"Someday you'll thank me, Eliza!" Mother's voice blended resentment and injury. She must have slept well or a more dramatic response would've ensued.

"I'm fifteen, Mother. And we are so newly arrived. Can't this wait a year?"

"Well, since you brought it up," she said disingenuously, "let me tell you my thoughts about Mr. Tilton. He looks sturdy, certainly possesses a gentleman's manners, and I have heard nothing ill of him." I grunted. Since when did the absence of negative rumors constitute a virtue?

"Well, we shall see soon enough, shan't we?" I snapped. With bits of straw strewn all over the tabletop and floor, my mother flung herself back into her chair as if my acerbic tone had physically shoved her.

"A year in these swamplands might bring us another epidemic," she said with weary resignation. "Our crops could fail. Your father could return to military service in the Leeward Islands at any moment. Do you consider any of this, Eliza, when acting the picky maiden? Lord knows, it's all a hideous gamble!"

Mother stared into the empty hutch, as if seeing into a future of ruin and then with a sweep of her arm, slid all the straw from table to floor. She grabbed one of the three brass bells at table's center and shook it hard. "Have July clean up this mess," she said, pushing herself to a stand. It was only ten and not yet stifling, but Mother appeared to be done in. I clenched my jaw, hating her posture of martyrdom, but also relieved at being rid of her. I'd be spared more critiques, like one of my recent favorites: Could I please stop moving around so much – it was making her tired just to look at me. Had I not an ounce of empathy?

From a stand, Mother rang the bell again, hard. When had a heartbeat become too long? She knew the Summer Kitchen was up the slope and sometimes noisy. She knew the house was often empty of slaves at this hour, which generally prompted her unmistakable relief – they were such a headache to boss, and so on.

July appeared. She smoothed her apron with a few quick downward strokes and slid the pocket door closed behind her. I surmised, by the way she arranged her features, that she strove to wipe away any traces of alarm.

"Rinse these pieces and arrange them there." Mother waved first at the crate and then at the corner hutch. "And when you're done, I want every last bit of this straw out of here. Not so much as a shred left at tea time. Not one shred!"

July looked down at the floor and then at Mother. "Yes, Mistress."

As she left the room, Mother added to me, "Eliza, make sure she knows how to handle such finery." Up the stairs she went in a sorry rhythm of defeat.

Moments later Saffron slid by, her footfalls barely making a sound. Pressed against her hip was the blue-and-white-flecked enameled basin, poised so as not to slosh its contents. In it, Saffron would moisten cloths for Mother's forehead. These cloths were draped over her shoulder. Though Mother's sick need arose often, I wondered how Saffron had known so immediately. Perhaps they kept a basin of cool well water in the pantry in readiness and recognized certain types of bell ringing as a sign of Mother's need.

Why wasn't it Melody heading up the stairs?

I generally avoided Mother's darkened bedchamber, but I'd been in it enough to be able to imagine the scene. The slave listening in silence, perhaps tut-tutting now and then. Mother alternately asking for care and refusing it. The slave would wear a neutral mask, perhaps trying to foster a measure of immunity to Mother's difficult nature. I don't often feel gratitude toward the house slaves, but how could I not today when they and not I bore the brunt of yet another of Mother's moods?

Back in April, I might have thought Saffron's percussive and nonverbal responses sprang from a limited vocabulary. After all, she'd arrived in South Carolina only a few months prior to our landing. How wrong I was! Saffron was my first lesson in the follies of underestimating a slave. A few days back, when I was gathering mint, I'd overheard a snippet of conversation through the Summer Kitchen window. It was Saffron peppering someone with questions, her desire to learn vocabulary palpable.

"What is 'migraine'? What means 'palpitation'? What is 'England'? What is 'Irish'?" I couldn't believe that Saffron had carried these words across a divide of many hours in order to conduct this urgent inventory. And then: "Tell me what means 'a headache to boss'?"

A long snort followed, whether of humor or contempt, I couldn't tell, but I was certain it'd been Melody. I retreated to the house, resolved to counsel my mother to guard her tongue even as I knew with sour certainty that such advice would launch a tirade – and not about the house slaves, either. Was I so mean-spirited as to put the slaves' feelings above hers, etc.

July busied herself with unpacking the porcelain, and in the next moment Melody came in from the back and headed upstairs, presumably to replace Saffron. Melody must've been mid-task, unable to minister care as quickly as needed. A relay team.

I left the dining room to play the harpsichord.

Tenderloin
Saffron, Wappoo Plantation

What changes? What stays the same? One night the heavens a-glitter with diamond after diamond in a glory show. The next night stars shine so cold and bitter you wonder how? What changed? The root cellar pitchpoled like that. One day fetching squirreled away pecans, it's just a dark closet. There's the peach preserves. There's the wrinklin' plums and two sacks of rice. But next time, it gawped like a hole of haunting.

Not long after the big gator cut-up, I stepped down into the cool dark, the floor squishy with tide that rose up through the ground, and got the goosies right off. I looked all round, half expecting to see a demon. Maybe Eubeline's spirit was wandering here – poor thing!

I was glad to have Melody's blue crab claw round my neck that morning. I patted it where it hung down to bring on its protecting power. But the shell just reminded me how we was flesh and bone and open to hurting while what creeps about sometimes wasn't flesh or bone and couldn't be hurt to bleeding.

Steps came behind me – flesh and bone, for sure. I'm cornered. First came Overseer's boots in the light on the top stair. Then his belt. Then shoulders come lit. When his face appeared in the sun, boots and belt in shadow, my heart hard pounded. He stopped at the sight of me.

"Get out!" He gurgled.

"Yes, sir." But how to get past?

"Get out!" he said again, this time from up his nose, whiny, which scared me just as bad. I started scooching by. Was he hiding brandy or rum down here? But why, when his cabin got a door? No one pass through his door without a knock and say so, not like slave doors which was doors by name only. The cellar floor squished as I cinched by. Gotta get to daylight.

"T'isn't you I'm a hankering after," he said. Did the fool man think I wanted a dance? He got habits of haughtiness, but just yesterday didn't I hear a guest buckra saying that the Scots were the darkies of the British Isles? Or was it the Irish? It's a lot of trouble keeping all their hate straight. Someone always lower than someone else, excepting for us – we get the bottom, every time.

"G'won now – and not a word!"

Back into daylight, I tried shaking him off like a bad dream. Never before smelt the stink of liquor comin' off him, but who's to say? Maybe the thought of a girl eaten by a ten-foot alligator bothered him too, even if she was a black girl. He didn't ask, but I'm guessing he could tell by the looks passing between us that we had a good idea whose arm that was.

Or was something else knocking him a-kilter?

Of late, folks going on and on about the numbers, how they's running against buckra. So many of us! What we gonna burn next? What slaves were itching to sneak and murder? Who got musket know-how? Whisper. Whisper. Like as if we can't hear when we were standing right behind the chairs at dinner.

Sipping sherry, they go, "Rebels taking 'vantage of sick months to run amok." It's the sick months now. "Maroons running crazy with machetes and gun powder, demanding treaties, taking up whole mountain tops in the West Indies. Trade, currency, and all." They shook their heads, but my heart leapt.

No wonder Overseer was sweating and pulling drink noontime. Maybe he was thinking on a rabble of blacks holding pine torches and running south, slaughtering any buckra in the way. Overseer don't got a thing to call his own, but I'm guessing he prized his own sorry hide. Who doesn't?

Back in Summer Kitchen, two big kettles steamed away. Inside: the giant shoulders. The kitchen smelt a little sweet, a little swampy. On the table lay the best cut, the tenderloin. July cut it into four long logs of tender, dark meat. "Fit for a chief," Indian Pete said. That was for the neighbors – Mr. and Mrs. Deveaux, the Gibbses, and the Woodwards. Oh, and the Jacksons. The Jacksons was Melody's idea, suggested all coy and sweet like she was considerin' neighborly relations. Some forms of vengeance run subtle and unspoken.

The boys was kneeling on the grass outside, scraping oyster shells at the gator's skin. Scrape, scrape. Benjie was best at it, but even Noah gave it a go. Where was Maggie? Before the skin got salted and stowed, all that fat gotta come off, every slimy white string of it. After a season tucked in the dark, it'd go supple and make someone a pouch of beauty or cover a book in elegance. In another world, sure enough not this one, that soft skin might've covered a Berber's Koran. How royal those nomads looked riding into our village! Robes and turbans blue as midnight, beautiful horses dusty with the desert. Prayer books fit for kings!

"Thank Oba Indian Pete still got knives and a gig," July said. She put her face in the meaty steam and drew it up her nose. Most slaves got no knives and no spears and no bow and arrows neither, but Indian Pete got 'em all. If Master took 'em away, I'm pretty sure Pete'd go out and find others – maybe trekking at night to find Pee Dee kin, what's left of 'em.

Even without blades, we'd catch fish in traps and trot lines or gig 'em with handmade spears, but for deer, coon, and wild boar – you gotta have arrows and a sharp blade for butchering. And gator? Well, now I know that takes two blades.

Noah stood on the skin and slipped and fell on his behind. He slid a little, looking surprised. Melody's head jerked up. Would he cry or laugh? He laughed. Next thing you know, all them boys was running 'long the grass behind that ten-foot alligator hide and then leapin' on it to slide its full length, squealing the whole way. Over and over, 'til they was greasy and giddy.

In between cutting up the jowl meat and the jelly roll, I spied Overseer coming along, his face grim. He brusht away a spider web – all mad-like – as if the spider spun the web just to wreck his day. I got to worrying about the men at task. Was liquor gonna turn Overseer's discipline rotten? Some sots go soft and forgiving, as if drink was a hinge that opened a door to secret bounty. Other drunks got darkly mean.

He hollered at the boys, "Ya radge wee shites! Get offa that hide or I'll hide *you*! Ya numpties!" Like a school of fish, the boys ran up the hill past the woodshed, the left-behind skin looking almost lonely. Overseer kept on shaking his fist, face turning red: "Rapscallions!"

Not lookin' like a soft souse. A gruff heart heading out to the fields. The men working didn't need warning, they'd see right off, but I still wished for a chance to give word. I sure hoped there'd be no brandy-driven stripes to tend later, the cowhide laid on hard for no reason. Probably not. Overseer got a sensible streak and everybody knew it. He can't spare a set of hands right now, and a solid walloping'd put him down a man for a week.

"Caesar'll ride out and deliver the meat," July said. She rolled the loins in dampened osnaburg and tied hemp around them. Then she slapped them onto old pages of the *Gazette* and rolled and tied 'em up again. A rucksack on the floor lined with pine needles, dried corn cobs, and stalks of rosemary was for traveling. She jostled it a little, tucked in the meat, kicking off the smell of rosemary.

"James!" she hollered up toward the woodshed. "You wash up now." When he showed, July took a wetted scrap of osnaburg and wiped down his arms and legs, wetted it again and handed it to him for his face. Then she tole him to run for Caesar. Benjie came in then. He usually'd be pouting 'bout being left behind. But he curled up under the table and fell solid asleep.

I told James to stay out of Overseer's way, but that was impossible. Mistress wanted a hand to leave rice weeding and deliver gifts of alligator meat. To tell Overseer what Mistress wanted, James would have to stand at Overseer's horse, look up, and ask for what Overseer would only grudgingly give.

"Benjie got a speck of fever, you think?" July asked.

"No. Whupped, is all," I said. Everybody knew somebody that done died from pox that season. We worried and kept a lookout for fever or bumps, aching joints. Pox could show up in a heartbeat, killing in less than three days. Turned out Benjie got a bad bellyache was all. Maybe he chewed some of that alligator fat. Hungry children will put all kinds of things in their mouths: leather, dirt, slugs pulled off the weeds by the creek, alligator fat.

July 1738

The Prophet and Migraines
Eliza, Wappoo Plantation

Throughout the month of July, stifling heat clamped down in a most oppressive manner. We were often flattened with fatigue by ten o'clock and still listless long after sunset. Worse, in the month since our visit to Mr. Dutarque, a new and unwelcome companion announced itself to me – heat-induced headaches, annoying at best and incapacitating at worst.

I would've thought the drenching summer rains would provide relief, but the storms that swiftly tore through the marshes didn't impart the hoped-for cool, instead often resulting in a clammy steam rising up from the soaked earth. There were days when it seemed as though we had stepped off our sloop from the West Indies into a fry pan of sizzling water. On top of that, with every torrent came worries about clogged sluices, damage from fallen branches, and possible losses due to the untimely wetting of crops. No wonder my head hurt.

In spite of feeling ragged and worn, I managed to think a good deal about our visit to Mr. Dutarque. I didn't ruminate about him, per se, thus confirming my initial impression that he was ill-suited as a prospect, but rather about some of the curious tidbits he'd shared, like about runaways and branding. Branding posed a conundrum. How was a planter supposed to protect himself from the substantial loss of a fugitive slave? And as an initial matter, what slave to buy was a difficult question. Slaves from the Carib were often foul-tempered ruffians with revolution in their blood, so a poor risk. The Angolans and Kongolese were reputedly runners, but these days brigantines arriving from Africa carried little else. Father had purchased Binah at a deep discount, she being both Angolan and a known runner. Would his investment prove worth the risk?

Father found branding human flesh repugnant and steered clear of the practice. He wondered what other deterrents were there, and if not deterrents, were there incentives? It was impossible to gauge the thoughts of the Negroes. Impossible. Our slaves, like so many others, were taciturn in the main, and I suspect generally duplicitous, such that even those that tended toward chatty disclosures, like Old Sarah, were likely dissembling. While I didn't go so far as to assume, as Mother did, that they all lied all the time, they were hardly reliable. Already, we'd had to impose two weeks of limited rations on Caesar for disappearing for a day and a half and lying about it.

As for incentives, perhaps in addition to providing shoes, we ought to host a festive party on the day after Christmas, with extra provisions handed out, etc. Ribbons and sweets? We could sponsor foot races. There might be dancing, hilarity – and, one dared hope, a sense of gratitude.

One morning towards the end of July, I woke with a clear head and tentatively laid out the day's schedule: a lesson on currency with Father, long delayed; needlework midday; then an afternoon tutorial with Polly, Phoebe, and Maggie. As it turned out by the time Father concluded my tutorial about debt and possible bank closures, I longed to be near the water and so abandoned my cross-stitch. I grabbed the Bible and called my sister from the back door. She peeked round the spinning shed's large opening and waved me over.

Inside, the spinning wheel squeaked its rounds as Melody made yarn from wool rovings. Against the far wall stood Phoebe, Noah, and all three of my siblings, looking at what appeared to be a giant bowl of mud. George stirred.

"What the dickens is this?"

"Ogre Stew!" Tommy bellowed, sprinkling crushed bark into the mix.

"Stew!" Noah echoed, dropping in little bits of crushed shell. Polly and Phoebe added flower petals, as if to prettify it.

I held up the Bible. "Well, who would like to hear a story about wicked men, slaves, and a prophet?"

"Oh! Moses and the Red Sea?" guessed George.

Like the Pied Piper, I led the troop of children around the house and down to the creek. I would read the whole Old Testament story, from enslavement to rebellion to the great prophet's journey out of exile across the divinely-parted Red Sea. I sat Phoebe and Polly at either side of me to follow my dragging finger, and when Maggie and eventually Melody joined us, I gave them each a turn. Maggie shucked corn and stared at the water mostly, but Melody kept glancing up from her darning, sticking herself with the needle once in what seemed a rather naked desire to follow along. George stayed for all of it, lying flat on his back and gnawing on a blade of grass, but after just a few verses, Tommy and Noah disappeared into the reeds, supposedly to hunt out baby Moses but really scouting for frogs.

When we were nearly done, Mother rang the bell. With a series of small grunts, Melody tipped her heavy form onto all fours and then rose to her feet. The birth could not be far off. She placed the osier basket of darning on her hip and crunched up the path to the house, and then, in anticipation of Mother's need, grabbed the long-handled fan off the gallery as she headed inside. It was stifling – Mother would want fanning.

"That's enough for today, then!" I too needed a lie-down.

Upstairs in my chamber, I stretched out on top of the cover, temples throbbing and eyeballs burning. Thankfully, Polly stayed out and about with Phoebe, as her restless stirrings would have been an agony. I didn't even have the wherewithal to ring for Saffron, though I too longed for the air to be stirred by a fan.

As I drifted off, misgivings gripped me. I probably ought not be sharing with the slaves Bible stories about release from bondage, much less teaching them to read. If I was sure enough to defy Mother on the matter, why have qualms now? It was as though in addition to clamping down on the jaw and eye sockets, the migraine pulsed doubt through my veins.

They Sought Him Out
Saffron, Wappoo Plantation

By the longest day, others started comin' round to Titus. Quiet, hungry for answers. Not all knew his ways, but it didn't matter. His power held strong and shone, and everyone could feel it. He changed to fit here, our place. No pair of chickens to offer? A pair of feathers'll do. No bowls of blood to mark the sacred circle? A single gill will do. A pretty pinecone instead of a jewel. The rare stolen peach instead of gold. The gods would understand.

Divining was a noisy, joyful, and serious business at home. But not here. Secrecy, exhaustion, and fear tucked us in tight. This was no life for singing or calling out. All spirit messages would have to arrive in whispers and light tappings, with a watcher at the gate.

I waited. By then, Maggie ate the odd mouthful and smiled some here and there. The haunted look still came over her often, and she froze many times a day. A bug stuck in amber. But less. Nightimes, she'd toss and turn and now and again, head off in a sleepwalk. During those night walks, she was fierce, as if hunting down her soul.

But grief over her stuck to me like tar on a summer-heated dock. What if nothing could help? What if whatever I offered the gods wasn't enough? What if the curse was too strong for this babalawo to lift?

July dished up good sense, how she do, saying the spirits weren't gonna ask for the impossible. The Ancestors were on our side, she reminded me. "Slavery's what is impossible," she said. "Why would they pile on more?" July wore suffering like a formal dress, something to keep neat and pressed, and by being neat and pressed, keeping misery off. She was what buckra call "well-seasoned." Buckra saw how quiet went with good service, but I saw how quiet went with survival. July's quiet was her way of hanging onto a slim peace, a calico-thin dignity. That's why she didn't talk about Before Times, I'm certain of it. She's Yoruban too, I know that, but nothing else. I didn't understand how she could turn suffering into generosity, but she did, nearly every day.

When she spoke, Melody and I knew to listen. About the Ancestors: "They were with us in the barracoons. They came up the planks onto the Guineas. They clung with us in the hold and on the isle of delousing. They hovered over the auction block. They must be here with us now." She sounded like Titus.

Melody was learning to read her Bible. Maybe being Carib-born made her open to it. On the full moon before the baby came, she laid the book open in a wedge of moonlight and leafed through the pages with care. How she loved that book!

July started saving up the blood of fowl. Had Titus told her to? She hid it in a bucket up past the woodshed, using a small board as a lid, weighted with two bricks to keep the animals out. Feathers started catching my eye, Maggie's too – jay, bobolink, and even duck now and again. I gathered 'em up and laid 'em out on the floor between the wall and pallet. Soon I had ten. Before the next full moon, Indian Pete gave me two owl feathers, each striped with white and brown. No hunk of gold could've meant more.

Mr. Tilton Calling
Eliza, Wappoo Plantation

Saffron put the final pin in my hair and left, quietly closing the door behind her. The muted voices of courtesy came through the floorboards. Mother's tinkling laughter. Mr. Tilton's low murmurs. I fluttered both hands at my temples, as if I could clear my disquietude as easily as one deters a fly. I despised agitation, particularly of the moist and anxious kind.

I recalled the barely disguised urgency with which my mother had made these arrangements. A simple visit! She rattled on about the slope of their property off the creek, the acreage. Her litany of details added weight to the already heavy imposition of her will. But these irritations were the mere threshold. Interactions with the man himself still had to be managed with the proper amount of interest and disinterest lest false impressions were made or unintended alienations caused.

With a force of will that I'd have rather applied to a grafting operation or to the design of a wind screen for silk worms, I smiled in the mirror. Mother would not turn me into a discourteous hostess. After a quick dusting of extra powder to hide my flush, I headed downstairs. For all Mother's imposing ways, she could not, after all, force a union. Or so I told myself. Someday I'd inform her of Mrs. Boddicott's indiscretions. I wondered how Mother's strategy might change if she knew that I'd heard about her own stubborn insistence in conjugal matters. Knowing Mother, perhaps not a bit!

As I entered the parlor, she was suggesting the gallery. "It is so stifling in here." She appealed to me with a look that said, "Please be reasonable." Mr. Tilton, meanwhile, kissed my extended hand. The moustache briefly tickled.

"Such a pleasure to see you again, Mr. Tilton." I would play my part. "Shall we?" I gestured to the porch.

"Call me Willard, please." At our first brief meeting in town, Mr. Tilton had insisted on using first names and I had resisted. I would continue to do so now. One of many clear signals.

As we maneuvered onto the gallery, where none of us expected to be a whit more comfortable, I noticed a certain cool smugness about him. His mouth smiled readily enough, revealing small and neat teeth, but it was not an expression of warmth. The neatly trimmed mustache reminded me of a whisk broom. His almond-shaped green eyes were probably his best feature, a little too small, but evenly set and unusually lashed for a blond.

"I'm long overdue paying my respects," he began. July arrived without prompting and delivered a tray of sweet tea and small sandwiches of ground ham and nettle greens. The mint sprigs in the tall tea glasses gave us all something to do with our hands while talk went to the usual subjects – the progress of Drayton's manse, how far upriver rice production now extended, the smallpox epidemic, and the weather, always the weather.

"How'd you like that storm two days back? A real frog washer!" Tilton's use of local jargon caused Mother to offer a tight smile.

Mr. Tilton, like almost everyone we knew, grew rice. Since his plantation abutted ours to the southwest, a union of our two holdings would create a large swath of creek front stretching from here nearly to the Stono River. I sat there fiddling with my sprig of mint, hoping that Father's hints about offering Wappoo to me as a wedding gift had not been broadcast.

"If you'd do me the honor of a return visit," he was saying, "I'd be most happy to show you our new sluices. Then I could take you over to Hutchinson's Depot."

I wondered if Mr. Tilton had heard of my passion for agriculture, which would make his sluice proposal a rather shameless ploy to appeal to a subject dear to my heart. "Hutchinson's?" I asked, mostly to block his attempt to engage me on matters for which I might display some enthusiasm.

"Oh yes, perched on Wallace Creek off the Stono, not much more than a shout from me. All sorts of goods. If y'all have been traveling to Charles Town for sundries, you might be pleasantly surprised. They've got luxuries like Hyson tea, porcelain, and silk, and the more usual stock, of course." Usual stock meant weapons, casks of whale oil, musket powder, fertilizer, seeds, barrels, and the like. Perhaps thinking he had offended us by suggesting that we were in need of luxury items, he quickly changed the subject, lauding the ham paste. "Did this come out of your smokehouse? It's mighty flavorful!" He flashed a smile, revealing those neat white teeth again.

At this juncture, Mother feigned a reason to enter the house. With all her perspicacity, she should have gathered that no amount of private time with Mr. Tilton was going to facilitate intimacy. I almost admired her tenacity. Apparently I lacked the flexibility that society required of unwed females. If the appropriate posture demanded an unquestioning and slavish welcome to any and all masculine attention as well as wholesale dismissal of one's intuition, well then, I would remain a stubborn virgin. Watching my mother's eyebrow perpetually reach for the heavens seemed a small price for integrity.

As soon as mother's hem disappeared round the doorway, Mr. Tilton leaned forward in an unearned gesture of intimacy. "I've heard a little rumor about you and your Negroes. You might be surprised how quickly matters get about in these parts. Teaching slaves to read – watch yourself!"

I leaned back as if from a stink. Our guest struck me as a mongrel, the sort of rangy, scrap-stealing mutt too mean to reform but too wily to banish.

"I don't know what you've heard, Mr. Tilton. I'm teaching my little sister her letters."

"Willard, please!" He leaned back, mirroring my posture.

"Is there news of which I have not been apprised?" I asked with feigned ignorance. "Has the Slave Code been revised of late?"

He shook his head. "The Assembly's shuttered against the pox. You know full well. But new restrictions'll be clapped on the Negroes soon, depend on it.

I'm willing to bet that in short order it'll be illegal just to have an educated Negro on your premises, never mind teaching them the alphabet." He picked up his sandwich and chewed thoughtfully before continuing.

"This part of the world's got way too many of 'em – and more arriving by the week. Ideal for getting rice to market, of course, but singularly treacherous in all other aspects. I shudder to think what might happen if more of those brutes could read and write. Imagine – sly buggers sending each other secret missives or reading the *Gazette*? Teaching a slave to read and write is like lighting a bonfire next to a munitions store, Miss Lucas. As it is, they can talk across the swamps with drumbeats and hoots, like a pack of wolves or a parliament of owls."

"Their capacity to spread news is a mystery, indeed," I said firmly, "but if the slaves can already speak across the night air without so much as a scrap of paper, why would possessing the craft of literacy help them in their plots? It's much more cumbersome to carry an inked piece of paper through a swamp than to whoop and tootle across the air."

"Ah," Tilton responded. "So it's true what they say. It pleases me no end to know that a mind possessed of such lawyerly skill lives so near!" Mother chose this moment to rejoin us. She sat down in a poof of fabric and dabbed her upper lip with a lacy cloth.

"Do you ever become accustomed to this heat, Mr. Tilton?" she asked somewhat vacantly. Her glancing appraisal seemed at last to take in the futility of her matchmaking.

"It takes time, Mrs. Lucas, as do so many things. You'll learn our ways soon enough."

Possibly staging a diversion, Mother suddenly called out, "July!"

As it turned out, Melody responded to Mother's call. Seeing the empty plates, she awkwardly maneuvered her bulk between the chairs to gather them up. Mr. Tilton's eyes followed her. I was by then familiar with the heightened awareness Melody produced in some men, as well as the variety of forms that attention could take. Before long, in fact, I'd come to use her as a gauge of a man's respectability. Needless to say, Tilton didn't fare well, even though his appraisal was cool, as if from a distance.

We sipped our tea in momentary silence until he said, "Some of these mulattos really get a man going. Just goes to show how improving white blood is! I would guess that one had herself a white daddy. Fifty/fifty. If the one she's carrying had a white daddy too, you'll have a valuable quadroon in your stable."

Mother blanched. "I really must check on something," she said lamely. Tilton had no idea that he had just dragged a nail across a scab and ripped it off.

August 1738

Starlight
Saffron, Wappoo Plantation

Melody trying to set herself down was a sight. First she sagged down onto her behind, then leant back, both hands behind her, sighing and shifting, shifting and sighing. Baby crowded her ribs, one day with its rump, the next day with its head. When it turned, Melody said it felt like she swallowed a butterfly. Last night she asked us to pray that he put his head down, "And keep it down!" A breech baby sometimes mean a dead baby. And a dead mama for that matter.

Her ankles swole up bad. After supper, July took Melody's feet up on her lap and eased out some soreness with her fingers. Our oak's shadow grew long, and a soft grey filled in around the grasses and fences. Fireflies sprinkled the creek bank. It was hot, and we were exhausted to a person.

One by one, people rose and went to bed. Indian Pete got up, only he wasn't going to bed. I watched his thighs flex, my heart skipping like I'd swallowed a butterfly myself. Where was he off to? Gigging for sturgeon, hunting for possum – or maybe heading off into the night to see a sweetheart?

The sky shined up like glass – azure, maybe? Finally, it inked into blue-black, everywhere 'cept where it curled along the treetops. It'd be full dark soon. Thinking on how I collected the word "azure" made me think on what the others save up. Collections. For James, it's shells. Benjie pocketed hemp from the barn and pancaked them into nests. Hercules got his crab claws and pinecones, July her ribbon scraps, cloth chips, and thread. Abraham scanned the river when paddling and gathered small chunks of wood, the smoother, the better. He saved up old newspapers too and papered the entire inside of his cabin. Time was he slept real bad, July said. Could barely make his body go one task, never mind four. But after the *Gazette* pages pasted up, he rested fine, the nagging spirits being too busy reading to bother him none.

There were Porch House collections too. For the pantry, Melody, July, and I gathered roots, seeds, and leaves. Some we plucked in the shade of the Deep Woods and some along the road twixt here and there. By August, even I knew where to spot wintergreen and snakeroot, snakeroot being good for snake bites and birthing women. We also gathered boneset and life everlasting for fever, deadshot for worms, and Jerusalem artichoke for sour stomach.

I could never explain how every so often a word fell into my ears and went straight to my soul, like "wintergreen." But now I see how it wasn't so different from Abraham spying a piece of worn-down wood and grabbing it out of the river or Hercules laying out his crab claws to whiten in the sun.

Some words I saved off to the side. Others I said aloud if a chance came along. Can't quite figure it yet. Take "magnificent." I was thinking that word was gonna rest between my lips and the sky 'til I heard Cudjoe whispering about Mo getting to learn a trade soon, rope making. It might be a long time coming, his apprenticeship, but the idea of it cast out a thin, beautiful line to freedom, like the trail of a falling star. Well, that was magnificent, wasn't it?

Maggie being silent for most of nine months twisted me hard, but muteness spoke my daughter's torment better than any words could. July, too, been busy showing me how a person can say a lot without spilling much more than a few sentences a day. How she did that from dark to dark, day in and day out, was worth thinking on. Caring doesn't require spoken syllables, it turns out.

I pointed to the treetops and dragged my finger along their curves. Was Maggie watching? The scrub and trees were so dark now they looked like black cloth cutouts. The sky pure glass. I was about to drop the word "magnificent" into Maggie's perfect little ear, like a sapphire plopped into spring water, when I felt her stir. And then, to my shock, she said, *"Elewa."*

That means beautiful in Yoruban. Yes! The sky was beautiful. My daughter's voice was beautiful. I wanted to bang out the rhythms of joy or loudly thank the Ancestors, but I knew better and with all my might, held still. Sometimes being still was harder than shucking barrels of corn or hoeing in the heat. Also, sometimes being still was the biggest gift you could give another person. I gave stillness to my daughter now, willing every little dot of my skin to open and listen.

Melody cranked an elbow under her ribs and propped herself up to look at Maggie. I kept listening, open and still, but oh how need rose up. I wanted more. A sentence. And then another sentence. I wanted my daughter back, the one who used to sing in her bed at night and who asked her mama "why" all the day long.

Melody flopped back down, probably because the baby wanted more room. But then she whispered, *"Elewa."* Was this an echo for Maggie or Melody's own commentary to the close of day? Or maybe it was for her baby, who must be listening by now.

Maggie went stiff. I dragged my fingers along the treetops one more time, hoping for just one more word, and then I poked at the fireflies as if I was making 'em light up. Maggie smiled! I couldn't see her face, but I could feel the smile in her shoulders. I could see the smile in her ears. Maggie smiled! My magnificent daughter crooked a magnificent smile at the magnificent fireflies. And then she leaned back and fell asleep almost at once, as if saying three syllables and then smiling done drained her. I sighed and hoped she was sleeping with starlight under her eyelids.

July asked Cudjoe, "Where would Mo live?"

"With my mama."

July jerked her head, "What?" Cudjoe having a mother in the city seemed to be news to her.

"She come by way of Barbados," he said, all somber. "Sierra Leone before that." His tone was heavy so I didn't expect much else, but surprisingly, he kept talking. "She live up on the Neck. Supposed to've been freed by will years back, but Owner died without papers, so she free by courtesy. She got herself a little house." How'd he kept this secret? A family member living free and owning property too! If knowing about his mother was healing to hear, wasn't it selfish to keep it secret?

Melody began to snore.

"But," I started, and then bit my tongue. I wanted to ask why his mother bought a house instead of Cudjoe's freedom, but it seemed beyond my knowing – too private, too complicated. And anyway, freedom for a black person was like a spider web waggling in the wind. One stray finger could tear it all down.

"She sells pastries at Market and Broad and to Poinsett Inn and the Fleur de Lis." Cudjoe smacked his lips. "Her beaten biscuits the best in the city!"

Herc, who often paddled with Cudjoe, slapped his knee. "That's you Mama's biscuits?"

That knee-slap called Melody back from her dreams. A star let loose in the sky, making a brief arc. I saw it. Melody saw it.

Was that Mo's freedom flashing overhead? Weren't we supposed to make a wish? I wondered what Melody'd wish for – a healthy baby probably. Maybe she'd wish for a baby so pale he could in some far-off time miles from here, walk straight into a white life. Forget the freeing papers or wills. Forget outrunning dogs to Florida. Forget white people's "courtesy." If your skin was light enough, running take on a different meaning.

It was suddenly time to sleep. No amount of pretty skies or treasured words or falling stars could push us past the punishing future.

Bird Minders
Saffron, Wappoo Plantation

The bird-minding boys were busy half a field away near the canal, banging pots, firing buck shot, snapping cowhides at the clouds. Bang. Boom. Snap. What a ruckus! Bang. Boom. Snap. Benjie and James clapped tin pie plates together. Tommy fired his new musket, Noah holding the powder pouch. The birds'd be fools to come near.

If bird-minding stopped even for the time it takes to squat and pee, the bobolinks would swarm back in dark clouds and do the devil's work. Mo said they could strip the stalks of grain faster than you could even say "bobolink." The boys weren't pretending to be important today. They were.

When I first came to this place, I wished for field task – to be far away from buckra voices clipping out need every hour of the day. But that was before I disappeared in a swarm of bugs, before the heat clamped down on me near to smothering. That was before Caesar's good ankle puffed up after a snake bite and he almost died. Now it seemed a tossup. Some days, task seemed better, other days, Porch House. But of course, on no day did what I like figure into it.

That day I was weeding. I was slow, either with hoe or hand. Abraham paced me a while, but just after the hour of short-shadows, I got behind by half a field. I worked along the scrub near the road, while the others were singing and moving in a line toward the chestnut trees yonder.

Dull thumping rose up out of the ground. I felt it in my feet. Then I heard it, the thudding. It wasn't the bird-minders. It was coming from behind. I froze. Thundering horse hooves, that's what it was. Thundering horse hooves didn't mean anything good for a slave. I listened for dogs and didn't hear any.

Overseer Mac, I remembered in panic, was over with Quashee at the Upper Field. I spied the long distance between me and the others. Running might get me shot, so I ducked into the near shade and crouched.

The horses came on like demons. Just how much hate hung in the trailing clouds of dust? My life depended on how much. We'd been catching sight of them three patrollers for days, riding along the edges of the fields like a twelve-legged monster, ornery and restless. Twice they met up with Overseer, dismounted, and clapped him on the back, talking in loud voices: the weather this, scurrilous darkies that. Whenever one troller was talking, the other two scanned the fields, like they were gonna spy some treachery that only their special slave-hunting eyes could suss out.

I was where I's supposed to be, pausing from what I's supposed to be doing – did it matter? One saw me and they all whoa'd and wheeled them horses round. I begged the Ancestors to watch over me.

I unfolded myself and got to weeding again, alert and casual at the same time, the dust biting my eyes. Doing task was no medicine 'gainst what they were sizing up to do, but I tried anyhow. I could tell by flinching of shoulders and slightly twisting necks that the men and women half a field away took note. Not one of them stopped working or turned fully around, and I knew why. The singing stopped, though, and the buzzing of cicadas filled the sky, as if they were happy to have the chance to sing alone. The rise and fall of their rusty cries called out my doom.

Down to the ground the men came, reins looped onto lower branches in swift gestures – they'd done this before. Maybe, too, they made it their business to know when an overseer wasn't around. The man coming up on me first unbuttoned his breeches, timing their drop to the ground just as he came face to face with me. He was tall, his cheeks ruddy. There was sweat popping out along his brow, and his tunic was dark at the armpits. I glanced down. That down there wasn't ruddy, but a sickly, shining grey, like a half-burnt branch that'd been soaking in water.

I thought I knew what was coming, but didn't. The patroller shoved me to my knees so hard my backbone jolted, his member bumping my face and then bouncing back up. The others found this funny. A gurgling laugh came from one, a dry hiccupping from the other. The half-naked man tapped my cheek with his cock's fluted end.

"This one look hungry to you?" he turned to ask his friends. To me, "They feed you enough round here? I'm thinking you could use some refreshment, what with all this hard work." He sneered the words "hard work" as if what I'd been doing wasn't really work. He tugged my head back with one hand, and with the other yanked my jaw down and shoved himself in. I gagged. He didn't move his hips at all to get himself where he wanted to go. Instead, using my ears like handles, he violently pulled my head forward and back. Forward and back.

"Watch those teeth, you dirty little cunt!" His voice turned to gravel.

Three. Four. Five. Five times? Very little spunk. Then the next patroller. And then the next. Three cocks, all fast, all near to dry. From somewhere far off I thought, why so little seed? Were they yanking morning and bedtime on their lonesome or maybe taking turns on each other in the bottomlands? It didn't dawn onto me until much, much later that there might be women willing to lay with them.

They mounted their horses, taking a minute to move their business in the saddles, getting comfortable, and then took off in a foul cloud. I fell forward onto all fours, but then I stood – to be standing if one of them looked back.

I was still dazed when three field hands wrapped their bodies around me and led me to a fallen log to sit: Binah, Abraham, and Herc. "Where's Indian Pete?" I asked. They traded looks. Binah undid her head cloth and wiped the sticky corners of my mouth. That's when I folded like a hinge and puked. Herc stroked my back. When I sat up, they kept their hands on me – on my shoulders, back, and neck. Binah dabbed off the vomit. Tears streaked through the sweat and grime on her face.

Thunderheads in the south, stalled all morning, now slid across the sky. The wind came up, rattling the palmettos and shrubs in angry sympathy. The rustling and twisting fronds knew how to hang on in a gale, but did I? I puked again, thinking about Maggie and all she'd been through.

We headed back to the street for shelter. Even the mighty chestnuts swayed in the wind, their leafy heads a froth. A late afternoon storm might bring dangerous lightning. It didn't do to be out in it.

They surrounded me, my feet hardly touching dirt. The rest jogged out of the fields and filed behind us in silent rage. They smoldered in such heat that someone standing by might have thought it was their anger making the clouds rile up in drama and not the wind.

I Hate Milton
Eliza's Diary, Wappoo Plantation

Milton bores me to tears – I can admit that here! All those meandering Biblical lists. Good Lord! But Lucifer and serpents, there's a pairing. Snakes are such a perpetual menace around here, the symbol gains potency. Note: Check pantry supplies of Angelica root, the snakebite remedy Old Sarah swears by. Just heard about a neighbor's slave losing a leg to mortification after a vicious bite and, poor Caesar, a water moccasin nearly felled him!

August heat disorients. Another intractable headache. How I long for a cooling breeze! I wander about, as if in search of something. Even the house slaves seem off – especially Saffron. This morning I caught her staring out the window in a stony moodiness, like a woman with a secret or a hidden wound.

In spite of vipers, I shall walk! Everyone knows evil resides in libraries as artfully as it does in rice fields. Mercifully, the racket to deter the bobolinks is over for now, a spoiling sound during yesterday's constitutional.

Mary Chardon comes tomorrow. Her company is such a tonic! Perhaps she'll dispel the disquiet left by Tilton. Such an odious man – I shan't waste the ink. But if I hear July tell me one more time to "let Mother's tongue lashings wash over me" – just like Bettany, by the by! – I shall scream.

Laundry
July, Wappoo Plantation

You'd be a fool to rest anywhere in view of Porch House, and don't touch the furniture unless you cleaning it! But out behind the laundry, there's a yard with the wood shed opposite and connecting the two buildings, scrub growing tall as a man. Side four faced the slope down to our cabins. In other words, it's private-like. Three gum stumps lined one wall, looking ready for chopping, but really they was waiting for our behinds.

Mistress call Tuesday Laundry Day. I call it Grunt Day because hauling water and clothes loggy wet from one place to another is heavy, steamy work – and Lord, in this heat? The shed got openings, but seem like no air ever pass through no matter how we wilt and pray. There's two kettles, the lye one for washing, the plain water one for rinsing. We use long paddles to stir and lift. Once we done hang clothes on the line, we move one kettle off and put a grill the fire on for heating the irons. Once in a while, we flap steam around with one of my palmetto fans. Melody calls 'em "virgins," cause they never once flapped to keep a white face cool.

When Melody first come, Caesar insisted on carving her a paddle, even though Quash coulda done in half the time. Most times Caesar jiggled and joked like a boy with ants in his pants, but whenever Melody come about, he go all moon-eyed. Quiet. At first no one said nothing, but soon the men took to ribbing him. Turned out Caesar didn't mind. Once it was out in the open, he could do more for her. Now that Melody grown big with child, Caesar was always helping.

The laundry hook had to be smooth for the good silks. No snagging! So there you got Caesar with a dreamy look, sliding his hand up and down the shaft, sanding it smooth. You can guess what jokes spilt out then. Caesar didn't care none. My guess is he took a mighty satisfaction knowing that where his hand labored, Melody's hand was gonna touch.

Today it was just Melody and me. We set to work before the morning conch-blow, hoping to beat the heat, even by a little. Melody's baby comin' any time now, so I fetched the water, walking to the creek and back, two buckets at a time. Melody used her apron as a sling to fetch wood for the fires. She could almost pile the kindling atop her belly and forget the apron!

That morning, the marsh held on to night like a stubborn mule, the sky wearing a nasty purple bruise. Mist curled up through the grasses like ghosts. By the time kettles were full and the embers glowing like angry tiger eyes, it was late enough to go down to Porch House and gather up the cloth. Miss Eliza was putting on her bonnet. She nodded and went on her way. Upstairs, I loaded the basket with skirts, breeches, and tunics. From the pantry: napkins and a tablecloth. I was careful to tuck the ends in. No tripping for me today.

In the laundry shed, the air smelled good. Melody must've dropped something in a kettle – lavender? Once the stirring, scrubbing, and rinsing done, we pegged everything on the lines out back, toting the cloth in what Mistress call a Moses basket. I asked Melody about that.

"Moses was a slave," she tole me. "When he was a baby, his mama put him in a basket like this one and set him floating down the River Nile. A princess found him and took him in. She claimed him but didn't want to nurse him, so she asked the neighbor's slave to suckle him. That was his mama, turns out. He grew up wise. Became a prophet and led his people out of slavery."

"That's in the Bible?" Melody nodded yes and tole me how the Good Book says we're all of us children of God.

"Good day for drying," I said, putting one peg on the line, one in my mouth.

"Good day for sitting too." Melody lowered herself onto a gum stump, hands on her big belly.

No place in Lowcountry give us sanctuary, but this come close. We wasn't grabbing at freedom by running, but we sure was taking pleasure in our small way. We stole time every laundry day, doing what we wasn't supposed to. We sat down. We idled. We tipped our heads back to the sun.

If Mistress was having one of her feeble days, like today, and if Miss Eliza was down in one of the new orchards, like today, we could sit pretty, leaning into buckra's ignorance as sure as we was leaning into the side of the shed.

After a while, I asked Melody if she was gonna mind the heat today, meaning the iron. You can ruin cloth in a heartbeat, scorching it with the shape of the iron's bottom. Lately, Melody liked leaving light toast marks in hard-to-see places – on a pocket or along a back hem. It was a dangerous game.

"Maybe." She gave me a sly look. "Maybe not."

I like rebellions that leave no trace, like us sitting shoulder to shoulder right now, watching clouds go by.

"You gonna make trouble for Saffron if you ain't careful, and Lord knows Saffron's got enough trouble," I warned. What if Miss Eliza noticed?

"Don't I get to leave my mark?" Melody asked.

I didn't answer. After a little, it was time to heat the irons. "That Mr. Pinckney visiting in a few days. Again," I said. Melody grunted, smoothed her apron, and shoved herself up off the stump.

"A head like an egg on that one!" she laughed.

"Miss Eliza don't seem to mind none."

"Miss Eliza don't like any of them. You know that," Melody snapped.

I stood and started scrunching the lighter cottons to test if they was ready for the iron. "Saffron say she blush when he come round. And you see how talkety she gets! She don't do that with everyone."

Melody considered this. "I can tell you who she don't like! That blond snake from yonder." She nodded in the direction of the Tilton place and shuddered. He made my flesh creep too.

For the rest of Grunt Day, we pressed and folded. Replaced one button. Fixed two tears. Midafternoon, we ate a peach each and shared a piece of cornbread. Just as the sun sat flat and orange on the marsh, we made our way down to Porch House, wands of lavender laid in the folds of cloth, cloth tidy and clean in the Moses basket.

The Full Moon
Saffron, Wappoo Plantation

A scalp-pricklin' tole me Melody's baby was coming tonight. At dinner Mistress said how the doctor was up on Goose Creek with another baby coming but she was sure his services weren't needed here yet, as if saying it made it so. But babies don't care about doctors' schedules and babies don't care about any Mistress's puffed-up sense of mattering and predicting. They come when they come.

Dinner on the street done, July helped Melody up. As she stood, a gush of water hit the dirt and her eyes went wide. July looked at the moon floating above the dark fringe of trees and barked at Melody, "Don't you look!" A full moon been known to turn babies into lunatics or sleepwalkers. "Don't you look at that moon!"

We led Melody to Old Sarah's cabin. A week ago, we'd scoured the pallet, restuffed it, and collected clean rags. A basin sat next to the pile of rags. Old Sarah smiled like she been waiting for us. Caesar hung at the door, wanting to help. Melody sighed. "You can go tell Mistress I'm laboring, but wait until the parlor goes dark."

Old Sarah did a quick check to see which way the baby faced. July tried to get Melody comfortable, holding a hand at her back, low down, counting through the pains. Baby was head down, face up. After a time, Old Sarah held the birthing bottle up to Melody's lips. Melody blowed and blowed during the next pain, then the next and the next after that. The bottle hoots lingered up in the rafters, sounding both spooky and holy, like a protecting owl.

Some time later, Miss Eliza showed up with two buckets, one steaming. She looked tense. July dunked a cloth into the bucket of cool water and offered it to Melody to suck and recollected about rolling suckin' cloths during the pox quarantine. Melody waved at her to be quiet and threw up. That's when Mistress come in.

"Sit down!" was her first order, but to Miss Eliza, not Melody. "Head between your knees. Now!" Miss Eliza was a little green. Old Sarah tole Mistress the pains was coming a little faster but birth might be three meals away. Or a lullaby. "Some come like honey through a oiled funnel," she said. "Others keep you waiting."

"Is the baby breech?" Mistress asked. Old Sarah shook her head. Mistress knelt, put a cool towel to Melody's forehead, and cooed, "You're doing fine. Just fine."

Miss Eliza raised her head sharp like someone done yank it with a string. She weren't the only one surprised by her mother's caring manner. Somehow the business of birthing gave Mistress a way to be with Melody that was more human than the day-to-day.

After what seemed a long while, Melody stopped hearing us. She went elsewhere. Mistress Millie kept sitting close by and talking in that soothing way. It was "Noah's going to be a big brother" this and "just a little longer" that. Mistress slid a damp clump of hair out of Melody's eyes. Old Sarah held Melody's hand.

Sometime after the darkest hour of the night, the pains came one on top of the other. Mistress and Old Sarah helped Melody lean onto all fours. "Eliza! Roll up the other pallet and slide it over here." Melody leaned her head on it. Damned if she wasn't taking teeny naps between pains.

"Isn't it supposed to be easier the second time round?" Melody yelped. A minute later, Mistress and Old Sarah, as if friends for years, said firm and loud at the very same time, "Push!"

"The head!" July said from across the room.

Old Sarah held out her hands. "Almost done now!"

"One more," Old Sarah said. "Push!" It was hard to tell if the words helped or even if Melody heard them, but Mistress and Old Sarah went on coachin' and encouraging like a team, and suddenly a baby slid out into the world. A boy! Old Sarah held his small, wet head in one palm and rubbed slime off his face with the other. He punched the air with itty bitty fists and mewed like a little lamb, but didn't even cry or scream. Melody looked over, a peaceful love written all over her face.

Seeing that baby didn't give no sweeping relief to Miss Eliza or her mother, though. Mistress slumped down onto the cabin floor, looking empty and used up. The flannel fell out of her hand. I was so taken with the baby's peace and poise that it took me a minute to account for his skin. Eliza's face crumpled. Was she gonna cry? Now I saw. Looked like this fella had a white daddy. The baby was more red than white at the moment, like he been burnt. That skin'd settle down and probably darken in the next days, but how much?

Melody collapsed against the wall in relief, maybe even triumph, and held her hands out. Once cradled against her bosom, the baby stared up at her and she peered back. She stroked his wet black hair – his very straight wet black hair – and she pulled him close and helped him latch on. Drawing down the milk would help the afterbirth.

A reverent silence married the night. New life had come.

Tally
Eliza's Diary, Wappoo Plantation

The scourge of pox makes it all but impossible to conduct ourselves in the usual manner, or even to understand what the usual manner might be in these parts. Surely there'd have been a swirl of invitations absent disease, but instead we are mostly confined to our bluff.

Thankfully, the mail wagons operate without interruption, allowing Grandmama to send missives from the peninsula. After declaring herself and Grandpapa healthy, she shares ghastly details. From her bedroom she can sometimes see open wagons loaded with corpses rolling past. Some afternoons, the church bells ring for hours on end.

Mother took advantage of the time to correspond with Mrs. Boddicott and firm up arrangements for the boys' schooling in England. A January departure seems likely. George acts like he's biding his time until his true life begins, while Tommy is miserable.

Aside from this productive planning, Mother wilted badly after Moses was born. Days and days in bed, tamped down and quiet. Less hostile, maybe. I can't tell if there's been a rapprochement between her and Father or if Mother feels too defeated to rally her grievances. Unfortunately, Moses did not darken, not even a little bit. In the right clothing, he could pass for a brother of mine. Over and over, I've made the tally from date of purchase to baby's birth: exactly nine months.

Meanwhile, some nights find me restless and whether wise or not, sometimes wandering like a wraith to the barn, dock, and back. One midnight I spied Saffron and Indian Pete emerging from the shadow of the barn. Another night: Saffron and Maggie returning to their cabin. I could imagine what might have Saffron and Indian Pete out and secretive, but Maggie and her mother?

September 1738

The Weight of Cloth
Melody, Wappoo Plantation

We were shelling peas, me and July. After sitting in the sun two days, the pods crinkled like old paper and when we cracked 'em open, little black eyes winked back. Being in the pantry, we could hear Mistress Millie and Mrs. Woodward yammering. Mistress sometimes sounds like a horse clopping on cobbles – clippety clop, clippety clop, all high and mighty.

"Why it takes them all the day long to finish the washing and pressing is simply beyond me!" A spoon tinkled on a tea cup, probably Mistress stirring in the sugar she liked so much. Such miseries! Just the two old biddies in there right now. Miss Eliza and Miss Mary out on a walk. Can you blame them?

"Laundry days test my patience, between the scarcity of service for a pot of tea and wondering what on earth they do up there!" Was Mrs. Woodward shaking her head in agreement? "At least I can attest to the results. Very fine, don't ask me how. They manage to press everything to perfection, in fact." Brag or complain – make up your mind, Mistress!

Sometimes such whining caused a poison to rise up, belly to throat. July kept on harping, "That jaw gonna get you kilt!" I didn't worry about myself so much, but what if rage was spoiling my milk? Moses was sleeping in the basket next to the sugar cabinet as usual, sweet as could be. The Lowcountry ways would poison him soon enough and I sure didn't want ire from my body bringing it on early.

Mistress acted like it was a hard chore to give out orders. "Go do the washing now," she'd say, then sit and sit, having tea and cakes. Sometimes I made faces when I was standing behind her. July hated that. I'd wrinkle my nose as if a stench was rising up or cross my eyes. Small satisfactions, small liberties.

Last laundry day, when Moses was maybe five weeks old, Mistress talked so speedy I felt like she was spitting watermelon seeds at me. "Press the pleats in the same direction! Don't forget, hot water is the ruination of silk! Are your paddles free of snags? Can't have you snagging our fine silks. Do you have any idea how much good silk costs?"

Why would a slave know the cost of fine cloth? Such a ridiculous notion. We don't own things. In my possession: a small Bible and the sack I carry it in. July? She owned the little rainbow coils of thread she picked up off the floor. But Mistress clippety-clopped on and on.

The morning of this particular visit, Mistress excused herself from Mrs. Woodward and stepped into the pantry. What happened to the bell? I stood behind her, my face like a stone, hoping Moses would stay quiet. If he fussed Mistress might give his care over to Old Sarah.

Moses was a bane to her, and we all knew why. I never said anything about him, not even to July. My secret held power, and I wasn't about to give it up. Actually, in addition to a Bible and a sack to carry it in, I own a wounding secret.

Since the full moon in August when Moses was born, Mistress had turned icy and bitter with Master again. Spats bled through the walls often, turning the air dangerous. Getting pleasure from their strife was one thing, but risking a bill of sale was another. Was I being foolish? The secret was mine to keep, for sure, but a lifetime of misery was theirs to dish out.

She stood in the pantry, fishing for fault, for any little thing – a slight delay in delivering another plate of sweets, the lack of extra biscuits. Didn't we know anything? To my surprise July rolled her eyes. Mistress was looking hard at me, so she didn't see. July probably rolled her eyes like you itched an itch, without thinking, but I took it as a victory, a sign of camaraderie. In that moment, I barely cared what Mistress blabbered about. July had rolled her eyes! We had to bake extra biscuits right then and there. Took most of an hour. And on laundry day!

After the ladies was set, we headed back to the laundry shed. Leaving the house was sweet, like biting into a ripe peach, and it was part-revenge too, knowing how we were gonna sit down. Sometimes we sat in velvet silence and sometimes we swapped stories – who's run off of Laroche's place, the size of the rattler Tommy saw, the chances of another dance come November. But that day, I was quiet. The small tear Moses made had eased, thanks to Old Sarah and her comfrey oil, but a sore feeling lay deeper inside.

I thought about my boys. Noah had yet to learn much about the nasty ills all around him. He didn't know how Tommy would one day turn. And sweet Moses! How he arrived so soft and quiet, hardly crying! The world's gonna chain him hard, and soon. Sometimes when I held him, tracing his tiny ear with my finger, hoping his guardian spirit was near, dark thoughts crowded round.

"Count your blessings," July said, as if she'd been reading my book of worry. "Those two boys."

"Yes," I said. I told July how blessed I was, too, that no Archdale woman, no Evan wife or lady Pitt had birthed a baby in these past weeks. Otherwise, I'd be suckling a white baby in addition to my own. July got quiet again and traveled off somewhere. Her losses were buried, like gems in a dark, dark mine. Most likely her private quiet helped her bear them. She wasn't like me, wanting to spit my pain out.

She must have children, but she has never said. Were they linked in the same coffle, separated in a barracoon? Did they cross the sea together but get sold apart? Then again, maybe they were still home, untouched by kidnappers, searching their father's face, wondering still, even after ten years: Where is Mama?

Phoebe came round to take Moses – a right little mother in training. She shot up over the summer, taller than me now. Lanky and loose-limbed, at Polly's beck and call, she nevertheless carried herself with a quiet grace. Cheerful, even. Who knows how she did it. I told her to stay in the shade. What do I know about burning sun on pale skin?

We pulled the cottons from the rinse kettle with our paddles, keeping skin away from the pot's rim – wrists being banded with scars already. Then we pulled the silks from the cool pot on the other side of the shed. We filled two baskets. Outside, we pegged the cottons on the line first because they took longer to dry. July threw me a look. She'd come back from wherever she'd been.

Out of nowhere, she said, "They'd be fools to sell him. Wappoo just gettin' going and the head rights help gettin' land. Even before Moses a man, he help the ledger and anyway, before you know he'll be two-three tasks."

"How do you know all this?" I spat, as if it was July keeping numbers on our heads, not Master. "If Mistress thinks Husband lifted my skirts, she could get him to sell Moses out of spite. Her sulking's got power in it."

July shrugged. "They don't do much selling hereabouts before Christmas. Plenty time to tell Master ain't the father."

I startled.

July looked at me with sorrow. That startled me more. Only once before had I seen so much sorrow and that was when Nell told me about almost breaking her daughter's finger as the auctioneer pried them apart. Usually July's face was smooth, like wood worn by a swift current, but now it seemed as though her features held not just her sorrow, but mine, and that of bonded mothers all up and down the Lowcountry rivers. Was this unique to slaves – the way grief leaked and gathered, spun and settled, without regard to origin? She wasn't telling me what to do. She wasn't badgering for revelation. She was sitting in the place of mother-worry with me.

A bird in the pines squawked, sounding like a hungry babe to the hollows and pillows of my body. Milk came out, soaking my tunic. Two dark spots.

Around here you've got knee babies with Choctaw cheeks and long French noses, slave children in ragged tunics wearing their master's profile, skin the color of pine. There were slave girls coming up as women with straightish hair and hungry hazel eyes. Nothing unusual. But you never knew how a Mistress gonna take it. Maybe I'd better tell.

Love's Quarry
Saffron, Wappoo surround

At first, I thought 'twas a shame to be sent off, 'cause Mistress Millie was in cheer – what she call 'up and at it.' But, with babies due up and down the Ashley and Melody's name floating from place to place as a right good baby-catcher, we needed herbs.

"Point of pride," Mistress said, whatever that means.

I was hunting out snake root, both roots and seeds. We pull out the plants, shake 'em off, but never take a whole clump, so it'll come back. For seeds, you just slid 'em off the stalk like beads off a string. Snake root helped with stuck births and all kinds of other female ills.

By the time I got to the edge of the Deep Woods for my short cut, Indian Pete was on my mind. What else was new? I thought of him as I stepped off the road. I thought of him as I walked in and out of the shadows of slash pines. I thought of his brow. I thought of his shoulders. His royal face. My belly warmed. Heat bloomed in my chest.

And so, when I cut across one field and started to cross the next and saw him yonder, it seemed like he came straight from inside my head. It spooked me. Either my thoughts conjured him or his being near flooded my head with thoughts of him, even before I knew he was there.

A posse of cock turkeys strutted into the clearing. How sure of foot they were, but strange — shoving heads out and back, out and back. Sun fell on feathers, lighting up some blue-black. Indian Pete crept the slow creep of the hunter and it looked like one of the gods melted grace direct into his body.

He looked like he was in a trance, but I knew he was alive like fire. He hugged the scrub. The turkeys didn't hear him. He stopped and for a second, disappeared. Was this another kind of conjuring? But no, it was just covering shadow from hickory trees yonder. He come back.

Should I turn and sneak away? Or stay still and witness his hunt? We only met hip to hip a few times and with time passing I wondered why he wasn't seeking me out. And why wasn't I looking to find his lips in the dark again? Twining suffering and joy into a single plait struck me as peculiar, impossible, maybe. Maybe we'd be better off without any spurt of happiness since it come with a jagged crown of hurt. I hoped it wasn't me. My smell? The way I laugh at times or my hard whispering in his ear?

I'm taller than Indian Pete, but lying down, we met up just fine, hip bones and mouths. I studied his long body now. Seeing him now struck me so hard, I think I could've turned into a hunter myself, tracking and snaring him, pulling him to the ground.

He reached one arm over his shoulder real slow, as if was moving through molasses, and drew out an arrow. The light caught the muscle running from wrist to elbow, breath snagging in my throat. How could a man's arm be so beautiful? He clamped the notch in the string and pulled them both back so his fist lined up with his cheekbone, knuckles just below the eye. Then he sank into the ground a little, bending his knees. Suddenly, I got that I wasn't breathing, so I let some air out real slow, not wanting to disturb him or the turkeys half a field away.

It come to me now how Indian Pete used his hunter skill to draw me in, but with glances and courtesies instead of bow and arrow. Did I want to be caught, hit, and made again? Everything was so new. Tongue and land was new. Opening up to someone not my husband: strange and new.

His hand let loose the arrow and it hit one of the birds, causing the rest to flee in a cackle of panic. Kneeling next to the still-fluttering body, he twisted the bird's neck in one swift yank. A violent kindness. Then, he pulled out his arrow, wiped its tip on the grass, and put it back.

It struck me now how that arrow made its kill – by Indian Pete opening his hand. It wasn't a hammering blow or hard stab. It was a hand opening up.

The dead bird was still. Indian Pete was still. I was still. He bent over, giving quiet thanks, I think -- Mustee habit.

I was starting to shake a little, thinking on how he'd bent over my pallet that night, tapped my shoulder, and led me out by the barn. Wasn't pleasure like letting go the arrow? You had a place to go, aimed your arrow true, pulled and tugged, pulled and tugged, but in the end, you just let go. Opened. How could shuddering in love and killing be so the same?

Maybe I should ask why he sought me out in the first place, not why he wasn't coming back. One question, good as the other.

All of a sudden, I felt dizzy, so I squatted down and laid my hands on the cool bark of a fallen cypress tree. My thighs was strong and could crouch a long while, but still I felt weak. I had no arrow to pull, no string to draw back, no flinty point to let go and hit its mark. I had only my apron and what lay under.

Could I slip away without Indian Pete seeing me? Seemed far-fetched that I could outwit a man who knew to look for a cottonmouth twenty feet up in a tree before anybody else even knowed to worry on it. He plucked one of the long brown and white feathers off his kill and tucked it in with the arrows. Was it for future arrows or was it maybe a gift -- maybe even a gift for me? A sweet offering that said, meet me later in the dark? And in the dark, maybe he'd take the feather back, ask me to close my eyes, and tickle my neck with it. Was I a fool?

I turned to leave, making a twig crackle underfoot. Indian Pete quickly crooked his arm over his shoulder for an arrow, nocked it, and pulled it back.

Then he saw me. He looked at my face, then down at the hollow of my neck. He looked at my hand sinking into my pocket. And then he looked back at my eyes. I felt shy, almost like he was touching me. He dropped the bow and then he smiled. Not just any smile, but the broad eager smile of a man in love. I waved a little wave, gave a little smile back and left, my heart skipping hard, satisfied.

October 1738

In the Ground
Eliza, Wappoo Plantation

Outside the clammy cabin, no refreshment, no relieving faith or logic either. Grief seemed an element, like humidity. Mother's face showed grim resolve, July's, bewildered loss. I thought my mother would issue orders, but instead she descended the cabin steps in silence, then sailed away as if propelled by a gust of wind. I jogged after.

"Burn the bedding," she called without turning round, waving her hand in that signature gesture. Imperial and dismissive. "The entire pallet!" I wasn't sure July heard, so I went back and almost choked to realize that before any bedding could be burned, something had to be done with the bodies.

Benjie and James were now "the bodies."

The blistering plasters and broken doses of calomel had been applied throughout the night. And the night before, poultices of comfrey. We hadn't known that either boy was sick. Not that we could have done anything – could we? Seemed some survived the pox and some didn't.

Just four days ago, I'd seen Benjie and James sweeping off the dock with small brooms, interrupting their chore to bat at each other. They'd died in the same hour right before dawn, mewling in fever. The pox struck them with a vengeance, pustules covering faces, torsos, and limbs, their formerly sweet faces disfigured. Those poor, poor boys!

Perhaps even more astonishing than their illness escaping notice was the fact that various slaves had attended the boys around the clock without our knowing. Further, they'd somehow procured calomel. That morning, I was not just grieving the little ones, I was questioning my powers of observation.

We had yet to establish a cemetery at Wappoo, for either white or black bodies. Other families had been less fortunate and paced out their plots months ago: the Draytons, Smithfields, Elliots, and Archdales. It was difficult, in fact, to turn in any direction without noting a recent death. Doctor Jackson upriver callously informed us last week that "no hand of mine will ever be buried within eyesight of this house." He consigned his pox-felled slaves – three of them – to the woods, some two miles distant. Unwilling to sacrifice a single minute of labor, he'd required that the burials take place at night.

I caught up with Mother.

"The bodies?" I asked, grabbing her elbow. She grunted, tugged her arm free, and disappeared inside. Since Father was attending to business on St. Helena's Sound, yet another decision was left to me.

I considered a small clearing about a mile into the Deep Woods, but there'd been a hootenanny there last year, and for all I knew, slaves gathered there still. How dreadful to bury the boys there, then. I rejected any land near the slave quarters, since proximity to the creek made the chances of dry graves slim. No, I would have Mo enclose a small plot up behind the woodshed. The graveyard wouldn't be visible from the house, but neither would it be remote.

Dinner passed in a grim mood. When July laid down my plate, I scanned her hands, neck, and the planes of her narrow cheeks for any signs of an eruption. She had now been doubly exposed, first during quarantine and now by the slave boys. Perhaps she was immune? If so, it wasn't on account of "jungle immunity"– just think on poor Benjie and James! What a dreadful way to gain empirical evidence for the medical debates raging throughout the Lowcountry that fall.

July laid a gravy boat down and turned to leave.

"Whose dress is that, then?" Mother asked, looking at the ill-fitting garb.

"Melody's child-carrying dress, Mistress."

"There's a bolt of Negro cloth in the back room. Cut out your and Saffron's new frocks tonight and you can stitch them up on the morrow."

July nodded and left.

Mother laid her fork down and asked softly, "Are they in the ground?" And then, before I could respond, "Such a waste of tallow! We'll need to burn at least three for the cutting session. Not at all what I had in mind when I had those candles poured." I chewed my cutlet without tasting it. There was no precedent for this loss, this inconvenience, but Mother's abnegation of duty earlier and now her failure of compassion irked me beyond measure. I left the table.

Digging Graves
Mo, Wappoo Plantation

I know axe. I know spade and blisters. But burning palms was nothin' next to grief. I worked all morning splitting wood, then pounding fence posts. I laid the long rails. Hickory split up good.

Grave-digging next. I got three buckets lined up, in case water seep in, how it do.

The plot ain't off in the woods, but it's near to invisible, up behind the woodshed. Always penning us in, keeping us out of sight. Like in the barracoons, in the dank holds of the slavers, and in the quarantine pens on Sullivan's Island. What's a binyah like me know 'bout all that, being born in the Lowcountry?

Plenty. Anybody born into slavery can tell you. We hear and we remember and we grieve and live like a single body. Big Joe burned alive down at Cox's place recently. It take all of us to hold news like that. You couldn't stop from hearing no matter how hard you tried.

No growing up for Benjie and James. No shoes. No kissing. But also, no being whupped or covered in honey and staked to a anthill. What was dying to them boys, good fortune or bad? Maybe they was the two luckiest fellas in the Lowcountry today. Felled by pox and heading back to the Ancestors. Fly free, Benjie and James. Fly free!

They died fast, but not fast enough. The crying. The skin pocking and oozing. Calling out about fire in the bones. At least their mama weren't around. There was that to be thankful for. Hard to even recall when she done gone missing – last fall? Or the fall before?

I heaped the dirt into two mounds 'til they looked like the bosom of mother ground. You could count on a thing or two in the Lowcountry, even as a slave, and this was one of them – we would always ache for the soil of the Ancestors, even men like me, the binyah.

A twinge run up my neck. I rubbed sweat in one eye and it stung. Everyone was on the lookout. Was that joint aching from task or was a fever comin' on? Was it threshing running you tired or sickness? The terror of fever blended in with grief. No bottom to the hurt.

Quashee and Caesar come up the slope, each with a small coffin resting on a shoulder. We put them boxes down in the graves. Out of his pocket, Quash pulled two small carved canoes and paddles and gave each boy a set to help them get back to the Ancestors. I grabbed the shovel and got stung with a splinter. I stared at it, shining and pricking in my thumb, as if I didn't know how it got there. Quash took the shovel from me and laid in some, but not all, the dirt. The sound of them thuds on the coffins hurt as much as anything else.

A slight chill come off the creek. Just as Quash laid the shovel up against the woodshed, the conch sounded, low and sad. Usually it mean rise up and labor, or quit labor and sit down and rest, but this time it carried news of death in its wail.

Benjie and James gone.

King George's Birthday
Eliza, Wappoo Plantation and Woodward Residence

As October came to a close, news of illness and death, so savagely routine throughout the summer and early fall, slowed to a trickle. Rattling cool breezes arrived at last and collectively, we breathed a sigh of relief. Life really seemed on the upswing when we received news that Charles Town was to host a King George's Birthday Gala. How exciting! During the ride to Woodward's for our usual Tuesday visit, I nattered on about gowns, how I might refresh my dance steps. Mother grunted and sat in opaque silence.

A restless Mary greeted us at the door, eyes aglitter. She took a seat and fidgeted. Her hands, so oft rhythmically occupied with quilting, waved and fluttered as she gave gay descriptions of former celebrations. The stylish appointments, the glorious repast, the ballroom aglow with hundreds of candles!

"Oh, and Eliza!" she sighed, "the music!" Mary's lyrical anticipation stood in such sharp contrast to her usual demeanor that I wondered if there was a suitor involved and if so who and for how long. If she was keeping matters crucial to the heart hidden from me, I may have badly misgauged our friendship.

"Mary's certainly ready to dance the night away," Mother ventured and then looked at me with the slightest of shrugs.

I eagerly awaited Mary's and my private walk along the creek, but on this of all days, she made no move to head out of doors. It wasn't raining and it wasn't threatening to rain, but there she was, glued to her seat, bringing up one memory after another. Before I knew it, the visit was over.

Out of nowhere in the carriage headed home, Mother announced that I would not be attending the gala. "Mother!" I hollered in such loud protest that a cluster of birds roosting nearby lifted off in alarm. "The eligible young suitors?" I prodded.

We'd not heard of a single new case of pox up or down the creek or along the Ashley since Benjie and James died, meaning any health caution was excessive. I knew she didn't believe much in the efficacy of inoculations, but still. Generally Mother's curtailments came with explicit narratives, footnoted to an obnoxious degree, so it seemed likely that there was some secret agenda.

"I'm sorry, pet."

Back at Wappoo, the harpsichord offered no solace. After I played the same four lines of music over and over, George yelled from the back patio, "Make her stop, Mother!" At that moment, Father clattered up onto the gallery with his favorite hound, Morgan. Mother, sewing basket on arm, quickly joined him, as did I.

"What do you think, Father?" I began with a casual air. "Should I wear the Watteau or the Robe Français to the Gala?" Pitting one parent against the other was beneath me, and the attempted ruse was patently ridiculous, for my father had no opinions about gowns and probably couldn't even tell the two frocks apart.

Father shot Mother a look. He reached down and flipped over first one of the hound's ears, then the other, exposing the tender pink undersides, stroking them gently. Quite a project, the dog's ears. We sat in a weighted silence.

"It's too soon," Father said finally. "Perhaps November? That's just a couple of weeks longer. I think that'd suit better."

"Suit whom better? Certainly not me!" But Father remained tight-lipped. Just in case he worried about the lingering effects of the inoculation or my migraines, I argued, "I'm entire in health and Mary says most of our acquaintances will be there. They're not worried about miasma."

He leaned down to scratch under the dog's chin. Morgan succumbed with a sigh, sinking into the porch boards and rolling over to offer his belly. Mother slid her notions basket closer to her chair with her foot and reached down for a bobbin of thread.

"Tell her, George."

"What? Tell me what?"

Father sighed. "You were spared the details last year, Eliza, because you'd only just come back from England, and frankly by then the ordeal was fully resolved." A knot formed in my stomach. "It wasn't just tensions with France and Spain that prompted our decision to leave Antigua."

Our decision? I thought with derision.

"Are you going to make me beg?" I asked. My mood now contained a curious and sour alarm. First Mary, now my parents – did I seem unworthy of trust?

Mother reached the end of a seam, triple-stitched in place, and leaned over to break the thread with her teeth. Her silence seemed to indicate a previously made agreement that Father would explain. This too rankled.

"Do you remember a slave named Tomboy?" I nodded. "And do you remember that he was executed? You probably don't know why." I'd heard vague references, but no real details. "Tomboy was an exemplary slave, loyal and well-seasoned. Highly skilled, endowed with intelligence, and trusted." Father ran a hand through his hair as if shifting the soothing gestures from the hound to himself. He cleared his throat. "Well, such was not the case. Not by a long measure!"

Mother held her needle up to the sky to poke thread through it. I watched her deftly knot the end as Father continued. "Imagine how deeply shocking it was when Governor Matthew discovered a plot – a truly dastardly plan for the violent overthrow of our rule. Tomboy was one of the masterminds." Father paused again, and now it seemed intended to allow me time to absorb the news. It was indeed disturbing, but how did it connect to Charles Town's gala?

"Led by one Prince Klaas, the rebels planned to claim St. Johns Harbor and then the island entire. Seems it'd been thought through in some alarming amount of detail and, here's the relevant part, the insurgence was organized around a gala for King George."

The news struck me like a blow. "What? When was this?"

"Roughly two years ago. Rumor had it that the rebel slaves had procured both gunpowder and weapons. The plan was to lay lines of gunpowder under the banquet seats and take out most of the island's elite in a single explosion. Gaining control of the harbor would have been fairly easy after that."

"One of ours was in on it," Mother inserted. "Caesar. The West Indian Caesar, that is. Did you know that one?" I did not. Mother went on to say that like Tomboy, Caesar had seemed the loyal slave, reading his Bible and so on. "So you just never know," she declared. "Some of the rebels eluded punishment, and suspicions lingered. Nothing puts a slave on the West Indian auction block faster than the stink of trouble, by the by. It doesn't take a quotient of genius to see that a similar plot here would be quite effective. For all we know, some of those very same troublemakers lurk about the Lowcountry as we speak."

"Oh my goodness!" I sputtered. "How many were caught? What was the evidence?" Without waiting for answers, I flung out a final argument. "The numbers aren't nearly so dire here, though, are they? And, just because one gala was targeted doesn't mean another one will be, especially in a different land with different slaves, and where on earth would they obtain gunpowder?"

Father ticked off his points. This ball, like the West Indian ball, would attract a good number of powerful landowners; two of the most devious Antiguan rebels, Jacko and Secundo, had been Catholics with close ties to their owners, and did I realize how many saltwaters were Angolans and Catholic converts, many literate in two languages? "I don't need to point out the aid bilingualism offers in the dissemination of a plot. Some of the Antiguan slaves were former soldiers, as well, knowledgeable about weaponry."

Mother gripped a pin in her mouth while lining up another seam. When she removed it to secure the fabric, her lips remained tightly compressed.

"Yes, well, and is there more?"

"Does Tomboy remind you of anyone?" Father stood and slowly paced the gallery. Mother looked at him quizzically. Apparently, she had no more idea than I what he was on about.

And then it struck me. "Oh! Surely you can't mean Quashee? He wouldn't harm a flea!"

Mother chuckled. "True! That one's so eager to please one nearly wants to bat him with a stick at times."

But Father reiterated how many of the Antiguan rebels had been by all outward appearances "eager to please," and how Quash, like Tomboy, was a highly skilled carpenter, often hired out and roaming the landscape with more freedom typically granted a slave.

"And then, of course, there was our first Caesar," Mother said quietly. "Executed for his part. Takes time to absorb a financial loss like that." I suddenly understood the glances that had passed between my parents on the day of our arrival. What I had taken to be revulsion at the hobbling of Wappoo Caesar had instead been a fearful reminder of the treacherous Antiguan Caesar. Morgan looked up at Father with the anxiety of a pack animal aware of a disturbance in the group.

Father continued. "The demand for skilled artisans – rope makers, sail makers, coopers, wainwrights, and the like – will remain desperate here until more European immigrants arrive. Until then, we have to use Negroes. No one's going to hold off a year's lucrative crop in expectation of a shipload of Swiss or Celts!"

"Lord," Mother groaned, "I hope the Irish never come!" Not this again! How many times had I heard her lament the absence of white household help, always making a harsh exception for the Irish. She'd take "the lazy, filthy Negroes" over the "blowsy girls from Cork" any day.

July emerged from the house. The table where she normally placed the tea service was occupied by cloth, so I offered to take the tray on my lap.

Father hiccupped out one last concern, "And let us not forget the damned Spanish! Very destabilizing."

"George!" Mother admonished.

"Well? Offering freedom for any slave making it to St. Augustine? That may end up being our powder keg in the end."

Mother looked at the tray. "What? Scones and no butter? Not a smidge of jam?"

"Damn the scones, Millie! I am making a rather serious point here."

"George, you've made your point. More than once, in fact. Do you take us for imbeciles? Allow me to go you one better and say that we weren't safe on Antigua and we're not safe here. Eliza will skip the ball and possibly be blown to smithereens while attending the theatre in one month's time."

Father blew out a big puff of air giving the impression that he did, indeed, find his women folk imbecilic. He abruptly left and set off down the road at a brisk pace, Morgan at his heels.

July returned with a small pot of butter.

On the following Tuesday visit with Mary and her mother, I hoped Mary would make revelations worthy of our former intimacy. In contrast to our last visit, she and I absented ourselves right away. Before we even reached the dock, she blurted out, "His name is Pastor William Huston and Mother has no idea!"

Both divulgences shocked me. Mary being swept up in romance seemed at such odds with her mien as somber widow. As for keeping news of such import from her dear mother, to whom she was so close – who would've guessed? Mary gushed on, with much fluttering of hands. They were secretly betrothed! No larger revelations would be made until her father approved the match

"How will you introduce your beau, then?"

Her plan was simple. They'd both be attending the upcoming comedy at Dock Street Theatre and would arrange to meet as if by chance at the Poinsett Inn afterwards. They'd ensure that her mother witnessed a lively exchange. On the way home, Mary would sigh his name out loud a time or two, after which she'd casually ask after his reputation. Simple!

Mary's plotting further shook my view of her. Integrity laced with guile? Perhaps I'd placed her on too high a pedestal. I realized that humans are complicated, with a strange mix of strengths and flaws. But never mind. With our close bond restored, we'd secretly talk gowns and Scripture selections!

November 1738

Five Things
July, Wappoo Plantation

Ever since Benjie and James done pass, the thick curtain of forgetting gone to shreds. Used to hold up sturdy and dark. Now it's a lacy frill with gaps so big memory slips through without asking. Here come my boys! Quaquosh, Obajani, and Ganda. They been stowed away, tucked behind. But not anymore.

Course I miss Benjie and James every which way. There they is in the woodshed, poking about and laughing. There they is lying down beside me or Melody at night. But it weren't just them, it was my three too, sometimes all five of 'em piled on my pallet giggling or sobbing in fear. Sometimes they be running from Mo down near the barn or begging for apple skins in Summer Kitchen or out at the laundry line, pressing naughty faces into clean sheets – all five of 'em! Everywhere, they was just everywhere. Benjie, James, Quaquosh, Obajani, and Ganda.

If I couldn't turn remembering into prayer, it was gonna end me. I stumbled around that season, scared, calling out to the Ancestors. I laid pecans in the hollow of the live oak, stealing two at a time, begging for wisdom. Under the Drying Up Full Moon, one of the long-gone mothers at last answered.

She whisper, "Five blessings. Every morning." I heard her clear, just as if she was standing under the live oak, with only hanging moss between us. "Name five blessings every morning. Don't labor, just do."

It don't pay to disrespect the Ancestors, so I took to it. Given how empty my basket of tricks was, what else was I gonna do? I was one recollection away from grinding up some trumpet vine flowers and mixing 'em with my tea.

Naming five blessings was like saying, "I am strong enough to remember." And strange enough, gratitude seeped in. The Ancestors probably thought me a fool, expecting so little.

Nothing gotta be grand — even the smartness in a hill of ants is a blessing, after all. And so every day I count five, pressing on thumb or finger with each blessing. Doing it every day is like winding a ball of wool: you start with a nub the size of a walnut and soon the ball was melon-size. When peace come to me now and again, it's the Ancestors lending a hand.

This morning in November, Blessing One is the gleam in Noah's eyes. Blessing Two is the sunrise, peach and orange today. Yesterday it was a hard rain, the day before it was the smell of pine. Tomorrow, maybe how air prickles before lightning.

Blessing Three always go to my boys. Every day, I say their names: Quaquosh, Obajani, and Ganda. I don't dwell, but I ain't avoiding anymore neither.

Blessing Four is the peach compote I made yesterday. Peach compote is goodness all on its lonesome, but it also stand like a flag for all the making I do. Rice flummery, terrapin soup, brandied plums, corn dodgers. Laboring give me something to count each day — smooth gravy, tender dough, seams felled as fine as any tailor in Paris (so say Mistress).

Even having every stitch and mouthful stolen don't take the making away from me. They can outgrow the breeches, give the cobblers away, eat everything I cook and leave nothing but a stink, and it don't change my doing one bit.

Walking to Porch House, I looked up at the sky, feeling empty. Many a day, I counted the Ancestors as the final blessing, but not today. I put the teakettle on the fire, and Blessing Five come to me: it was death. Blessing Five was death!

Death's a gift everybody get one time. Maybe it's sudden-like or maybe it's slow, like after a wasting fever. Maybe it take you when you is but nine-year-old, maybe when you past sixty, but whatever way death come, it's a blessing. Clouds, figs, and love, them other blessings, make you want live, but the blessing of death make you want to let go. Letting go is a blessing, a relieving rest, all things beautiful and brutal done.

The Theatre
Eliza, Wappoo Plantation

It was settled. We would stay the weekend with my Grandparents and attend Dock Square Theatre. The comedic piece, *The Recruiting Officer*, had been well-received and, after the trials of small pox, we were all in terrible need of a good laugh. We would eat well, dress well, and be in society at last.

On the appointed evening, the play came and went with a great deal of jollity, so it was with a light step that we headed toward the Poinsett Inn. The briny air off the Atlantic mixed with the tang of horse dung and hints of tar as shouting and laughter rang out. The sheen of silken gowns catching the light from lanterns held high by gallant men made for a scene both beautiful and mysterious. Day had fledged into night, but not quite fully – bands of luminous turquoise lined the horizon, as if reluctant to let darkness hold sway.

We walked alongside Suzanne and John, or "the young Draytons," as Mother called them. As if on cue, together they launched into boisterous descriptions of the inn's cuisine. Turtle fin soup this and oyster pie that and chicken fricassee as good as anything served on the Continent. John looked at me as if to gauge my appetite. "Oh, and don't get me going on the sweets!"

His father sniffed the air and interjected quickly, "One brisk breeze could turn our city to char. That rope house needs to be moved up peninsula." He said this with some sense of urgency, but perhaps it was merely to prevent his son's discourse on sweets.

Suzanne looked lovely if not ethereal in an ivory silk Watteau, but when John stepped closer to place an arm around her, his lantern revealed a hectic complexion. I wondered if all this talk of food was stirring up a healthy appetite or if she was perhaps with child. Another alternative crossed my mind, one both harsh and inescapable after a season of epidemic: was she sick? I scanned any and all exposed flesh for signs of an eruption.

Like many of the structures in Charles Town, the Poinsett Inn ran its length away from the street, showing only a narrow gable end upon approach. Sounds of conviviality emanated from one and two stories up, where iron-railed porticos ran the entire eastern side of the building. I took a last look at the sky. The heavens had gone velvety black except for that blue at the horizon which had deepened into sapphire.

The second floor housed the main gathering, so up we went along a curving mahogany staircase. Framed botanical prints lined the walls, each lovelier than the last. Upstairs, the rooms were so well-appointed that I swore I could hear Mother's internal click of approval. In the parlor to our right, two fireplaces crackled with warmth at either end of the long, narrow room. A series of three deep niches on the long exterior wall featured French doors opening out toward the harbor. On the facing interior wall, several long tables draped in white linen were lit by ornate candelabra, blue and white porcelain and silver at the ready.

Negroes in livery deposited two large tureens on a buffet near the far fireplace, and more slaves entered with platters held aloft.

I claimed a seat near the middle, facing a massive mirror tilted against the wall. Father wanted to know if the ornately carved frame was made in France or England. Imagine our surprise when we learned that the work was recent and done by a slave – one of ours, no less. Quashee, of course. Mother warbled with pleasure and boasted that Quashee had carved an ornate frame for us, also for a large mirror.

"We're just waiting on the silvered glass to arrive. It's taking an age!" she added, but with pride, not annoyance.

I'm embarrassed to admit that I was distracted by the sight of myself in the mirror. Who was that woman in the glass? I wouldn't turn sixteen for another six weeks, and yet the face looking back at me was unexpectedly mature. My features looked sharper, more clearly rendered, as if the artist responsible for them had returned for a second go-round. Some layer of childhood had vanished when I wasn't paying attention.

Meanwhile, Suzanne filled my ear. "The secret ingredient to baked shad is allspice. Do you keep it in your pantry?" We sat quite near, her right hand near my left, her breath over my plate. "And do you know how to remove the bitterness from palmetto cabbage leaves?" I was soon informed. Eventually, Suzanne leant closer to me and in a husky whisper revealed that although she could read, she'd not been instructed in history, the classics, or French. I glanced at her rouged cheeks and hoped she blushed with embarrassment and not fever. Recipes forgotten, she peppered me with questions about education, all on behalf of her children, ages two and four.

Dinner was a success, barely a morsel left on any plate. There would be a pause before dessert. Many headed downstairs, but I wandered about on the second floor, hoping to find Mary. I found my dear friend by one of the fireplaces in the other parlor. Next to her sat Pastor Huston, whom I recognized from a service she and I had attended at Independent Church a while back. He was looking at her solicitously as she quietly related something. I wasn't about to interrupt.

In any case, soon the evening was winding down. At the front of the inn, men donned hats or replaced wigs they had abandoned upon entering. Women wrapped capes or mantillas about their shoulders, pulled gloves on. Through the doors came the moist smell of impending rain. Father announced, "That breeze'll stiffen on the morrow!"

On the street, relief overcame me – what an exhausting business society was! – and then gratitude for the refreshment of air, the freedom to walk with energy! I couldn't wait to step out of my petticoats and unlace my confining stays. Mother slipped a hand into my arm and I leant into her as she hummed a familiar lullaby, the one about the mockingbird.

She interrupted herself to say, "Looks like our Mary's found herself a beau." I nodded. *"And if that looking glass gets broke, Mama's gonna buy you a billy goat."*

The Dance
July, west of the Deep Woods

I was set against going. I skipped supper, laid down, and fell hard asleep, missing all the primping before they tromp off. Woke before deepest night to a thrum in the air. Was it a dream? Was it the blood running in my limbs? No, it was drumming, a pulse and commandment, a call home. How could I refuse? I made my way there.

Faces warmed by firelight greet me at the clearing. Bodies stomping and slapping the rhythms of home, calabashes dried and shaken, empty hogsheads beaten as drums. To get here, people walked along paths stamped by patroller horses. A three-mile walk, a five-mile walk. Some paddled, hiding rafts in grasses along the Ashley, risking alligators and punishment. But here in the clearing near the Deep Woods, gladness sparked and glowed. Memory collected up gay skirts in grace. Music bowed the night air in happiness. I thought to myself: joy is the best rebellion of all.

There in the circle was Cudjoe dancing with his wife, Mo's mother. Even though he got the honor-badge of key slave, he risk all being here. If found out, Overseer might take an ear or take his life. There was Cato from up Goose Creek handing a slip to a young buck. How that boy grin! Cato's forgeries was well-known.

My jaw drop when I spy Saffron. Uh, oh! Were she really wearing a calico dress of Miss Eliza's? My heart raced. What's she thinking? How and when she done sneak into Miss Eliza's chamber and put it on?

Saffron wore a flirty air, as if putting on the frock give her a new way to be. Made sense. It was for sure a fine garment: pearl buttons and inset lace, never mind a waist that gather up yards of cloth so it bell out in a twirl. Was it worth the risk of whipping or sale to feel pretty and alive, not herself exactly, but not a slave neither?

The possibility of me taking a turn in the circle, slim to begin with, vanished under the weight of a future brung on by that calico dress. I fingered the worn edge of my cuff. Good for me for keeping barren this side of the sea. I been lucky and quick on the count too – them smelly pastes and so on. Been here more'n ten years and produced nary a head for the ledger. Talk about rebellion!

Saffron and Indian Pete took their turn. I tried to look away but couldn't – love declared too beautiful to behold. I suddenly saw how a steely will tugged right beside Saffron's vanity, and I admired her will, but it weren't necessarily gonna bend her in the direction of survival.

The Dance
Eliza, Charles Town

When we arrived at the Regan household, the dance was in full swing. What a scene! In one corner stood a harp, like a static butterfly, in the other, a cheery fire roared. In between, an elegant harpsichord chimed out the familiar melodies of the quadrille. Lines of dancers stepped back and forth, then grabbed hands and promenaded down the room's middle. There was a rainbow of silk skirts. There were lace-cuffed arms held high by eager men, their satin brocade jackets catching the candlelight.

"Planter's Punch all around!" Mr. Regan said by way of greeting, with a mention of "the young bucks" in attendance. He gave me a bawdy wink, and at the approach of Mr. Tilton, he whisked my parents away. My neighbor bowed and smiled, as gentlemen do, but it was all courtesy and no feeling. The music struck up again. What was I to do but take his hand and smile and hope that the flower Grandmama had so carefully tucked in my hair remained in place?

We danced and paused and danced again. If only I shared a fraction of the exuberant delight Sarah Hext and John Rutledge took in each other! There they were, aglitter in affianced esteem, high color on all four cheeks, eyes alight. It seemed too much to hope that I might one day share a dance with a man whose hands were as elegant as John Rutledge's. With a man who looked at me like that.

I feigned delight when Henri Dutarque cut in, but better him than the odious Tilton, who offered him an icy glare. Were two "young bucks" in competition for me?

After another number, the harpist and the fiddler left the room in search of refreshment. Guests wandered into the other parlor or the library or out onto the long candlelit second-story gallery. I looked for Mary Chardon and came upon Mary Bartlett instead.

"Wasn't that just divine?" she gushed. I laughed and allowed myself to agree. Mary sidled closer and said in low tones, "Have you noticed how tall the second Regan son is?" What a surprise! First Mary Woodward, and now Mary Bartlett in a twitter over a man! Until tonight, it wouldn't have surprised me if she chose to devote her life to horses – husbands be damned.

"What's wrong with the first-born?" I asked. Everything, apparently – hadn't I seen him rising up off the harpsichord bench, hardly taller standing than when he'd been sitting? Mary discreetly pointed to the taller, younger sibling.

"Well then," I pronounced in solidarity, "And such a nice head of hair."

In need of liberation, we snuck out the front door in a more radical kind of solidarity, daring to be out on the street near midnight unaccompanied, gossiping in gritty detail about the party's guests. Had I seen Mr. Gibbs trip upon entering the parlor, nearly knocking over the elder Middletons? And what about Christopher Gadsen bragging about his champion cock? How had everyone maintained a straight face? We snorted, no decorum needed! I was refreshed by the cool air and by the frankness of our friendship.

Soon the glittering Regan structure drew us back – a ziggurat of light, an emblem of civilization. After our little jaunt, we were eager to re-enter the party's convivial warmth. A block shy of the house, we saw Henri Dutarque exit a side door, alone, and head off in the direction of his city dwelling. Moments later Willard Tilton emerged, not from the side door but out the front. He swiveled his head round this way and that, attempting to look casual, and went off in the direction of Henri.

I shuddered. Mary's jaw dropped.

Neither of us were prudes, but the subject of sodomy didn't exactly come up. "Perhaps there are things I ought inquire about Andrew Regan," Mary whispered, as if the notion of Dutarque and Tilton doing unspeakable acts together now required her to reconsider all men.

"Indeed," I whispered. However disgusting this discovery was it had the redeeming consequence of making sense out of formerly inexplicable gestures and moods, Tilton's caustic tone, for instance, and the decidedly distant manner of Dutarque.

By the time we slipped back upstairs, mantuas and hats were being donned. Best to let the strange and disturbing news settle. I was exhausted and sleep was in order.

The Morning After
July, Wappoo Plantation

When we stepped into open field, birds told us dawn weren't far off. We was listening for dogs even if we didn't know we was. The Jackson slaves peeled off before long. I feared for them – Doc Jackson was as mean a man as ever walked the earth, and now we knowed his wife was worse.

Saffron bumped shoulders with Indian Pete before he headed into the woods. How was I gonna get that dress laundered without Miss Eliza finding out? There was time, right?

Just then: a snap, like a twig breaking, and suddenly there was Overseer, frizz poking off his head as if anger shooting through every hair, the usual hat missing. Seeing him bareheaded scared me almost as much as the musket and the coils of rope hanging off one shoulder.

Cudjoe stepped to the front. Caesar limped to join. Saffron wrung her hands and whimpered. I snugged next to her, as if touching shoulders could spare anybody anything.

Overseer snarled, "Git! Go on now, git!" He walked a wide arc to get behind us and jabbed Hercules in the back with his musket. "Git, boy!" He herded us down the street and across the road to their live oak. He told Cudjoe to take the dress off Saffron and tie her to the tree.

Cudjoe fumbled with the rope 'til Overseer shouted, "Titties first, up agin the bark." Saffron pressed herself to the tree, turned her face to one side. Overseer handed the whip to Cudjoe, who looked at it, dread hidden behind a stone face.

"Twenty lashes! Go!"

Cudjoe trembled, stepped back, and then with clenched jaw began. He flinched with every snap. We all did. Even as blood begun to spray, I looked round for Maggie. No sign of her. After Saffron, Caesar – why? He already got the clipped ear and ruined heel. Overseer grabbed the cowhide back, as if Cudjoe's pace couldn't match his rage. He whupped Caesar hard. Melody and me was spared, and I'm near to certain it was so service keep going. Overseer picked up the dress with the musket muzzle and shoved it at Hercules.

"Put it on, boy! You'll make a fetching lass, you will."

Hercules looked like he'd a rather taken the lash. The dress's back had to be left open, the hem fell to mid-shin, and the waist seams wasn't gonna last 'til noon.

By now the sun striped orange bands along the horizon, looking like violence instead of beauty. Overseer stormed off, tamping down his hair. Did he only just now miss the hat?

Parlor Announcement
Eliza, Wappoo Plantation

A loud rap at the door signaled that Mac had urgent business. Father grabbed his cup of tea, gave Mother his "have no fear" look, and welcomed Mac into the parlor. I followed. Without preamble, Mac spit it out: a slave assembly roughly two miles out last night.

"A real hullabaloo. I whupped three – Cudjoe, Caesar, and Saffron."

"Saffron?" I asked. Mother, sensing dramatic news, joined us.

Mac eyed me with a nervous glare, and then blurted out, "She'd stole out in on one of your frocks, Missie!"

"What?" Mother sagged onto the sofa as if she'd been punched.

"One of my dresses?" I mewled. When I asked which one, he sputtered something about navy with white dots. Ah! My scoop-necked blue calico with the white sprigs.

"How will I ever look Saffron in the eye again? She put me in that dress a dozen times. Did up the buttons. Pressed it to my liking. Or maybe to *her* liking."

Mother straightened herself. "She could be gone by week's end, you know, never to touch another Lucas button!"

"Yes, yes," I said slowly, as if considering Mother's idea even though I was thoroughly opposed to it, "but that would mean putting two seasons of training to waste. You know how much sewing needs to be done before the boys set sail." Mother's vengeance might be impetuous, but she wasn't one to take a casual approach to domestic efficiencies.

Here Mac bid an awkward farewell. Mother and I sat without words, listening, trying to ascertain if any of them were in the house. We heard nothing, not even that prickly silence that was the hallmark of a slave endeavoring to be quiet. Why might they sneak about? To overhear a conversation, to remain undetected themselves? To steal a dress.

Calico Burning
Melody, Wappoo Plantation

A secret can be possessed, even by a slave, but at what price? Ever since the dance and what came afterwards, I wondered what my secret might cost, now or down the road, and was it worth it. Easing the fears Mistress held in her bosom certainly wasn't my duty, nor did I owe her a jot of courtesy. For all I cared, her hand-wringing could last all season and Master could stutter denials 'til he was blue in the face. Let them suffer together and let them suffer apart.

Silence as rebellion. Silence as power.

My secret wounded them if I was in the room or away, whether I slyly nodded or kept mum. And I knew it would gather bitterness over time as doubt and jealousy did their bits.

Master Lucas knew the baby wasn't his, but he deserved this misery. Not just for the leering but for the concerts, the talking about me like I was a table. Overseer thought Master fathered Moses, 'twas easy to see, and he didn't much care. People up and down the rivers hereabouts would come to the same conclusion without a shivering whisper of scandal, it was so common.

July came bursting round the corner. I looked at her, and the fear in my gut bloomed. She was scared.

"What's wrong?" I asked.

Wordlessly, she dragged me out in front of Summer Kitchen, where I could smell the stink of fire. Smoke stung my eyes. What was that hanging from the near live oak?

"It's the dress," July said.

Indeed, there it was: the borrowed calico sagging off a rope like a sister freshly lynched. Someone had stuffed a melon-sized piece of fabric and stuck it on top like a head. Below, a pile of tinder and fatter sticks was catching. We watched in horror as flames started licking the hem. Five people stood on the other side of the fire: Overseer, Cudjoe, Caesar, Indian Pete, and Hercules.

Herc must've scratched at the dress in a fury of shame out in the fields, but he'd worn it because he liked his ears, his privates, because he didn't want to go through life walking like Caesar. He'd worn that dress because to take it off was to invite death.

Mistress and Miss Eliza marched round the front corner of the house, Saffron pinned between them. They each held an elbow, as if – what? – Saffron might run away? Whupping her raw wasn't enough. They had to stage a mock killing and make her watch. Flames waggled up the folds of the frock until a violent burst took the entire skirt in mad fire. I tensed, waiting for the head to go.

Saffron looked on with dead eyes, chin jutting. Sometimes that was all we could do – deny them the satisfaction of our fear.

Mistress, on the other hand, looked sharp like a bird hungry for seed, eyes going from face to face. She gave Saffron's elbow a yank now and then, as if to jerk her into terror. It didn't work. Miss Eliza, on the other hand, looked weary, possibly disappointed. Was she against the violent display or was it only about her dress being sacrificed?

The head burst into flames with a pop and crackle. Long, burning ribbons of paper sailed up and away in wavery heat. Suddenly, there was the barn to worry about. My heart skipped. Was it too much to ask for this show of primitive dominance to go terribly wrong? I caught Herc's eye and saw a faint flicker there, making me think he was having the same idea.

Saffron's back hurt, I could see. The heat from yesterday's flogging probably throbbed extra from her being so near actual heat. Later I'd send Caesar off to find a thick branch for Saffron to bite on. I'd need to clean the welts again if she wanted to live, saltwater first, then witch hazel water. Then I'd anoint her back with indigo paste made by Tilton's slave Hannah and it would soothe.

The fire burned through the rope, and what was left of the head and dress fell to the ground in a splash of sparks. Overseer dashed over and stomped on the fire, not out of any concern for Saffron – he was aiming to save the barn.

Week After
Saffron, Wappoo Plantation

Even though I perched 'tween waking and sleep cause of the sting-throb of welts, he startled me. He stood in the open door like an invitation. I looked him over, then at Maggie. She was breathing the raspy breath of deep sleep. He waited quiet-like, never a man to fidget or rush. Even his stillness pulled like a tide at me, never mind that hip, slung down and leaning into the door frame.

I went to him. He took both my hands. He whispered in my ear, the heat of his breath nearly buckling my knees, "We'll stay near."

We walked to the blocky shadow made by the barn. A slim privacy come to us here, but I'd see Maggie if she left the cabin. The dogs inside must be twitching in dreams, cause if they knew Pete was near, they'd rouse in eager joy.

Before he leaned in to kiss me, he turned me round so his back was up against the barn and not mine, thinking on the welts. I cupped his face in my hands and kissed him deep. Indian Pete circled his arms round the small of my back, pulling me in hard and close. I groaned. With quick strength, he grabbed my hips and hoisted me up. My legs latched on. He kissed me with the kiss of a man lost. I kissed him with the kiss of a woman found. With quiet hurrying, I moved my hips up and down, feeling his wanting there, proud and hard. My rubbing was catching pleasure over and over, so by the time he let loose the drawstring and came inside, I was as wet as the marsh yonder and nearly gone.

We found it – a flow, a tug, a flow, a tug – 'til he say my name over and over and send me right over the edge. The whole time, his care to my back was part of the dance, but the stolen dress and the shaming fire and lash cracking had nothing to hold on to here.

Panting into my collarbone, Pete slowly slid me down. I stroked his crooked nose as he gently pulled my tunic over my head and turned me to take a look. Some skin had pulled, even with our care.

"You're bleeding." He led me down to the water, stripped off his tunic, dipped it into the salty creek, and dabbed at my back. I flinched. Dab and flinch. Dab and flinch.

That was the second loving.

"I wished they whipped me instead," he said. "I wish I had six frocks to give you, covered with flowers, pearl buttons. I'd have Quash make the prettiest wardrobe to put 'em in." I'd never heard him say so many words that weren't about what was here, what we could touch, or what the seasons foretold. The grasses waggled in a small wind.

"Ssh. You just gave me the moon – ain't that enough?"

December 1738

Labor
Melody, Silk Hope Plantation

The pounding of horse hooves sounded like a dream. I rose to look. 'Twas no dream. A liveried messenger leapt off his mount and flew up Overseer's steps. I saw the froth at the bit, heard the banging on the door. Two heads met, one close-cropped and dark, the other a'frizz. In a heartbeat, the slave leapt back on his tired horse and wheeled away. Message delivered.

Blackened on the horse's haunch, clear as day: "TW." If the slave had been bare-chested, I knew the same letters would've been visible under the collarbone. Thomas Wright. Silk Hope Plantation. My heart sank, for all the hurried lather meant a baby was coming.

During the long water passage, I struggled to stay awake and so acting the midwife came like a cool glass of water. We were lucky to arrive in time. Inside the stuffy bedchamber, Missus Wright rocked from side to side, moaning. As soon as she saw me, she screamed for everyone to get out. Right off, I got the birthing bottle from my bag and held it to her lips. On the third or fourth puff, she made the bottle sing and actually smiled. I pressed my palm on her belly. Head down. Good. In no time at all, she'd be ready to push.

Sure enough, a little boy squeezed out before even another log had burned down. I wiped off his wrinkled face and he let loose a reedy howl. What blessed relief! The Mistress held out her arms and laughed. Then she nodded for me to open the door and in crowded her mother, younger sister, aunt, and dressing slave.

The newborn looked like an old man sucking on a lemon but still he won all the hearts in the room. They cooed and talked names and I hardly listened, letting things roll along as if I wasn't there, which was easy enough seeing as how to them, I wasn't. No matter – birth was its own reward.

Catching babies was the only effort I ever made on white women's behalf where I gave it my all and it was the only work white women took from me that gave something back.

Bloody Cloth
Saffron, Wappoo Plantation

Maggie and I sat on the dock, listening for paddles. Light shined up the grasses. Was that a laugh or a bird yakking on the wind?

If the birth had gone well, Melody should be on her way back from Silk Hope. A while ago, when Old Sarah wilted with fever on the day of a neighbor's labor, they sent Melody instead. To everyone's surprise, she delivered a breech baby, with both mother and child surviving. News like that got around, and now Melody was oft called for, to the satisfaction of Mistress, who liked having a midwife to loan out for reputation and coin.

Melody had promised to bring me an offering for the gods, and if it pleased the gods, Maggie might turn toward grace. Maybe destiny's good side would force destiny's dark side off. Maybe she'd sleep again. Maybe she'd grow like a girl instead of like a pine stunted in the wind.

Was it true that nothing but death would ever take the chains off for real? I remembered Titus's twin, Kehinde, the sound of his body slapping the sea, the silence after, and then the harsh opposite of silence – feet pounding, sailors shouting, and sharks thrashing.

Freedom might cost everything – every secret, every muscle, every kiss, every dusky sky, every scant meal, and seduction, but wouldn't it be worth any price? A few new words lined up while we were sitting there on the dock: penalty, barter, amnesia. And a really good one: maroons. I'd heard it before, but now it sank in. I'd heard that maroons gathered and thrived not just on the mountaintops of Jamaica but west of here in the swamps. Maroons was a name I liked, but I liked better what some others called them: free wilds.

The boat came round the buckle bushes all of a sudden. Melody looked a little sick, and I ran to help her off the boat. There's only so much we can do, one for the other. We can hold someone up when they collapse, we can block ugly views for a heartbeat, swirl up baby-ridding herb pastes, give pats of affection. There's storytelling and song and listening so deep it goes towards the gods, but nobody's humor or hug gonna stop most of it. Nobody's smile will put three or four snarling hounds down before the savaging begins. Nobody's embrace will shoulder epic grief on Hiring Day when a child is sold away. Nothing will shield all the brutality, insult, smearing and wiping off of dignity, but we tried and the trying mattered.

Melody leaned back and pulled something out of her apron pocket, eyes showing a glint of old mischief. That look was gift enough, but there it was: the cloth soaked in afterbirth blood.

Did it matter to the gods that the blood was white lady blood?

I held the scrap in one hand and laid the other flat on my heart.

Shining Silver
Melody, Wappoo Plantation

The next morning, when I looked down at my sleeping boys, my bosom tingled with the memory of nursing. Maybe Moses could tell, because his eyes popped open and he stuck a thumb in his mouth. The conch sounding woke Noah, who reached out for me. Darling boys!

Outside, I smashed peas with the back of an oyster shell for Noah. That Caesar and his courtesies! He'd planted a row of late-season legumes a while back just for us. After breakfast, I swaddled Moses and wrapped him round my back, both of us liking the warmth. We headed over.

In the pantry, I was buttering a warm biscuit for Polly when I felt sudden relief at not having to nurse any buckra baby. Catching their babies was one thing, nursing them another thing altogether. White women acted like it was no inconvenience to bosom-feed unless it was their baby and their bosom, and then it was some kind of chore. Fobbing off babies robbed buckra of newborn tenderness, and they didn't even know it: the smell of an infant's crown; the sweet feel of tiny fingers clutched round your thumb; watching sleep come on, rosebud lips wet with milk.

Stupid, stupid white women!

In these parts, cruelties popped up so often they got to seeming ordinary. No white person felt the need to hide what they did, however monstrous. Wickedness was just another thing they took as their right. Branding, ridiculing, accusing, binding, pouring salt and tar on wounds, hacking off a man's sack – everyday business.

The silence we had to wrap ourselves in was punishment too. Speak out, you could get killed. My jaw ached with holding it all inside. Sometimes on the street, I'd spit out a day's worth. Others would laugh or worry, depending. It wasn't like I was saying anything instructive because the evil was so plain to see, but sometimes my words spoke for all and tripped a relieving gladness.

I looked at Moses sitting next to the sugar cabinet, clutching two wooden spoons, and knew all at once that my rage spoke pure and that it was a gift to him. July could scald-eye me all she wanted but my bitter furies weren't going anywhere. What if my anger was the only thing keeping me alive? Did July ever think of that?

After breakfast clearing, Saffron headed out to the spinning shed, while July and me set to buffing silver. Wan December light shone on the counter and then bent straight up the wall where it crinkled from the glass and looked like water. Miss Eliza played harpsichord. Mistress sewed. There was a lot of silver to shine, so we set to it.

Panther Moon
Saffron, Wappoo Plantation

Scritch, scritch, scritch. The blade flashed in morning sun. July held the knife up and ran a finger along the edge. The turkey Indian Pete kilt hung out on the clothesline, sagging that rope hard, neck dripping where the head used to be. July said we'd get the gizzards, but it was the neck I wanted. Maggie and Phoebe would take turns spinning the roasting spit. Maggie should get first pick on what side to stand on since burned skin can prickle in heat like it's remembering the first burn.

Earlier, Caesar had flopped the big turkey on the table for plucking. There was a hole in the breast, just a little slit, but big enough for death to sneak in. I remembered how Indian Pete lifted his closed hand to his cheek and let the arrow fly.

Took better than an hour to bald that bird. We saved the long feathers, the pretty brown-and-white-striped ones. Phoebe stuck two in her hair, making July mad.

"Gimme here! Trust me, child, it ain't no picnic being red round here, if that's what you're thinking."

"Yeah, except they can disappear," Melody said.

It was well known that natives made terrible slaves because they could melt away. They knew the swamps, the bogs, and the woods, what roots to eat and what ones to avoid, and like as not they had family scattered here and there.

Later, the Panther Moon shone through the knuckled branches of catalpa, leaving skeleton shadows on the ground. Maggie and I had the turkey neck in a bag and found Titus on the far side of the garden fence. He took the neck, our second offering, the bloody birth cloth being the first. He started calling out the prayers. Maggie rubbed her arm, tired from turning the spit. Was she afraid?

Titus leaned over and whispered something to her, and she leaned back and answered. It was between them. Then he threw his opele and made the strike marks in the dirt, taking his time with each toss. A strong hush came on, almost like someone had clapped a big bowl over us. At the last throw, Panther Moon cleared the nearest cabin. It was big, bright, and nosy. Titus gave Maggie her oddun in a whisper, like before, but then he told both of us that her spirit lingered out over the sea, back where the evil was done. Maggie had to call it back, he said, and whispered to her some more.

For most of us, love might make us foolish or careless, but a babalawo's love always went to the greater good – a good that shone brighter than the Panther Moon, mightier than arrows that kill turkeys, and wider than the sea. Looking at a broken child, a babalawo can call up all the laughing children of kin and gain their help, and the powerful aid of the Ancestors too. What other kind of love can do that?

Trusting Titus was important, I already knew, but now I saw how trusting Maggie mattered too. Even at eight, she had her own path through the night.

Madagascar Rice
Eliza's Diary, Wappoo Plantation

Bands of light sparkle on the creek evidencing either the mercy of beauty or the cruel indifference of nature – I can't tell which. Suzanne Drayton died. She succumbed to the pox about a week after the gathering at the Poinsett. Even more heartbreaking, both young children followed her to the grave. Poor, poor John!

In the meantime, life does go on. Received shipment of Madagascar rice from Father's newly purchased Waccamaw Plantation: two hogsheads for Wappoo and the rest on a brigantine bound for France. Father's factor arranged lucrative terms. How lucky South Carolina is! Exempt from the British law mandating making port in England before heading to the prime rice markets to the south. Also, unlike other colonies, we're not restricted to British ships, meaning we were able to hire a Dutch snow with more favorable terms. No wonder our northern brethren complain bitterly about the Mother Country.

Mother's excited about serving the delectable grain at our holiday repast. Along with it, we'll serve a clove-studded ham, okra à la daube, and guinea squash. For dessert, a sweet potato pudding with orange-flavored Chantilly cream. The fact that the meal's centerpiece will be the pig that Polly formerly referred to as "Mrs. Pinky Winky" will have to be dealt with at some point. Fortunately, my sister'd been at Cross Winds on killing day.

Wedding
Eliza, Charles Town

"Go get your sister!" Mother's breath left a trail of fog. The boys stood on the dock next to her and huffed in unison. Whose cloud was bigger? Could they make the vapors collide? They had never seen breath condensed by cold before. Polly appeared and joined the game.

In spite of it being Christmas, we had decided to attend the Rutledge wedding. Our holiday meal would hold a day, and we would be in church after all. I'd made peace with this union: Sarah, recently fourteen, and John, twenty-five. Step-niece and step-uncle. One imagined scenario after another had played out in my mind, but I'd been alone in coarse objection. Now I mulled over the choice of wedding day. Surely, the decision to wed on Christmas was neither casual nor made out of piety. Maybe meant to keep the gathering small? Maybe but of course, there could be a cruder cause. If they were racing against the calendar, a wedding date of 1738 would raise fewer eyebrows than one in 1739, even if mere weeks separated them.

Cudjoe, Indian Pete, and Caesar steadied the boat as we climbed in. This was only our second trip to the peninsula as a family and the first time a neat appearance was required. The morning was cool but clear, the sky a pale blue, flat and brittle, as if it might shatter with a wrong move. The boys continued to huff and puff with such vigor that I feared they might pass out. Six white egrets, startled by our approach, launched themselves skyward, like a collection of hankies taken by the wind.

Father gave me one of his amused looks. "So, what do you want for your birthday?" Dear Father! Perhaps he anticipated my disappointment, for this year my December birthday competed not just with the birth of Christ but also with this wedding.

I had no answer, or not one I could share. I desired plenty. I wanted the pressure exerted by him and Mother regarding suitors to stop. I wanted fig and oak trees thriving in lush lines. An indigo crop. I shrugged.

Soon enough, we saw the tall, thin Negro called Ducas standing next to Grandpapa's carriage, waving. Once on board, Father began to whistle. How he loved our trips into town! His chance to mingle with men of intelligence and social standing, I suppose. Polly held the wedding gift with the seriousness of a court treasurer. And indeed it was a lovely gift – six sterling silver salt spoons, each bowl crafted as a botanical leaf, each handle like a stalk.

Emerging onto East Bay, we were exposed to a sturdy gale. Whitecaps frothed, swayed, and jerked, the sea's color running to dark grey. Father commented, "Looks like we're in for a little rain." Mother raised an eyebrow as if to challenge the understatement.

The first drops peppered the road just as we entered St. Philip's. The service began shortly thereafter and was brief. When heads swiveled and smiled at Sarah's entrance, I kept my gaze fixed on John at the front. His clasped hands signaled dignified restraint, but everything else about him spoke of barely contained desire. How he glowed! How eager his pleasure! He stood with the confidence of a man sure of his choice. And how could he not be? Along with beauty and sparkling wit, Sarah came with a significant fortune.

She played the demure bride. Never had I seen her sustain a mood of delicate and mature sobriety for so long. Her garb showed exquisite taste in every detail: a pale ivory gown with Flemish lace at the cuff, perfectly matched silk shoes. She was the picture of grace and beauty. What had I expected? A twirl at the altar, flirtatious banter with the priest? Truthfully, something like that.

By the end, both of my brothers were squirming. They were not up to the reception at the Poinsett Inn and since we had no tag-along, Mother asked me to walk them back to Cross Winds. "If I'm late in returning," I said, "please explain my absence?" At her raised eyebrow, I grabbed each boy by the hand and set out under a sky surprisingly clear. Even the weather seemed gladdened by the felicitous union of Sarah and John.

Day after Christmas
Saffron, Wappoo Plantation

Doc Jackson, hear tell, puts the slave children's food in a trough. Bend and snort, what? Here we got shells to use like spoons and food goes into bowls, and today it's a Christmas Hol-i-day! They call it a feast. "Feast" came as a new word, but I refuse to use it. This is Wednesday for them. Why should it get a special name just cause it's landing on our table? Do they think we don't know?

Long boards under their oak got loaded down with casseroles, breads, buttermilk for the children, ale for us. A platter of chitlins, a big bowl of red rice and beans, okra deep-fried, pig's feet, pickled radish tops, corn pie, and peach preserves. We sat on stumps round the table, jollity and hunger having a time together.

After a bit, Miss Eliza came out with cinnamon jumbles on a tray like she was queen, but she's no queen. Heard tell of two – or is it three? – royals hereabouts. Not whites, mind, but people from villages back home. Who knows what flung these whites off home? Anyone can see Mistress doesn't want to be here. Who knows what made Master haul her out into them fierce ocean currents and sail so far from home.

Woodwards came early and with their people, too, so it got cheery and crowded. Miss Mary and Miss Eliza shared secrets up on the gallery. Miss Mary was newly spoken for and looking shinier than before, even wearing a frock with color. After more food than we done eat since I landed, it was time for dancing and a foot race. Neighbor Tig pulled out a fiddle. Phoebe and Polly grabbed hands and twirled. They were like twins, those two, except one treated like a royal, the other treated not always but in the end, like dirt. Oh, how they giggled, though! Joy matching up even if skin didn't.

Tommy looked ragged and pale. He curled up in Mama's lap on the gallery, eyes half closed. George took charge of the gift basket, held it high, wearing a glad smile, ear to ear. He's the one! Out came bags of pecans, packets of tobacco, and clumps of ribbon, tied up nice. A few new pair of shoes – Hercules, Mo, and even Caesar were still growing – yes, even Caesar needed shoes though he hardly landed on the one foot. Seems torture don't stop a man from growing.

Master and Miss Eliza looked like two peas in a pod today. How they stand. How they take stock. In and among. Mixing, showing grace – but let's not go overboard. Their grace costs them not a jot. With everything they possess, how little they let go. But I'll give Miss Eliza this: she flared glad and hale in a new blue calico frock. Ha! Somebody gained something outta my waywardness!

Calico and fire – for me, they forever will go together. The pall cast by calico is dark, for sure, but it arises from grief and not shame. I gave back the shame long ago, laid it on the parlor hearth when they weren't looking. They think they can load us down with bad feeling as easy as they stripe a back. Fools!

"That frock fit better than the last," I said out the side of my mouth to July. She flinched. Maybe it wasn't as easy to set down worry? Oh, how July worry!

George handed July a bundle of ribbons, me a lace cap for trips to town. Head rag for here, lace cap for town, it seem. So I'll say it simple and true: the gift was for them, not for me: tag-along's garb saying this or that about the owner. Not anything I cared on.

George upended the basket. It was empty.

I kissed Maggie on the head. She followed Mistress into Porch House cause it's her night for tending fires. It's a Wolf Moon, Indian Pete says, taking my arm. His skin warm. Look at that: my stomach so full and my heart so full. I breathed out.

Part II

January 1739 – September 1739

January 1739

The Source of her Distress
Eliza, Wappoo Plantation

Our Epiphany gathering was rather uneventful until around four, when I spied an unfamiliar couple across the parlor. What a mismatched pair! The husband stood tall and lanky, the wife short and squat, like Jack Sprat and his wife.

"Mr. James Whittaker," our neighbor Mr. Deveaux announced, "and his wife, the lovely Mrs. Rebecca Whittaker, come from the continent by way of Philadelphia. Old friends of ours from Barbados." Mother greeted the couple warmly, quickly ascertaining that the purpose of their trip to Europe had been acquisition. She grabbed Mrs. Whittaker's hands and held out her arms.

"Forgive the intimacy, Mrs. Whittaker," Mother cooed, "but I really must take in a full view of your exquisite gown. Parisian, I assume?" Mrs. Whittaker nodded with pleasure. Mother asked her to turn, continuing a complimentary but genuine patter about the dress. Oh, we wouldn't see such styling for at least another season, if only local dressmakers had an ounce of the taste and a quarter of the skill of those in Paris, etc. More back and forth, during which Mother mined for details about their continental purchases. What size Belgian tapestry did you say? And the sideboard's provenance – Renaissance or medieval?

Meanwhile, all I saw was a pretty pink gown draped on a decidedly unattractive woman. I'd never known Mr. Deveaux to be facetious or unkind, so I wondered at his choice of the word "lovely." Her features crabbed and creased as if she perpetually sucked a sour lozenge. Compressed lips sat atop two chins, the lower one large enough nearly to cover her entire neck. All that made her unappealing enough, but it was her nose that truly spoiled her visage. It was, quite simply, giant.

She and Mother chatted like a house on fire. God love my mother's social graces! Sarah caught my eye from a chair next to the fire and crooked a conspiratorial smile before casually but distinctly making a gesture indicating a large nose. Others might have seen her waving a stray lock away, but I knew better.

July came through the pantry door with a platter of savories, Melody trailing behind with sherry. Mrs. Whittaker's eyes widened and she snorted so loudly that heads as far away as the front door turned. Melody walked quickly past to serve the guests in the foyer. Mr. Whittaker, meanwhile, abruptly interrupted Mother's description of the lutestring silk recently arrived from London to take his ashen-faced wife by the elbow and lead her to the sofa.

"Water for our guest!" Mother barked.

By the time Mrs. Whittaker consumed half the glass, she had somewhat composed herself, but now Mr. Whittaker began to fidget, first with the lace at his cuffs, then with the hair at his temples, as though apoplexy had passed from wife to husband – or perhaps he, too, was thirsty, for he kept glancing over at the foyer where Melody had disappeared with the sherry. Before Mother could make a soothing comment, Father came over and boomed, "My friend! Is everything alright?"

My friend? Mr. Whittaker left off stroking his cuffs and held his hand out for a hearty shake. Well met and so on. Inquiries, brief and sociable were made – their Atlantic passage, the weather in Philadelphia – and then they were reminiscing about slave purchases. With what seemed like misplaced pride, or worse, bravado, Father nodded toward Melody in the foyer. "Of course, when she was in your stable, she was Sally," he said.

At the mention of Sally, Mrs. Whittaker, rather indecorously, held her glass straight up in the air for someone, anyone, to take and refill.

"Make it sherry this time," our guest dictated.

Before we could be further embarrassed, Mother glanced at me, decisively plucked Mrs. Whittaker's glass out of her hand, and pulled her off the sofa, bumping Mr. Whittaker in the process, no apology offered. We exited the house and claimed the back terrace.

At Mother's nod, I knew to natter on a little, as was sometimes our arrangement to afford her some interval in which to sort out the subtleties of a social interaction. "How do you like this dappled shade?" I asked Mrs. Whittaker pointing to the new pergola. "We find the heat much stickier here than in the West Indies, I'm afraid. Enjoy your ocean breezes when you return!"

In the meantime, Mother rang Melody's bell. The slave's appearance at the back door did not cause our guest to start fitfully again, but the way she narrowed her eyes erased whatever doubt remained about Melody being the source of her distress. Mother's prompt removal of the aggrieved guest from the parlor had suggested an instinctive female alliance, but purposefully calling Melody round suggested something else. "We'll have our syllabub out here," Mother said to Melody. "And Mrs. Whittaker still needs her sherry."

Sarah, always one to gravitate toward the most complex and potentially scandalous interaction, joined us. To my great relief, she took up the task of providing chatter. Mrs. Whittaker relaxed in the flow of Sarah's charm, as did so many, and might have thoroughly recovered herself had we not heard a soft mewling from one of the Summer Kitchen windows. Melody's month of nursing was long over, but whenever possible, she fed Moses herself, so it was likely that Saffron would come looking for her.

Sure enough, Saffron appeared in the kitchen doorway holding Moses. Melody kept her expression bland as she handed round the glasses of syllabub, the one glass of sherry. "Oh, delightful!" Sarah said. "But where's the rosemary?"

"Good grief!" Mother exclaimed. "Saffron, put the boy down and bring us four stalks of rosemary! They should've been inserted prior to pouring, but we'll just poke them through the foam."

Saffron laid Moses down on the path flat on his back, where he commenced waving his fists about. As she handed the rosemary round, Mrs. Whittaker dropped her spoon.

I offered our guest my unused utensil and then clownishly wiped the fallen one with my hem. "Good as new!" I hoped my antics would divert attention from the baby up the slope, who even at this distance could be seen to have wavy black hair and nearly white skin.

"Whatever will our sassy hostess do next?" Sarah joked, but the glint in her eyes showed no humor. I knew she saw the complexities of the moment and had made the correct assumptions – that Mr. Whittaker was the father of this boy. Emotion clouded Mrs. Whittaker's face and it seemed that with each spoonful of the milky, sweet dessert, another silent calculus took place, as though she were rewriting her personal history right before us, revising the story of her marriage to account for a new and grievous detail. I wasn't sure of this, but one thing was abundantly clear: Mrs. Whittaker was devastated.

The catapulting of Mrs. Whittaker into heartbreak sent my mother in the opposite direction, into her own healing dispensation of doubt. Mother was too skilled a hostess to let any sudden buoyancy of spirit show, but I'm afraid that her attitude of soft sympathy slid into its cooler cousin, pity. To victims, one handed out pity disguised as tender inclination out of fear of joining the ranks of the broken. Some primitive fear of contagion clamped down on compassion in moments like these.

"Awful, the numbers of mixed babies running about our plantations," Mother said emphatically, and then she took an amazing social risk and asked in quiet voice, "You didn't know, did you?"

Mrs. Whittaker could have tendered a denial with disdain, but I think the great need of her caved-in heart aroused what I can only assume was uncharacteristic honesty. "I had my suspicions, of course – what wife doesn't?" We all nodded, even though I had no experience and I doubted that Sarah had been given cause.

Our guest continued in measured speech. "It would explain a series of turnabouts within the household, particularly some well-timed acts of generosity. I refused to speculate – to what end once she was gone?" Mrs. Whittaker nodded toward the pantry, where Melody was working, and asked when the baby was born. The confirming count was made. "If I didn't know better," Mrs. Whittaker continued, "I would've said I was looking at my daughter ten years back, so similar is the babe's hair, the shape of his face."

Mother's directness had surprised me, but perhaps having sat with the very same devastating inquiry, about the very same object, she understood the woman's need better than anyone. A strained silence fell. Eventually, Mrs. Whittaker held up her half-empty dessert glass. "Tell me, do you steep your lemons in wine before assembling?" And with that, we moved on to the most ordinary of topics, as women do, as if infidelity and recipes carried equal weight. And indeed, who is to say they don't?

Before I knew it, the guests had departed and the house's quiet was restored. We sat and enjoyed the crackle of the fire. Mother reviewed the evening in a thoughtful monologue, as she was wont to do, but didn't revisit the revelation of paternity. I couldn't help but wonder what, if anything, she would have to say about it later, privately, to Father.

Portraits
Eliza, Wappoo Plantation

Months ago, Mother commissioned a painter recommended by the Izards to make portraits of her sons who were soon to leave for England. Their upcoming departure highlighted so many matters of the heart, including that a daughter could never occupy a mother's heart the way her sons did. How she seesawed, my mother, between worry and sadness, pride and devotion!

The boys fidgeted and squirmed through their sittings, Tommy more than George, but at last the portraits were finished. I viewed Mother's insistence on them as another of her vain yet understandable attempts to control something in her life, anything.

I watched the painter for a while and then retreated to the barn. I was currying Sir Raleigh when Father joined me.

"I have news," he began. "All of the mortgages have been approved." I froze, holding the brush a few inches from Sir Raleigh's withers. Approved mortgages meant enough money to purchase a commission on Antigua.

"How soon? Before the year's out?" He nodded and held my gaze. Some wordless transmission of authority and love occurred. I felt, along with my quaking sadness, a sterling resolve, one that hadn't existed a moment prior, and I knew that whatever else happened in the months leading up to Father's departure for Antigua, he would help me formulate the strategies necessary to act from that resolve.

I recalled the painting of Tommy, the cuffs of his jacket a rich midnight blue, fashioned from linen imported from England and dyed with indigo from South America. Some of our land was not quite suited to rice, and since the labors of indigo efficiently dovetailed with those of rice, Father and I avidly discussed indigo as a possible fill-in commodity. Rice prices were falling, and as if any more justification were needed, shipping bricks of indigo cost a fraction of shipping hogsheads of rice. I could see it: fields filled with the shrubby splaying branches, leaves collected in verdant piles, big watery vats aerated and acidified to perfection, and the precious blue dye-stuff settling to the bottom. Blue bricks being fashioned and turned as they dried, then stacked for shipment, all of it translating into a long and healthy asset column! Others were trying – why not us? In a flash of recognition, I saw that indigo could become for me what the paintings were to Mother. An attempt to bring order, to make sense of absences.

After both portraits were framed, Mother busied herself with deciding where to hang them. She auditioned the parlor's southern wall, then the wall along the stairs, but finally settled on the interior wall of the dining room. Morning and midday light flooded the room, and the painter had cautioned about the damaging effects of light, but Mother would hang the portraits where she could enjoy them with every meal, sunlight be damned. Her philosophy of life often placed the value of daily, casual pleasure above an object's long-term survival, unlike Father who would choose conservation every time.

One afternoon not long after Father's disclosure in the barn, I closed the drapes in the dining room, hoping to protect the paintings for at least a little while. For the first time since they'd been hung, I looked at them in the solitude of my own thoughts. There was George, chin thrust out, well on his way to becoming a man. It was easy to imagine how he'd look in two or three years. The cheeks would be thinned, perhaps, the hair darkened, but he would wear an expression essentially unchanged.

Tommy was another matter altogether. For the entire sitting, I'd wondered which of my younger brother's fluid moods the artist would attempt to portray. Even though Tommy had squirmed and whined and flared in annoyance, the artist had seen past all of that to my brother's vulnerability and incredibly enough, captured it. The sweet eyes on the canvas revealed tenderness, regret, and fear – the true attitude of an eight-year-old on the verge of leaving his mother for many years.

For all Mother's talk about daily viewing of these pictures, I suddenly wasn't sure that being reminded of her younger son's very apparent lack of readiness for a long voyage and extended separation would in fact be pleasing. How could Tommy's eyes, rendered so close to tears by the artist's skillful hand, do anything but haunt her?

The Mirror
July, Wappoo Plantation

Now days comin' cold, I wear shoes to Porch House. I like to sit on the cabin stoop to tie 'em up and look about for a minute. Today two jays squawked across a silver sky, and their beauty jarred me hard. Think on it: lifting into the sky and going. And then going some more.

I knew I wasn't going nowhere, and unlike some, I wasn't aiming to try. Them that talk on about Promised Lands was either speaking on the hereafter or a place on this earth mighty hard to reach, even though for us bonded folk, the Promised Land didn't need no riches or rivers of honey. All it needed was to be rid of the canker of slavery. There's heaven! "Heaven on earth" weren't no made-up paradise. It was a real place where white people didn't own black people. How long would that take?

"Twelve generations," whispered the loblollies. Wasn't that what Titus said?

Who knows where runners go? If there weren't no Cane Creek to the west, no St. Augustine or Ottawa to the south and north, they'd conjure a place – Zion, the River Jordan. They'd follow blue jays or the starry calabash, keeping the constellation over one shoulder for Florida, over the other for Canada.

On this and any morning I can name, no planter's foot gotta to slide into cold leather without stockings, but mine did. Buckra got linsey-woolsey stockings, ribbed, clocked, argyle, and plain. I shrugged. Hardly worth a gill of thought. Not when I imagine Eubeline's eyeball rolling across the floor or Big Joe screaming through flames up at Archdale's place, or when I see Saffron's heart breaking over Maggie, dawn to dusk.

Anyway, plenty of Lowcountry bonded folk got no shoes – even in January, even working in the fields – so wasn't shoes something to be glad about? They wasn't jay wings, but they was something. I count 'em as my Number One Blessing today. Not evidence of buckra kindness, hah, but a blessing just the same.

The stiff grasses along the creek ghosted up with rime. They be my Number Two Blessing – how they silvered with light. This time a year, it got hard to believe the sedges'd ever spike up again, pointy, green, but they was gonna. Trees'd leaf and crown again, yes sir, and cypress tops gonna poke at the sky with yellow again – believe it. Believing in spring was my Number Four Blessing, my three boys being always Blessing Three.

That frosty grey morning, I thought of jasmine. That was something. A memory with perfume.

My pockets were empty. Having pockets at all was my Number Five Blessing.

I headed to Porch House, the grass stiff underfoot. The house sat quiet and dark, the family not due back 'til evening. Melody clomped in. This was her first winter.

"Look see," she said, pointing to the frost on her shoes. "Look!" I saw it melting there and melted a little myself on how I adored Melody, sometimes even her ragging.

Later in the day it warmed up enough for us to settle on the back gallery for sewing. We both slid off our shoes. On my lap: a shirt for Georgie who'd grown like chickweed over the fall. On Melody's lap: breeches for little Tommy sized to last two years. We was sewing clothes for England, clothes for days and years to come.

The boys' passages was booked. The Mistress hired a artist to paint pictures, as if a painting could take the place of them. England was important for learnin' and all, they say, but I couldn't for the life of me understand a mother putting an ocean between her and her children by choice.

When the crash come, it made me jump – a violent thud and shatter from the house so big and loud I felt it in my feet. I leapt up and ran inside, bare soles slapping. When Mistress and Miss wasn't home, I left my shoes on the gallery from time to time, even in January. Who was even here?

It was Maggie. Maggie! There she was, shoulders 'gainst the wall, eyes wide, neck straining so hard the muscles stood out like couched yarns on a gown. In front of her: the toppled mirror, frame empty, glass scattered everywhere.

"Don't you move now," I said, low and steady. "You be just fine, long as you don't move."

I knowed as sure as I know anything that things wasn't gonna be fine, but no need to scare her more. What a fuss they made over the mirror – especially Mistress! Like it proved she was loved or important or something. Like she owned sunlight. The long talks over breakfast, waiting on the mahogany, then waiting on the glass, Mistress cursing the trade winds, impatience breaking out like a rash.

I held two corners of my apron sling-like and loaded big pieces of glass in it. Clink. Clink. All the while, I kept talking to Maggie, sounding like Cudjoe settling a spooked horse. Melody walked in, making a wide path around the slivered glass and frowning at my bare feet. She went round the other side to scoop Maggie up.

We wasn't ever to sit on Porch House furniture, but Melody did now. She held Maggie tight. Saffron told how even though the girl flinch and cower, 'twas best to hold her tight if you was gonna hold her at all. It seemed Saffron was right, because Maggie took a deep breath and leaned into Melody's collarbone.

Melody started singing. That butterscotch voice: "Peas and the rice / Peas and the rice / Peas and the rice, done, done, done . . ." Talk about taming a spooked horse! Melody could sing the wind right out of a hurricane.

I left to fetch a broom, shooting a worried look to Melody. The fear drained out of the girl's face, but it was back to wooden absence. What now for her? The girl's night-roamings done slowed of late and the pouches under Saffron's eyes was nearly gone. Maggie'd taken to eating regular-like with a oyster shell instead of sneaking pinches off her mother's plate. She still spent every evening sitting between her mama's knees like she got a fortress round her, but still, it got to seeming like somebody home. I wondered if all the blessings that tried to gather round the girl would ever bind her spirit and what would the bad coming off this accident do to them small bindings?

What's natural? Nothing hereabouts, that's for sure. Sleeping and working in the same tunic four seasons running wasn't never gonna be natural, and that was just a little matter. Having to wait 'til dreamtime to hear your own tongue wasn't natural, and that wasn't no little matter. Whips and insult so common you'd think they'd come to seem natural, but they wasn't ever gonna. And how could having an ocean between me and the Ancestors' burial grounds be natural? What I wouldn't give for a morning on the banks of the Niger River, the Strong Brown God, patting silt on my face to soften my skin! What I wouldn't give to see the weavers' bent over long strings of indigo thread, making cloth for a new baby, knowing how the same blue cloth would circle his shoulders come wedding-time and wrap his cold body at death.

Back in the parlor, Melody still singing. "New rice and okra, eat some and lef' some. Peas and the rice, done, done, done." Then she made something up, pulling notes out of the air and giving 'em back to the air, pure and haunting. Maggie fell asleep.

Why didn't the mirror get nailed proper to the wall? They left it tipped 'til Quash come back from his loan-out – everybody wanting his skill, Lucases wanting the sterling. Otherwise, that mirror never would've fallen. Maggie must've found the small space behind it and hid there. Maybe when she stood up to leave, she bumped it.

Because so many mens was digging a canal over at the newest rice field, Saffron toiled as a field hand that afternoon. It'd be two tasks before she found out. Before the pox, I'd holler for Benjie and James and send them hustling to deliver word. Remembering sliced like a blade.

Just then, Phoebe poked her head in. "Hightail it to the closest rice field," I said. "Find Saffron and tell her about this" – I pointed at the remains of the mirror – "but before anything else, you say, 'Maggie's fine.'" I gave Phoebe a stern look and asked her what she gonna say first.

"Maggie's fine," she said over her shoulder, flying off. Was that the spirit of Benjie racing in her legs? How long was every little thing gonna make me think on Benjie and James?

Just after every sliver of glass was swept up, I heard Missy's horse snort and the boat thump the dock at the same time. Soon, too soon, they come inside and the Mistress set to wailing. "Good God in Heaven!" Miss Eliza face go to ash. I told 'em I done it, but I could tell they didn't believe me. I made a pot of tea right quick, scared about what was coming.

Oh How They Lie
Eliza's Diary, Wappoo Plantation

I've seen July catch an egg rolling off the counter from two meters away. I've seen her plait palm fronds while simultaneously dictating to Melody how to prepare a soufflé. And that time she was nearly kicked by our mule? July'd stepped out of the way with lightning reflexes. Oh no, it was not she who bumped the mirror. I suspected that July knew I didn't believe her and worse, that she didn't care.

Waving from the Rail
Eliza, Wappoo Plantation and Rhett's Bridge

The night before their departure found George aglow with excitement, Tommy agitated. After tea, they both pored over our precious map of the Atlantic with Father one last time. Tommy rattled off questions Father had already answered dozens of times. What size wave would threaten a ship's seaworthiness? How many years had the Captain of the *Hound* been sailing? How did currents run this time of year? My little brother sounded more like a nautical student than an eight-year-old whose expertise ran to reptiles, ants, and honey cakes.

"We sail on the *Hound*," Tommy said brightly, looking at Father. George rolled his eyes. For days Tommy had made the same announcement to anyone who would listen. "We sail on the *Hound*," he'd say, as if the ship's name carried luck or royal dispensation. But I understood. It was a name he could relate to, unlike *Hezekiah* or *Dambia*, say, and it carried none of the doom that names like *Defeat* or *Bury* did – actual vessel names I'd seen in the *Gazette*.

Last night, I'd talked George into giving his gold cross necklace to Tommy. I meant him to offer Tommy a token to allay his anxieties, yes, but even more I meant to seed in George the idea that Tommy would need him, and perhaps need him greatly. Some of George's preparedness for life, I'm sorry to say, involved a rather profound disinterest in his younger brother. Tommy's moods had cost George dearly over the years, so who could blame him for a certain lack of sympathy? I pointed out that their lives were about to change drastically. I might have said something about George's innate generosity, his older-than-his years competence, how Tommy would rely on him. I think he heard me.

The next day, my parents, Polly, and I stood on Rhett's Bridge watching sailors hustle the last of the hogsheads onto the *Hound*. I held Polly's hand, while Mother stood slightly apart. Father positioned himself at the very edge of the wharf in front of us, legs spread, hands clasped behind his back, as if at any moment he might shout out suggestions to the Captain or nod his approval to the industrious sailors.

Even before the ship began to move, George waved from the rail. Then he disappeared and reappeared, holding Tommy up in his arms. The two of them waved enthusiastically, like children at a parade. To see their faces beaming with excitement was good, but more, I was heartened to note how naturally George had offered Tommy this simple accommodation.

The riggers untied the ship, and the pilot began his slow maneuvers. A wind kicked up. I was reminded of the gusty air the day we arrived almost a year ago and wondered what happened to the lace cap that had blown off my head that day. Did it lie in a soggy heap somewhere at the bottom of the harbor, or had it been swept out to sea?

As it departed, the ship came alive – men climbing the rigging, muscling ropes, and unfurling canvas. Eventually, the majestic sails of the *Hound* were tugged open and favorable winds powered the vessel out into the Atlantic. What a sight! Father came away from the wharf's edge and put an arm around Mother. With a sad longing, we stood there a while longer, as if by watching the sails diminish in perspective, we might retain the previous configuration of our lives just a bit longer.

The Graceful Nephew
Eliza's Diary, Wappoo Plantation

I am newly spiteful when it comes to Tilton. The other day he stopped in while exercising his mare and I taunted him with mention of Dutarque. Never has a twitch of the cheek given such satisfaction.

Mary's wedding service – what to say? She looked radiant in garnet silk, white flowers pinned to her crown. The groom's chest puffed in pride and anticipation. As a pastor, William couldn't help mouthing the words along with the deacon. Awkward, but followed by such a happy gathering at the Izard manse that it was soon forgotten. A spread worthy of a king! We dined in merriment. Well, all of us except John Drayton, of course, who wore grief like a haunting. His mother, Abigail, stayed by his side all evening.

Noticeably absent were Mr. Tilton and Mr. Dutarque, which is perhaps why Father led a gentleman I didn't recognize over for introductions. The harpsichord struck up a quadrille. I handed Mother my hat and gave Father a sour look before taking the chalky hand of a man who looked to be a few years my senior. A Middleton nephew, Arthur.

He stood average height and possessed average features, but oh how he danced! Like a bird in command of the wind! Not only that, but he somehow exported his fluid grace to me. I was flying! So this was why people dance! Even Mother's approving looks couldn't knock me off my perch of gladness.

But then, Arthur told me that he lived in Philadelphia and was visiting for the month of January to escape the frigid winter. Alas!

August 1739

Apprenticeship
Saffron, Wappoo Plantation

When he came back from ferrying Mo to town, Cudjoe was full of it. "Alligators so thick, you coulda crossed the crick on their backs." I looked at Maggie, like I always do. Waiting on a flicker. Fear or joy, no matter – just some sign she dwelt among the living. "That Mo lay his paddle 'crost his knee and stuck his hand in the crick, dragging it along like he King!" The scolding didn't fool anybody. This moaning was pride, pure and simple.

"I tole him, 'Get your sufferin' hand out the water!' He gave me that boy-grin, jess about begging me to clobber him with the paddle." Cudjoe paused to eat. Tonight it was greens mixed with ash cake. A little ribbon of chard hung off his oyster shell, and he stared at it.

"Well?" Melody asked. "Did he?"

"Did he what?"

"Take his hand out of the water?"

"No he did not! So I splashed him good, like this." Cudjoe set his bowl down and acted out flinging creek water with a paddle. "Then I tole him if he didn't start paddling, I'd *feed* his sorry backside to them gators." Cudjoe sat back down, ate up what was left, and looked at the empty bowl. We all knew that feeling.

After months of bird-nibbling, Maggie wiped her bowl clean. Then, when Cudjoe showed how he flung water, she covered her mouth and giggled. I couldn't believe it. Melody grabbed my eye and offered a small smile.

Mo's apprenticeship for rope-making, when it got firmed up as a plan, felt like a victory for one and all. By now we knew about Mo's mother up on the Neck, selling jams and jellies on the odd Sunday down near Rhett's Bridge. She gathered berries up along the scrub lines and took up windfall too. How she got sugar or glass, I got no idea, but probably not by stealing else she'd be a long time dead. And then there was Cudjoe's mother, Nana Lucy, baking and making enough coin to pay head taxes and buy a proper house.

Cudjoe been saving too. He and Mo sell fish in certain seasons. They got secret traps and a sturdy cypress raft hidden past the smokehouse in the reeds. Now and again on a Sunday they'd raft out to secret spots along Willis Creek or Hut Creek, or out past the barrier isles. They knew where to go. They knew which tavern-keepers'd do business with darkies.

What I'm saying is, Mo got it special. He was gonna get rope-making training. He got family saving coin and cheering him on. If ever there was a path to freedom in the soggy misery of these parts, he was on it.

The rope Mo was gonna twist and tar would rig slave ships or dangle from trees with brethren in the noose, or even tie our kin into coffles across the Atlantic – nothing he could do about that. I hoped this didn't worry him none. If a man born a slave could twist and ply to freedom, well then he ought to twist and ply to freedom.

The dream of freedom waved like a banner on that summer night, flapping out hope. Not glaring hope like summer sun on a barn roof, but soft hope like moonlight wobbling in a bucket of water. Freedom for a black soul was rare and easily broke. Any slave who got it knew to take care. One cruel wink could rip it away – freedom undone in a flash, leaving a man naked with nothing to do but survive. Still, a fragile plan was better than no plan.

Announcement
Eliza, Wappoo Plantation

On a stifling August afternoon, I entered the parlor in time to share rice bread and peach compote with Father. He scarcely looked up from the *Gazette*.

"Is there troubling news today?" I inquired, hoping political tensions befouled his mood, not domestic ones. Father folded the newspaper and met my gaze.

"There's always that." He smiled but didn't elaborate. "Have you tried these peaches?" He held up a teaspoon heaped with glistening wedges.

"Oh yes! Heavenly!" I waited. He crossed his legs and dabbed a napkin to his mustache.

Father looked away and then back and announced without preamble, "On this day a week, I shall sail back to Antigua."

I straightened my spine as if to signal to both of us that I was up to the charge his absence would impose. "Is it official then? War with Spain?"

"Not yet, but it's only a matter of time." Grim determination lined his mouth, while a strange combination of pride and regret pooled in his eyes. The tensions with Spain had been escalating since our arrival in the Lowcountry, but none of us expected that he'd receive his commission and ship off quite so soon. The risks to his person were not trivial: yellow and dengue fevers rampaged through the West Indies; Spain had a well-appointed navy, much better than ours.

There'd been the affront of Jenkins' ear, of course – but years ago now. We knew how it went: the Spanish violently boarding one of our ships, swords drawn, the offending captain slicing the British captain's ear off and the subsequent presentation, by Jenkins, of the pickled appendage to the House of Commons in England. It seemed so long ago.

"King Philip pricks at our pride!" Father stood and paced. "All this St. Augustine nonsense! Passels of 'em keep making a run for it!" By then we all knew how the outrageous offer of freedom to any Negro who reached Florida was more disturbing to Lowcountry peace than even their harassing ships along the coast of Georgia. "Purposeful fomenting of insurrection! He knows how outnumbered we are." Father paused as if recalculating the ratio of dark-skinned to white. "It kills me to leave you here, but obviously there'd be no advantage to your coming along."

I wiped tears from my cheeks. Father glanced toward the parlor doorway as if to address, albeit silently, the problems posed by Mother's perpetual retreats.

"Does she know yet?" He gave a short nod. I now understood what precipitated today's migraine. Poor Mother! Not only was she stuck in "the wilds of Carolina," but soon to be abandoned by Father. And without her boys as well – they'd be gone for at least two more years, maybe three. She was going to have to manage. As was I.

I asked, "Is it true King Philip promised the Negroes an acre of land and the right to bear arms? I've heard talk of a former slave named Moses who walks the streets with a pistol tucked in his sash."

"Mac tells me the slaves are full of talk about it." Father sat back down. A peaceful urgency entered the parlor and remained with us for the rest of the afternoon. There was a lot of business to discuss.

At one point, he unlocked the top drawer of his secretary and pulled out a pile of papers: the mortgages, letters of credit, a power of attorney in my direction, and the slave inventory. When we finished reviewing them, he returned to his desk and pushed a darkened nub of wood on the edge of a carved rosette. To my surprise, a small panel sprang open. I'd always believed the panel to be purely decorative, and I suppose that was the point.

Inside lay currency wrapped in a piece of paper and tied with a pink ribbon, an oddly feminine touch. Off came the ribbon. A count was made, the written figure on the covering paper double-checked. "For emergencies," he instructed. "Best to forget about it – almost." Then, he formally handed me the household keys. I raised my eyebrows, imagining Mother's umbrage.

"It's up to you," he said. "If Mother is well, it might aid domestic peace to hand the liquor and sugar keys over to her."

On and on tumbled his advice. Obviously, I would rely heavily on Mac, and since rice prices were falling, best if we got on with indigo. Father and I had discussed indigo casually many times, but never with such urgency. I wasn't to forget English demand. He would proffer ongoing assistance from the West Indies, not just in terms of seed, but also in the eventual hire of a dye expert. He'd already corresponded, in fact, with a reputable dyer on Montserrat.

By then, the sun was setting. The overwhelming amount of detail hadn't dragged me down – quite the opposite. Father's holding me in such high esteem bolstered my confidence. I felt clear and determined.

Just as the dinner bell rang, Polly ran up the steps to the front, Phoebe in tow. Father embraced me. His affection could always calm me, but at that moment his embrace forced the realization that in very short order he would not be around and it saddened me.

The tantalizing scent of roasting pork drifted into the parlor. In the dining room: Mother's empty chair. She didn't descend for that meal, nor join us for a single repast on any of the intervening days leading up to Father's departure, which arrived with what seemed impossible speed.

Blonde and Black Plaits
July, Wappoo Plantation

Cotton see-through-thin be the devil to stitch. How it slip and slide! Even in good light, I go cross-eyed. Stabbed my thumb already, drops of red to suck. That cloth refuse a pin like a bad baby spitting out supper and it won't take a finger press, neither. But then I got it. How to roll up a short bit and hold it tight between thumb and fingers to make a tiny stretch of cloth tight where I work the needle. Trick turned needle and cloth from enemies back to friends. Roll, clamp, and stitch – now 'twas easy. Or I made it look easy, cause Saffron can't get the hang of it, Melody neither.

With a bang and a hoot, here come Polly, popping out the back door bright and blonde, how she do. Why she rooting through the notions basket like that? I had half a mind to slap her hand away.

"Who's got the scissors?" Polly got to know. Phoebe come then too running down the hill, breathing hard. Why was those girls apart this morning?

Saffron found the scissors and go to hand 'em to Polly but Polly shake her head and point at me, grinning. I took them scissors, but didn't know why until she come right up to my knees and turn around, holding up a plait and waggling it.

"Papa needs a charm for when he goes to sea!" I set my cotton square down and opened up Polly's braids. "Take a little from everywhere," Polly say, so I do, cutting off hunks from all along the bottom. Then I think: Should I've asked Mistress first? But then: Why? Everyone know Mistress never say no to the girl, and anyway, she hardly up and around of late.

I tuck the hair in my apron pocket and tole Polly to run along and get me some sweetgrass out of the spinning shed. We'd be weaving fanner baskets soon enough to get ready for harvest and the rice winnowing that come after.

Polly trot off and Phoebe take her place. "My turn! My turn!" Her hair was plaited in pretty rows all along her head with two little pigtails jutting over her neck. I didn't have time for undoing them now.

"At supper," I told her. Never one to argue, Phoebe trotted after Polly.

Polly brung me the sweetgrass, then run off with Phoebe again. By the time they returned late afternoon, I done twist the white tresses and sweetgrass into a charm. Polly's hair stuck out the bottom like a brush, with grass wrapped around the middle and a loop at top for hanging. Polly clapped.

"It's perfect!" She about knock me over with hugging and then dash inside. Phoebe stayed behind. In a small voice she ask if her charm gonna be pretty too. "Course," I tell her, "for sure." Phoebe's charm would be full of what we left behind. Every curl and twist of it would call up the Ancestors. They'd would point to Saharan dust, to the rains of Benin, to the rice terraces of Gambia. Her charm'd echo the call of the babalawo, the voice of the Koran called out by Berbers, the drumbeat of soldier warriors. And it would be hers, all hers.

But there weren't no father for her to give it to. Nothing was gonna make the world right enough for Phoebe to ever see kin again.

At dinner, Polly squirm like eels in a bucket. How she hold off for so long? After I laid down the pudding plates, she jump off her chair and onto Master's lap, handing the charm over. Master took it like a judge takin' important papers – serious. Sometimes he knew how to make his girls feel important. He ate the sweet with one hand and held Daughter with the other.

When at last we was done clearing up, Phoebe was waiting by the fire. I'd never let down a girl living every day with disappointment tucked in her ribs. How she keep the cheer on was beyond me.

"Get over here, l'il sunshine," I tole her, and started untwisting her braids.

Nettles
Eliza, Wappoo Plantation

After Father's announcement, the house, so recently recovered from the boys' departure, became deeply unsettled again. Mother retired most afternoons but spent a few vigorous hours each morning supervising the care and packing of Father's garments. There were breeches in need of new buttons, a vest lining that had come loose, a nightshirt with a hole under one arm. Mother cut two dozen handkerchiefs and put the slaves to work rolling the hems.

She snapped at everyone. No one could do anything right – not the slaves, not me, not even Polly. Morose anticipation of Father's departure cast such a pall over everything, I began to wish he'd leave.

I followed Father around like a lost whelp, half-hoping that some pearl of wisdom would fall from his lips, one that I could live by in the coming days. I tried not to worry, but how? I couldn't read, even briefly, prayer seemed a rote practice, and needlework, an exercise in wounding my fingers. Even music failed me.

The transition might've been marked solely by anxious grief were it not for a nettle plant. Several baskets of washing had been hung, dried, pressed, and packed in the last days, but there were a few late additions so I went up to see how they were coming along. Saffron was tending to Mother, so I expected to find Melody and July.

A couple of yards shy of the shed, a nettle caught my dress and scraped my ankle, causing me to bend and fiddle with my hem. The slaves' voices became quite suddenly audible. I had not meant to listen, but after a few exchanges I was glued to the ground.

"Woe is me, oh woe, woe, woe," Melody half-sang. It would've sounded like a nursery rhyme, if not for the venom. A loud scraping sound followed, perhaps a shifting of one of the big kettles. I thought I heard July murmur agreement. Did she agree?

"What's Mistress got to cry about? How'd she feel, I wonder, watching her sweet little Polly feeding the horses while wearing rags?" Melody said.

"Or naked, like the day she born," July added. "Better yet, eating out of a trough naked."

How silly of me to have equated the silences the slaves inhabited in our presence with some sort of acceptance. And sillier still to have believed that I was even remotely acquainted with their thoughts on any matter.

"And how about Christmas," Melody continued. "They'll be doling out necessities wrapped up with ribbons – a blanket, ten yards of cloth, shoes – as if they were gifts. My Lord, how they deceive themselves!"

"Mm, mm," July hummed. And then – had I moved and made a sound? – she added, "Now hush! That jaw gonna get you kilt." I stared at my feet, frozen like a hunted rabbit.

"We're pampered, did you know?" Melody continued, not inclined to heed July's advice. "Why? Because we wear shoes!"

Offering shoes to all but the very young was, in fact, a point of pride at Wappoo. It may have been mentioned in company.

"Oh, I know. But hush now," July said.

"Pampered!" Melody shout-whispered with disgust. "They think themselves *kind* – just because they don't have a hanging-hook in the barn like old Doc Jackson."

"Huh!" July again. It was hard to believe I was hearing the same slave who nodded and smiled and cooed and fetched with astute dedication. The same slave who tended us with care when we were sick. A paragon of seasoning! But here was July, agreeing with Melody's contemptuous characterizations.

July shushed her again, but Melody was not yet done. In a high and whiny voice, she sang, "We're doing the Lord's work – look, see, slaves in shoes! Mistress crying 'bout Master leaving. But what if somebody stole him, sold him, and he disappeared, never to be seen again?"

After a pause, July said, "Best be holding back now."

I uncurled from my crouch and ever so slowly headed back to the house and into my utterly changed world.

The Pants
Eliza, Wappoo Plantation

I finished tucking the clumps of crinum along the laundry shed foundation and stretched my back. The heat gathered up its hem like a tyrannical mistress aiming to sit and smother the entire Lowcountry. It was getting harder to breathe by the minute and the way my vision creamed along the edges, I knew a migraine was imminent. I availed myself of the shade of the shed interior for a moment.

A slight spell of dizziness o'ertook me. Maybe this was no oncoming headache but rather the pained remembrance of the overheard condemnation between the slaves. Then again, maybe it was anxiety brought on by Father's departure. He was one week gone. Just seven days ago, Mother, Polly, and I had stood at the wharf, much as we'd done when my brothers sailed off, waving and feeling stunned disbelief at the disappearance of Father's schooner over the horizon.

I'd worked hard to earn his trust, but perhaps it'd been all show. The speckled air about my head offered no answer, but there across the shed hung another reminder of my father's absence: a pair of his pants. They startled me, holding only air, empty of person, and yet so spookily full of the man.

I approached the pants warily, as if they might rebuke or prank me. A fine wool gabardine, they featured deep pockets, a five-button fly, and mid-calf cuffs. I inspected them. With some hesitancy and sense of impropriety, I felt something in one of the pockets. Cool metal met my fingers: Father's small penknife. So familiar an object! Running my finger along the nacre finish, I missed him overwhelmingly. His warmth and affection, the sense of protection his keen intelligence and presence provided.

Many an evening I'd seen him employ this very knife to cut a cigar end, or if among family alone, to scrape his fingernails clean. A gift from his father, he'd often announced, one he'd carried on his person since the age of thirteen. How he must miss it! I resolved to get it on our next shipment to the West Indies.

The other pocket seemed empty at first, but upon further inspection, I found something there too. My heart sank. It was Polly's talisman – the one she'd so ceremoniously presented to him. Finding it triggered a sense of foreboding. What if it was this very amulet that would keep him safe, whole, and healthy? Living in the Lowcountry had made me superstitious.

Now my head throbbed. I stepped out to the small lawn at the shed's back and sat down on a gum stump. There were three of them, lined up in silent congregation. Even through my mental haze, three observations arose. One was to note how seamlessly I'd slid into self-pity. The second was to change my mind about the knife. I would not send it south. It was mine for the duration of our separation, a symbol of him to hold fast. Father got his commission. I got his knife. I would send Polly's charm, his memento of filial affection, and let him make what he would of his lapse in attention.

The third observation concerned the convenient positioning of three gum stumps along the wall in a spot hidden from view of the house. I wondered who had put them here and who sat on them and for how long.

The Summons
Eliza, Wappoo Plantation

The morning the summons arrived, the crinum lily along the gallery's foundation trumpeted the air with perfume. Such a heavenly scent! I drank in the sweetened air, knowing that soon enough the atmosphere would clog with damp and swarm with biting insects.

According to Mac, crinum bulbs grew to the size of small cabbages. Mother pshawed, but I wasn't so quick to disbelieve. This much we knew: the crinum flowered early in the season, mid-season, and in the autumn too. Such largesse! Their trumpet-shaped flowers were delicately striped with pink and reminded me of an angel's instrument – Gabriel's horn, perhaps. For plants possessed of a near obscene amount of riches, they required little care. In fact, they were rumored to be indestructible. We should all give as much with as little fuss.

The sound of the pettiauger thunking against the bollards disturbed my reverie. There was Cudjoe returning from Charles Town, dressed in livery. He'd traveled to the city after the blow of conch last night. I knew of no other slave who would consistently brave the waterways in the dark. The summons we'd sent him to fetch probably occupied the same inner vest pocket as his ticket, the one I signed yesterday, with all the requisite specifics: "Cudjoe of Lucas Plantation, on Wappoo Creek, permission to do business in Charles Town on Thursday and Friday, traveling by waterway, no excursions elsewhere."

While I was impatient to read the summons, Mother eagerly anticipated another of Cudjoe's deliveries. She craned her neck to watch the two polers unloading the skiff. We weren't sure what to look for. Would it be wrapped? If so, in what? Would it yet be alive?

During last week's visit to Sarah Rutledge, Mother offered her blancmange recipe in exchange for Sarah's turtle soup recipe, which was really her mother's, of course, but then, Mother's tried and true dishes were really her mother's as well. I had little enthusiasm for the trade, as I was holding Sarah's exuberant conjugal happiness against her. Small-minded, I know, but ever since it became clear that she was with child, my resentment had grown. As had her gloating. How thoroughly Mother approved! And if it's a boy – what exaltations will ensue!

All sourness aside, I'd sampled the turtle soup and found it divine. Definitely worth a little trouble. It was a testament to the soup's creamy and lustrous qualities that Mother was willing to overcome a deep-seated squeamishness about reptiles in order to prepare it. She'd made Oyster Pie and Shrimp Soufflé a time or two, but neither the shucking of oysters nor the peeling of shrimp involved quite the amount of skinning, tugging, and gutting that turtle soup required. She'd go through the process once with the slaves and July'd likely learn the recipe in a single demonstration.

Perhaps July already knew the recipe?

Suddenly, a commotion erupted. With a great deal of splashing and yelling, the slaves hauled a netted bag out of the creek. Inside: a large turtle. Mother stood. "Good Lord! We needn't feed the King's Army!"

Mother sat back down as Cudjoe approached. He presented us with a basket of figs from the Middletons, a sack of oranges from Grandmama, and an etui filled with needles and thread, which Mother quickly examined and deemed to be as ordered. Lastly, he handed Mother the much-anticipated summons and descended the stairs to stand on the spot where he typically offered up news from the city. I asked about the new drainage law.

"Some grumblin' Miss. Some favoring canals, some not. The planters none too pepped up on account of not having hands to spare, harvest and all. And them that can't spare a hand can't spare the coin neither." For some reason, Cudjoe turned to Mother and added, "And no letters or notes allowed."

Cudjoe was generally economical in his speech. Mother raised an eyebrow, I think more at the length of his address than at its content, but maybe she was also taken aback at the news that credit would not be accepted were we to refuse to supply a slave for drainage construction.

For my part, the possibility that our key slave knew enough about the family's finances to recognize the hardship the law might impose disturbed me. Either we were the subjects of gossip over on the peninsula or he had discerned the situation in some other way. Neither prospect pleased. For the first time, it occurred to me that Cudjoe was literate. Why this possibility hadn't occurred to me before was puzzling, especially since it would explain the alacrity with which he conducted our business.

"Well, privations shan't be imposed for long!" Mother made this oracular statement with an imperial impatience, as if her uninformed optimism, as long as it was enthusiastic enough, would magically diminish the consequences of the riverways law. Or maybe she was just thinking about turtle soup.

"Who knows, Mistress," Cudjoe responded, "what with the Edisto, the Stono, the Cooper, Goose Creek, and the Ashley all needing canals." He counted off the rivers on his fingers like a barrister making his case, and then, as if realizing he'd overstepped, shifted his gaze downward and slumped his shoulders. While we were all well acquainted with Negroes' poses of deference, I had yet to witness a slave slip into one right before my eyes.

Mother handed me the summons and resumed sewing but seemed to sag with the effort. "I think I'll take a little lie down before tackling that turtle." She disappeared into the house.

I was about to dismiss Cudjoe when his slight look of consternation made me pause.

"Is there something else?" He seemed to make a quick calculation and shook his head no.

"Well, that'll do." I waved him away. At last I could read the summons. I already knew that the drainage law required every slaveholder in the region to offer one or more slaves for canal construction and if that were not possible to pay a fee instead. What I didn't know were the precise numbers: how many slaves and what fee?

The law required that Wappoo loan out one slave. One.

Given that the freak frost in April devastated our ginger and cassava crops, too little sat in the general purse to pay the fee, so one slave it would be. I'd forgotten to ask Cudjoe if he'd heard anything about enforcement. Perhaps, as with the prohibitions against educating the Negroes, no real clout would be expended to uphold the law? But this much was clear – the penalty for noncompliance was higher than the fee so it didn't make sense to take the risk.

In a flash I realized that the obvious slave to pony up was Mo. Of course! Having begun his apprenticeship, he was already out of circulation. In a very real sense assigning him to the canal effort would cost the plantation nothing in the short term. I recalled Cudjoe's expression with the sudden understanding that he'd already thought this through and it bothered him. Why?

For some number of weeks, perhaps months, his son would dig ditches and slash undergrowth with a passel of other slaves, all of them belonging to different planters, but then he'd resume his apprenticeship. The interruption to training was one thing, but it struck me that Cudjoe's worry spoke to something else. Surely the seven-day work requirement couldn't be concerning for a slave as young and strong as Mo. Snakes? Maybe. So much care was required to avoid cottonmouths and copperheads near the water, even while riding in a boat. Working ten hours in the muddy banks and rivers, surely some number of the men would be bitten, and some of the bitten would die.

It dawned on me that other plantations might not have a slave as cost-neutral as Mo and would therefore be assigning slaves otherwise expendable, those who were lazy or disobedient. Bad influences. Dutarque's concern. Maybe they'd all be saltwaters, hustled from auction block to drainage crew, a gathering of Negroes with little or no seasoning, limited supervision, and nothing to lose. Perhaps we all ought to be worried. Unlike Mo, who had a trade to learn and family in the Lowcountry, others might set their sights on St. Augustine.

September 1739

Basket of Cottonmouths
Eliza, Wappoo Plantation

After reading a single passage of *Paradise Lost* too many times to count, I donned my bonnet and left the house, the early tremors of headache affording excuse enough, but did I need one? The slaves' breakfast conch had sounded, but no one in the household had yet risen, so I slipped out unnoticed.

The air was sticky. Down at the dock I took off my shoes and stockings. I trod along the path that paralleled the creek towards the Stono a good distance before approaching the water's edge. Where the scrub thinned a little, I lifted my skirts and waded in. Ah, how cool the water! In two or three strides, the cranky girl struggling to read Milton vanished, along with any trace of a migraine. I would remember this next time – the healing powers of Mother Nature!

The cicadas rang out. Other insects thrummed. Before long a new sound wove itself into the chorus. Singing? Yes, it was – and a slave song, no less. Perhaps I should've turned immediately around, but my expansive mood coalesced with their haunting refrains and made me curious. I crept forward. I couldn't tell if the tongue was Spanish or Portuguese, but it was one of the two.

From behind a tangle of dewberry bushes, I spied a cluster of a dozen or so men with shovels and machetes. One of the newly formed canal crews, no doubt. Some dug at the creek bank, while those with machetes hacked at the undergrowth. All worked in that African way, in unison and in a rhythm measured pace by pace to their song.

In the creek itself, detritus was floating about, perhaps scrub from the slashing efforts. Out of each cluster of waste extended a long split branch, which I soon recognized as too regular to make sense as debris. In the next instant, one of the rounder pieces of floating wood turned and revealed itself to be a man, eyes and nose easily seen at the water's surface. Ah! But what use was a dousing stick to a man neck deep in water?

A sudden splashing commotion made everything clear. Alarmed shouting, harsh directions yelled out. Mayhem. And then there it was: a snake, at least three feet long, held aloft on the forked stick, writhing in a vigorous attempt to escape. It opened its mouth in fury, revealing the signature white throat of the cottonmouth.

The slave hoisted the snake above his head and emerged from the water. First his bare shoulders, then back blades and bare waist, and then hips and thighs wrapped in soaked breeches. I was glad his back was to me. He held the stick off to one side, then dropped the venomous creature into a large basket. One of the machete-wielding slaves came over and slashed this way and that within the basket. Snake dispatched!

By that time, a swarm of flying pests had found me. I'd also taken a moment to count – six slaves in the water, eleven on land, one of them our Mo. Self-preservation dictated a swift departure – I was a mere bowshot from almost twenty unsupervised slaves. They started to sing again, not a mere song of labor but a hymn of devotion, I thought, perhaps to one of their gods. Or to the Virgin Mary? I thought I caught the word "Maria."

I turned slowly as sour fear pooled in my belly. No one heard me, did they? My hem fell into the creek, but nothing seemed to matter but returning home unseen. Once back on the dock, stockings and shoes back on, all I could think about was Cudjoe's seeming anxiety about Mo being on one of these crews. His apprehension blended with some unnamable fear of my own.

Rope Hopes
Mo, Near the Stono River

Sixteen of us swung, flung, and heaved, scooped and slashed like we was one body. Digging canals. Clearing scrub. Catching up snakes and killing 'em. We was parched. Bugs bad. Bites went puffy and raw with scratching 'til every back carry a diseased map of the stars between shoulders and hips. Oh, but wait, heaven don't show up on black backs round here – only hell.

Highway Commissioner Gibbs sat atop a dappled grey like he got a piece of empire, but to hear Hercules tell it, and he finds things out, the post don't pay but a pittance and nobody wants to do it. We was nowhere near a road, so his title, Highway Commissioner, swaggered about with a special brand of stupid. Maybe to square up the paltry pay, Gibbs never stuck around for long. That morning, he was biding his time and we all knew it. We was relying on it hard, in fact.

Plans were afoot.

The mare snapped her tail fierce but useless, trying to keep the bugs off. If I had a tail like that, I'd smack the smug look off Gibbs' face. He smoked a cheroot, part of his claim to sitting high and mighty, but probably hoping to keep off the midges too. The horse tail failed. The smoke failed. We was all getting bit.

Gibbs puffed away, now and then hawking up something nasty and launching it our way. Cato was a good target. He was big, for one thing, easy to hit. For another thing, he was planning a revolt, something Gibbs didn't know for sure but feared. A pecan-sized gob landed on Cato's shoulder and I watched it slide down his back. The gob and its trail shined – badges of hate as bad as any lash mark.

No fancy title was gonna keep Gibbs cool or free of itch. That made me snort and then fake a sneeze, what with Gibbs lookin' hard my way. The man got suspicions and he was not wrong.

The men from the Kongo and Angola lived free just months back, so they hate Gibbs sharp and hard. Their hate lives close to the surface. They don't yet know all the ways a white man can cut a black man down. I actually hated Gibbs more, I think, but showed it less. Today that hate ran white hot down my middle. What else do that but love?

Jemma plucked a fiendish snake up with his forked stick. Those buggery rogues dropped out of the buckleberries from ten feet up. On the ground, they slithered away into the weeds, but in the water they came right at you, on duty for the devil. All this digging and slashing pestered 'em bad, making 'em ornery and vicious. Two men got bit last week. One died, the other still puffed up and laid low with fever. Being harvest time, Gibbs'd be hard pressed to find a replacing hand if a snake bite sent another man home to the Ancestors. He can't afford that.

Gibbs got plenty to worry on. He clamped the cheroot in his teeth and snapped the air with the cowhide. "Keep on it, you lazy bastards!" He pose like a lord, but I could smell the stink of fear coming off him.

Before short-shadow hour, Gibbs announced to nobody that he just might mosey on over to Hutchinson's Depot. "That Bathhurst might be stupid," he chuckled, "but he keeps some mighty fine brandy on the shelf." He tongued a last goober over. It landed in the water near my knees. A soft sound. How could so much hate land with a plop so quiet?

Jemma's jaw go rock-hard, but he got to humming again and soon eight or nine others joined in. I'd heard the song before – a praise hymn to the Virgin Mother Mary they told me. They sung in Portuguese, but with the tones and beats of villages across the sea. Those melodies made me homesick for places I never been.

Last week, Jemma spelled out the song's meaning. "We ask for Her mercy. And for lukangu too." That's the Kikongo word for liberty. Tomorrow, September 9, was Mary's birthday, making it a blessed day to ask for Her help. Her birth was pure, he said, and carried no taint of sin. This seemed important to him even if it made no sense to me.

Jemma stands tall and willowy, but strong. There's pride in his bones, courage in his flesh. Even though he don't yet know the full punishing ways of buckra, he knows running to Florida could end his life and it wasn't gonna stop him.

Cato, a binyah, born here, stood big and broad like an ox. No buckra ever looked at him and thought, "There's a fella who can read and write," but read and write he did. He worked his learning for others for years, forging passes for folks up and down the Edisto and Stono Rivers. A house slave stole paper and ink for him and he wrote those liberatin' slips, helping some run, helping others meet up with family for a night. And on account of reading, he often knew things.

Because of Cato, we knew a new gun law was coming. Starting at the end of September every white man gonna have to carry arms to church. Yellow fever delayed things in our parish, but it was already happenin' over in Wiltown. Hear tell, it's starting hereabouts on September 23. Today was Saturday, September 8, meaning there was only two more Sundays 'til buckra nearby would be toting pepper pots and muskets to church. To Cato, asking the Virgin Queen for her help was one thing, but getting a rebellion going before guns was handy was another.

Every side and length of Jemma, resting or moving, showed he was ready to die for liberty. He crouched like a panther. He stood like a god of fire. He sang with lungs built for speed. Jemma would lead the running, and Cato, knowing the lay of the land, would tell the direction. Together, they were like a mountain with legs or a thunderstorm with a soul.

As for me, I'd run with the others for a bit and then melt away. I was aiming to stake my odds for freedom in the Lowcountry, not in St. Augustine. Unlike most these men, I got family here, a girl I'm wanting to know, and an apprenticeship waiting.

The dream of freedom was gonna help me endure the jeers of Irish and German ropemakers in the hemp house. Help me stand the stench of tar and the hand-shredding twisting. As long as the others didn't cover me in tar and light a taper at my feet "by accident," I'd get my training. Why run?

Standing in pluff mud in a buggy marsh next to Wallace Creek, I looked off toward the Stono River. I could taste freedom.

September 9, 1739

The Depot Steps
Hutchinson's Depot

Tired but satisfied after the first brisk day of trade since the outbreak of fever back in May, Robert Bathhurst, the Sunday clerk at Hutchinson's Depot, silently reviewed the day. His boss would be pleased. There'd been sales across the board. Sundries – butter, cloth, tallow – and essentials, especially powder and balls now that the deer were fattening up. But specialty items had sold too – Peruvian bark packets, two hornbooks, and many a draught of rum and expensive Madeira. He'd even sold two sets of porcelain. No wonder his mother often crowed, "You, young man, could sell ham to a pig!"

Such an industrious day merited an unusual liberty for Bathhurst. A nightcap. His companion, Thomas Gibbs, had arrived many hours earlier, to escape "the pitiless insects and dumb Negroes." Gibbs had lent a hand now and again, proving especially helpful packing the porcelain sets in straw.

"On the house!" Bathhurst announced magnanimously. Midday had been hot, but round sunset, the temperature dropped, bringing hints of fall, so he'd built a fire in the store's small hearth. It glowed with a heap of well-tended embers. What little light remained in the sky did not penetrate the velvety dark of the store's interior, making the orange crackling coals especially welcome.

A sound from outside disturbed the peace. "Hear that?" Bathhurst asked, sitting up from his slouch. He twisted in his seat but his companion, with an air of quiet satisfaction, held his glass up and stared at the embers through its mahogany-colored contents.

"One of the reliable pleasures in life, wouldn't you say?" he mused, taking another sip.

"A critter looking for scraps, maybe," Bathhurst said uneasily. He might be a man who could sell ham to a pig, but he'd long since accustomed himself to disregarding his deeper instincts, particularly in service of avoiding confrontation. In this pairing, he was the lesser man. Gibbs, after all, had surveyed and memorialized more than 2,000 acres out in Colleton and owned a passel of slaves. He'd also been awarded the prestigious post of Highway

Commissioner, an important position for the new riverway project, and one that required experience disciplining Negroes. Authority.

Another shuffle. A clank.

The peace would not hold.

At the risk of offending, Bathhurst muttered, "You had to've heard that!" Now Gibbs turned into the darkness as well. The brandy bottle on the makeshift table between them was nearly empty, the companionable drinking session interrupted. Gibbs started at the next sound.

In a silky panic, he recalled a series of what now seemed like ominous conversations. Just last weekend, one of the other municipal agents had mentioned that the canal slaves were grousing about missing their Sundays off. Two days later, Izard, sharing the head count of saltwaters on his crew, openly worried about their lack of seasoning, musing that maybe, "going straight from the auction block to remote locales was not advisable?" And there was the brief exchange with the Wappoo overseer, Mac. "Watch them Angolans and Kongolese. They're runners, sir, and not a few of 'em know their way around a musket."

Gibbs now regretted how he'd waved off these comments as inconsequential, even girlish. He'd given Mac a punch to the shoulder and jocularly asked, "What're they gonna do, wade to St. Augustine? They don't know their arses from a hole in the wall, never mind where to cross the Savannah."

But now these casual rumors and admonitions sparked in his brain violently, swiftly. Bathhurst grabbed his sleeve, and the two remained frozen, all ears and terror. They heard the nickering and sidestepping of their horses, then a clink of harness metal and more shuffling. Something larger than a possum and more dexterous than a deer was out there. In a final desperate bid for normalcy, Gibbs whispered, "A flock of turkeys, perhaps, scrapping around?"

"Jerking the reins of my mare?" Bathhurst rejoined, terror stripping him of habits of deference.

The ground vibrated, and both men sprang to their feet. "I'll bet it's them crew diggers after food and liquor," whispered Bathhurst, patting his hip for a weapon that was not there. Gibbs glanced at the clerk. Saw the sheen of fright on the man's face. Looked for his weapon, but before he could grab it, what seemed like an entire tribe of Africans stormed in.

The slaves looked around, breathing hard. A nod and grunt from the largest Negro Bathhurst had ever seen, the one Gibbs knew to be Cato, and the men surged forward. Cato skewered Gibbs through the middle with his machete.

Another man used his shovel to smash Bathhurst's head open, splattering his brains onto the hearth like a bloody Milky Way. Gibbs slid down in a heap at Cato's feet, first sitting like a school child and then slumping to the side like a rag doll, eyes open and going glassy fast. For an eerie pause, the rebels stood still, breathing, staring down at the dead men. It wasn't respect, regret, or fear in their silence but rather an acknowledgement that this was the moment when everything changed.

A scuffle followed, hands grabbing muskets and balls, powder and tampers, biscuits, rum, and brandy. Jemma's face lit up when he spotted a bolt of white fabric high up on a shelf. He pulled it down with a thud. When it fell right next to Gibbs' body, it narrowly missed the pool of blood. Jemma tugged at the bolt, thumped it round and round, bit a notch in it and tore off a strip, then did the same thing again and handed the strip to Cato. Two white banners for the rebellion, a color associated with the Virgin.

The cloth shone in the glow of the orange embers. From the way it draped and shimmered, Mo knew it was dear cloth, the kind buckra turned into gowns with lace and tucks and all. Expensive, just like freedom.

More of the men crowded in, eager for a weapon and for food. Juno found a crock of peaches near the back and flipped the wires up on one jar after another. Squatting, he scooped out the dripping halves and handed them round. There was slurping and moaning at the sweetness. Jacko found strips of jerky, some handed round and eaten, some tucked into waistbands for later.

Jemma tore off shorter strips of cloth to serve as belts. These would hold lead balls and packets of powder. Cato called out, "Flints? Strikers? We need at least one set, better more." Mo rifled through a drawer and found a half dozen sets. Cato looked at Mo and Jacko with a small smile and made a slashing move at his throat, nodding down at Gibbs and Bathhurst. He handed Mo a machete. Jacko still held his from earlier.

After a second's hesitation, Mo swung the machete high and brought it down hard. It gashed into Gibbs' throat just below that smug face, smug no more, but the head hung on. Two more whacks it took to free it from the body. Bathhurst required four. "Set 'em on the steps," Cato ordered. Their heads would make a grisly warning to anybody coming by. Mo hesitated again, not wanting to pick that gory head up, but after looking down, up and down again, did as he was asked. The head was warm and heavy, like a calabash before it dried out. He tossed it up and down a few times, then made his way outside and held dead Gibbs's face up as if to talk to him, but what to say? "You had it coming"? Or maybe, "Hope you enjoyed your last drink!" In the end, Mo set the head down on the top step in silence, turning the blue eyes to stare out toward Wallace Creek. Something stirred in his groin. The sweet scent of Binah breezed past him from the pines along the road – but how? Mo tried to shake it off, but knew that death with its violent crush and rot sometimes brought desire along.

And there it was: desire, Binah's face in front of him clear as day. He could see the space between her teeth, the small curves of her ears beneath her head wrap, her smile, shy and alive. Mo saw his hands clapped to the sides of her head in a strange echo of gripping the dead man's head, but tender, not brutal. If she was here tonight, he'd ever so gently pull her close, rebellion be damned! In a second, the vision of her was gone. The night closed up around him. Would he live long enough to kiss those lips? If Mo hadn't been sure where to head next, he was sure now. There was no way he was about to hoof it to Florida.

They clustered outside, waiting for Cato and Jemma. Time to count: how many guns, how many powder packets? There were two empty hogsheads to use as drums, and those two long white strips of cloth for banners. Good! Two horses and two lanterns. Good!

With Cato on horseback in the lead and Jemma right behind, they headed south. The rest ran as a single body, Jemma's lone voice calling out in Kikongo, "Lukangu, lukangu!" Liberty.

The night flashed by in a bloody and fiery rush. Mo took to grabbing lanterns in buckra's parlors or libraries and dumping oil onto floors and porches. After the machete men walked away, he'd spark the fires. Houses whooshed into flaming balls, killing anyone inside not yet dead. They spared one tavern keep on account of kindnesses well known. They ran and ran, to the next house and the next, until dawn brushed the sky and they stopped in a clearing. Mo thought Jacksonboro Ferry might be near. He hung near the tree line while Cato waved all in and praised them. Jemma started the military exercises. Having covered more than fifteen miles and killed more than twenty people, the men were exultant and tired.

Slow and easy, Mo walked away. A last look showed him the white banners held aloft and the men moving in unison. He heard the African rhythms beat out on empty hogsheads. Some rebels were drunk on rum, some on brandy, some had not touched a drop, but all were drunk with the promise of freedom.

Would they make it across the Savannah River? What about the horses? If they got that far, the coast of Georgia stretched a long treacherous way to Florida. Even though slavery wasn't legal in Georgia, hunting slaves sure was, so how would they avoid capture or execution? But Mose had made it — why not them? Rumor had it Mose walked the streets, armed, and that near to a hundred former slaves lived there — blacksmiths, carpenters, coopers, bakers, and seamstresses. They ferried goods through the marshes. They farmed Florida soil, no one claiming the food they grew. No one stopping them.

Asking how hard it was to get to Florida was like asking how hard was it to be free. Maybe ignorance moved the rebels more than bravery. Mo understood all the ways it could go wrong: dogs and patrollers, drowning, rattlesnakes, hunger. There were waterways that twisted and sagged into holes that'd swallow men and horses entire. Tides that ran smooth one way but tugged fierce in the other. Thickets dying to rip skin off. And all along the way, men with twisted alliances, dropping whispers into the wrong ears for the wrong reasons.

So many ways to end up dead.

The more distance Mo put between himself and the rebels, the more their doom seemed a certainty. Hard sorrow landed like a rock in his chest. He headed away from Wappoo, west into the swamps. He knew better than to show his face any time soon.

Part III

September 1739 – December 1739

September 1739

The News
Eliza, Wappoo Plantation

After a long day, I was craving the sweet extinction of nap when rapid hoof beats announced a visitor. I stepped outside in time to see a harried rider dismount swiftly and nearly lose his balance on landing. Not at all graceful – embarrassing, in fact. Mr. Tilton?

His face wore the sheen of physical effort and something else. He barked, "Call the overseer! Now!" I jangled the big bell that was affixed to the clapboards for this very purpose. Mother emerged quickly but Mac was likely far afield even at this late hour, given the harvest.

"Whatever's the matter?" Mother asked. "Mr. Tilton – are you quite alright, my friend?"

"Never mind that!" Tilton snapped. "I have news, Ma'am," he added in a slightly conciliatory tone. "I don't have time to relate it twice. Others must be alerted too." Mother appraised Mr. Tilton's sweaty agitation just as I had just done. I now recognized that it was fear in his face. He came with not just bad news but calamitous news.

Mother invited Mr. Tilton inside, but he declined and instead gripped the reins tightly in one hand and crushed the brim of his hat in the other. Too impatient to wait another moment, he spit out the news. "Up near Wallace Creek, a passel of slaves stormed the Depot, stole rum, lanterns, and muskets, and then rampaged all night. John Gibbs, Robert Bathhurst beheaded. The rebels drummed up others as they ran, mobbing up to nearly a hundred. They burned houses all along the Pon Pon Road. They're probably hoping to get to Florida."

Our jaws dropped. He continued. By the latest count, twenty settlers were dead: Colonel Hext's wife and daughter; Thomas Gibbs and his two children. Others. Mother placed a hand on my shoulder, looking faint. Mac, who had joined us by now, offered his arm, but she was frozen.

"If Lieutenant Governor William Bull hadn't just happed upon the insurgents on his way back from Beaufort this morning, who knows how many more would've been killed."

"Wait, what's that?" Mac asked.

Tilton looked anxiously at his horse, as if he was risking something by tarrying so long. He sped through the last of his account – how Bull and his three companions had come across the rebels; the hasty call to arms; an impromptu militia. How the Negroes were drunk. Dancing. Easy targets. "It's a good thing Wiltown already had the Securities Law in place. The men at the nearest church were armed. Ready." The rebels fired off a shot or two, apparently, but otherwise were easily dispatched. Close to thirty executed on the spot. A few ran off – whether back to their owners or toward St. Augustine, currently unknown. Bull had already hired native trackers and doubled the patrollers along the riverways.

"Good Lord!" Mother exclaimed.

"They won't get far," Tilton asserted. "Don't you worry about that."

Mother looked at me, and I could read her thoughts: How in heaven's name were we not to worry about that? Murderous rebels on the loose, desperate armed men who, having already committed a series of capital offenses, now had nothing to lose. It didn't bear saying the obvious, but it was inescapably felt – our household lacked any male protection. No husband, no uncle, no grown brother.

"The militia determined some were unwilling participants, don't ask me how, and let 'em go. I'd have shot 'em all. It's suspected that any escaped runners have covered some ground, likely ten to fifteen miles by now."

Mac mused aloud, "Now I understand – 'twas a mood yesterday I could na' fathom. They all knew. The buggers knew."

"Of course they knew!" Tilton snapped. "What's essential now is that they not sense your anxiety." Rounding his way to a conclusion, Tilton regained his smug authority. "Don't let them see even the smallest degree of fear. And two other pieces of advice. Seeing as how you have no men folk in the house, you might want to rethink letting any slaves hunt." Tilton glared at me. Yet another of his rebukes.

"And the second?" I asked neutrally.

"Well, you might be interested to know that one of the rebels – the one called Captain or Cato – was literate. I'm sure his master regrets letting the brute learn to read now!" And with that, Tilton thundered away on his horse.

A Storm Rolls Through
Eliza, Charles Town

At first our travel was as pleasant as could be under the circumstances: the soothing, rhythmic sound of the paddles dipping and dripping, the choir of marsh birds, the sparkle of sun upon the creek, pretty. Even the thunderclouds heaped up along the horizon seemed benign. And then a ghastly sight. Rebel heads skewered on pikes. Four of them. The heads had withered into ghoulish shapes, with dark holes for eyes.

We recoiled in horror and disgust. I looked at the slaves accompanying us – Cudjoe and Abraham paddling, Melody and Phoebe tending to Mother and Polly – their faces inscrutable.

The rebellion had changed society in ways we had yet to discover and surely harsh deterrents were required. But this? For such a hideous display to be placed where every decent family traveling down the Ashley to a funeral would have to see it seemed a step too far. Four more grisly heads assailed us near the peninsula, one of them slightly rotating on its pike as if deliberating on whose shoulders to deliver a torrent of curses. Mother hid her face. We scrambled out of the pettiauger, eager to be away.

After such a grievous landing, we looked forward to the Hext memorial. It would remind us of what mattered: civility and faith, our traditions. A genteel wife in her prime, Mrs. Hext, felled by a ruthless mob of unseasoned slaves; her daughter, a twelve-year-old girl taken from this earth untested in pleasure or sorrow, now never to be so. And why? Because the two were unlucky enough to be in the path of savages bound for Florida. Because the Spanish had seen fit to meddle in our affairs.

Inside St. Philip's, the sweet, woody fragrance of cedar paneling quieted my spirit. How we all needed reminding of the Lord's mysterious ways! The pastor was speaking to exactly this point when a commotion erupted in the front, in the Rutledge pew. How dreadful if the baby was coming at this inopportune juncture! Sarah leaned heavily into John as he ushered her down the aisle, every eye in the place watching them. As it happened, the moment passed and the memorial proceeded, though not before Mother elbowed Melody to follow them out, in case her skills were required.

The reception at Poinsett Inn unfolded in a cheerless manner and not just because of our collective grief – lightning had started to flash out over the harbor. People gathered up their things and said their goodbyes rather sooner than was polite. Our surrey deposited us at Cross Winds just as the first large raindrops pelted the walkway.

Taking off her cape, Mother began her usual post-gathering commentary. The reception was fine, if overly abbreviated. Sarah held up well, all considered, and wasn't John looking peaked? People were rattled. She placed her cape in Nell's outstretched hands, which shook a little. "That poor Colonel Hext," Mother continued, shaking her head. "Would he prefer to be laid to rest alongside his wife and daughter, I wonder?" And then she continued about the reassurance of ritual, and so on, especially at times like these.

"Isn't it our faith that upholds us and not the rituals?" I asked, seeming to forget that not an hour earlier I'd had the very same thought.

"I'm just talking, Eliza. No need to snap."

Grandmama sat near the hearth, where a small fire glowed. She started when Mother bent to gently kiss her crown and then blinked her way back into the room. Silence took hold until Nell brought in the tea tray, but somehow it was a comfortable quiet, not a prickly one. Pouring my cup first, Mother said casually, "Don't forget, Eliza, you weren't there in '36." She went on to note that while the plot in the West Indies hadn't cost any planters their lives, it was just as unsettling, and in some ways worse, because it'd been planned by well-seasoned, loyal slaves – even a few converts to Christianity. Saltwaters couldn't be expected to behave better. "But whoever the villains and whatever the causes, that makes two slave uprisings in three years for us." Point made. Mother seemed to weigh the cost of continuing and opted to change the subject – to what else? – the weather. The rain that had started moments ago had stopped.

"Gonna be a frog washer!" Grandmama chirped.

Large periwinkle clouds towered out over the Atlantic. From this distance the slants of rain looked like the shadowing lines of an etching. Wind swept the thunderheads across the harbor and then, in a formidable show of force, the storm was upon us. The atmosphere darkened and the rain hammered down, pocking walkways and battering the roof. Steam rose up off the street, and in no time the gutters streamed like shallow creeks. Gusts of wind battered the palmettos to a frenzy.

Recent events had bruised us, left us dazed in shock and fear. Now it was as if the heavens growled out a response to our anguish, or maybe spoke the anguish itself. At the same time, the storm's swift and retributive power diminished our plight into insignificance. Nature always offered the better sermon.

By the time we sat down to supper, it was dark as night and still raining hard, but the center of the storm had moved inland and the worst of it was over. Grandpapa surprised us all by returning in time for the meal. I forgot where he'd been – even Grandmama didn't seem to know – but how welcome his ruddy, cheerful face! Rather than being harried or inconvenienced by the weather, he seemed energized by it and sat down without bothering to change out of his damp jacket.

"Oysters and greens! How delightful!" he announced. Polly came in looking rosy and refreshed. She must have slept.

"Oh yes, ever so tasty," agreed Grandmama.

Grandpapa launched right into politics. "I predict an immediate tax on all imports from Africa." The crystal goblet fractured candlelight on the way to his lips. His assurance, indeed, his sparkle, so reminded me of Father that I felt both heartsick and comforted. I glanced at Mother to see if she might be feeling the same, but she was already formulating her response.

"Surely, tariffs can't be the answer given how many more hands are required by the week?"

"At the cost of treachery? We stand now three to one. Should we risk four to one?"

"It was six to one on Antigua," Mother observed.

"Yes, well, and look what nearly happened there."

Mother wasn't the least cowed by Grandpapa's authority or his roughshod pace. She was about to reply when he declared, "I have a prediction." He glanced around the table to make sure he had everyone's attention. "Governor Bull's column in the next edition of the *Gazette* will skip all mention of the rebellion. You watch now. It'll be rogue galleon this, rogue galleon that. The black market. Spain, Spain, Spain." He looked at us with a raised eyebrow, daring us to ask why. No one did. "Because of his rather dubious role in quelling the insurrection, of course."

Mother looked up from her oysters in surprise. "You don't mean to suggest –
"

"Indeed I do!" Grandpapa replied, right before a loud crack of lightning. Rain clattered in a violent gust against the windows, prompting Nell to draw the heavy drapes. "Leave them be!" Grandpapa boomed. "We should revel in the power of Nature."

"Yes! Let's!" agreed my grandmother, her gusto at odds with her narrow, shrunken shoulders. She held her knife upright in one hand, her fork in the other, resting the sides of her clenched hands on the table, exactly like a child awaiting supper – a real statement of her readiness to enjoy life. Like Mother, by being married to a certain kind of man, Grandmama was acquainted with power and knew how to be near it without cowering.

Something tickled my mind, the way a forgotten birthday or a task inadvertently neglected might. I strained to remember. It was important and had to do with masculine authority. I scanned the afternoon's events, with the mild urgency that attends this sort of forgetting. And then I remembered. And when I remembered I felt a stab of embarrassment, for surely it wasn't so important a thing after all: Charles Pinckney.

Charles had impressed me yet again just hours earlier when I'd overheard him speaking to Colonel Hext, offering kind remembrances of his wife – recollections both particular and glowing and likely to stay with the Colonel for years. Charles Pinckney was a man of sweeping knowledge, steeped in the rigors and elegance of logic. His broad intellect! His clear articulations! All while maintaining a most amiable manner.

Mr. Pinckney's authority was less bombastic than Grandpapa's and more fluid than Father's. He was equipped for discourse at any level. He was literary as well as grounded in politics and the law, and yet he spoke without rancor or stuffiness or even any need to convince. Grandpapa was a bit of a provocateur, Father tended to want to be right, but Charles Pinckney could tease and instruct without ever condescending or raising his voice. For the first time, I recognized that I felt something more in his company than the satisfaction of an argument well-made.

Grandpapa was still going on about the governor's about-face after encountering the rebels in the clearing. "What would I have done if I'd come upon four dozen drunken rebels? Frankly, I'm not sure – half of 'em trained soldiers too, you can be sure. Who in their right mind assumes a black man doesn't know how to handle a weapon? Maybe it wasn't obvious how drunk they were, but still, to turn tail? How else to say it?"

Mother pointed out that there were only four men in the Governor's retinue. "Surely those odds do not speak to cowardice? Imagine the wholesale slaughter that might've ensued had the Governor been killed." Since Mother had not given the least impression of wanting to talk or even think about the rebellion, her acuity stunned me.

"No, no, of course you're right, Millie. A dead governor would've been a disaster," Grandpapa conceded. "Massive retaliations and tremendous economic losses. Still, aren't you a little perturbed at the image of him wheeling his horse away?"

Because avoiding the topic of the rebellion had been dampening and isolating, the discussion at dinner served as a tonic. Conversation about troubling matters was always better than avoidant silence. By the time I scraped the last delicious, crumb-filled clump of whipped crème from my plate, I felt renewed. The rain pounded on.

The Lost Ones
Melody, Charles Town

The water ran high, pulled strong. We slid along the creek toward the Hext funeral, moving in and out of lumpy shadows of scrub. It was almost peaceful. Nobody talked. Could be the way the oars splashed a watery lullaby. Or maybe it was how death crowded round from all sides – the uprising one week past, the next week rebels hanging from gibbets up and down the Pon Pon Road, or shot, burned, and buried rough in a mass grave.

In my bag, I carried clean cotton strips and a salve wrapped in catalpa leaf for Cudjoe's back. Mac had whipped him raw right after the uprising, said he'd caught him running off. Cudjoe poled at the rear before sitting to paddle. All this moving didn't bode well for the welts. If the wraps he already wore slipped, his tunic would stick, unstick, and stick again. No end to the hurt.

The dreamy quiet did not last.

Phoebe gasped and Polly's face crumpled. Quick as a flash in the pan, Miss Eliza grabbed her sister and shielded her face. I put an arm around Phoebe and pulled her close but didn't try to cover her eyes. Abraham laid his oar across his knees, and Cudjoe stopped paddling too. We drifted a little toward the bank where the pikes rose up out of the earth. Vultures had done their nasty work, leaving dark holes caked with blood where once there'd been eyes. We were close enough to hear the insects, buzzing and busy. A pale purple cloud drifted across the sun, hanging there long enough to smudge the creek with shadow, as if even the sun couldn't stand the sight.

No one could find a word to say. Or maybe, there just weren't any words that any one of us could say that would make sense to all of us. Phoebe sat frozen, eyes wet with fear like a rabbit hoping to outwit a fox. I stroked her cheek. Polly whimpered and rocked herself.

When the men picked up paddling again, it was with hard grace. I'm guessing it looked like a courtesy to the family – speeding the women and girls away – but I knew better. It was fury, plain and simple. Cudjoe and Abraham paddled fast and in perfect time for an impossibly long while. Rage gives a man power and rage long tamped down gives a man power he didn't know he had. Over and over, hard stroke by hard stroke, it seemed like the men were saying, "I'm here! I am here!" I sat straight and received their rage as best I could. A duty. An honor.

When we entered the Ashley, a moist breeze blew in from the Atlantic. I winced thinking about Cudjoe's back. It was a small hurt compared to all the rest, but still, I wished I could cool the cuts with salve. With a gentle touch. With love.

Gulls wheeled overhead, squawking about the coming storm. Ducks skidded down into the water along the reeds. We skirted overhanging buckleberry branches and startled off a wedge of egrets that flew off like the Good Lord's answer to death. But then we came in sight of four more poles, poking up like grotesque reeds. Someone groaned – was it Abraham or Miss Eliza? Polly swatted off the clutching female arms this time and stood and looked with naked determination. Now and again she turned fierce like this, and Mother and Sister knew not to interfere. Phoebe's lower lip quivered and I pulled her close. Down at our feet, the yarn from the game of Catch Cradle she'd been playing with Polly swayed in a small puddle on the bottom of the boat.

One spiked head drifted back and forth as if some spirit held on. The others were stiff, fear or surprise frozen on their faces. Which was worse – the secure heads, gaping at us with shriveling mouths, or the swaying head, defying its soullessness? There was no question in my mind but that buckra knew full well about our beliefs – about how an intact body was necessary for crossing over. Just this past summer we'd heard about a planter decapitating men who'd committed suicide, to keep others from doing the same. Punishment upon punishment was buckra's way.

When we arrived, Abraham tripped stepping onto the dock and very nearly fell into Mill Pond. Mistress and Miss Eliza scurried toward the carriage as if late for something. But Cudjoe kept his wits about him, perhaps holding up against the pain of his ripped back?

Oh no. No.

It hit me like a slap that Cudjoe'd already seen the heads. Just two days ago, he'd gone abroad looking for Mo. That meant not only had he seen these heads before but he'd studied them to make sure none of them wore his son's features.

October 1739

The Absence of Words
Eliza's Diary, Charles Town

Still no word from Father, though I wrote to him the very day after the rebellion. Why does he deny us? Even before the ink even dries on that thought, I worry. He could be suffering from a fit of illness or worse. Mother's exchange with Grandfather at Cross Winds recently made me think we'd keep trying to make sense of our changed world together, but ever since our return, she's been cloaked in a stony silence. Malaria or a pointed and personal withholding? It's always so hard to tell.

K-I-S-S
Eliza, Wappoo Plantation

"On the dock – please, please?" My sister's braids flounced as she hopped and twirled. It was before ten and pleasantly sunny, so I agreed, Phoebe and Maggie to join us. The slaves sat cross-legged, erect, and attentive. Polly, on the other hand, whipped off her shoes and stockings and dangled her feet in the water, flopping down onto her back. As I removed the slate and chalk from my basket, she tipped her chin up to ask, "Can I read upside down?"

Phoebe and Maggie eyed the basket with undisguised interest. They enjoyed the biscuits as much as the lesson, I'm sure.

"Nothing for you then, missy," I said to Polly. My sister waved one of her delicate hands in a gesture reminiscent of Mother. "The queen refuses today?" I jibed.

"The queen rules the creek, you mean." Polly's laughter opened a glad gate. Since the ninth, a pall lay over everything, including mundane exchanges with the slaves. What commonly passed between us was superficial, expediting, but now everything was layered with mistrust. Mother and I took to reviewing our day in whispers, evaluating any and all possibilities of menace. Was that look laced with anger? Was the burnt soufflé intentional? Where exactly were they all after sundown? Slaves and owners coexisted in a landscape marked by an unfathomably deep divide, but a lopsided one. They shuttled back and forth constantly, giving them broad, daily, and intimate access to us, but we knew so little about them. I continued to grapple with whether to continue to teach the slave girls to read.

Time had split in two, like a halved loaf of bread. There was before the rebellion and after the rebellion. As catastrophic as two back-to-back summers of pestilence had been and as difficult as it had been to say goodbye to my brothers and then to Father, those events were nothing compared to the revolt: to marauding, armed Africans, hell-bent on traveling to St. Augustine. Numbers varied. Some said there'd been sixty in the mob, others reported eighty or even one hundred. Nobody knew how many were still on the loose.

We munched on biscuits while neighbors and friends up and down the Pon Pon Road buried their dead. Some families had only partial, charred remains to inter, remains they'd been forced to scrape out of the ashes of still-smoking homesteads. I shuddered to think on it.

I opened the pages of *The Distress'd Orphan*. Polly immediately squirreled herself round. "No Bible today?"

"Enough of slaves rising up, I daresay." I said this before thinking, but truly – tales of Israelites rising up against their oppressors seemed ill-advised. Better to follow the plight of a young heiress and orphan whose step-uncle plotted to steal her fortune.

My sister claimed her seat by my side and dragged her finger along the words as I read so that the slaves, to the extent possible, could follow along. Phoebe was gaining vocabulary, but whether Maggie was, I couldn't tell, given her penchant for silence. I wondered if being mute perhaps made a person hungrier for the written word?

As the morning warmed, the novel's romance also heated up. Polly squealed when she came to the word "kiss" and spelled it out, as if to speak it aloud was forbidden. "K-I-S-S." They all giggled, even Maggie.

After another chapter, I sent the girls over to the spinning shed where they could help July, more or less. Instead of returning to the house, I went to the barn. Ah, Sir Raleigh! He met me with a juddering snort. I patted his soft, whiskered nose and wondered about Mo. We still had no word.

Making Seams
July, Wappoo Plantation

Mornings and just before tea make the best stitching times. You want good light. Noon glare get you bad and candlelight turn threading a needle into a headache. Outside better'n inside no matter the hour. You gotta see, especially when it come to knots. Hard to undo rascally knots blind and you can't be leaving 'em behind. Nobody likes rippin' out.

Sewing's bending-over work, so Melody and me sat on the gum stumps out back. Being low make reaching the sewing basket easier and don't give the cloth as much room to tug down and wrench a wobble in a seam. Cloth got a mind all its own.

The climbing vines overhead waggled, dimpling the light.

"Never dip the needle one time when you can dip three or four," I told Melody, tipping my work to show her. "Try a thimble if you want." I don't like thimbles none, they slow me down, but Melody gotta decide for herself. I nodded at the sweetgrass basket.

Old Sarah made the sewing basket a while back. She gettin' on in years, but those gnarled hands still plait the sweetgrass beautiful-like. Now the grass gone dark with age, but the sweet smell held on. Every time Maggie came round during stitching, she put it to her nose, like it was medicine. Maybe it was. She never spit out many words, but sniffing sweetgrass said something bold and sad.

Basket got a patch of felt stabbed up with needles, a darning mushroom, bobbins of worsted wool and cotton floss, scraps of calico, two pin cushions, and thimbles. Thimbles like to sink, so Melody dug down.

Last year, burning all the pox cloth and sewing for the boys' trip put a big burden on us, but it's less now. Today: a frock for Polly and a nightdress for Miss Eliza. On my lap: butter-soft brown calico. On Melody's lap: even softer cloth called cotton lawn, to be gussied up with frippery and lace – for sleeping, mind.

I was teachin' Melody how to top stitch along a placket, how to pull a single thread through a waist for gathering, and how to make buttonholes. She dropped the thimble back in the basket. She didn't like it neither.

They didn't teach Melody a lick of sewing on Barbados. She was making a nice stitch, pulling some, but not too much. Maybe she was taking to it. Good grief. You mean to tell me the girl can sing like a angel, catch babies, shows promise working stews, *and* got the knack for sewing? The littlest meanest part of me wanted to see a mess of puckers and knots, but she pulled that thread just right.

There was one thing Melody was real bad at. Keepin' her tongue. She wasn't even tryin' half the time. I seen her hooded eyes, heard her soft snorts. With Mistress in the room! No matter how good Melody get at catching babies, putting up dewberry jam, or putting in a collar, her eye rolling might get her kilt.

I used to hold steady real good, but ever since Benjie and James cross over, grief pecked at me hard.

Miss Eliza now, she liked a thimble. Speakin' of, where was she? Earlier, she talked up seam-felling. She was gonna show us how. I already got the knack, but when one or t'other get to teaching you, you best sit quiet and act all thankful. We'd been sewing for better 'n an hour and still no sign of her. I put both Polly's sleeves in. Should I fell the seams or wait?

"You doing good," I said. Melody smiled a tiny smile, but it go by quick. She was watching the thread. Keeping the stitches even. No knots.

Just then, a burst of harpsichord come out the window. Chunky chords, pretty but hectic. By now, we all knowed to listen to Miss Eliza's playing as a way to see into her. Was the song tinkling like a bird or stomping like heavy boots? Today come like a dazed chicken, stumbling this way and that. Miss Eliza clean forgot about sewing.

Later, during tea, she asked how it went, chipper, like the plan all along was to skip it. If I could borrow one thing from white women, it'd be that – the trick of acting like a mistake was meant. Owning it, just like they own everything else, as if forgetting was beneath them and only for idiots or slaves. You gotta wonder where they hid shame – in the harpsichord or maybe in the bookcase, in between them gold-stamped spines. They don't even seem to pause for mild regret.

A Fickle God
Eliza, at Pinckney's residence

Mary Bartlett tapped a blade of grass in the pond and dimpled the water's surface. The day was mostly clear with the kind of startling blue sky that only autumn can produce. A few puffs of white clouds, like confection. You'd think such a scene would cheer a person, but Mary was distracted and I was morose.

Out of the center of the Pinckney's reflecting pool rose Mercury, the keeper of the place. Silhouetted against the intense blue, his classic pose seemed elegant

– one sandaled foot lifted as if in fleet pursuit, one arm holding aloft the caduceus.

"What would he say, do you think?" Mary asked, following my gaze.

"Nothing. That's the problem, isn't it? Sometimes the gods say nothing, even in our dark times."

"Dark times?" Mary grunted. I looked sideways at her. My friend's proclivity for avoiding unpleasant matters surely hadn't managed to gloss over the events of September so soon, a mere month later? Life had charged forward like a wayward horse since then, it's true, but in some other essential way, it had barely moved, as if we were ants suspended in a chunk of amber. Maybe, in fact, we resembled the statue of the fleet-footed god, poised to dash into our futures but stuck suddenly in a stony stasis – all promise and swift attainment one moment, stymied and full of dread the next.

"Now they're talking about cancelling the Gala altogether," Mary said, standing and flinging away the blade of grass. It landed noiselessly on the pool's surface. The Gala had been delayed once already.

"I can't say I'm disappointed," I told her. "Who feels like dancing?"

"I do!" As if eager to demonstrate her readiness for the quadrille, Mary paced along the water's edge. "We've had our funerals and our overly long sermons. Most of the rebels are dead. Shouldn't we now have our music?"

Overly long sermons – oh dear. When I acquiesced to Mother's plan for this visit, I forgot about the dissonance that sometimes dwelt between Mary and me. Given the recent tragedies in the Lowcountry, my friend's brisk desire to return to life as usual struck me as very nearly bizarre. Such a view certainly wasn't going to cheer me up, as Mother intended. Instead, I sat in a stunned and lonely judgment of my friend.

Rather than disagree, I asked, "What gown will you wear?"

Mary clapped like a child about to be given a bag of sweets. "Auntie Elizabeth thinks that at my advanced age – well, she didn't use those words, but I'm over twenty now – that I ought to wear something mature. I've chosen a brocaded pale blue silk, with flowers embroidered in a tumble down from the waist. Auntie thinks it flatters my skin. It's at the dressmaker's or I'd show you. No tassels. No ruching. No puffed trim." She paused and sighed. "My mother's pearl choker would be the most divine accessory…"

With this lament, Mary plunked herself back down and my friend came into sharp focus. Foolish, selfish me! Here I'd been missing Father, not pausing to remember that Mary's father was long dead and her mother half a world away in London.

"Oh, but I have pearls and you shall wear them!" I said with rather more enthusiasm than I felt, but what harm? It wasn't likely there'd be a Gala this fall. They were saying the last of the rebels had been rounded up and executed, but many suspected that the Assembly overstated their successes to calm the public. Services for the victims had concluded, but mourning relatives were saddled with the business of property transfers or lengthy restorations. Headstones were being carved, Bibles passed down. I thought of Colonel Hext's wife and daughter, buried just three weeks ago.

A chill came in off the river and the sky bronzed orange. The shadows flattened the snake-twined staff into calligraphy and soon Mercury's dark shape would meld into the night.

On the Banks of the Stono
Eliza

The next day slats of rain striped the windows and I welcomed the dark, cocooning atmosphere. How it suited my unshakeable melancholy! I even would've welcomed one of Mother's morose moods, but leave it to her to show up at breakfast peppy, as if in defiance of my need. She'd had correspondence from her old friends the Royalls!

Mother waved the letter. "All the way from Massachusetts!" Reading page two, she chirped, "They've built a folly! Oh, and Eliza, guess who graces its top? Guess!" I refused. "Why, Mercury!" She paused as if for applause. "Isn't that the god Pinckneys have in their pool? What are the chances? Course both are such good families."

Mother kept musing aloud: What must it be like to live with such bitter cold, how nice to live where slaves don't run amok, and however do they make money without cotton, tobacco, or rice? After a pause, she crowed, "Penelope's being courted. By Henry Vassall, no less! Do you remember him?"

"Henry Gambling Vassall of Jamaica?" Mother tensed and rattled off notions that even she didn't believe: how marriage settles a man, how marriage alchemizes a weak character.

By midmorning, I needed air so headed out to the barn and saddled up Sir Raleigh. With a cluck-cluck, my ever-devoted roan and I headed west. We would follow Wappoo Creek for its length toward the now infamous Stono River. It was not, perhaps, the best idea to ride out alone that day and maybe an even worse idea to head toward the Stono, but I was determined to go where I pleased.

I kicked Sir Raleigh into a smooth canter and then a thundering gallop. What pleasure! We splashed through puddles, I ducked low-hanging branches, wind stirring both mane and frock, mud flecking Sir Raleigh's hocks and the hem of my pantaloons. It wasn't until the path curved slightly away from the creek that we slowed.

A splash about bowshot's distance ahead caused Sir Raleigh to stiffen, me too. It was likely an alligator, but given September ninth, I had to allow for other possibilities. The rebels wouldn't linger here, so close to the place of their fellows' demise, not with patrollers scouring the landscape night and day would they? I could never pretend to understand how or if Negroes organized their thinking, but surely the need for forward motion would be obvious? Heading south at all costs?

Sir Raleigh gave another snort and a prancing sidestep. I scanned the water for the telltale bump of eyes and found none. A little further on, we passed one of the ditches that the now disbanded drainage crews had started. I suspected most of those slaves were dead. Was Mo?

I thought about the dead. Some twenty rebels had been cornered near the Jacksonboro Ferry and killed on the spot just hours after the rampage began. It was said they sang, marched, and waved their banners until the very last. Some untold number escaped. A week-long, massive manhunt caught a passel thirty miles away and killed them. How many dead was that? There were conflicting accounts.

Along our southern border, a militia currently occupied Purrysburg. Scout boats cruised the barrier islands. Native trackers were hired and sent into the scrub, both west and south. The *Gazette* published the bounties: forty pounds for a live black male, twenty for a scalp, as long as it included both ears. No wonder the patrollers exhibited such a frothy persistence.

We still had no word on Mo, not a single hint of his fate. Perhaps we would never know what happened to him. If he'd run with the horde, had he done so willingly? If not, why hadn't he returned? In hindsight, I should have paid the Riverway Act fine. The penalty was inconsequential compared to the replacement cost of a healthy male, a cost we couldn't afford without securing more credit. Father and his mortgages!

At the creek's intersection with the Stono River, I reined Sir Raleigh to a stop and admired the broad sweep of the river. Completely unbidden, I shouted, "Take it back! Dear God, take it all back!" Before I could stop myself, I leaned into my horse's neck and sobbed. Sir Raleigh stepped in place and turned toward me as if to offer solace.

Just as suddenly as the tears o'ertook me, they were done. What powerful relief! The Stono River — witness to rebellion, a carrier of blood, a home for my grief.

Cricket Lullaby
Mo, on the way to Wappoo

For two long weeks, I walked away from Wappoo, away from the cinders of rebellion. A lone black man, no slip, blood on my tunic, I was a walking death sentence. Even if I made it back, Overseer might kill me quick in a temper or maim me bit by bit, never once strayin' from the law. The loyalty of my return would count about as much as a candle in a hurricane.

I ate hickory nuts, wild plums, and clumps of sorrel. Memory flared and pinched. Houses aflame against the night sky, hoots of celebration mixed with the screams of the dying, fury meeting panic. I'll never forget the feel of Gibbs's head in my hands, or the sorry look of surprise on Bathhurst's face. If every hard listen to the wind paid off, if I survived hunger, if no rash or cut go to pus, if the snakes, boars, panthers, and alligators let me be, I would offer the gods whatever Titus say to. But if I was to die, the memory of Gibbs's head, fear-frozen and bug-eyed, would make it almost worthwhile.

Almost. I spat into the grasses and called up another face: Binah's. How many times did thinking on her deliver strength? The idea of running a finger across her eyebrows and then her top lip kept me moving, kept me smart. When muscles ached in torment, I imagined how soft and warm her breasts would feel when at last I hugged her. How small her shoulders! I recalled the bold roundness of her knees. That missing tooth. The thought of her was keeping me alive. How could I die without kissing her?

I kept up my tricks, never traveling for long, always listening hard, padding in and out of water, smearing pitch on heels and ribs whenever I passed a slash pine. At any sound, I dropped, tucked small, slowed my breath. Footstep or wind? If six, eight breaths passed, I knew it wasn't dogs because a pack comes at you in swift howling rackets. But Chickasaw or Catawba? Harder to tell. The trackers crossed the land like ghosts.

Eventually I headed back, and when I came to what I thought was the Stono River, I knew I was near home. I pulled soggy leaves out from between my toes. A wincing hurt. My feet were battered. My heart sore.

The marshes rattled. Shoulders tensed. Couldn't tell what it was, so I crawled under a dewberry bush and pulled sticks over me and prayed no reptiles found me. After about an hour, I fell fast asleep. That's how tired I was. The thundering gallop of a horse woke me up, I don't know how much later. I rolled over in panic. Were there dogs? More horses?

No. Just one horse. No dogs.

I listened hard. Panting. A voice called out, "Take it back! Dear God, take it all back!" Miss Eliza?

I needed to know if she was alone, but getting a better look was risky. I heard a gasp – was she crying? Seemed unlikely – word on the street was that Miss holds herself tight – but she was, she was crying and hard. Had the rebels come back east before going south and struck dead her sister or mother or burned their house or barn? And was she armed? Before September, surely not, but now? She might have a pepper pot inside her jacket.

She was alone. I was sure of it, but I couldn't show myself. She'd take a scare. No way I was gonna let a strange coincidence ruin everything. Wappoo couldn't be far now. For the first time in weeks, I felt a little luck come to my side. Maybe it'd been there all along. Maybe the Ancestors were moving me along. Maybe Binah and our unborn children were keeping me safe. Maybe it was Binah herself, putting the luck of love on me.

And sure enough, after Eliza wheeled off, I followed the river path and was back to the street in no time at all. First thing I see as I rounded the last cabin – Binah. Orange clouds gathered round her head like she was holy. I stumbled. She heard. Turned and gasped. Ran to me. I fell down on my knees and grabbed her apron. She rubbed my head, then knelt down too and hugged my rail-thin body. I couldn't die now – I had somebody to live for.

Others came round, looking glad, but nervous too, going foot to foot. Where was Overseer? Somebody behind me – July? – pulled off my bloodied tunic and slid another one over my head. Abraham handed me a bowl, but more'n food, I wanted to see my father. Where was he?

I ate and Binah kept a hand on my shoulder like she wasn't about to let me get away again. Saffron gave a shy smile. I wolfed down the hominy, July cautioning to go slow. Hercules piped up, "Your daddy's in town. Been looking up and down every river for you, some of 'em twice."

Abraham added, "Never did give up. Not one time." Herc and Abe exchanged nervous looks, so now I knew my daddy's been punished. Beat close to death most like. I called up the memory of Gibbs's head as a tonic.

July come up from the crick with a bucket of water, and she and Binah put my feet in, tender as can be. Ooh, it stung good and hard! Melody fetched Old Sarah's healing sack. They was gonna clean me up. I didn't know Melody'd done the same for my father.

I near to passed out, relief at being back, being alive, being cared for, the water cooling my feet. I made it. Binah held my hand. She was the sun. She was the moon.

I got foggy tired. Abraham picked up my bloodstained osnaburg and laid it on the embers, with two hickory sticks placed on top. Overseer Mac'd show up soon enough, and there was no reason for him to see blood stains from a white man.

The crickets kicked up a lullaby. I couldn't keep my eyes open. No matter how bad I wanted to drink up Binah's face – every crease, curve, and dimple, that gap between her teeth – no matter how fine a sight the fire and the fat oak, grey-green moss swaying, I couldn't keep my eyes open. I was home. Or, at least I was as much home as anywhere. Leaning into Binah's side, I fell fast asleep, feet still soaking in the bucket.

Shoulder to Shoulder
Eliza, Wappoo Plantation

Mother and I waited anxiously for word from Father. Pestilence, we knew, was making its ugly rounds throughout the West Indies. Barracks like sick bays. Soldiers felled by yellow fever or the bloody flux instead of battle, weakening both infantry numbers and morale. Meanwhile the Prime Minister's formal declaration of war with Spain was imminent.

Finally, towards the end of the month, a proper missive arrived – six pages! Cudjoe brought it directly to us before unloading the pettiauger. Kind man. I slammed shut the Greek tale I was reading and arranged myself on the sofa next to Mother. Her fingers shook opening the envelope.

"Should we wait for some tea?" she asked. Oh dear, no. I would let her dictate the pace of reading but could not abide the delay. And so, rather than take turns, we read simultaneously, shoulder to shoulder.

Much of his reporting, we already knew. Tensions with Spain escalating. Severely limited access to lucrative southern markets for British merchants, making the Spanish-English treaty signed ten years ago more and more unpopular. Situation volatile, with Spain's right to board British ships particularly destabilizing.

Britain had set its sights on Spain's four strategic ports: Havana, Vera Cruz, Porto Bello, and Cartagena. Our strategy was to bring the full might of the British military to bear, with Havana as a top priority because of its deep-water harbor. The other three ports were important as critical gateways to trade in South America.

Father detailed the formation of a mighty British assemblage. Troops even coming from New York! All the island outposts would cooperate. The idea of battle, though politically inevitable, caused both Mother and me to shudder.

Father did not mention the threat of local slave uprisings. Jamaica had suffered a large one, and renegade maroon communities on both that island and Domingo grew by the year, some of them operating efficient black markets, including arms trading. In this one way, the French, British, and Spanish were very much united, sharing a constant anxiety about black revolution.

Of Charles Town's recent peril, there was no mention, unless I counted a sardonic comment that perhaps our safety would have been better preserved on Antigua, after all – a remark he'd made in his previous letter. Was that humor? A sidelong apology?

Mother folded the sheets carefully and slid them back into the envelope. In silence, we continued to sit side by side. "If only he weren't so far away," she said at last.

November 1739

Cloth for Maggie
Saffron, Wappoo Plantation

The day my bloods came, Mama took me to the river and blessed me with palm oil. Holy quiet. Sweet river. How Mama's thumb felt on my forehead. I hear her voice even now. "You're a woman now." What can I give Maggie when her time comes?

If it comes while she's picking peas for street supper, that'd be fine. Woman-blood meeting earth-body. If a coin of blood hits the floor of Summer Kitchen, we would all be there to act as witness, also fine. But what if her bloods came in the parlor while holding out a plate of jumbles for Polly? Their precious rugs. Their polished floors. Such misery to think on.

Time to save up scraps so July could make Maggie a second pair of drawers and some cloth strips.

Bow and Arrows
Maggie, in the Woods near Wappoo

I been learning. July showed how to gut a fish. Old Sarah showed how to mix the baby-spoiling paste and how to coil a fanner basket. Mama's showings were not the same as the others. She showed me where azure dwells and how to name the moon. Her showing was more like sharing breath and mind, so it counted both more and also less.

Indian Peter's teaching came with tools, wood and metal, and was special since the skills go toward hunger and survival. All summer past, he shared hunting tricks. He made me a bow and a batch of arrows. I'm guessing he tended me out of love for Mama, his sheltering care generous and wide enough for both of us.

I loved him, oh, I did. But I loved what he been giving me even more – power.

Even though I'm growing fast, my bow's smaller than his. My arrows go in a cloth tube, his slide into leather. But my knees bent as good as his, and my fist drew the arrow and string back as good as his. Aiming will take more doing yet, for sure. Good lord, his eye! How he struck where he wanna strike just about every time. But me? Some Sundays it look like I'm hunting slash pines, turning trees into porcupines.

So it was cause for a little hoot and holler when I felled my first bird – a fat turkey. I shot him – or her, Indian Peter says – right in the breast. She went down hard and seemed dead to me when I knelt by, but Indian Peter showed how to wring the neck for mercy, just in case. I bowed my head when he bowed his head. We gave thanks.

I knew I gotta bring a word back to mama – *wring*. Wring hands. Wring cloth. Wring a neck for mercy. Maybe she could hear it even now, going across the fields to her thoughts? Or, for all I know, she was wringing laundry right now and sent the word to me. I'm trying to remember if Indian Peter said *wring*. Did he?

He let me carry the bird back to the street. It hung over my shoulder, a prize. I didn't know what I was lookin' forward to more – roast fowl for dinner or all those feathers for my collection.

December 1739

Indigo Seeds
Eliza, Wappoo Plantation

Mother had just risen from a nap and I was practicing etudes when a lone horse approached.

"Are we expecting anyone?" Mother asked.

I didn't think so, but there came Charles Pinckney atop a beautiful shining roan, alone. Mother unlocked the liquor cabinet and rang for July. We would have sherry and a tray of savories. "And slice up some of your pound cake too, July – is there any left?" Happily, there was.

What a genial afternoon ensued. We delighted in Charles's company for all the usual reasons – his charm and intellect, his warmth – but also, I think, because Mother and I both missed Father so very much. After queries regarding his wife and niece were answered, Charles supplied us with news from the peninsula, starting with the status of the Slave Code revisions.

"It's being expedited. Ought to pass early next year." The new measures covered matters of punishment and restitution, as well as many of the more ordinary conditions of slave life. Some freedoms currently enjoyed by Negroes – gardening, the right to carry money, literacy – would be outlawed, for we now knew that small freedoms could lead to murderous liberties. To impose greater control on their movements, the law strengthened the chit system, requiring that each travel slip specify destination as well as the time allotted. Very little wiggle room. Hunting might still be permitted during the week, but there was going to be a complete ban on weapon-use from Saturday night 'til Monday morning. Period.

"Long overdue," he said in conclusion, perhaps sensing Mother's fatigue.

I hopped out of my chair. "Would you like to see the indigo seeds we've harvested for next year?" I asked. Of course, of course. I disappeared down the back hall to retrieve them, but not before hearing Charles say to Mother, "So, how is Eliza – our Little Visionary?"

The words clobbered me. *Our Little Visionary?* Mother's response was muted, but her laughter rang out clearly enough. I stood still and listened.

"She needs to come in to Charles Town or Belmont more often. Mary'd love it, as would Elizabeth. I've promised Mary and Eliza an afternoon at the horse races. It's quite a spectacle — lads aglow with speed, pounding two miles down the Neck on beautiful mounts. We're talking March or April?" July entered the back door with the pound cake. I quickly bent over to fiddle with my shoe, wondering how I'd re-enter the parlor with my head up. Turns out I needn't have worried, for when I returned, Charles was mid-sentence about the fugitive rebels.

"Four, maybe five. Two might've made it to St. Augustine, but no one knows for sure. The slaves certainly wish it to be so." This confirmed Mac's recent reports. I sat down and looked intent, though the small sacks of seeds shook in my hands a little.

"What about Georgia, then?" I asked. "With Oglethorpe refusing to legalize slavery, why don't the runaways just decamp there?" A Little Visionary with political speculations.

"Too conspicuous," he answered, then asked to see the seeds with what seemed genuine interest. After a decent interval, he reached into his satchel. "I brought a book for you — *City of God*, by St. Augustine — the saint, not the city. I apologize in advance for his views on slavery." I scanned his face for signs of condescension and found none. "Our renegade saint believed slavery a sin. But his views on faith are well worth the read. Like you, he saw rationality as a proper approach to God."

Such keen observation and kindness rendered me speechless. Mother barked out a laugh and asked, "Did the Spanish know his views on slavery, I wonder, when they named their town?"

And suddenly the visit was over. With a bow and a broad smile, he was off. I turned the book over in my hands. I would begin that evening.

Part IV

December 1740

The Nature of My Affection
Eliza, Wappoo Plantation

The house was sure to sparkle for the party, but would I? It'd been a fairly solitary year since the rebellion, many letters written and received but few visits. Even though four whole seasons have passed since the awful night of the insurrection, in some ways it felt as though time had stood still. Epidemics didn't help.

I suppose it was a sign of normalcy that I inventoried who among our guests I most wished to impress. The Middletons. The Pinckneys. Always them. What if Charles Pinckney teased me in his avuncular tone and called me "Our Little Visionary" in front of others? I wondered if his good opinion mattered so much because of Father's absence or if it was something about the man himself.

Though the river route was shorter both by distance and time, the Pinckneys planned to come mostly by carriage. These days Elizabeth can be sickened by water travel, and naturally her comfort trumped convenience. We were pleased that they're making the effort at all, given how intermittently feeble her health. We put July on notice, with a stole, foot warmers, and herbal tinctures at the ready.

Yesterday, attentive hands damp-mopped up clusters of wind-blown dust, giving the pine floors a warm luster. Silver polished to a faultless gleam, rugs beaten, windows freed of smudges, and a fir tree brought in and decorated with candles. Lovely! We'd planned an elegant meal – molasses-glazed ham, cornmeal-encrusted turkey cutlets, and Madagascar rice flavored with thyme. In the Continental style, we'd finish with dressed greens, though Lowcountry style – sorrel, wild scallions, roasted benne and pecans. It was July's pound cake for the sweet course, a raspberry compote on top. The cuisine was sure to satisfy, perhaps even impress.

The Rutledges would be here, of course, and the Draytons, father and son, the Manigaults, Izards, and Middletons, including the elder Middletons, William and Margaret, from Crowfield Plantation. The Governor planned to grace us with his presence, bringing his wife and one of his daughters, Charlotte. Many of our neighbors were coming as well – Mr. Deveaux and his wife, the Woodwards along with Mary and Pastor Huston, the Holmans, and Willard Tilton.

I took a final look in the glass, hoping my calico gown wasn't too summery with its blush pink background and chocolate-brown floral repeats. Perhaps the occasion called for more formal attire, like my cherry-colored brocade or even the silk moiré. No. This was fine. My best lace tucker would dress it up, as would the pearl drop earrings.

"Saffron!" She came in, grabbed my silver-handled brush, and tended to my hair and scalp with hard strokes. An efficiency not without its pleasures.

"Top or side, Miss?"

I tapped my crown nervously. "Why am I so agitated?" I asked the air, but to my surprise, Saffron answered.

"Why, it's the company, the Pinckneys and all." She said this matter-of-factly and I froze. What had Saffron noticed and when? She instantly recognized her error and tried to distract me with patter. "And you know how Mistress likes everything perfect. Her nerves could give a stone the jitters." Saffron removed one hairpin after another from her mouth and worked swiftly. "Nothing to worry on, Miss Eliza – the house spotless, ham roasting up good, and July's cake batter the best ever. You know that cake takes top prize in all the Lowcountry." The next and last hairpin scraped a little too hard against my scalp.

I wondered if Saffron spoke about the pound cake by reputation or whether she had actually sampled it. More to the moment, I couldn't help but think that the slight wounding by hairpin was intentional.

"We want the evening to be special for all our guests, not just the most esteemed," I said.

Saffron nodded and fetched my silk pumps out of the armoire. I should have let the topic lie, but like a child with a scab, I picked at it. I would die a thousand deaths if any of our guests suspected that I carried an extra reserve of esteem for Mr. Pinckney, especially he himself or his wife. "Charles Pinckney's often been our guest," I ventured.

How strange if Saffron had come to a clear conclusion about the nature of my affection for the man before anyone else did. I couldn't resist knowing the source of her clarity, so asked her.

"You pace before visits," she said with reluctance. "Your face lights up talking with him." She plucked a blossom out of the vase on my vanity and stuck it into my coif. "There!" She was clearly satisfied with her efforts and wanted, no doubt, to end the conversation. Shaken, I left the room.

Mother waylaid me in the upstairs vestibule. "You're wearing *that*? Oh no, it simply won't do," she said, and herded me back into my bedroom. "John is already here." She referred to John Drayton, her latest idea of a suitable mate. At the armoire, Mother slapped through the hangers and selected one of the frocks I'd rejected earlier.

"Too fancy," I pouted. With my eighteenth birthday mere days away, surely I was old enough to pick out my own frock. Saffron appeared and bustled about, straightening accessories on the vanity, tugging the comforter tighter at the bed corners.

"Too fancy, my foot. You take that summer calico off this instant." Mother spoke as if meeting resistance, but I was already reaching for the uppermost buttons along my neck. Saffron quickly stepped in.

"Get the panniers and the stomacher," Mother directed Saffron, and took over undoing the buttons. The calico dropped to the floor, and Saffron handed me first the wire apparatus for my hips and then the quilted underskirt. Like a lion tamer, Mother draped the evergreen satin Robe à la Française over my head and tugged it into place. Then my mother stepped over to the window and looking out, rattled on, "Suzanne's been gone —"

I finished her sentence, word for word, having heard it before. "For well over a year now."

"Do not sass me, Eliza!" Mother snapped, clearing wanting to say more. Instead she turned and gave me a swift once over, grunted, and pronounced me ready for a Christmas party.

We descended the stairs to greet the early arrivals. I wasn't sure how festive an occasion this would be with Mother's hawk eye following my every movement. With a mild shock, I realized I'd prefer to be under the watchful eye of Saffron than that of my mother. Saffron observed the actual me. What irony! That my slave possessed a keener sense of me than my own mother afforded no pleasure.

Soon the parlor clattered and hummed with merriment as more and more people arrived. A fire blazed, adding cheer. The slender red candles that Melody had clipped to the tree made pretty flickers. There was the delightful aroma of pine. John Drayton stood next to the tree conversing with Mary Huston who caught my eye and smiled. Pastor Huston was across the room talking religion with one of the Middleton sons.

I accepted a glass of punch and then another. Surely, this was one way to manage.

Over by the harpsichord, Thomas Drayton stood next to his wife and regaled the elder Middletons. A more charming group would be hard to imagine. Near the hearth, Charles and Elizabeth chatted with Mother. Elizabeth looked reasonably well. Charles raised his glass to me with a broad smile. Mother did so as well, with a slight nod in John Drayton's direction.

I defied her and joined the Cornwalls instead. Near neighbors of the Pinckneys on the Cooper River, they had just given my sister a gift. Polly looked particularly angelic, dressed in vermillion silk, with evergreen satin ribbons plaited into her hair. Adorned like a gift herself! At the age of seven, Polly still exhibited the quivering excitement of children at Christmas. She pulled off the wrapping in a flurry.

"Liza, look! Look!" She held up a jointed wooden duck. A pull string hung down.

"Gumwood," announced Mr. Cornwall proudly. Pinned together with copper brads, the duck raised and lowered its wings when pulled along by the string. Polly did so now with glee, people clearing out of the way. Guests smiled down at her shining braids and the cleverly flapping bird.

"Thank you, thank you, thank you!" Polly sang over her shoulder as she sailed out onto the verandah. Mary Huston waved me over. I steeled myself. It wasn't as if John Drayton repelled or bored me, for he was as well-educated and distinguished a gentleman as one could hope to meet. Rather he was tainted by the oppressive matrimonial interests of my mother. If only she knew how counterproductive she was.

I asked after the progress of construction. The skeleton of Drayton Hall, we learned, was now visible from the river. Paneling being carved as we spoke. Flankers framed. Soon the Boone Hall brick would arrive to supplement brick that had been recovered on site. John recounted the designs for the plaster ceilings with some particularity.

"Here's to our hostess!" he suddenly announced, raising his glass, but his glance slid past me and landed on Charlotte Bull. Ah! The younger daughter of the Governor, a pretty study in calico – pine green and red calico, but still. Off he went to her. Two years my senior, Charlotte was about as attractive as I, which is to say, no great beauty. The fact that John seemed to have set his sights on her put me suddenly and wholeheartedly into holiday cheer. I gave Mother a nod, then looked at Charlotte and John with raised eyebrow. Now I could comfortably join her and the Pinckneys. I would thank Charles for the recent loan of *The City of God*.

"Why, it's our Little Visionary!" Charles said jovially. Oh, dear.

"Oh, 'tis I, through and through." No matter, conversation quickly turned to the recent conflagration now dubbed "the Great Fire." We had briefly considered cancelling our party on its account, but Mother eventually decided that an elegant night of entertainment could provide much needed merriment.

"Mary Bedon and her three children took house where Mr. Carr lately kept his tavern," Charles informed us, "so they're sheltered, but there's no end to the struggle. A basket for charity in the vestry at St. Philip's has been refilled many times, but the need remains great."

Hearing discussion of the fire, a Mr. Daniel from Wiltown joined our circle. "Smell the sleeve! Smell it, go on." He held his forearm up to Mother's face. She sniffed with a delicate reluctance. "Cost me a pittance," he boasted, "Hill & Geurard's fire sale. There was a mild acrid odor initially but after time on the line, nothing." Mother's face suggested otherwise.

"Henry Williams' house on the bay is gone," Elizabeth lamented.

"A pity that," her husband added.

There'd been no evidence of arson, but many were convinced it was yet another act of treachery by one or more malcontented slaves. At least three suspicious fires flared every season in the Lowcountry, each generally believed to be ignited by black hands. And of course, last September's slave revolt was still very much on all our minds.

"They gave Elliott's Negro his freedom, you know," Charles said, referring to the slave who had hidden his master and his master's two daughters under the floorboards of their summer kitchen the night of the rebellion. "A proclamation of the Governor."

Elizabeth laughed a silvery laugh. "A pair of breeches, shirt, hat, stockings, and a pair of shoes were awarded as well." It was as though one of the couple submitted the first half of an idea, the other the second. So simpatico!

Though it was old news, Mother pursued the topic. "And what will he do, this free black? Wouldn't he be better off a slave?" But no. The shortage of white labor, particularly for nautical businesses, meant there was work aplenty for an able-bodied man, no matter the color of his skin. He would learn a trade.

"He's said to be living up on the Neck and working on the wharves. Apprentice to a wainwright, I believe," Charles said.

Mother: "Oh? And the other apprentices will stand for it?" Mr. Pinckney remained silent on that point. "They say that at least one and possibly three of them made it," Mother added in a lowered voice.

"Oh, I've come to view that as myth," Charles rejoined. "You know how slaves cling to their notions. Of course they want to believe some made it. St. Augustine, the shining city!"

I wandered off. While exchanging pleasantries with a couple from Goose Creek, the longest night of the year laid its claim, turning the windows a glossy ebon. Laughter rang out. Crystal sparkled. The windows reflected the candles, at times giving a false impression of an exterior blaze. I caught a number of guests sniffing the air. Across the room, Mary Huston was gazing at the reflected candles with a frightened look.

Eventually, our elaborate dinner was served, enjoyed, and cleared. A success by any measure. Political views were aired, silly jokes shared, flirtatious glances registered. The ham was declared tasty, the pound cake delicious. By the time port was being poured, we were all standing again, conversations going and laughter erupting, but the party's swelling peak had passed and its inevitable arc to closure had begun.

Before long, guests went off into the night. We stood on the verandah, saying our farewells and hollering out additional Christmas cheer. Slaves carrying lamps and paddles and poles appeared as if out of nowhere, following or leading their owners to the dock or the barn. For the first time since the rebellion, I felt the long sway of optimism. As the final "g'nights" were yodeled across the air, I felt wed to this land, fully and without reserve. Perhaps, like a slave with two years' experience, I was now "seasoned." Or maybe it was the third glass of punch. Mother slipped her arm into mine and declared the party a success.

Jump the Broom
Saffron, Wappoo Plantation

Queen shone out glad, hair coiled up by July. Binah wore a necklace of cockle shells that Maggie collected and knotted together so that when she shook her shoulders, the shells jingle-jangled, calling out, "Here I come and ain't I beautiful?" Yes. Yes, you are!

We stood at the end of the garden huddled for warmth, waiting on the groom. The inky night sky stretched and spangled like a poem to love. Couldn't see nary a plank of Porch House and that was on purpose. Hear tell, some buckra did up slave weddings big, loading tables with casseroles and pies and hiring ministers to say the words. We didn't need any of that, or want it.

I caught Indian Peter's eye and smiled.

At last Mo came through the gate wearing a cape made of palm fronds. He didn't need anything extra to make him fine, but the cape sure made him look royal. Have you ever noticed how love turns a face and a body beautiful?

And hate does the opposite.

When Mo come back last fall, he seemed a shadow of hisself. Overseer put a bad beating on him, took two weeks to heal. And of course living on sorrel and sour plums made him rail thin with ashy knees and elbows. Well – love's got reviving power. Nothing drawn in about him tonight.

July laid out two brooms, an old one from our cabin and a new one made special for the day. Mo and Binah stood back-to-back outside the brooms, he on the outside of the old broom, she outside the new.

Titus spoke solemn words at first. "Ancestors! Orisha! Spirit guides! We call on you!" Arms high. A singing voice. But after a few more blessings, he looked at Mo and Binah and talked more like a father. "You about to leave old Mo and old Binah behind. You about to pledge to a new body – a third, because marriage makes a third body. Slavery gonna deny each body – well you know – not just food and rest and dignity and the futures of your children. More. They always find ways to take more. But today, we turn our backs on wickedness. Today, we celebrate you."

Before I could wipe away my tears, Mo and Binah jumped backwards lickety-split – hop, hop – into the space between the brooms. Oh, there was clapping and hollering. Maggie squeezed my hand and a wash of joy spread over her.

"You married now," Titus said with a big smile. July leaned over and picked up the new broom and handed it to Binah – the first married gift.

"For health and joy," she said.

Was anybody gonna point out how Binah's hop landed between the brooms first and how that made her the boss?

Finding love always came like a star falling in the lap, but for Mo it was specially blessed seeing as how after the uprising, Miss Eliza canceled the rope work. No slave of hers was leaving the plantation for training, no how. The dream of freedom papers withered away. One of many things killed in the rebellion. Turns out, Binah didn't want Mo out of her sights anyhow.

Quash handed Mo a bowl he'd rounded out of black walnut. Hercules took off his crab claw necklace and laid it over Binah's head, and Old Sarah did the same with hers for Mo. Maggie stepped close, all serious and true and gave each of them three perfect polished grains of rice.

Maggie said, "Put 'em in your pocket for long life."

Herc pulled out a pair of spoons and rattled out a tippety-tappety pattern. Where'd he come by those? We all clapped and joined in, and whispers of choruses sung by the Ancestors wove through the air.

Covering the Tallow
July, Wappoo Plantation

Cudjoe dead. Drowned.

How plain a day it go to start! So many candles melted down at Mistress's party, that we was outside the spinning shed rendering tallow for new ones and also for soap. Maggie and Noah off gathering bayberries 'cause Mistress like the smell. Course she do – bayberries burn sweet and tallow burn rank. Moses played with a new litter of orange kitties in the corner.

In the time it took for the tallow fire embers to burn bright, the wind started hassling the treetops, making leaves flip and flash. Rain coming. Every now and again, a howl sweep across the land. Then spooky moans. My skin pimpled in fear. I should've known death was making the rounds.

Coming from Porch House, Melody almost stepped on one of them red and yellow snakes. "A storm coming," she shrieked, hopping away. "A storm coming!" Well, it didn't take no snake to tell that, now did it? The grey clouds puffed and raced, a hurrying doom. It weren't time to strain the tallow yet, and now it looked like I was gonna lose a whole morning of boiling. We'd have to start all over tomorrow, and sometimes a second boil don't render right.

It wasn't cold for December, but since a big storm about to deliver, I told Melody to call the children in. She pulled up her skirt and ran. I put out the fire, embers hissing in disappointment. With my apron folded round my hand three times, I brung the pot into the spinning shed. Melody rushed in, Noah on her hip and Maggie by her side, the basket of bayberries half full. She set the basket down one minute and knocked it over the next. She was panting. Maggie looked scared through and through.

Melody plunked down on a bale, and Moses come over from the kittens to climb on her lap. Noah snuggled in too, eyes big with fear. A loud rumble of thunder growled overhead, and the wind came up fierce, moaning, howling. Then, just as if a gate opened up, the rain came slashing down, hammering so thick you couldn't see the horse fence across the yard. It was deafening. The palmettos near the shed were dipping and swinging like crazy ladies with fans.

Nothing you can do then but witness. A mighty storm demands it. We was struck dumb, afraid one minute and full of awe the next. Lightning crackled and thunder roared just as if one god was chasin' another across the sky. The goat pen turned into a pond. Loud streams poured off the corners of the shed.

A storm delivered flooding and downed trees to everybody the same – to the red-skinned, coffee-skinned, cherry, black, freckled, high yellow. The sky don't care who you are or what you own or who you own. For that reason alone, I'll take a killer storm over a cagey buckra any day.

Cudjoe and Caesar was gone a whole day now, meant to come back ferrying rice barrels from another plantation south of here. If they was on the water when the storm heaved up, would they find a place to pull in and wait it out? Rice barrels make a boat top-heavy, and they carried a big load – eighteen or twenty barrels, we heard.

"River rising," Melody said. Was she thinking on Cudjoe too?

I nodded. "Water'll be collecting deadfall – whole trees even."

A door slammed at Porch House, and there was Polly standing out in the yard like a crazy angel, getting soaked. Phoebe come round quick after and dashed into the shed.

"Polly, come in. Come in!" she pleaded, but Polly froze, and her face crumpled as if it was melting in the rain.

"Get in here now, Polly!" I hollered, but she just stood there, arms straight down, hands balled into fists, eyes squeezed shut.

Melody tried. "Get in here, child!" Polly kept standing out there, crying. She and the heavens seemed to be agreeing on something.

A confirmin' fear shot through me. For a long minute, I done hoped she was just cryin' for the moss coming off the live oaks, but then I knew: the girl was crying for somebody.

The wind tore up a small palmetto and sent it cartwheeling across the yard. Should I fetch the girl in or leave her be? Polly looked fierce, and the way she give over to the storm made it seem as if she was the safe one, not us.

Even at five, Noah was a regular little ox. He jumped off his mother's lap, stepped out into the squall, grabbed Polly's hand, and brung her in. Polly fell in a heap next to Phoebe, who put her arms around her until the storm finally rolled off, taking its noisy bother north.

At supper, Overseer stomped up the stairs and come in wet and worried. He had news. We already knew it was bad news. Saffron and me stood next to the sugar cabinet with our ears pressed to the wall. He left right quick.

"So, to review. What did Mac actually say?" Mistress.

"The boat capsized. Why must I repeat his words? Probably struck something submerged in the river. Then the weight of the barrels toppled it over."

"How many barrels, again?"

"Twenty."

"How can they be sure Cudjoe's gone? Mightn't he have swum downriver and crawled out somewhere?"

"We won't know for certain for days, but Caesar saw him go under and didn't see him come back up. And for all his talents, I don't believe the man could swim." A heavy pause. Our hearts were breaking in the space between words.

Mistress again: "Why couldn't it have been Caesar? What a terrible irony – the young man that can hardly walk swims to safety and our strongest slave goes down." A chair sliding and scraping. Miss Eliza objecting? "So, we've lost an entire season of rice," said Mistress. "And our most valuable slave. How does one even go about replacing a key slave?"

We stepped away from the wall. I felt sick. Melody needed to know. We headed up the path to Summer Kitchen to tell her, found her rubbing cornmeal in the iron skillet to clean it. When she saw us, down she went. Everybody'd seen the way Melody looked at Cudjoe. She seemed like a different person around him, all quiet-like. Shy even. Melody knew all about his wife, but I think that suited her just fine, since nothing could come of her feelings.

It was nearing time for dessert. After what she said, I wished I could deny Mistress her sweets. I squeezed Melody's shoulders. "I got to get back."

"Of course, the stack cakes need serving," Melody said, laughing the bitter laugh of someone so stunned by grief that she'd come out the other side for a minute.

Bear Claw Pattern
Eliza's Diary, Wappoo Plantation

Mrs. Woodward, her daughter Mary, and Elizabeth Pinckney came today. Mary B. couldn't, she was looking at horses on Johns Island apparently. Only two things of note, really, coincidentally both involving fire.

When Melody knelt to light one, she sparked the flint three times but failed to ignite the kindling. In her ire, Mother grabbed a page of the Gazette, violently crumpled it, and flung it in Melody's direction. It bounced off her shoulder. She couldn't wait one more minute, my mother?

And then there was Mary's response to the fire. She pulled out her beautiful Bear Claw quilt, but instead of threading a needle per usual, she looked lost. Out of nowhere, she asked, "What about the horses – when there's fire?"

Mother changed the subject, sharing news about Father's hire of an indigo expert. Elizabeth stepped in next and talked about recent controversies about currency and possible bank closures.

But Mary spoke nonsense again. "The banks, the tribes, and the King – watch out! Demons'll be next!" Mary's mother twisted her handkerchief and looked down at the rug which is when I realized she had yet to speak a single word that visit.

After they left, I sat at the harpsichord, tired and in need of music, but also reluctant to interrupt the darkening quiet. From the couch, Mother asked, "Whatever is the matter with Mary?"

Part V

May 1743 – May 1744

May 1743

Athena and the Owl
Eliza, Crowfield Plantation

There were reasons to feel hopeful in the spring of 1743: a fresh crop of indigo, Father's promise to hire a West Indian expert to help with this year's harvest, and Father's promotion. He was now Lieutenant Governor of Antigua. We were so proud. Of course, such a prominent position meant that it was only a matter of time before Mother, Polly, and I would be summoned back to the isle of my birth. I tried not to think about it.

Two offers of marriage had come my way in the last year. I'd written to Father, "The riches of Peru and Chile put together could not purchase a sufficient esteem for either to become my husband." Nothing more was said, perhaps suggesting that Mother and he were finally permitting my preferences to dictate.

The Spaniards have continued to hassle our coast. When called upon to aid our brethren in Georgia recently, our ships failed to engage, purportedly marooned on a sandbar. Grandpapa was having none of it, calling the commander, a Captain Thomas Falkland, a coward. "He might as well have said the sun was in his eyes." Such boisterous condemnation assured us that Grandpapa was on the mend. We'd lost Grandmama in February, and he'd been subdued and ashen in his grief.

My brother George recently joined Father's regiment on Antigua, while Tommy was still in England, holding off any travel until he was well enough to make the journey. More than once in these past years, Tommy's health had faltered such that I feared we might never meet again on this side of death.

Polly remained fey and sweet and was nearly as tall as Phoebe, who was less tag-along and more house slave now, being trained by July and Melody. For at least a year, both girls had been able to read passably well. Melody's literacy was coming along too. Further, though Melody hadn't said, I was pretty certain she'd been tutoring her sons. Since Moses could pass for white, his literacy concerned me some, but not enough to discontinue.

There were other changes worth noting. Since the birth of her third child, Sarah Rutledge had rarely been about, choosing instead to devote her considerable energies to family out at Boone Hall Plantation. Meanwhile, Mary Bartlett had become my closest friend, and I grew closer to Charles's wife, Elizabeth, too. Mary Huston, it grieves me to say, I lost to madness. She who was incapable of any disguise, with cheerful temper and pleasing vivacity – collapsed into the gutter of insanity. Wild barking and rambling narratives took the place of her sophisticated wit. Her mind paranoid and deranged. Gone was Mrs. Woodward's only child and my dearest friend. I don't pretend to understand the origins of her madness, but I did know that three miscarriages – one of them occurring in our parlor, a horrific scene – had applied a lasting and irredeemable hurt.

Spring was poised in its verdant glory, just about to fledge into summer, when I received an invitation to visit the elder Middletons at Crowfield Plantation. Charles had arranged it. Whether he sought to take my mind off serious matters or to advance my knowledge of local flora or to re-introduce me to the couple hardly mattered. The change of scenery would do me good.

My boat arrived at the dock on Goose Creek early in the afternoon, and right away the alleé of young live oaks stretching for at least a quarter mile, took my breath away. The Middletons' two-horse carriage took me down the drive and through an iron-worked gate where there was a spacious marble basin surrounded by greenery. Then, a little further on: the house itself, adorned with graceful vines twisting up the façade, mantling it in green. How beautiful!

My hosts greeted me in an airy foyer. William and Margaret Middleton were so alike in appearance as to seem more siblings than man and wife, both lean in aspect with sharp and narrow noses topped by slate grey eyes. William wore a small brush of a grey moustache, while Margaret's silver hair swept off her face in stylish waves, pinned neatly to her crown. They couldn't have been more gracious.

An early tea was set for us in an elegantly furnished room with sweeping views of the river. Here I was gladdened to see Elizabeth and Charles, who had arrived earlier. Everything charmed, but even so, I could barely contain my impatience to see the much-touted gardens. William finally stood and extended an arm toward the exit.

"Shall we?"

Stepping down a sloped lawn, Elizabeth stumbled and very nearly fell. She mumbled something, perhaps embarrassed, while Charles, grabbed her elbow and conferred with her in low whispers. I looked away. Elizabeth's health had declined rapidly in recent months, and she'd been pale and silent for most of our tea.

Eventually it seemed that the fresh air revived her. And no wonder. The sky shone, and a variety of airy choristers poured forth their melody from a thicket nearby. On our right, a murder of crows pecked about a sunken bowling green. Were they the source of the name, "Crowfield Plantation"?

As if reading my mind, my host uttered a disclaimer. "Crowfield's an old English name, by the by, on my mother's side. And if you don't know, crow's as good as squab." I did not know, and hoped that it wasn't on the evening's menu.

At the first bench, Elizabeth sat. That she tired so quickly was heartbreaking, to be sure, but even more so was how slowly she lowered herself onto the planks – as if every shift of her spine caused pain. Charles sat beside her and took one of her hands. She waved us on graciously, but he looked only at her.

Mr. and Mrs. Middleton and I continued a lengthy way, and I'll confess that in very short order I thoroughly charmed William. He indulged me with a little harmless flirtation as we wandered along serpentine paths edged with buckleberry bushes. We paused at the edge of a small pond straddled by a red lacquered bridge at its narrow end, and there enjoyed the dappled shade of a double row of catalpa trees in full flower.

Further on, at the banks of Goose Creek, my hosts' warmth and solicitous regard drew me out. Private details, including those about my many indigo trials, tripped off my lips. Generally, I would have excluded such operational concerns from polite discourse, especially with new acquaintances, but already I trusted them.

"An expert from the West Indies will surely help," Margaret said. "Your journey is forward, my dear."

William concurred. "Yes indeed, sweetheart, you must shake off failures like a dog coming in from the rain. And speaking of moving on," he said with a mischievous wink, "have you any suitors?" When his wife gasped, he quickly added, "Let me restate: how many suitors have you – at least a dozen, I'm guessing? Why, if I weren't married to the lovely Margaret here, I'd be in line myself!" I laughed and hoped that was the end of it, but he persisted. "Perhaps unrequited love, then?" Without meaning to, I looked back at Charles and Elizabeth, and something must've passed over my face, for the two of them exchanged a look.

William tucked one of my hands in the crook of his right elbow and one of his wife's hands in the left, and said softly, "I thought as much." We returned to the house in a silence that seemed filled to bursting with my secret.

Throughout the following days, Elizabeth languished and peaked in hard-to-anticipate rhythms, but one afternoon she regained enough strength to join Margaret and me on a stroll to a glade devoted to Athena. Along the way, Elizabeth gathered flowers. In the clearing, the marble Athena towered over us, one hand extended, as if she would touch and heal any ailment, whether of the soul or body, if only the stone would liberate her grace.

Elizabeth laid her bouquet at the marble feet. Yellow primrose, swamp rose mallow, and orange butterfly weed shone in a warm array, making for a lively contrast to the white stone. The gesture was puzzling for such a devout Anglican but it pointed to unknown depths, perhaps depths with which even she was unacquainted.

Disease led Elizabeth down a solitary path. No matter how constant the conjugal care, how many friends attended her bedside, she would meet her Maker alone, as we all must. What secret prayer did she make to Athena that day?

Midweek, I managed to slip away to the library in hopes of finding Palladio's treatise on architecture, which William had once loaned to John Drayton. I found it. Could it possibly be only five years since I first looked at these renderings? So much had come to pass – lives lost to pox and rebellion, children born, houses erected, houses burned. Suzanne and the two young Drayton children gone and buried, John remarried to Charlotte Bull almost two years now.

Charles entered the library and my heart jumped.

"She's asleep," he announced, and offered up a rattled speech. "It really could be any time now. The doctors can do little but keep her comfortable. Her bravery in the face of it all. Her bravery…" He rambled on, nearly incoherent. His words were so full of private revelations and tender regrets – about life, about Elizabeth – that I began to feel like an intruder.

"I am most sorry for your difficulty," I said at last. "How it saddens me to contemplate a world without her." He looked at me, seemingly more lost than ever. I asked if he would like to be alone.

"Oh no, dear Eliza. It does me good to ramble on in someone's company. Can you bear it?" Charles's eyes were liquid with sadness. Of course I would not deny him – but "someone's company," as if any warm body would do? Finally he paused and looked at me with a penetrating gaze that made my hands shake, my breath go shallow. But there were to be no more confidences. He made polite excuses and left. I resumed my examination of the architectural illustrations, but my heart was no longer in it. It wasn't even in the room, it had gone right out the door on the heels of a man old enough to be my father. A married man with a sick wife. That man.

The rest of the week passed in a bit of a blur. I took much pleasure in the floral extravagances everywhere, in the long, lovely vistas, and in our hosts' charming company, but the visit drained Elizabeth. Therefore, on the eve of departure, in spite of plans to the contrary, it was decided that I should travel back to Wappoo alone. Just as well. I didn't want to sit close to Charles just then. Once underway, the idea of a Lucas family reunion in Antigua came rushing toward me.

Only last week, Mother had gleefully recited from a letter: "Tell dear Eliza, if all goes well, I could wish her 'Happy Birthday' in person this year." Whatever glad prospects lay in the plan, they were not mine. I belonged to South Carolina now – did Mother really not see this? The Lowcountry had infiltrated every fiber of my being. The figs and indigo. The egrets. The expanse of sky. The ever changing marshes. My friends.

And, I was in love with Charles.

Flip
Melody, Charles Town

"Nell! Stop, Nell!" I chased after her down the dark hall – the same bony body as all those years ago when we met. Of course! How could it be otherwise? It wasn't like she dined at the Bacchus and Vine once a week. She trotted right out the back and down the steps into the dank kitchen. I followed her.

She sat. Clasped her hands. Stared at a point behind me.

"I didn't mean to make you worry," I told her. "Mistress nearly never comes back down after a nap when she's been drinking." This was my lame apology. I'd snuck out of Cross Winds earlier after hearing old Master Lucas mention that the Poinsett Inn was serving their specialty drink, "the flip." Ganda, handsome Ganda, was the local master of the drink. What harm, I thought – Mistress three sheets to the wind and Miss Eliza not due back from Crowfield Plantation 'til the morrow.

Nelly looked at me hard. "Won't do them boys no good if you dead." She wasn't saying anything I hadn't already thought a thousand times. It was selfish to forge a slip and sneak out, but I'd wanted to hear Ganda's mahogany voice calling out, "Flip! Flip! Who wants the next flip?" I'd wanted to watch his elegant moves – pouring rum, brandy, and sugar, whipping eggs in a pewter mug, topping it with beer, and best of all, at the very end, inserting a hot fire poker for a hissing rise of foam. It was drama. It was grace. Buckra loved to watch the drinks being made and I loved to watch him.

This time, I noticed his dimples. How had I not seen them before – either at the Panther Moon dance years back or last year when Miss Eliza came for flips with Mistress Rutledge – or was that two years back? Hadn't seen that wily Missus Sarah in ages. Time curled round in strange ways. You'd hardly know Cudjoe'd been gone for three years now or that the uprising was four years back already. Ganda reminded me of Cudjoe. Seeing him was a way to see Cudjoe again.

As it turned out my rogue outing came with a lucky encounter. I ran into Cudjoe's mama, Nana Lucy, when she delivered a tray of her famous pastries. I'd met her once, years back, but everybody at Wappoo knew about her, how she was free by courtesy, how flaky her biscuits were.

Before she left, I tapped her shoulder and reminded her where I was from. We talked in the way of people who have but little time left on earth. Much slave talk went this way. Quickly intimate. Deep and wide, but hurried. She told me how much she still missed Cudjoe. I nodded, trying not to tear up myself. Back in the day she only saw him but now and again, but it did her good knowing he was alive and living just across the Ashley. I didn't say how much I missed Cudjoe too. Seemed Nana Lucy needed my listening more than my sharing right then.

"These days," she whispered, eyeing the back door. "I watch my back. It's gotten worse lately. I can feel them watching me. I draw curtains tight evening times now. Disdain or jealousy or hate, does it matter? It's the same old story, our success turns us into brighter targets." She looked at me. "I'm scared."

I grabbed her hand and held it to my cheek. As if her skin touching my skin communicated something, my mind lit up with a plan. Not a thread of an idea, not a whisper of a thought, but a full-out plan. I didn't say anything to Nana Lucy then, but I would soon and I knew she'd agree. If she survived long enough, that is.

I did tell the plan to Nell in the kitchen's half-light, though, maybe as a kind of atonement, or maybe because by saying it out loud, it seemed I gave the plan bones and energy. "Nana Lucy could pose as slave to Moses," I said. "We'd train him how to speak white, gaze white, wave and snap white. Getting money for passage'd be easy enough, I know about a secret cupboard in Master's desk. Booking tickets'll be harder, and deciding where to go – who knows? But possible."

Turned out Nell had heard something useful that afternoon. Before Mistress got too soused to see straight, she'd read a letter out loud from a niece up north. "Mostly about concerts, gowns, and whatnot," Nell said, "but something caught the one ear I got left. Free blacks up in Philadelphia – dressed to the nines, running businesses, getting married. *A shocking number*, the letter said."

"Phil-a-del-ph-i-a," I echoed. Just like that, five syllables turned into a prayer, maybe even a song of freedom. I looked at Nell. As so many times before, I felt her sorrow and understood now that it went with her everywhere. There was no shaking off or getting under or over the loss of a child, especially when that child was taken in brutal, mercantile circumstance. Nell stood and ladled out two glasses of water from the well bucket.

She handed me one, raised an arm, and said very slowly "Here's to Moses walking the streets of Philadelphia, a free man!"

Clink. Clink. She knew better than I that such a dream of freedom, if successful, meant I would never see my boy again.

Calls Home
Eliza's Diary, Wappoo Plantation

Father beckons us to the West Indies while Angels assemble in Elizabeth's sick chamber. "Come home, dear one. Come home," the heavenly hosts must be whispering. Who would be called home first – Elizabeth or me? Such grim and taboo calculations turn me into a ghoul, pitting Elizabeth's march to the grave against the speed of the trade winds. My desire imposes staggering complications and there seems no decent way to think about it. About him.

Since my return from Crowfield, Mother's extracted every conceivable description of the place, of the hosts, of the land, but her blindness to my feelings for Charles remains. Eventually, I'll have to reveal myself, but not yet. Imagine if she counseled silent withdrawal or worse, charged me with indecency. I could not suffer her rebuke. Not only did I hope to marry a man freshly widowed – I truly hoped not just for my mother's blessing but for Elizabeth's as well. How selfish!

Think on it. Elizabeth dwelling in a cloudy, pain-hazed gloom, in the midst of the greatest struggle of all – that of leaving this world – and me requesting the favor of her benediction. And why – to ease my conscience? Perhaps I'd read one novel too many, for I could picture it: one heroine fringed in lacy nightclothes, near death, husband standing by; the other heroine looking on, eyes glistening with sorrow as well as an eager vitality that she hopes does not offend. From the pillow, the hectic face whispering, "Dear Husband, you must find happiness after I'm gone – with Eliza." Tears all round. A sigh and a passing.

Two mortals would be left to grieve, shoulder to shoulder, his sorrow more easily borne knowing that at some point, certainly not immediately, but soon, he would turn and face the doe-eyed lover. They would press against each other in grief, yes, but also in the passion allotted to the lucky living.

If only Charles had given the smallest of signs. Had he?

July 1743

Smart Breeding
Melody, Wappoo Plantation

Peepers sang out a holy wobble, cries rising up, greeting the sky. Pie cooled on the big plate near the pantry window, ready to slice and serve. July held the knife. Metal caught low-hanging sun and flashed off it just as we heard Miss Eliza through the pantry door. "Did you read Father's letter yet?" A grunt from Mistress. Miss Eliza kept on. "He wants us to breed Melody."

"Yes, yes." Seemed like Mistress wanted to be spared the talk. We all knew from way back how Master Lucas cut her with rude talk about me, a "fine specimen" and all that. Years back now, and here he opening up old wounds.

Miss Eliza: "He wants her bred with Indian Pete. He thinks the Pee Dee blood will make any children more resilient to the cold."

Saffron was staring at the pantry door as if she might set it afire with her fury. Four years ago, Indian Pete placed his heart in Saffron's hands, and for all that buckra's blind to, even they knew it. Maybe they think Saffron can't carry more children. They don't know about her careful moon marks on the wall or about Indian Pete's courtesies, abiding by the marks. And, how could they believe it of him anyway? Him being half savage and all.

They already get to count my two boys, quadroons no less. Binah's baby-making is going strong. Isn't that enough? Why even ask. Nothing's ever enough for them.

July gave the pie plate an angry tap and got my attention. She cut and slid wedges onto dessert plates. We took turns dropping a gob of spit onto the shiny peaches spilling out of the crust.

"How is it," we heard Mistress ask in a hard whisper, "that no one's managed to get her with child all these years? And Saffron too?" A whisper wouldn't shield us from harm, and it didn't hide Mistress Millie's old feelings, either. She was insecure and she was scared. I'll bet you that even the peepers could hear her jealous fright.

July served the pie. They ladies went silent. Ha! They know we can hear them from the pantry, but it's inconveniencing for them to act on that knowledge, so they pretend otherwise. White ladies shine at this, making meaning any way it suits them, then acting as if the physical world agrees.

Saffron trayed up the teapot and the rosebud cups, but her hands were shaking. Indian Pete's strong and he's been true, but still. They're going to force-bunk him and me? I shoved past Saffron and threw up into the big bowl where we'd stirred the supper greens. July rubbed my back while Saffron kicked the pantry door open so hard that it slammed into the liquor cabinet on the other side. It sounded like musket fire.

"So sorry," Saffron lied. "I tripped." Wished I could see the ladies arranging their faces around that. I put a hand to my belly. How was it possible to want to kill and to die at the same time? Even years back after being torn up by white men twice, I didn't feel this way, but maybe suffering and torment were like river debris jamming against a log during freshet, causing unspeakable trouble as time went on.

July saw me staring at the pie knife. I put her mind to ease by taking a sweeter lane to rebellion: I started to sing. I sang louder than I'd ever sung in Porch House before, even on those nights when Master made me perform like a show donkey. I tipped my head back and let out a bawling, lilting song, loud and sweet. It was honey and scythe, fanner and hoe. It was peepers and panther, turpentine and prayer. It was peach pie and the sharp knife that cut it. If they wanted to silence me, Miss or Mistress would have to put down a fork, rise up out of a cushioned seat, and come hush me. I knew they wouldn't.

Palm to Palm
Saffron, Wappoo Plantation

Overseer barked at Melody to move her pallet into Pete's cabin. His freckles flushed, lightning bugs skittering across his face. A prude? I wouldn't have figured, but he showed his back right quick.

Melody folded up the pallet, slow and sorrowful. In a whole new way, we were sisters. A connecting pain. Soon Indian Pete's body would connect us too.

When Pete came to me three days later, I lifted his hand to my face. Could I smell her on his fingers? I wanted to know: did he grip her hips, did he make her moan out the way he made me cry out?

"Where'd you do it?"

"Don't."

"No. Tell me."

"Nowhere we go." His voice was bitter as a peach pit, but soft too, like the sweet flesh around the pit. He took my hand and rivers of thought flowed from palm to palm, more dream than conversation. He was red-tailed hawk flying overhead, screeching "Saffron! Saffron!" He was crab coming to me sideways. He was dog panting out heat, and he was turkey fanning feathers in a strutting love. Palm to palm, how it came through.

We found our shadow and lay down across the night's middle. Grasses wet ankles and neck. With each kiss, I grew softer, bigger, harder, and smaller, his tongue finding mine, offering more heat, more tribute, 'til I was hawk and turkey too. We slid across the sky, out over the marshes. We tugged off raggedy cottons and tucked into a rhythm so right it pulled us back to earth, now letting sky serve as guardian. We were fellow makers of the world and not just specks living on it, owned.

His lips found nipple and caused down below to spark and beg. And when he let me surround him, pure pulse and wet to his hot push, another faster course took us all the way to the end, him falling off the edge first, me just after with a screech I hoped others would think was a panther crying out in the night.

When he rolled over, our breath still touching, I knew I would not lose him. Not to Melody, not to any woman. Snake bite, whip, or auction could take him. Pox, fever, or abscess. But not another woman. With all his body and spirit, he told me so and I was satisfied in the telling.

September 1743

Under the Catalpa
Eliza, Wappoo Plantation

Waiting in the shade of the catalpa the morning Nicholas Cromwell arrived, I made a quick count. I was in my fourth year serving as the deputized manager of my father's three plantations. Twenty years old. The responsibility had enlarged my horizons, but also taught me the limits of individual influence. What youthful hubris to have believed that I ought to be able to make sense of everything.

Out on yesterday's flatboat went foodstuff for Father: two hogsheads of rice, two of corn, a box of eggs packed in salt. Coincidentally, goods from the West Indies were due to arrive this morning. An unlikely symmetry. Father was sending: rum, muscovado sugar, coffee, and our indigo expert, one Nicholas Cromwell.

Indigo was more important than ever. Not only did we lose an entire season of rice three years ago, but the same storm deprived us of our key slave, Cudjoe. The bundle of notes in the escritoire's secret cupboard might have covered the expense of another male slave, but caution dictated not spending it. Instead, I elevated Quashee. Another loss of income, because we couldn't hire him out.

My crops of indigo hadn't yet fared well. I lost the first harvest to frost. Another withered in an early cold snap, but I did manage to salvage the seeds. Those cold-hardened seeds now flourished in a field near the alfalfa, coming up like verdant flags of promise. With rice markets still sagging, slave imports at a standstill, and a British market eager to be rid of the bickering Indian farmers in the East, indigo was poised to become a profitable commodity. A subsidy from the Crown didn't hurt. I dared to hope.

Father had extolled Nicholas Cromwell's virtues: he was knowledgeable, fit, prepared to "save the day." When we heard the tell-tale thumps of a boat pulling up, Mother and I made our way to the dock, curious and excited. And there he was – a middle-aged man greying at the temples, with clear blue eyes and broad shoulders, dressed head to foot in blue cloth. He doffed his hat and gave a quick smile. He kissed Mother's hand and then mine.

"I have heard such pleasing things about the Lieutenant Governor's women, and now I see why!"

"From Husband, I hope?" Mother laughed and invited him inside for refreshment. He would love to, but was there a place to make himself more presentable first after two weeks at sea? Mac joined us. From inside his vest, Cromwell produced a contract and handed it over to Mac. Just spying Father's signature gave me a jolt. Evidence of his care, evidence of his person. We would not have to rely on local knowledge now, and we certainly wouldn't have to rely on any old indigo-dabbling Negro. We were after the precious blue bricks, and Cromwell was here to help.

Mac led him away, and when Cromwell returned not long later, he looked tidier and acted pleasantly enough, but I thought I detected a cruelty about the mouth.

"How is Colonel Lucas," Mother asked right off, and then made the same inquiry six more ways to Sunday.

Cromwell replied repeatedly that Father was well and eventually turned the conversation to indigo. "Word is," he said, "that it takes four to five times the amount of Lowcountry dye to achieve the same result as a West Indian or South American product."

"Good gracious, not so!" I snapped. "What a falsehood to circulate given how conveniently it dovetails with preserving foreign markets at the expense of ours. Ridiculous."

"More tea Eliza?" Mother slid the teapot toward me, as if my irritation was a function of dehydration. Undeterred, I added, "I can assure you, Mr. Cromwell, that Lowcountry indigo has all the quality it needs to compete."

"And have Wappoo's blue dye bricks found favor in London," Cromwell asked. There it was, the cruelty in the mouth.

"You know they haven't."

Dessert arrived and a satisfied silence ensued. Sometimes a distraction served the common good.

Not long later, he bowed his goodbye, somehow managing to turn the gesture into a mockery of good manners. Or was he merely inept? As I watched him head over to his cabin near the smokehouse, I felt my shoulders drop, unaware of how tense the man had made me.

Mother raised eyebrow. "Not sure he's someone you want for an enemy."

Indigo Expert
Eliza, Wappoo Plantation

Processing indigo was a messy, stinky, tricky business. It required a commodious drying shed and three linked vats. The leaves had to be harvested at exactly the right time — when they showed a blue sheen – and then stacked in piles to rot a bit. After that, they were dumped into Vat Number One, or the steeper, to soak, which helped precipitate out their precious juices. This liquor was then drained into Vat Number Two, also called the battery. Slaves carefully agitated the battery liquid, helping the necessary reactions along. At this stage, limewater, or sometimes crushed oyster shells, was added to encourage the chemical process. You watched for foam and a certain viscousness. When ready, the liquor was drained out of the battery into Vat Number Three, with the precious blue muck left behind. The paste in Vat Number Two was scooped up into cotton bags, hung to dry, and then molded into blue bricks. Roughly fifteen slaves were required, start to finish.

Indigo matters did not proceed in a cooperative vein with Cromwell, to say the least. For starters, he opted to build the vats out of bricks over the customary preference for wood, never mind the fact that our holdings offered nearly limitless free lumber and we owned a slave with superior carpentry skills. Bricks, on the other hand, would have to be purchased and then transported from Boone Hall, a costly and difficult process. Further, I worried that trace minerals in the bricks might upset fermentation, a process well known to be finicky.

In the meantime, the indigo was almost ready for harvest and lengthy delays could be ruinous.

Turns out I needn't have worried about timing for just two days after Cromwell's arrival, two pettiaugers loaded with bricks pulled up to our dock. Father must've approved the choice before the indigo expert's schooner even set sail. Cromwell would get his way, then.

Since we could only spare Caesar and no others for the bricklaying, Cromwell hired tradesmen from the peninsula, three Irish masons. Mother fumed. "I don't want them lurking about. Worse than Negroes! They so rarely bathe! Not one of them is to set foot near the house, do you understand?" She bounced out of her chair to pull the russet drapes closed, as if the offending Celts might be crouching at the foundation that very instant. "Eliza, for the duration, lock the silver in the liquor cabinet."

Fortunately, the Irish hands built the vats quickly. I inspected progress daily and was impressed with how efficiently the crew turned a chaotic heap of bricks into neat, connecting rectangular vats. I wondered how "a race bedeviled by idiocy" (Mother's words) could work with such dispatch and skill.

Mr. Cromwell maintained a polite decorum, but by mid-September, when we were hip-deep in the indigo field looking for the leaves with the all-important blue shine to them, I could see that the slaves regarded him with a wary vigilance. His cowhide remained stuck in his waistband whenever I was around, but that meant nothing. Clearly, Cromwell governed through fear.

Just before the vats were finished, Tilton came by. The solicitous neighbor. Ever since the Regans' party, I had viewed him with curious wariness, as though he were an exotic insect pinned to a collector's page, still fluttering, not quite dead. To think that a marriage might've been arranged between us!

He, Mother, and I sat on the gallery rockers and I mentioned the mineral content of the bricks as a worry. Tilton asked condescendingly, "Surely, they'll hold water as well as wood?" How like him to side with a man, even a man of lowly status whom he'd never met.

"According to Cromwell," I said, "the minerals in the clay enhance the fallout of the dye, but I have no cause to believe him."

"Shall I consult with him, then? Perhaps find out too if he knows how to gauge the correct amount of limewater to add, come time."

"That'd be most appreciated," Mother piped up, possibly because she wanted the man off her verandah, but I was suspicious and wondered if perhaps our visitor had his own reasons for wanting the encounter.

Mr. Tilton twirled his hat, his version of gracious exit. On impulse, I decided to accompany him. I bolted to the foyer to fetch my bonnet and told Saffron to have someone saddle up my horse. Mother looked a little confused, but given that it was nearly time for her lie-down, mustered no resistance.

So off we trotted, Tilton and I, side by side. "What news of the Natives have you to report from Mr. Dutarque?" I asked casually. Tilton gripped his reins a little more tightly but kept his voice steady. Resettlements going apace, land apportionments being made, etc.

Thereafter, we heard the cicadas buzzing long and raspy across the fields but did not converse. Soon enough we heard Cromwell's shouts piercing the air.

The first two of the three vats stood complete, the final and third vat about halfway done. Tilton dismounted, shook Cromwell's hand, and walked around the structures, appraising them, rubbing his chin, apparently approving the dimensions, the level changes, the mix of mortar. I'm not sure what he knew of such things since he only grew rice.

Cromwell gave me a brief nod and tip of his hat, pulled two cigars from his vest, and used a flint and piece of straw to light them. The men puffed away. What need had they of words? Such easy mutual regard sickened me. There was so much exclusion in it.

Caesar had proved skillful with hob and scraper, easily keeping pace with the Irishmen, placing each brick with the right amount of pressure, sliding and scraping the mortar off the hob, applying it along the top exposed surface, not too much, not too little.

"Their hand is decent enough anyway," Cromwell said, nodding at Caesar, as if I was not there.

The Irishman mixing the day's last batch of mortar was bearded and scarecrow-thin, wearing a tunic with ragged sleeves. Cromwell made as if to inspect the work near the mason's elbow but instead blew a large cloud of smoke into his face. The worker coughed, to derisive laughter from Tilton and Cromwell. Caesar, in a rare undefended moment, glanced at me with a look of naked rage.

Cromwell was cruel and everyone knew it.

Tansy and Pennyroyal
Saffron, Wappoo Plantation

Melody plunked down next to me after supper and asked, "Where's Old Sarah?"

Old Sarah's eyes have gone rheumy, but she could hear well enough. From two cabins down, she lifted up her head, pointed her face our way, and waved. Slow as time passing under slavery, she rose up off the stoop and fetched her medicine sack before disappearing behind the cabins somewhere back by the garden. Melody followed and of course I went with her. She was my sister in this, with natural love on one side and unnatural, scalding shame on the other.

Sarah's fingers were bent and knobby like a catalpa branch, but she pulled the strings on the sack just fine. Inside was a little bit of everything: jimson weed for worms, cobweb balls for wounds, snakeroot for monthly cramping. Also inside: one piece of red cloth, tied up tight, holding dried tansy, pennyroyal, and cotton root bark. The baby-killing powder.

"Open up," she said.

Melody lifted up her hem, and Old Sarah laughed. Her laugh sounded ancient, like three-hundred-year-old tree roots, maybe, coming as if from deep down under the earth. Her laugh had something of the hot Saharan winds in it too, winds that used to scorch through my village, scouring sleep and carrying news from afar.

"Open your *mouth!*" she said.

Melody let go of her frock and stuck out her tongue.

"This gonna be bitter." Old Sarah took a pinch and dropped it under Melody's tongue. Then she dunked a dried calabash into the water bucket by her side and gave it to Melody to drink. "Finish what's in the bag and finish the water." Old Sarah rose up like her bones had other ideas and all of them were about staying put. "All the water," she repeated, and hobbled away.

Melody looked at me. "That's it? Not how soon or how bad?"

I shrugged. "She didn't bring the cotton strips, so maybe not soon?" Halfway across the street, though, Melody took a hard tucking breath. I grabbed the pallet and July took Melody by the elbow and walked her the rest of the way over to our cabin.

A curious moon rose up over the cypress tops. What was it hoping to see? I didn't know the Pee Dee name for it. Corn Moon? Wolf Moon? Not Panther Moon. I knew that came later, after frost. I'd have to ask Indian Pete.

Melody didn't care about the moon that night, even though the sight of a fat one usually got her humming. She went inside herself, almost like a woman giving birth. We arranged her under the blanket and rubbed her legs, but she truly seemed gone.

By morning it was over. Melody lay quiet, awake, looking like someone tugged her spirit out her collarbones, but I knew she was back because she wore a small, satisfied smile. Her pallet a bloody mess.

The next day when we were trading daylight for dark, the Heavens opened and rain came pounding down. We were aiming to dash all the way back to the street when a ruckus come up. Branches cracking off? Trees whistlin' to fall? No, it was musket fire and horses and baying hounds.

Quashee had been acting overseer that day because Mac done gone to St. Johns for horse business, and now three horses came galloping past, their riders yelling, casting out the cowhide just for fun, snap-snap, leather cracking, then lightning cracking. Was the storm on buckra's side? We stepped aside and let 'em pass, rain running down faces and backs.

Quashee was probably deep in the rice fields or up near the alfalfa. Storms meant trunks needed minding. The rains cleared off to the north, but the worry tugged at us like another heckling gale when Quashee didn't show for supper.

The Trial
Eliza, Godfrey's Place

By the time we stepped onto the dock, quite a crowd had assembled. Thankfully, Mr. Deveaux had agreed to accompany me, as had Mary Bartlett. Mary gripped my elbow and murmured words of encouragement: "You're articulate, the facts are on your side, never mind the crowd," etc. But my nerves were raw with worry. How much Wappoo Plantation stood to lose today! Our prize slave, Quashee, had been erroneously picked up in a patroller sweep.

Apparently, a little over two weeks ago, some number of slaves had gathered near the woods flanking our Upper Field – the infamous spot where Saffron once upon a time danced in my calico frock, a scene I shuddered to think on even now. This time, patrollers heard a thumping ruckus and worried it might be the Negro call to arms – just as it had been the night rebels stormed Hutchinson's Depot almost four years ago to the day. The patrollers stormed the clearing. Most of the slaves scattered, and all but seven got away. The patrollers asked round for slips, found not a one, and bundled the slaves up into a makeshift coffle. As they were leaving the woods, they came upon Quash, who'd been checking on the alfalfa crop not far from the entrance to the woods. Acting at the time as both driver and trunk minder, Quashee was oft in the fields past the sounding of conch. He checked water levels and pressure near the sluices, assessed the readiness of harvest, performed other important tasks. Surely patrollers and magistrates alike knew that effective plantation management did not arise out of ignorance.

Since he was on plantation, Quashee could not produce a slip either. The patrollers took this as proof of guilt even though it could have just as easily been proof of innocence. It made my blood boil to think on it. Quashee's repeated suggestion that they ride a quarter mile down the road to confirm his identity was rebuffed, and off he went with the others to the jail on the peninsula. Only by the grace of that swift and mysterious grapevine among Negroes did the message of his capture reach us early the following day.

I was utterly certain that Quashee'd had no part in the illicit gathering, whatever it was, but whether the others' actions constituted the early stages of a rebellion I had no way of judging. I hied myself to the jail as soon as I heard, but my pleas for Quashee's release fell upon deaf ears. In fact, my well-articulated indignation about his wrongful capture was met with looks of hostile disdain, as if my temperament was the problem rather than Quashee's unjust imprisonment. Had Father, or even my brother George, nearly two years my junior, made the same appeal, in the very same language, Quashee's release would have been arranged within the hour, I'm certain of it.

There I was, soon to be twenty-one, being condescended to as if a child, or worse, a lunatic, like my poor friend Mary Huston. Recalling sweet Mary's great adversity offered a helpful perspective, granting me a modicum of calm. The guards' skepticism, while insulting in the extreme, was nothing compared to the utter and devastating loss of one's senses. With a storming heart, I left.

Charles had kindly met with me last week to draft an affidavit in support of Quashee's release. Gave me his vote of confidence. I have no doubt he'd have accompanied us today were it not for the precarious state of his wife's health. Dear Elizabeth was now nearly an invalid.

People crowded Godfrey's parlor and hallway, such that we had to shoulder our way to the chairs reserved for parties with legal interest. The rising heat was worsened by the throng, so the suggestion was made to move the proceeding outdoors. People grabbed their bags and jackets and jostled out, some holding pints of ale above their heads.

In the shade of a gum tree, a pair of slaves set up a table to serve as judicial bench. I was surprised to see a lone chair behind the table, thinking there would be at least three freeholders on duty. More chairs were hastily lined up along the riverfront, presumably in the vain hope of catching a trace of a breeze off the water. Bales of hay afforded additional seating. We sat near the front.

As a slave serving ale passed, I leaned over Mary to ask Mr. Deveaux, "Is this common, the circus-like atmosphere?" Not only did the festive air strike a discordant note with the matter at hand, the idea that someone was profiting off the day's proceedings bothered me. Mr. Deveaux assured me that it was indeed common. Judging by the way he eyed a passing tray, he approved the custom.

I sagged back into my chair in sorry recognition of the strange tribal behaviors of humankind. I knew we could be a superficial lot, but truthfully, I was less worried about treating law as entertainment than I was by some of our other foibles – self-imposed blindness, for instance, or a predilection toward vengeance. When it came to controversy, people often saw what they wanted to see in the face of countervailing evidence. Rough justice could be dished out when the more suitable fare might be mercy. I hoped it wasn't too much to expect an equitable result today.

"I thought there were supposed to be three freeholders," I said to Mr. Deveaux.

"Actually, there are supposed to be five in capital cases," he informed me, "but two succumbed to bilious fever over the weekend and two are down with bloody flux. Rather than delay the proceedings, it was thought best to get on with it."

Best for whom?

My hands were clammy – nothing to do with the temperature at all. At the same time, my commitment to repossess our slave made me taut with purpose, like an arrow nocked for a shot. Because of Charles Pinckney's help, I had some notion about what to expect, but I'd been unable to lay to rest my apprehension that the savage history of the rebellion might sway today's results. I looked around. The house that stood here in 1739 had burned to the ground that fateful night. The rebels killed the former occupants, Colonel Godfrey and his two children. The late Colonel's nephew inherited the property and by the following September had buried the dead and built a new house for his own family.

I had no reason to doubt Mr. Godfrey's integrity. In fact, I'd never met the man. But he would have to be made of stone for the violence inflicted by the Stono rebels not to have imparted a lasting and particular grief. Even the most moral of men might be swayed toward vengeance. At the very least, Freeholder Godfrey might be predisposed toward viewing a cluster of Negroes off plantation as a menacing threat, even in the absence of any real evidence. At worst, the man could be feeling a sly sense of gratitude for the way Providence was affording him the chance to serve up retribution under the cloak of justice.

At last the accused appeared. Led by one of Godfrey's slaves, the coffle of eight men made its way from the rear of the house. The slaves were made to stand against the exterior of the house, as if lined up for the firing squad. The morning light smacked their faces, causing them to blink and squint and attempt to raise hands to shield eyes, only to find themselves tugging at their neighbor's arms with wrists bound by hemp.

The sun was indeed harsh that morning. In a morbid turn of thought, it occurred to me that if this was my second-to-last morning on this earth, I might welcome its uncompromising glare. Shadows met the house and bent up in crooked forms. Even these fleeting indices of embodiment might be rendered dear by the imminence of death. I tried to will the men to turn and look, as if the memory of how their bodies blocked light might ease their final suffering at the gallows.

I glanced over at Mary to gauge her reaction, but she was staring off into the distant scrub with an inscrutable look. Mr. Deveaux placed a hand on one of hers and squeezed. She appeared to be willing herself to be elsewhere.

The prisoners were of varying heights and colors. One of them was a particularly large specimen, as Father might have said. Quashee stood two from the right, looking composed and terrified in equal measure. He might have been the only mulatto in the lineup. With a slight turn of the neck, he scanned the rows of attendees, found me, and gave a simple and dignified nod.

Mr. Godfrey came out and assumed the designated chair. The heat rendered him casual – no wig, no jacket, not even a vest. Given that this was a capital case, the law required at least two witnesses to give evidence. I wouldn't be surprised if this measure was also relaxed. I wondered who would provide evidence against the accused besides the patrollers.

Godfrey called out a name and nodded to his slave to loosen the ropes on the man furthest to the right. He possessed very little English but managed to make clear his meaning: the large man had been the ringleader. I thought Godfrey looked relieved, perhaps because the case for insurrection had just been made for him. The slave was released because "he has become material evidence for our Sovereign Lord the King." Godfrey jotted some notes, I suspect about restitution. Compensation for labor lost would surely be demanded by each innocent slave's owner.

The second man called forward was the purported ringleader. He stood with tall and resolute, with shoulders back. Everyone sitting there knew we were looking at a dead man and indeed, Mr. Godfrey, with very little interrogation and no corroboration beyond the first slave's testimony, declared him guilty with a slap of his hand upon the table. Mary jumped.

"Death by hanging! At dawn tomorrow," Godfrey added. The slave was taken into the house before I could see his face.

It was bone-chilling to consider that a revolt might have started so near our property. Had they rampaged like the Stono rebels, surely Wappoo would have been in the path of destruction this time.

A hush fell upon the crowd. The reasons for the sudden stillness could hardly be unanimous, but at least for some, the quiet surely arose from knowing that the man who'd just stood a bowshot away would be dead this time tomorrow. I looked at Mr. Deveaux. His eyes, so often the repository of kindness and lively curiosity, showed flat gray. He continued to hold Mary's hand.

The next four slaves were released to their owners, each looking more penitent than the last. Mr. Godfrey didn't make notes about these four. Had he forgotten about restitution? The seventh man asserted that he wished he'd been part of the plot but had only happened through. Such impertinence! Godfrey slapped his hand down and bellowed, "Forty lashes, to be administered by another slave on plantation."

Finally Godfrey called Quashee. Judging by the truncated shadows, it was near noon. Normally a tidy and well-composed figure, our bondman looked done in. Half-moon shadows darkened his eyes, and his tunic clung to him in sweaty patches. I laid aside my fan and gripped the affidavit.

"State your name for the record." Godfrey was perfunctory now, perhaps tiring in the heat.

"Quashee, Master Godfrey," our man replied. In spite of his wilted appearance, he was composed as he pled not guilty. After a nod from Godfrey, Quash continued, "As driver, I get back late. I do all that needs doing. I inspect one field or t'other, check sluices. That day, I was inspecting alfalfa. I didn't have no slip, sir, as I was on plantation." Quash paused. "Where I stood," he continued, "was where I belonged. I didn't need a slip, sir."

"Enough! Anyone here to give evidence?" Oh dear. Had Quashee appeared impertinent?

"Miss Eliza." Quash pointed at me. Godfrey was new to the area, but I didn't think it vain to assume he might have heard of me.

I leapt to my feet and flapped the affidavit and then, as if trying to catch the attention of an imbecile, yelled, "Here, Mr. Godfrey, I am here!" I took a shallow breath. "My father serves at the King's pleasure on Antigua, where he is Lieutenant Governor. I'm deputized to speak on his behalf." I could feel my heart pulsing in my temples.

Godfrey raised his eyebrows. I wasn't sure if his look was condescending or laudatory, but at that juncture I hardly cared because the lifted eyebrows under the bald head atop a neck extended in my direction produced a comical resemblance to a tortoise. The image melted away my anxiety. My voice rang clear and steady. "I have an affidavit, sir."

He signaled for me to approach. I handed him the paper, hoping he noticed the prominent seal affixed at bottom by Charles Pinckney. He read through it, glancing up once to look me over and a second time to look at Quashee.

"The overseer was off plantation at the time?" Godfrey asked me. I affirmed. He chewed his cheek for a bit and then slapped his hand on the table. "Not guilty!" He nodded for the untying of ropes and gave me a tired look that was surely part relief but also seemed part confusion as to why I continued to stand before him.

I said, "This slave's absence lasted sixteen days, sir."

"Yes, yes," Godfrey replied, sitting back down and jotting a note with a slight air of grievance. He slapped the flat of his hand down for a final time and honked out, "These matters are now concluded."

Godfrey made his way round the back of his house in a slow trot. One had the sense that the proceedings had interrupted something he was eager to resume, or perhaps, some urgency of digestion plagued him.

Quashee rubbed his wrists where the hemp had scratched his skin. He didn't smile, but I could see relief spelled all over him as clearly as if a calligrapher had inked it there. He joined us in a thrice and we quickly achieved the dock.

The ordeal was over.

Witness to the Dumping
Saffron, Wappoo Plantation

The day Cromwell dumped limewater into the vat, it was so hot even the grasshoppers went still. At half-morning, sweat soaked my tunic dark. Paddling the indigo water was punishing in any kind of air, mind, on account of the stench. Bugs too. First the bugs came to swarm the rotting piles of leaves, but then they stayed on and pestered and nagged, even after we sunk the leaves under water and pinned 'em down with logs.

But heat, stench, and bugs didn't keep me from dreaming of blue. To think on it – blue head rags, blue aprons, blue ruffles, blue pillows and pockets – peppered me with a rare gladness. Maybe a dunk here wouldn't equal the shiny dark indigo of the Tuareg traders, cloth they rubbed with goat fat and pounded 'til it glimmered in the sun, but it would make for some kind of blue. Dusty blue. Storm cloud blue. Cloudy creek blue. Unnamable blue.

Was a thing there if you couldn't conjure a name for it?

We paddled air into the mix, making essential bubbles. Phoebe and Caesar were standing in the vat, the rest of us working from the sides, the shorter paddlers standing on stumps to reach. Every so often, Master Cromwell came round from his smokin' perch behind the drying shed to inspect.

"Get more air in there," he barked, as if we weren't doing that already. "Gently! Gently!" What did he know about gentle?

He'd recently grown a beard. I thought it might hide his mean jaw, but somehow it just made him look even more unkind. And his eyes? How they glint and shine with hate! Worse than most of us seen in a white man before, and most of us seen plenty bad. I glanced at him hard once to check on the color of his eyes for my own sake of naming. Were they grey? Oh no. They were ice blue, devil's blue, as cold a blue as you ever wanna see.

Round about noon that swelter of a day, Master Cromwell took off. It wasn't the first time. Punish and vanish, return. Punish, vanish, and return. It got me remembering Mo's stories about the rebellion years back – how that canal overseer punished and vanished too. Now years later, in the deadly heat, with fear of what might come next, I liked remembering what else Mo said – how good it felt to have a white man's head in his hands, still warm, eyes open and full of fright, body gone. Punishing and vanishing didn't work out so good for him, did it?

Some people deserve to die. Before being nabbed, shoved on a ship, and force-sailed to this marsh of misery, I never thought such a thing. In my village, I'd seen people prickle and steal, hog, cheat, and hurl insult, but nothing like here. The rebels didn't deserve to die, but I'm pretty sure that canal overseer did. Pretty sure Master Cromwell does.

Like a sour burp, he showed back up some time later, trotting along the road with a bucket. Limewater? At the vat, he dumped the entire thing out faster than you can say jackrabbit. Splat. Mr. Deveaux's words come back to me, how the liming needed to be just right. Not too much and not too little. The vat stirrers next to me both flinched.

What was Devil Blue Eyes gonna do next? We knew how one violence often fathered another.

Quashee shot me a look and mouthed the words "bad, bad." We all knew how hard Miss Eliza relied on this year's indigo. Thwarted year after year, and now this? Cromwell grunted and flung the bucket away, nearly clipping Caesar in the head. He sauntered off, fishing in a pocket for his pipe and flint. No hurry now.

"Go tell Miss Eliza," Quashee said, low and urgent. "Tell her the batch gone."

Dismissal
Eliza, Wappoo Plantation

The batch was ruined.

Shells crunched under my feet. I hurried. Gnats poked at my face, an emblem of my ire. I pulled a large handkerchief out of my pocket and tied it round my neck. The bugs. The coming stink.

Saffron had burst into the back pantry ten minutes earlier, eyes wild, chest heaving. I entered just as my sister slid her a glass of water. "Here," Polly cooed. "It's straight from the well-bucket."

Saffron's angular arm, hardened by the recent labors of aerating the indigo vats, set down the empty cup and grabbed the amulet hanging around her neck. I suddenly understood that it was no primitive adornment, but a talisman against malfeasance. A few weeks back, all of the indigo slaves had taken to wearing them – either crab claws or tiny red cloth bags. I knew my worst fears were about to be confirmed. Recently July had called Cromwell "a stink up my nose," emphasizing, "and t'ain't the rotting leaves." When a taciturn slave enlarges on her point, it was best to take heed. Why hadn't I?

My stomach churned. Saffron said in a rush, "He dumped it all, Miss Eliza, the bucket – the limewater. Every drop. Not pour and check, pour and check. He done dump it all!" If this was true – and why would Saffron fabricate such a thing? – I'd just lost another year of work, not to mention profits. By the time I broke into a trot at the sight of the vats, sweat beaded my forehead. What was I going to say? I should've formulated a speech, but rage cauterized my lungs.

Hoofbeats charged up the road behind me. The swift and nearly invisible spread of news among slaves, so often a source of aggravation or fear, this morning well served my need. Someone had alerted Mac.

He pulled his nag to a stop beside me, the reddish frizz of his hair haloing his face. My knight in shining armor? Where was his hat? It was then and only then that I shuddered to realize that as a twenty-year-old woman, I had no business confronting Cromwell on my own. A man with no scruples, at that. Mac nodded toward the vats. "Shall I go ahead, then, Miss?"

I agreed and he kicked his horse back to a canter. The ensuing dust cloud spoke to the need for rain – rain that had held off for days, which had until that very morning, seemed like a stroke of fortune, making all the indigo labors possible. We'd been so close this time! I'd dismiss the dyer on the spot! Surely, this was not an occasion to seek out Father's permission, a communication that could easily take six weeks. Mac could escort the black-hearted knave to Charles Town this afternoon – this very hour! Mr. Cromwell could swim to back to the islands for all I cared.

As the vats came into view, the sunken shoulders and tense faces of the idle slaves told the whole story. They had formed themselves into a line, hands behind their backs. Mac stood facing Cromwell. I didn't address the traitor at all, for the act of speaking exclusively to Mac in the wrongdoer's presence delivered a strong message of contempt. "Supervise the collection of his things and escort him off the premises by sundown. I don't care if the next ship to the islands doesn't depart for a fortnight. He'll not spend another night here!"

Mac looked surprised, but not for the reason I supposed. "Miss Eliza, come aside." Out of Cromwell's hearing, he said softly, "So ya dunna know."

"Spit it out – what? What?" I had never spoken this way to our overseer before. In subdued and nearly apologetic tones, Mac informed me that Cromwell had been hired on with a two-year contract. We could fire him, but the man would still be owed payment for the rest of his term – some twenty-plus months more.

I looked at Mac with incredulity, delaying response by pulling my hankie back up over my nose. Was I going to cry? How could Father have failed to inform me of this arrangement? I pulled down the hankie. "Well, what shall we do?"

"Ship 'im to Waccamaw. Let Starrat suffer his putrid hide. He'll keep the swine busy and his paws'll never taint another batch of indigo." He snickered and added, "The more grimy and back-breaking the better, yeah?" I enjoyed Mac's inclination toward vengeance, but his ready solution suggested that he'd seen this coming. Yet another sickening comeuppance for me. "Waccamaw sits a goodly distance. Like as not, you'll never lay eyes on him ag'in."

Before returning to the house, I inspected the vats for myself. With one of the long-handled scoops, I dished up some liquid and slid it around in the spoon. Sure enough – a dead batch. Proof, right there in the spoon. Even with my lack of expertise, the signs of an uncohered brew were clear – a flat, grayish blue instead of the signature yellow green running to teal along the edges, no foam anywhere in view, a thin liquid with no body whatsoever.

The wind gave a little kick and I knocked the ladle inadvertently, spilling its contents onto the hem of my frock. Imagine my surprise to see the edge of my dress turning from a pale green to blue right before my eyes. Well, then! Perhaps the liquid was spoilt for dye bricks, but viable enough for an hour or two of dyeing? Who doesn't want to salvage some slender good from disaster?

I waved the slaves to come round to see my blue-tinged hem. Eyebrows went up. A few tongues clucked. They looked at each other and then at me. "Have at it," I announced. Before I'd even made five paces back toward the house, head rags were being unwound and carefully submerged into the liquid with the long-handled paddles. Walking down the road, I sensed rather than saw men twisting out of their tunics.

Quash passed me on my way back, carrying a crock of vinegar. To my query he announced, "It might offset the lime." Ah, Quash, with intelligence to spare. I waved him on with a smile.

Later, Sir Raleigh and I made our way along the edges of drained rice fields, enjoying the fresh breeze that had begun to blow in off the Atlantic. To all the world, I must've looked like a planter's daughter surveying her father's land. No one would have seen how the stains of perfidy undid my person – how stiff my spine, how clenched my jaw. No one would have seen what I really was that day, a young woman wrestling with the first big betrayal of her life.

October 1743

Inward Flowers
Eliza, Wappoo Plantation

Charles and I walked my fig "orchard" this morning, Elizabeth ensconced with Mother at the fire. We talked poetry and politics. He made inspections, offered his expertise. Nothing remarkable about our exchange, in other words, until he tugged a ripe fig free, pulled a knife out of his pocket and cupping the fruit in his left hand, split it open with a precise stroke of the right. Any more pressure and he would've bloodied his palm, any less and the fruit would not have fallen open. The pink centers glistened.

"Hold out your hand," he said before sliding the fig onto my palm. He supported my hand with his, as if the weight of the fruit required it. Continuing to hold my hand, he used the tip of the knife to point. "The fig is not a fruit as commonly thought," he said, "but rather a flower growing inward. Look." After a pause: "Brown Turkeys are self-pollinators or we might find a dead wasp here." I gave a quick nod, flustered at this intimacy.

He removed his hand and returned the knife to his pocket, lesson over. I stared at the fig nested in my palm. Were my cheeks as pink as the fig flesh? I didn't think I could bring myself to eat it in front of him. My ever-considerate guest grabbed the fig halves and flung them afield. "There's one for the bugs," he laughed.

On our return to the house, I described my scarring and burial propagation method, how I hoped for independent shoots in a few years. "Eventually, I'll cut them free and plant them elsewhere. Or give them away. Perhaps you'll be a beneficiary!"

The reference to the future must have reminded Charles of his wife, for it effectively ended our pleasantries. Of course, I was guessing at the cause of his mood change, but I was sure of this – Elizabeth wouldn't survive long enough to be the recipient of any future fig trees.

Fig Preserves
July, Wappoo Plantation

"Figs gotta sugar on the tree." I held one up and twirled it round. "Not like peaches. Them we sugar on the counter." I pointed to the stem. "Stem gotta come with. You tug. Not hard. Just hard enough."

That fall Maggie was thirteen. I was hopin' they wouldn't task her in the fields so I could keep on teaching her. Who else I gonna teach? The branches bent low with fruit, so Maggie didn't need no crate for reaching. She was near as tall as me by that season anyhow. "You feel it? It's a feel."

Maggie shrugged. When she reached up, the sun shone on them burn blotches from years back. All scars got histories – moods, even. Hers look angry. They say, "Hey – look at me." And so you look, unable to turn away. Just where you hope the scarring might stop, it kept on going. Other scars, like Saffron's crisscrossed back, made less demands 'cause they was hidden.

I held up another fig. "Should look like Old Sarah's face." Maggie smiled. She smiled again when she tugged one off just right. She truly got the best smile in all the Lowcountry, maybe 'cause we waited so long for it.

After we filled two small baskets, I tugged off two more figs, one for Maggie and one for my own self. Maggie look scared, but I nodded. "Go on." We was far from Porch House, but we turned our backs anyhow. Old habits. Maggie ate slow, curious. Me? I moaned.

Back at Summer Kitchen, we rinsed each fig, pulled off the stems, and put 'em up to cook. Once they's soft, you crush 'em with a spoon. I showed Maggie how and told her to take care on account of figs being dainty, not like apples or potatoes.

Maggie tried, pressing her lips together, but the figs slid out from under her spoon. Like so much in the kitchen, weren't as easy as it looked. She mashed with her right hand and kept the left arm wrapped round her back on account of how the fire tingle up the bad arm. Maggie's scars might have authority, but they also was a root cellar of pain, full of memory.

Before I added the sugar, Maggie piped up, "What's gonna happen when the household breaks up? Is Miss Eliza gonna marry or go with her mother?"

"Who's saying anything about weddings? Missy's particular and by the by getting long in the tooth."

"But if Miss Eliza does marry, she might take Mama with her and put me in her pocket."

"Nobody's putting you in their pocket," I said, too loud. Maybe by being too loud, I showed Maggie her fear got sense in it.

In went two cups of sugar to each pot. I turned the hooks away from the fire, wishing I could turn away from the future as easy. After lugging the pots to the table for the night, we draped flour sacks across 'em to keep the flies off.

"Be syrup in the morning," I told her. "Then we cook the syrup, long and slow. That's how you make fig preserves." Maggie'd had a hand in blueberry jellies, peach jam, compote and even blancmange, but never fig preserves. "I'll show you how we warm the crocks before filling 'em. You'll be licking your fingers."

That smile again. What she gonna do with her fearful questions? Roll 'em and stuff 'em in her apron? Line 'em up with all the feathers she found over the years? Maybe I let Maggie down 'cause I didn't have no ready or true answers. We all was speculatin' how Miss Eliza might marry Mr. Pinckney. We'd seen his doting ways, her flushed-up chatter. And if she did marry him, seemed like she'd move to Belmont. And then there was all this talk about a ship coming from the West Indies? Why, I could end up in Mistress's pocket!

The next morning, the heavens opened up. Saffron, Maggie, and me dashed to Summer Kitchen. Oh how I grinned to see a bag of persimmons on the table.

Melody said, "Caesar brought them."

To Maggie, I said, "Simmons a delicacy." She was surprised, I bet, me with a word like that. Delicacy. But simmons need a special word, for my lord, what a molasses they make! Course we hold dear all the fruits, nuts, game, and fishes we gather: the rice tended in a squishy bog half a mile away; the okra and sweet potatoes in our garden; chub fish, whiting, and shrimp caught or netted, mostly on Sundays. Some evenings, the flavors of home filled our bowls and drifted all the way to the dining room. Sometimes delighted buckra slurped flavors from across the sea, not even knowing. That was a kind of pleasure too – them not knowing.

But food only go so far. Even when turned into molasses, fruits won't be fixing the hurts we crash into, fall under, or get burnt and strangled by. Ever since Maggie's bloods come down, we all been worrying about buckra's swampy-sick notions of breeding. What if they force Maggie with Indian Pete? How fixed they get on a notion – like mixing black blood with native – as if it make 'em men of science instead of what they is, monsters. They know about Saffron. They know. Would they make Daughter bed down with Mother's Lover? Make a man bed down with Lover's Daughter?

Stop. I know the answer. No amount of bread with simmons molasses gonna heal the wounding of this place.

November 1743

Dream of the Bottomlands
Maggie, Wappoo Plantation

Come the cooler time, we add basketmaking, barn chores, kindling collection and the like to our labors. On the stoop between me and Phoebe: palmetto fronds, long pine needles, and sweetgrass. Sweetgrass is a word to love. I love the smell of the blades too and how with enough coiling they turn into flat, elegant fanners, something useful and necessary to take rice to market.

A year ago, Old Sarah showed Phoebe and me the up and under, over and around of coiling. She couldn't see much, Old Sarah, but her hands held memory, and sometimes that's enough.

Phoebe and me worked side by side until I couldn't abide her noisy cheer a minute more. I gathered some sweetgrass and left. She's sweet, Phoebe, so it hurt to walk off but better to accept I have my ways and she got hers. I headed up to the laundry line.

Melody and July were pegging petticoats and tuckers up to dry. I sat on a gum stump and busied my hands. Melody and July chit-chatted like blue jays even with clothespins in their mouths. They were making fun of Caesar's pledge to protect Melody.

"What's he think?" July hooted. "He a wall? A pair of slicing blades? A white man?" She huffed and shook her head. Melody laughed. I felt bad for Caesar, how he cared so steady all these years, getting nothing but mockery back.

"Hey, fools got hearts too!" I blurted. Both of them stopped, turned, and gawked. Because of what I said, or because I piped up at all?

"Oh, just you wait, little woman," Melody finally said. "When some man comes tagging after you moon-eyed and pie-faced, you might mock him too."

"How do you know some man hasn't already?"

"Ooh, look who sassing us," July teased.

Talking still came hard, never casual. It came with barrows of fear. I worried my talk would run silly or false. I worried that when it really mattered, words'd hide from me. And, what if people wanted me to shut up?

July came over and knelt in front of me, quiet-like. The air got still around her, so I knew she was serious about something. When you don't talk for most of five years, you learn to listen to more than words. The positioning of someone's hands. The attention of dogs nearby. The air around a person's body.

You also learn how people treat words in all kind of ways. Some toss 'em out like trash, some speak 'em with care to show themselves and others make shields with them. Some, like Titus, use words to call down the gods, to make a moment sacrosanct.

Knowing a word like "sacrosanct" proves in three quick sounds that I am my mother's daughter.

I am my mother's daughter is a group of words I like.

July pulled her eyes up from the basket and stared into my face. I guess the skill coming through my fingers made July see me in a new way. I've known for a long time how pride and skill kept July alive. Kept her sitting up, standing, and walking. Kept her from howling out the names of her three sons and wading into the creek with bricks in her pockets. Pride and skill weren't just stand-ins for what was lost – they stood good all in themselves. Her labors gave something back to her. They were all hers and sacrosanct, even though just about everything her hands turned out was stolen. By them.

Melody started humming. She was draping Mistress's bed linens over the shrubs. Her humming was her something. A voice rare. A voice that made one white man change his mind about everything. Or so it was said.

That night I dreamed about ridges making paths through hardwood bottomlands. Indian Pete'd told stories about places watery, mysterious, shifting, and not well known by buckra. In the dream, I flew above the ridges. The berms looked like hems on a dress, holding back rivers and swamps. Then I walked on the ground. I was going toward something and I was going away from something and I was stopping to feel my head every now and again.

Some dreams catch up loose ends from days past. Other dreams go forward into time not yet seen. This dream traveled ahead, I was certain. In all my walks to Hell Hole Swamp, I never did see a bottomland like that one.

Just yesterday at breakfast, I heard Mo tell Binah about a treaty between the maroons and the King. On Jamaica. "What's maroons, Mama? What's Jamaica?" Mama whispered the answers with her mind. No words spoken.

That's another thing five years of barely talking will give you. Hearing the thoughts of your mama.

January 1744

Conspiratorial Glee
Eliza, Wappoo Plantation

Mother yodeled from the base of the stairs. I stood up without looking out my window or I might not have been surprised when Mother flung open the door and Mary Bartlett, Mrs. Woodward, and Mary Huston shouted out, "Happy Birthday, Eliza!" A week after a subdued and disappointing birthday, turns out I was not forgotten after all.

What a hubbub of affection! Capes hung and gloves set aside, we enjoyed a luncheon of delicious savories: fried sweet potatoes, creamed palmetto cabbage, stuffed blackfish. Mother had outdone herself! I truly had not known. July brought out a cake topped with six white candles – five for every four years of my life and one extra to equal twenty-one. Mary Huston watched the candles warily.

I blew out the flames with gusto, hoping to vanquish Mary's fears at the same time. We all knew about her husband's association with George Whitefield's disciple Hugh Bryan, whose false prophecies about the coming ruination by fire grabbed hold of her thoughts. According to her mother, she sometimes rattled on about fire and avenging angels for hours, calling out to a phantom Bryan.

July lifted the cake to the sideboard to slice, while Mrs. Woodward straightened her spine. She exhibited the alert caution common to those caring for unpredictable, lost souls. No one expected Mary to sit through an entire visit, but the eruption, when it came, nevertheless shocked. First she spewed incoherencies to the ceiling, then to the tablecloth. She laughed maniacally.

With grim resolve, Mrs. Woodward corralled her daughter to the door. Mary yelled over her shoulder, "It'll be fire next time!" Mrs. Woodward waved hastily. Mary kept up her wild speech. "Kongo beasts one year, angels of retribution the next. A burning barn is the Devil's work. Watch the crossroads!" Their carriage slave bounded forward to help. As scuffling and indecorous departure as ever there was.

Stunned silence. Finally Mary Bartlett said, "Surely, there must be something Mrs. Woodward can do."

"If there was a remedy, my dear," Mother said stiffly, "Mrs. Woodward would have procured it at any cost."

Thankfully Mary next leavened the talk with stories about what a terrible invalid her uncle made. He'd broken his arm falling off his horse recently and was refusing to follow doctor's orders. "They recommended rest, but heaven forbid anyone tell Uncle Charles what to do," she chuckled. "But you know, he's not twenty anymore." Mary next painted rather too graphic a scene of her uncle inserting a dinner knife under his plaster to relieve the itching.

July set down a tray of wrapped presents on the table. With a gleeful clap, Mary demanded that I open her gift first. The box revealed a pair of lovely tortoise shell combs. "Put them on," she yelped. I did. Next: a volume of plays by Hallam inscribed "With lasting love and affection," signed by both Elizabeth and Charles. Mrs. Woodward had left behind a package of two kinds of Venetian lace, both exquisitely made and in significant yardage. I was nearly in a swoon.

Mother nodded at July, who disappeared and came back through the hall door so as to stand directly behind me. "Turn around, Daughter, dear." Oh my goodness! There was July, beaming, holding an exquisite gown by the shoulders. Mother rose and pulled out some of the skirt's volume to showcase its drape and luster and the beautiful handwork along the hem.

"What? How?"

"Try it on! Try it on," chanted Mary.

The frock was an exquisite moss green brocade with tiny pleats at the neckline and a long row of buttons along the back, each covered in a matching moss green silk. "The two of you?" July and Mother nodded.

"It'll look stunning with your quilted chenille petticoat," Mother said. "The lace from Mrs. Woodward and Mary is for the cuffs." July turned the gown to show the back, clearly proud of her work.

Stepping out of my calico frock upstairs, I imagined July and Mother sitting in chairs near the bedchamber windows many an afternoon and stitching away in conspiratorial glee, probably under the cover of a migraine. Mother would've enjoyed colluding with a slave whose needle skills very nearly matched her own. Who fetched the fabric and threads? Had Hercules been in on it too?

Until today, I had not believed my mother capable of keeping a secret. She will ever disappoint and surprise me in equal measures. I descended the stairs, taking care not to trip, feeling every inch the queen. Oohs and aahs all around!

Chance Meeting
Eliza, Charles Town

Halfway back to Cross Winds from the dressmaker's atelier the next week, Mother and I met up unexpectedly with Charles. It was a dank day in January, but no gloom of atmosphere could possibly outdo his dismal aspect. I hardly recognized him – face drawn, pallor running toward ash. His wig sat slightly off-kilter, making the broad expanse of his forehead seem misshapen instead of dignified. Poor man! The gentle charisma had taken leave and in its place the shadowy sentinel of death had taken up residence. He was waiting for his wife to die in the only way he knew how – with all his person, in the slow measure of time.

No business took place during the early weeks of that year. I suspect that Charles could hardly have attended even to minor matters, brilliant mind or no, so it was just as well. Politics, plantation affairs, personal comforts – all on hold. Even in his burdened state, however, he managed to inquire after Father and George.

"Father will be sending George for us in the wink of an eye," I said.

Mother stiffened. I did not intend to elicit Charles's opinion about the changing circumstances of our family, and I most certainly could not let the man see how ill-inclined I was to leave the Lowcountry or why. Mother took hold of our worried friend's elbow and asked after Elizabeth: Was she comfortable, could she still receive visitors, did he require assistance of any kind? Meanwhile, I felt such a pull to help him through this grim phase that I hardly knew myself.

No mere impulse toward courtesy, this need to care. It tugged like a tide at the full of the moon. Was it desire, pure and simple?

Moments later, we mustn't hold him back and so forth, we watched our esteemed friend depart. He headed north. Mother grunted. "I never thought I'd say this of Charles, but the man is undone. He lacks all composure."

"Well, he did have the presence of mind to inquire after Father and George."

Mother qualified. "Yes dear, but he was utterly elsewhere during our response." She seemed surprised that a man of his station would show himself to be so out of sorts.

"Death has a way of barging in at inopportune times, Mother. Would you confine him to his parlor?"

"Now, Eliza, your testiness is not about me, I happen to know," she said with a sly look.

"What?"

"Polly's no spy," she began. My heart sank. Maybe my sister had at last discovered my diary under our bedchamber's floorboards and read it. Such an act alone would pose no threat, so innocent was her curiosity, so redemptive her compassion – but if she'd mindlessly reported a detail or two to Mother, there might be no end of embarrassment.

"Apparently, you left a letter out to dry," she continued. "A letter to Charles which you signed, *Eliza Pinckney*." She saw the look of horror on my face and rattled on, as if this was not a major social gaffe, but rather the kind of minor mishap that occurred all the time. "Slips of tongue, or in this case, slips of the pen, often reveal the true status of one's heart." She chuckled as if her clever wordplay could mitigate my embarrassment.

"Surely, Polly read it wrong?"

"You know the girl has no guile."

I moaned, "Oh dear Lord, how shall I ever face him again?"

"But you just did, sweetheart." True enough, but I hadn't known of my gaffe then. Mother patted my arm and waxed philosophic about the folly of worrying on matters that cannot be undone. "Sometimes, like death, truth comes at the least convenient of times. When the dust settles – and in this instance I'm afraid we're talking about the dust of the grave – I think you'll find that your faux pas did you a great service."

I didn't ask her to elaborate, but she did. "You think I haven't seen the way you look at him? You can be sure that if I've noticed, he has as well." We arrived back at Cross Winds. She stopped me at the base of the stairs. "It wouldn't surprise me," she ventured, "if Elizabeth and your man Charles −"

"Don't call him that."

"Hear me out, child!" Mother's blue eyes turned a dark grey. I couldn't tell if they darkened with sorrow at Elizabeth's imminent passing or with the seriousness of her message. Perhaps in that intuitive way of hers, she understood that if my heart's no-longer-secret wish was granted, we would soon, mother and daughter, be parted, and once parted, not likely to see each other again. "I wouldn't be surprised if the affectionate bonds between you and Charles were a topic of conversation between them. Do not tug away, young lady! The love between spouses sometimes runs deep enough that it can be elastic and transcend the particular needs of one or the other. Death finessing the rules, if you will." She looked out over the harbor. The dark waters and her eyes seemed made of the same liquid. "Of course Elizabeth has considered what will come to pass for Charles after she's gone. I would expect nothing less of her."

"Mother," I mewled, my voice shaking with vulnerability.

"You've been no more or less a fool than anyone who's ever been in love," she said matter-of-factly. It was like a lid on a box snapping shut. "We shall help him bury his wife. We shall grieve the loss of our dear, dear friend. And then we shall see about the two of you. Now how about some tea? It's a frightfully good day to sit by the fire."

Funeral
Eliza, near Belmont

We gathered under a sky hung close with charcoal-colored clouds. More rain? Perhaps even the sky would weep at Elizabeth's passing. I hunched my shoulders against the chill and traveled a circuitous route around gravestones, the frozen ground offering a soft crunching commentary, one both sweet and reverent, somehow. The headstones, erect or canted, seemed decorative only − a visual rhythm of curve and stone. When Elizabeth's open grave came into view, though, my breath caught short. The large, gaping orifice struck me as volatile and offending − a gash in the natural order requiring immediate and drastic repair. Inside rested the still mahogany coffin. I found Mary Bartlett and leant into her with wordless sympathy. Mother stood behind me as if to shelter from the disturbing sight of the grave.

Mary slid her hand under my arm and whispered, "At least her suffering is over."

"Indeed, though his is not." I nodded toward Charles, who stood in rigid attention opposite. Mary squeezed my arm. Charles seemed to have aged years over the last several months, the strain of watching his wife's decline etched in his haggard face. Even so, he cut a fine figure, cloaked in an elegant black linen jacket with silver buttons, ivory silk folded at his neck, a single orange-red flower inserted into his lapel. How lonely his coming days would be!

I peered intently at the ground and struggled to give the droning minister my attention. A long low growl of thunder rumbled to the east, however, distracting us all. The gathered company, nearly to a person, scanned the horizon with apprehension. Did others think, as I did, that nature offered the more apt commentary? The minister began to rush.

"Heavenly raiment now clothes our sister in joy! She has released the mortal cloak. Let us give thanks." Mother leant her head into my upper back. The simplicity of her gesture belied its power to convey the whole of grief. I teared up. Mary noticed and pressed a palm against my upper arm again. Her eyes were red-rimmed and puffy, and no wonder – Elizabeth had been her favorite aunt and very nearly a mother to her these many years.

The pastor concluded just as a closer rumble of thunder gargled along the horizon. Even though not inclined to hurry, Mac broke away from the now restless and murmuring mourners and trotted to retrieve the borrowed carriage. Abraham and Hercules peeled away too. Although it was a short buggy ride to the water, our travel home involved a paddle down the Cooper River, navigation around the peninsula, and crossing the Ashley before making our way down Wappoo Creek. For a variety of reasons, we had no desire to stay at Cross Winds that evening.

Looks of consternation flashed across faces already shadowed with grief. As surely as death came to each of us, storms barreled through the Lowcountry. Lightning flared as I approached Charles to say a few sympathetic words. My heart raced. I'll admit that the need for a truncated farewell suited my nervous aspect.

I grabbed his hands. "We shall be praying for you and for Elizabeth." His eyes welled up in sadness and though I couldn't be sure, perhaps some other emotion as well? He held my gaze a bit longer than was strictly necessary and then lowered his head to kiss my hands. The moment I felt the warmth of his mouth through my gloves, I added in a broken voice, "Anything you need, please let us know. Anything." He dropped my hands as another mourner approached. I turned briskly to leave.

Mac waved us all into the carriage. Mother and I sat facing Polly, Abraham and Hercules on the front bench with the overseer. In no time at all, we exited the small copse surrounding the church. The grasses lining the road waved in hectic patterns. I thought perhaps the grasses were responding to the death of our dear friend too, their wild and swift waggling offering up distress at Elizabeth's death. Why not?

Polly sat in a calm quiet. As a rule, I didn't like to rely on her special sensibilities, but this seemed a good time to make an exception. Surely if any of us were to join Elizabeth in the heavenly quarters today due to dangerous travel, my sister would sense it?

By the time we reached the Cooper River, the rain was pelting down, pocking the river, drenching bombazine and wool challis alike. The spiky palmettos lining the river banks jiggled their leaves in fanatical disarray. Polly remained bland and distracted and if you hadn't met her before, you might have mistaken her for a dunderhead.

Once in the pettiauger, we made speedy progress, the current in our favor. Mother forbore, gripping Polly's hand. By the time we reached the mouth of the Cooper, all of us were thoroughly drenched. The harbor frothed with chop and the sheets of rain made even White Point invisible. Abraham and Herc paddled in a synchronized fury.

Polly turned her gleaming visage toward me. "The next time we visit that church, you'll be dressed in ivory."

March 1744

Magpie
July, Wappoo Plantation

With a nail I found on the barn floor, a potato sack, and years of scraps saved in secret, I'm making a rag blanket. A poking and knotting business, there's not much skill in it, but the tufts of cloth add up 'til it starts to look like a horse mane cut short and dipped in a rainbow. Beautiful, in other words.

Life made strange flips. Maggie showing a chatty side, Melody holding onto a new secret. Binah having one baby, then another. After Melody took the baby-killing herbs a second time, Master gave up on pairing her with Indian Peter and insist on Binah instead. But Binah just made babies with Mo. How was they gonna know?

At sunset, Titus tossed his bag of bones and the opele up and down. I could tell he felt the coming change and it weren't good.

April 1744

Ambrose
Eliza, Wappoo Plantation

Paper hexagons scattered onto the gallery as I stood to peer down the road. I smelled cheroot but couldn't yet see Ambrose. If the new wooden vats were complete, it was just possible that the stars were aligning this year. If so, how providential! The rice crop at Garden Hill turned out ill last year, producing but a hundred and sixty barrels, Wappoo a mere forty-three. Furthermore, rice markets continued to sag, recently fetching only thirty shillings per hundred.

Ambrose came into view, slightly slouched, wearing his signature blue jacket. By the time he stood at the base of the stairs looking up at me from under graying eyebrows, my heart was racing. "The building's done," he said with quiet authority. Ambrose was steady, contained.

"Well, let's see, then," I said, and yelled out to Mother that I was going to the vats.

Father had assured me in letter after letter that this hire was sound. A free man from the islands, Ambrose was descended from Benin masters and thus well versed in all aspects of indigo. "A thousand years of craft behind him," Father'd written. Privately, I referred to Father's first hire as "that treacherous bastard," so Benin history or no, experience had left me wary.

Over the last week, I'd barely kept wild impatience at bay – taking on another of Scarlatti's sonatas, overseeing the barn attic organization, and assembling hexies for a quilt. Even as I folded the tiny scraps of cloth over the paper hexagons and stitched them in place, all I could think about was indigo. Well, and a certain gentleman on the Cooper River. A tiny part of me dared to hope that the Grandmother's Garden quilt might grace a marriage bed.

Ambrose picked up his pace. He was forty-five, maybe fifty years of age? The graying hair suggested older, but it was so hard to tell with Negroes. His skin was smooth and his eyes deep set. He moved as if to a secret rhythm, unusual in any person, but strikingly so in a black man. Such assurance. Such independence.

From Father, I knew that Ambrose had been freed by testamentary disposition while still a young man. Born on Barbados, he'd eventually made his way to Montserrat and worked as a small-time merchant. Father found him selling spools of hemp on the wharves with nothing but the rich color of his jacket to advertise his skill. After a mere half hour's dialogue, Father hired him. This time the contract was at-will, and this time I knew the terms in advance.

When we started cutting through a field of young okra, Ambrose pointed to the ground. "Careful, now. Fire ants love okra." I took off my apron, hiked my frock up a few inches and retied the apron over the gathered cloth so as to see where I walked. I'd already had an encounter with fire ants and did not care for another.

We arrived at the vats. The slaves stepped back deferentially, another contrast with Cromwell. The three-tiered wooden vats were configured just like the former brick vats, but spoke to a better understanding of the finicky process of indigo leaf fermentation. My chest expanded with pride and a sense of hope.

Later I resumed my hexie paper-piecing, now and then lifting my head to watch Melody's sons playing on the dock in between mucking out the horse stalls. The catalpa blossoms had rained to the ground in gentle flurries a little early this year. Noah kicked through them, Moses dashing behind. Mother had taken the trouble to make Moses garments more befitting a plantation son than a slave, which was concerning for obvious reasons. Through a series of not-so-subtle hints, I'd convinced her that it was strange to dress one boy so much better than the other, but rather than give up the effort for Moses, she took to sewing on Noah's behalf too. Something for her to do.

Moses stood tall for a five-year-old, further proof of paternity if more were needed, for Mr. Whittaker had stretched lean and lanky, taller than any other man at our party when we met him five years back. Though both boys were quadroons and shared a mother, they hardly looked related – Noah with his dark eyes, tawny skin, and slightly coiled black hair, Moses with his hazel eyes, a mop of black wavy curls and skin so pale as to look white.

I was about to head inside when I heard the soft, repetitive splash of a paddle. Mr. Tilton appeared, alone in a canoe. What was he doing here?

He reached into his vest pocket and pulled out a letter, holding it aloft. "Forgive me for not tarrying, but I've got another letter to deliver."

"But why are you delivering any letters at all?" Apparently, when his post arrived this morning, he'd offered to take over since he was heading out in our direction anyway.

"I'm on my way to Dutarque's," Tilton said.

"He's home, then?" Dutarque was often peripatetic this time of year, making rounds to buy and sell with tribes further inland. Tilton nodded with a look of eager anticipation. Did he not realize that a little dissembling was in order? It was one thing to adopt the role of the perpetual bachelor, a role even Mother now accepted as unbendable in both of these men's cases, but it was another thing altogether to wear such naked emotion on his face.

As he lifted his paddle to depart, Moses ran a big circle under the catalpa in full view of the dock. Tilton gave me a stern look, taking in the jacquard. "I'd brand that one straightaway. And not on the chest, mind, but here." He tapped his right cheek. Though intrusive and condescending as usual, his advice was not without merit – especially since the little tyke wasn't wearing Negro cloth. What was Mother thinking? Missing my brothers, of course, but to treat Moses like a doll and dress him for her own pleasure was not without risk.

Watching Tilton's canoe recede, I exhaled, always relieved to see him leave.

I opened my letter. It was an invitation to tea at Belmont. Charles was ready for company, at last.

Anticipating
Saffron, Wappoo Plantation

April bloomed her pretty skirts, but we were tossed high and low with not knowing. Letters came from Antigua like weapons. Talk about reunions seeped like poison through the pantry door. Seemed Master George, a child no longer, would sail north to fetch them back. The future started coming at us, harsh and dangerous.

Phoebe'd go with Polly of course, but what about the rest of us? Would Mistress take Melody, and if she did, what about Noah and Moses? Would Miss Eliza take me, and if so, what about Maggie?

Miss Eliza paced that week, all churned up inside. Clear as day, she wasn't hankering for the West Indies. She and Mistress closed doors, put heads close, trying so hard not to be heard.

Soon enough, they went off to Master Pinckney's. Miss Eliza had asked for extra hairpins and wanted to know were the pearls too much? "No, Miss. You look fine." She wore a flirty air, even though Mistress Elizabeth dead but four months.

Open the Curtains
Eliza, Belmont

In the Pinckney house, all the curtains were drawn closed. A small fire crackled, but instead of offering cheer, it seemed timid and withdrawn, as if it too were constrained by woe. The sight of Elizabeth's empty chair caused a shudder of anguish. Wasn't she just there?

Our host sprang up from his seat near the hearth and attempted a courteous greeting, but it came across as dutiful and marked by surprise, even though he had invited us by letter days earlier. Perhaps his slaves were falling down in their duties.

"Sit. Sit my friends." Neither Mother nor I chose Elizabeth's chair, so Charles scooted his seat round to face the sofa. A house slave made her way to the first of two tall windows, gathered up volumes of burgundy damask and pulled them to the side. How long had it been? Charles blinked. We pursued superficial topics until it seemed more impolite to avoid discussing Elizabeth's absence than to broach it.

"We all miss her so," Mother said softly, glancing at the empty chair.

"Indeed," Charles sighed, and then, looking at me, said, "You were like a daughter to her, you know." His tone was sweet and genuine.

"She was the dearest of dear women," I said. "Such worthy friends are rare in life. I felt as much tenderness for her as for any woman in the world – my own good Mama excepted, of course." I laid a still-gloved hand upon Mother's arm. She gave me a tight, unreadable smile and nodded. Tears gathered in my throat.

Now that Mother knew about my feelings for Charles, she shared my sense of urgency. The subject would need to be brought up this instant hour, in fact, if there was to be even the slightest chance of attaining my heart's end. George's sloop was aimed at our shores at that very moment.

"We've had another letter from Father," I began. Back came the slave with a large silver tea tray. She placed it on a mahogany table near the fire. I hoped the distraction of service would embolden me, but it did not. Mother tapped her spoon on the edge of her cup like a merry host chiming a champagne flute before making a toast. "Speak up daughter," the tapping seemed to say. "Speak up."

"He's sent George," I continued, "and as soon as tides and hire permit, we're to accompany him back to Antigua." I glanced at Mother, who winked. Winked! Charles held his teacup between two palms and gazed at the embers. I couldn't tell if he was even listening.

I took a breath and said, "Father has changed his mind about South Carolina after all. We are to join him in the West Indies."

"Life can change with a rapidity that disturbs, no doubt," Charles said. He still wasn't looking at us.

"We're to depart within the month." I might've made this statement a little too loudly. "After nearly six years, Father, Mother, and Polly are overjoyed at the prospect of living together again." Now I too stared at the embers. It was perhaps too much to expect a man in the throes of grief to hear what I was not saying. Mother sat straighter in palpable expectancy. For once, I wished that she would advance my cause. She echoed my words, but with a heavy-handed emphasis on my sister's name. "Polly will be better off in the West Indies, I am quite sure."

Charles barely moved, but something in his manner shifted, almost as though a mild shock had coursed through his limbs, animating him from slumberous unhappiness. Mother all but nudged me. He looked up and met my gaze. While still looking at me, Charles asked my mother, "And what about your other daughter? Will she too be better off in the West Indies?"

"Heavens, no!" Mother exclaimed. "Eliza belongs here now." Mother's tone expressed mischief, but I suspected she dissembled to disguise the high stakes at play. "Ever since the arrival of Father's plans, she's been quite unbearable honestly," Mother chuckled.

Mother did her bit of nattering now, perhaps to give Charles time to absorb this message. It was my beloved orchards, my indigo experiments, my skill in running three plantations, etc. "She's not one to abandon projects before their conclusion, isn't that so, my dear?"

I nodded, my cheeks flaming with color. Mother might be verging on the heavy-handed, but at least we were talking about it now. The conversation felt daunting and perilous beyond anything I'd ever experienced – and yet we were just talking about travel and households. Clever Mother.

Charles scooted forward in his chair and leaned onto his elbows, closing the distance between us. Mother sprang to her feet. Such an actress! Never one to mind making a bit of a fool of herself, she chirped, "Oh aging parts! I'm off." She left as if for the privy in a flutter, her skirt billowing in the door frame.

I struggled to breathe. I'd been alone with Charles many times before, of course, but never after having been so laid bare. My pulse raced in equal parts dread and excitement, knowing how much my happiness depended on what he said next. He pulled his chair forward again and took one of my hands in both of his.

"Is it true, then?" The soft look in his eyes melted my fear. "I am not alone in these feelings?" I managed a nod. He stood and walked the length of the room a few times. I wondered if he paced to gather courage or to march out the grief before pivoting toward joy. Before I knew it, he dropped to one knee in front of me and asked for my hand. He proceeded to slowly tug each finger of my glove loose before very deliberately removing the glove entire. He laid it neatly on the arm of the chair before asking for the other hand. Again, he slowly tugged each finger free. Warmth fell down the column of my torso and gathered below my waist in inexplicable and saturating delight. I'd yet to experience any feeling such as this, apart from the strange shuddering dream here and there. He laid the second glove upon its mate.

Holding both of my now-bare hands in his, he asked for my hand in marriage. I barked my yes and then burst into tears. We made our first embrace as suitors ever so awkwardly, nearly knocking over the table and tea set. Laughter.

Laughter, and ecstatic relief. One soul finding its way to the other! In spite of the age difference, in spite of the terrible loss of Elizabeth, in spite of fluctuating fortunes, we made the proper and eternal pledges right then and there. What followed would be mere window dressing.

Mother waltzed back into the parlor. Sizing up the scene, she clasped her hands and yelped in mock surprise, exceedingly pleased with herself. She very well might go through the rest of her life telling everyone that this union was all her doing. I didn't care.

In a flutter of cheer, we departed. In an ideal world, or even in England, such an abbreviated courtship would be deemed inappropriate – the pall of mourning, the insufficient passage of time and so on. But colonial life imposed its unique dictates, exigencies that our entire society well recognized. We expected no judgment.

We left soon after. From the walk, I looked up to see Charles opening the curtains in his dining room. He would let the spring light in. He would resume his place in the passage of seasons. And he would have me. Climbing into the carriage to return to the Ashley Ferry, I had the sense that my life had just begun.

Rattle and Burn
Saffron, Wappoo Plantation

I felt the thudding hooves in the floor first and heard the harnesses jingling a song of doom next. Like always, we tidied aprons and lined up on the gallery, hands behind our backs. But it wasn't like always – Melody with her bit-up nails, me with knuckles rubbed raw, July pole-straight, tense.

"Welcome home, Miss. Welcome home, Mistress," July said all chipper, trying so hard. The ladies stepped off the carriage, grinning. They'd just come from Belmont. Miss Eliza was to marry Master Pinckney. And soon.

After serving glasses of sherry, we clung like ghosts to the pantry door.

"Here's to your upcoming union!" Mistress sang. "You could not have made a better match, Daughter. Perhaps I should've trusted you more."

"Why, Mother, I do believe you're trying to apologize." The two of them playing, no cross words today.

We all knew how debt and auction blocks can rip a family up, but a wedding or funeral can do just as hard. Sometimes wills wrought ugly change. When a Master died, after giving out linens, books, and land, he might give a slave mother to his niece, a slave father to his son, and their child to his cousin. And if the relative needed money, even a family willed together could be mercilessly split after to settle the ledger.

That's why the wedding shone like rainbows for the white ladies but came over the horizon like a wicked storm to us, clouds and wind aching for damage. Who would be ruined and who might march toward summer, heart in hand? Nobody knew. Our days were slashed sideways by fear. Soon the orders would come: *You – you go on the sloop. You – you go to Belmont*. No way to stop what was coming.

Waiting was no friend.

At supper, Miss Polly popped up and down like a mad cricket. Mistress just smiled.

"Flower girl. Flower girl," Polly sang. Miss Eliza nodded, glowing. Polly twirled, tipped off center, caught the curtains and tugged 'em down in a heap. She was quiet under the cloth.

"That's enough, Polly. Finish your dinner." Mistress barely blinked. "After dinner, let's fancy up your champagne-colored frock with some ribbons, shall we?" Mistress nodded at Melody, who slid a chair over to put the curtain rod back up.

"Will you like seeing the West Indies, again, Melody?" Mistress said to Melody's back. Miss Eliza snapped her head as if someone slapped her, but Melody turned round and smiled. Her pleasing singsong voice hid all kinds of fear and contempt, I knew.

"What does it matter what I like, Mistress?"

As the wedding day came closer, the live oaks swayed and whispered with gossip and dread. It didn't occur to them that we had a stake in things. To make plans clear.

Maggie had come round a slow curve, mostly sleeping at night, mostly eating at meals. Her voice gave suppertimes a new pleasure, sometimes even rat-a-tat-tat with stories. She was stretching into her body and playing at times with wit. But wouldn't she backstep into that bleak and damp slaver's hold if we were separated? The questions rattled and burned.

Sounds like Mistress wants Melody. Makes sense 'cause Melody got the knack of filling her bath just so and sponging her neck the way she likes. Mistress being ever so picky, why would she leave Melody behind? Unless she was worried on Master and the old failures of trust, that is. Some bit of peace settled in before he sailed long ago, but was it a lasting peace? Maybe their peace was like dirty clothes folded nice and tucked back in the wardrobe, looking fine but apt to stink when worn again. And then there was how almost five years sagged on Mistress's face but bloomed on Melody's.

If any hate lingered, Mistress could dish nasty now. She could take Melody and leave Noah and Moses here. Or she could just take one of them. She wouldn't even have to sell the boys to ruin her. So many ways to break a slave mother's heart!

Melody and July turned into cloth thieves, secretly making another pair of linen breeches for Moses. Something's up, but Melody ain't sharing yet, which tells me it's a plan freighted with risk.

I been dressing Miss Eliza all this time. She relies on me for more than hair pinnin' and frock pressing 'cause of how I guess at her notions, even those she does her best to hide. And a fancy Master like Charles Pinckney was always wanting two more female hands, right? If you asked me, and no one was, it'd be easier for Miss Eliza to take Maggie to the wedding house 'longside me than to go to the bother of putting her in her pocket. And besides, Miss Eliza can't need the money, marrying a rich man?

A nasty new word slapped hard on my tongue in those tumultuous spring days: dowry. Dowry was a bride price. Dowry should be lace and linens, pots and dishes, night frocks and fine woven wraps. Surely, not people. A donkey, a wagon, a spinning wheel – maybe even a house. But human beings? What a cold word, dowry. Probably why buckra liked it so much. Cold words helped keep scorching truths at bay. Cold words helped hide the evil of trading bodies, helped keep off the stink of charred hearts.

We were all unsettled. Crates crowded the hall and parlor, but still somehow emptiness crept in. Melody started gnawing on the skin round the nails now 'cause there were no nails left to chew. Caesar disappeared into the scrub for three days. Recently, Maggie took off to Hell Hole Swamp – the first time in so, so long, and for the first time on her own.

And then there was Indian Pete. He was strong at task, the best with dogs and tracking and hunting, but he ain't no paddler. If I ended up the Cooper River, I'd be a crick, a river mouth, a harbor, and then another river away. Tides coming and going. The freshet. Would I ever see him again? A soft hoot floated out over the back terrace, an owl looking for her mate. It sounded like my grief calling out.

A week later, we lined up at the smokehouse for rations: peas and corn, bits of jerk, molasses, and some clabber. Hercules spilled out gossip. The dowry, he told us, was Wappoo Plantation and all us living on the street. All twenty-two of us, except maybe Quash. We were, each of us, a wedding gift.

Later on, we heard arguing. This time they weren't trying to keep it quiet. We shelled peas and made bread. July was starting on wedding sweets already. "Like we were soup bowls," I whispered to no one. "Am I a tureen? Have I got a ladle? My bones might be made of clay, but a stew pot I am not."

I patted the dough into a ball, dropped it into a larded bowl, draped a towel over, then set it to rest in a sunny spot by the window. Melody finished the peas and started helping July peel oranges. We were sugaring citrus curls for the wedding cake.

"Is the dowry a piece of paper, like a will?" I asked. They didn't know. "Was Master's letter the dowry, or is it something else? Do they have to go to court, or is a handshake enough?" More shrugs. One thing was clear as orange peels curling on white porcelain, dowry brought division. Even a dowry made of flimsy paper got the power to cut.

Planning a New Life
Eliza, Wappoo Plantation

"Well, it's settled then," Mother said with a satisfied air. "Wappoo and the slave inventory are yours." She set down Father's letter. I'd already read it twice and made some rough calculations. "Of course, Phoebe will sail with us and I'll want Melody too, which means Noah and Moses'll come too, naturally." Even though I was flush with newfound happiness, Mother's presumptions rankled.

"Perhaps I ought make a more thorough examination of the inventory before we come to any hard and fast decisions," I said. Mother huffed. "Well?" I continued. "The ink on Father's letter's hardly dry, and yet here you are divvying up the dowry as if it were your due."

"So this is how it's to be, then? The world is your oyster and you would deny me small comforts? How quickly you're prepared to make me a poor relation. Well, I shall not beg."

Egad! My measurement of loss ought to have been done silently. Would I never learn? "Oh, Mother. Can't I have the satisfaction of my dowry for ten minutes before you lay claim to pieces of it? You know how heavily mortgaged the property is." Indeed, by the time the debt was accounted for, there would be very little left.

Mother stirred her tea with a loud tinkling but said nothing more. As numbers weren't her strong suit, it was possible she hadn't considered the mortgage. It's true I hardly needed a generous gift from Father to establish a comfortable future with Charles, but I'd yet to fully absorb my disappointment at such an encumbered dowry without having Mother immediately carve off big pieces of it. Mother entitled to more than a fifth of the human capital and why? Simply because it suited her need. How galling, how typical. When hadn't a critical portion of my life been about Mother's need?

Melody's absence would present one kind of loss, but Noah and Moses another altogether. I certainly wasn't going to be the one to tear the family asunder, but Melody's sons happened to carry more potential value than all the other children on the property, both being quadroons and male. Maybe in the next breath Mother'd lay claim to July too because the prospect of living without the slave's Beaufort rice bread or Charlotte Russe was simply too much to bear.

I swallowed the Assam brew and my resentment. In a softer tone, I asked, "Surely, Charles won't object to Saffron and Maggie?"

Mother offered only a stony silence.

I worried that our two Wappoo slaves would duplicate the labors of others. I couldn't predict, either, whether Charles would take issue with Maggie's silences or the unsightly scarring on her arm. If he erected even the slightest resistance, I had no idea what asserting myself might cost.

Oh, and Quashee. Charles had recently purchased land on East Bay as the site for our new home. How excitedly he noted that Quash was "just the man for the job, nothing out of his league," etc. Charles's sketches included one Quashee specialty after another – carved pilasters, ornate mantels and balusters, the finest mahogany paneling. Because of Quashee's skills, including literacy, owning him meant we'd also be able to save on the hire of a contractor. The trouble was Father wanted him too.

"And then there's Quashee," I said to Mother, waggling the last page of the letter, where in a squirrelly postscript Father had carved out the exemption. In this way, my parents acted in accord, giving away and taking back in the span of a breath or a page.

"So? He's your father's to do with as he will."

"Charles won't be pleased." This was meant to be an appeal, but Mother remained mute. Midday exhaustion or spiteful withholding? I decided right then and there that if push came to shove, I would simply refuse to put Quash on the sloop, possession being nine-tenths of the law, etc.

Just then I realized that even more than plaster medallions or carved balusters, I wanted my girls, Saffron and Maggie. Charles and I'd often volleyed opposing views on a point of literature or philosophy, but if this came to a disagreement, it would be different, more significant. Marriage suddenly seemed a dark tunnel without a handrail.

May 1744

The Secret Cupboard
Melody, Wappoo Plantation

All morning, I patted apron pocket. *It's empty. It's still empty.* Porch House was upended. Most things were staying put since Mistress and Miss were both headed to well-appointed houses, but naturally we packed all of Mistress's clothing and most of Miss's. Miss Eliza had already crated up her leather-bound books with care, her harpsichord music double-tied with ribbons. So far no one had touched the secretary.

My apron pocket was empty, my head full of ideas.

Nana Lucy sent a message a few days back, so I knew what passage for two to Philadelphia cost. Mo gave me a few coins, since Nana Lucy was his grandmother and he had taken over Cudjoe's stash. Thank goodness Saffron had spied Cudjoe burying his coin sack that night when she and Maggie came back from Hell Hole Swamp, otherwise the treasure might never've been found.

A crash of notes from the harpsichord. I dashed from pantry to parlor. It wasn't Miss Eliza, it was Morgan scrabbling for scraps of breakfast left on a plate above the keyboard. "Shoo," I hissed. The dog skulked away.

I paused and listened. Nothing. Mistress and Miss were in the barn sorting out the horse leathers, equipment worth a small fortune. Wouldn't do to leave them behind for the slaves to pilfer. If that ruckus from the harpsichord hadn't drawn them in, maybe this was it, time to act.

I went to the secretary and with a trembling finger pushed a carved square on a piece of pretty molding. Pop. The secret cupboard door opened – the money was still there. My hands nearly shook too much to untie the ribbon, but I did and counted out, one, two, three bills, then one, two, three bills more. Enough to aid in purchasing passage, but not enough to be noticed – I hoped. I took care to tie the ribbon back just as I'd found it.

July came down from Summer Kitchen out of breath. "You can't hide it in a pallet," she said as if we'd been talking it out. "That's the first place they'd look." We put our heads together. Digging a hole like Cudjoe had all those years back wouldn't be practical either because I might need to grab the money in a hurry. "Hide it in plain sight," July offered.

There was a tureen up high on the Company Shelf that wasn't likely to be touched anytime soon. July helped me hop up onto the counter. I lifted the lid and slid the bills into the big bowl. I was so nervous, so worried about getting caught or breaking the porcelain, so scared that Moses might be caught eventually, all of it, that I forgot to worry about my balance. I slipped and fell and landed right on July, who looked up at me from on the floor and laughed. She laughed, and I did too, and when I shifted onto my knees and offered her a hand, it came to me: I'd never heard July laugh before. Oh, there was the sly grin, the toothy flash of a smile, hu-humming agreement, but laughter? Not once in six years. Such a simple thing, such a natural thing – laughter. They'd taken that too.

Packing up the Porcelain
July, Wappoo Plantation

The ladies hiccupped joy, but our pockets filled with mud and ash. I'm stuck in Porch House packing cups and whatnot, wishing to be away in the laundry shed 'cause here I'm privy to the glad chattering. Every giggle and sigh stung like a bee.

The pretty porcelain. Roses tripping 'long the rim pleased me a time or two, but now the glamour gone ugly. Change be like that sometimes, more for slaves than them – sweet gone sour, the steady thing gone rogue.

They sat for tea. Saffron serving. I faced the hutch, working in my shadow.

If you learned to bear one weight of suffering and got loaded up with more, you might fall, and once fallen, never get up again. I'd seen it time and time again. How strong was I?

Along the way, something inside slumped when I wasn't looking. What I took for resilience turned out to be more like dulling of sense. Blurring losses allowed me to go day to day, but clear seeing pierced like a needle under the fingernail and it hurt every time.

"Careful. Careful" Mistress say again. The dishes was sailing to Antigua, possibly to sit on another mahogany table like this one. I couldn't put up a picture of tomorrow for myself, but somehow I could see table settings for them even in a place I ain't never been.

We overheard tidbits, but mostly it's what they don't say that drag us down. Every time they talk, the door's left open for the boogeyman. I can feel him haunting the creek right now, rolling in pluff mud, blood in his eyes, about to cough up the bones of black people. The hutch was filling with evening or was that the boogeyman's shadow? I listened for his rasping breath.

They was on about veils, dainty cakes, and shoes. The coming schooner. The ladies wasn't feeling a speck of dread. Too much joy. They don't know how hungry the boogeyman's getting. I looked inside the teapot before wrapping it. Maybe it housed secrets I could use?

One thing's for certain – if Maggie loses her mama, that girl would walk right back into darkness, never to return.

Maybirds
July, Wappoo Plantation

"We'll serve small plates of pickled fruits for variety," Mistress said. Miss Eliza wanted to know if the hog been kilt yet and the answer was yes. Last year's squashes, plus this year's butter and herbs. A yellow cake with three layers. All this need making and carting to the inn.

After tea, Saffron helped put final touches to Mistress's new gown, just come from the dressmaker. I stitched ribbon roses on Miss Eliza's wedding purse, a task taking a sure hand. Usually I could make 'em in my sleep, but that day one knot after another clutched at the ribbon. A mind of its own. Or worse? The boogeyman standing too close.

Another letter arrived, saying the sloop'd reach our shore in maybe 'bout three days. George might get here for the wedding. The ribbon knotted and then broke. A first. Meanwhile, it weren't the pins in Saffron's mouth making her clam up tight. She was worried sick. Sleep closed off its doors most nights.

The next morning, the same tea served at the same table, but halfway through Miss flew out in chattering like a mockingbird. "July, look at the time! Run and tell Indian Pete to ready the carriage." I hurried out. Was she late for another dress fitting? Maybe she got a tryst with the devil to discuss my future.

The first dress fitting was here a bit ago. It took all of us plus a dressmaker from the city to make the marks: me with the pin cushion, Melody with the tape measure, Saffron giving Miss sips of water and handing over new pieces of chalk. The gown was patterned silk, the best. Strips of lace got sewn in the arms like fancy windows to the body. Down the front, silk zigzagged just like icing on a cake. Mrs. Tully, the dressmaker, must have mighty sharp eyes and needles.

Some simple affair they having.

Later, outside, I could breathe better, but how the birds chit-chattered. Maybirds back. Every year, just after the rice was tossed onto the fields, dug under by heel, covered by toe-slide, them birds showed up in big dark clouds. I remember how Benjie and James set about bird-minding with Tommy and George – waving rakes, banging pots, shooting pellets at the sky. None of them here now. Who'd do it today?

Thin wooly clouds stretched across a sky otherwise clear 'cept where the birds swarmed dark and jerky. Angry nitpickers at heaven. Me and maybirds share a frantic hunger. Their flit-flatty flying blotched the blue bowl of heaven in sweeps like the fear that churned in my chest.

Even so, I felt a tiny stab of gratitude. All the wrapping and hoisting we got going on, the peeling and sugaring, the pampering and adorning – imagine all this laboring in the choking, clamping heat of August. Least we getting the sweet breeze of spring every now and again.

Back and Forth
Melody, Wappoo Plantation

With the wedding fast approaching, I spent more and more time at Cross Winds, which cramped my style, trickery needing to be planned and all. For instance, how was I going to fetch Moses at the right time and in secret? How was I going get him to the ship with no one noticing? I bit my nails to the quick. I wasn't sleeping.

Miss Eliza required trips to the dressmaker and to the Bacchus and Vine on the peninsula for foodstuffs. Boats went back and forth from Cross Winds to Wappoo fetching crates, some bound for Antigua and some for Belmont. The sheltering chaos made my continued scheming possible.

Using a straw man, Nana Lucy very quietly sold the land her house once stood on to another baker. Yet another friend, a man who studied in the new Negro School recently started by Reverend Garden, asked the Reverend to arrange passage for two to Philadelphia. The friend's cover story was weak, but we hoped it held – something about how his Master and lad were going north, no time to run all the errands, etc. The tickets would be hard to trace back to Nana Lucy and harder still to trace to Moses or me.

So far it had worked. With passage squared up, we were left with the hardest part of all – the actual departure. While I could rely on all the wedding hubbub to put up one distraction after another, it still puzzled me how to spirit Moses away from Wappoo and board him on the ship bound for Philadelphia without anyone noticing. I struggled night after night and eventually came up with a simple ruse. I'd say that Overseer loaned Moses out for a week to Mr. Tilton – a little extra money for the newlyweds being welcome, no time for permission, and so on. Did Mistress want the money or should I pass it along to Miss Eliza direct? It was a bit of a stretch

As it turned out, the Philadelphia-bound ship entered Charles Town one week before the wedding, set to sail in forty-eight hours. A message was sent to

Abraham back on the street saying he might have to use the hidden cypress raft to get Moses to the wharf in time. What excuse for that? And would I be able to say goodbye? Did I want to say goodbye?

In the end Miss Eliza's horse, Sir Raleigh, gave us our ruse. Miss Eliza, Saffron, and I returned to Wappoo the day after the Philadelphia-bound ship arrived. Hercules was appointed to ride Sir Raleigh up to Ashley Ferry, take the ferry across, and deliver the horse to Cross Winds. Oh, you should have seen him – Hercules, that is, not Sir Raleigh – trotting off, unable to stop grinning. You'd a thought it was him going off to be married!

Meanwhile, Miss Eliza saw to the last crates on the dock. Abraham was to deliver them to the peninsula. She'd travel back to Cross Winds by carriage. Caesar would drive me in the carriage late tomorrow afternoon so that we could bring some remaining boxes. Saffron and July were to take one more day to close up the house. Then Saffron would be ferried to by pettiauger for the wedding preparations, along with the cake made by July, who would remain here.

What a perfect stroke of luck. Tomorrow, we'd put Moses on the boat with Abraham. Nana Lucy'd meet him at Mill Pond, and together they'd maneuver on foot to the wharf, steering clear of Cross Winds and the Bacchus and Vine. And then they would walk clear into a new future.

It was probably my last night on this earth to be near my younger son, but I could not dwell on it. If all went to plan, he'd be on a ship to Philadelphia on the morrow and I'd be on a sloop sailing to the West Indies next week, none of the Lucases any the wiser.

Cane Creek
Saffron, Wappoo Plantation

Time twisted like hanked yarn or lay out shiny like a field flooded before the rice in shuck. Time snuck up behind like a Master's nasty son pranking or it clobbered you right hard like a rolling pin to the head. Summer was coming at us like a wall of molasses. That kind of suffering we knew. But Miss Eliza's wedding was carrying suffering we didn't know.

In the mess of taking apart Porch House, even while fears harried us, wild ideas crept in. It was as if all the scrambling let other notions enter – notions of running, sailing, flying off. In other words, freedom came calling. Freedom huddled at doorways and tapped at windows, rattling treetops, chatting with the boogeyman. They were trying to get our attention.

Meanwhile, happiness turned Miss Eliza's mind to melon just the sickly-sweet side of rot. She kept on forgetting the time, her other petticoat, where her new fan was. How's she gonna act with Master Pinckney? Sweet and coy, going day to day forgetting, or steady and sometimes bullish, like she's been all these years with Mistress?

We pressed linens and cleaned shoes. We cooked up syrups for the wedding table, glossy and sweet. We cleaned out the root cellar, putting tubers and such into baskets for the boat. But mostly it was heartbreak we were prepping for.

After supper one night, Melody marched Moses about the cabin. "Repeat after me: 'Come here slave! Mop this floor!'" Come here slave?

Moses shouted with glee, "Come here, mop this floor!" Noah was confused, not by the game, but because he was left out. He marched around with his brother, just to be part. Maggie understood before I did, 'because she started acting the part of Moses's slave. She wrung her hands. She looked down. She peered up. Said all girlish, "What was that, Mastah?"

"Come here, slave. Come here!" Moses barked at Maggie. Melody and Noah clapped.

As for Maggie and me, a few futures hung down like moss off the live oak. One put me and Maggie with Miss Eliza, leaving Indian Peter behind. In that case, if I was lucky, I'd see him maybe one or two times a year, and what slave was lucky? My ribs stitched up in knots, missing him already. Other futures showed Miss Eliza taking me and leaving Maggie, or taking me and selling Maggie. That was a heartache so big it needed some other name, like soul tarring or living death.

Would Maggie survive a separation? Or would it put her right back in that hold on the ship of damnation, the one where that captain stained her soul. She can't go back. I can't let her go back. I'd feed us trumpet vine root before I let that happen.

Look how she rose up to help Moses! Did she understand she was working on Melody's heartbreak, for if that boy goes off north passing as white, Melody won't ever see him again. Such a little goober too, the drool still shining on his chin.

Before we laid down to sleep, July pulled the cloth away from the windows, letting in the joyful creaking of the peepers.

"Mama?" Maggie whispered. "Them rumors about Cane Creek. How true?" Indian Pete told us the Cane Creek stories, so I believed them. Stories about people livin' out in the swamp west of Hell Hole – black people, red people, living without any buckra near, living where little grew and nobody went to hunt, not even slave catchers. "I bet they sleep under the stars," she said. Maggie wanted to know if they was free.

I whispered, "As free as a slave can be without papers or courtesy or Canada." My thoughts and Maggie's thoughts started to beat in time. Maggie shut her eyes. Her chest rose and fell. She was sliding to sleep, dreaming on freedom. The slant of her collarbones, the shadows beneath, the delicate breath escaping her lips made love bloom in my chest.

Funny how sometimes it's the timid and meek ones who turn out to be bravest of all.

That was how freedom snuck in, restless and impatient, on rumors, in dreams, with peepers singing. Freedom got fed up with lingering along the cabin walls, feeling death an empty challenge. It was done stalling and it came right in.

In the days after, we talked with Indian Pete. We got to stealing jerky and nuts. July grabbed ribbons and pins. "Like a magpie," I said, airing an old joke. Abraham made a small wooden bowl for Maggie. Melody gave her a cloth to carry things in and July made benne wafers on the sly. July also supplied ribbons for tying on shrubs so Maggie could leave a trail for me.

With tears in his eyes, Abraham watched me braid Maggie's hair. How we all wanted freedom for each other even when it came with loss. The braiding looked like plain old grooming but was anything but. Indian Pete talked us through. "Turn the plait here, straight for a while, curve there." With each change of direction, Pete whispered landmarks. We were making a map.

"At the lightning-struck tree is where the Choctaw trail shows up." He touched the braid above Maggie's right ear, took her hand and traced her fingers there. "This is where you turn south for a spell. The bog's too deep to stay due west." Anybody watching would think Maggie had nits, how we tended her scalp.

Indian Pete went over it again and again, whispering the routes, the landmarks, the days it would take. By the time Maggie lay down for sleep, her head was a map to Cane Creek. The next night it'd be my turn and by twisting the same braids in the same patterns on my head, Maggie'd learn the routes even better. All them tiring walks in the night to Hell Hole Swamp suddenly seem like training. They gave Maggie a sense of what she was going into. They made her less afraid.

There was one upfront trick to the plan. We would fake Maggie's death. We'd lay her head scarf in the reeds to make it seem like she drowned or a gator got her. With all the comings and goings, it might take days for them to see she'd gone missing. I practiced tears at the telling.

Titus threw the opele for her one last time. I sat at the far end of the garden, hearing only the music of the words, not the words themselves. They were for Daughter alone. But even from across rows of peas and green beans, it seemed clear that Titus's words gave Maggie strength. After, he opened up his red bag and pinched out dirt – the very same soil that traveled all the way from Yorubaland, mixed with grave dust from Benjie and James's plots. Maggie took off her shoes and he sprinkled a pinch in each one.

Time now coiled and sparked, as if about to catch fire.

At dawn the next day, we set out together. I'd go as far as the fork – Hell Hole Swamp one way and the Choctaw trails the other. Hell Hole Swamp called up the past, the other way called up the future. "Ewa," I whispered. I could've stayed there all day, breath and skin linking us. Next time Daughter moved, we'd be cleaved apart – would we meet again? Does a daughter live inside her mama always, no matter what?

I reached in my pocket for the oyster shell I'd been eating with since coming here six years ago, a gift from July. "Here." Maggie took it in both hands, like a jewel. I whispered, "May food come to you and may sunlight and health be your friends. May the Ancestors protect you. May the demons of slavery pass you by. May love find and crown you."

"Don't talk that way, Mama," Maggie said, and kissed me and walked away.

"Wait." I pointed to her head scarf. We nearly forgot. She unknotted it, handed it over, and then pulled out one of the strips of ribbon from her apron pocket.

"Every time hunger pull my stomach tight," she said. "Tie a ribbon at eye-level."

I nodded. "Now go." She turned. And she went. Just like that. No more words. I held the scarf to my nose. The scent of her. I stood there like a lone tree rooted in the ground, watching until her tunic, a ghost glow, disappeared into the shadowy thickets.

Tickets and Abscess
Melody, Wappoo Plantation

I drew in a sharp breath. What was I going to do without Moses? He waved his hand. "Bye, Mama." His voice carrying the sweet honey of knee baby. He kept up a brave face, wanting more than anything to please his mother, and turned forward as if heading off for a day of plantation marketing. What did he understand? More than he let on, I was certain.

Of course, my baby wasn't a baby anymore. Five, with stiff, wavy black hair, hazel eyes, skin the color of an Irish sail rigger keeping his face perpetually shadowed by a hat. Everything was planned, down to the last detail. For the boat trip into town, supposedly to Cross Winds, I oiled and braided his hair and dressed him in tattered garb. Slave clothes. Nothing to see – for all anyone knew, he was just a dowry item being shipped from one plantation to another. A transaction. The brocade jacket Mistress made for him months back and the linen breeches July and I made in secret were folded and hidden in a bag set at his feet. It also held strips of gauze.

Sturdy calculation, money stolen and given, and a near holy cooperation had stitched this plan together. I'm a crypt for secrets and ready for any punishment, but it's bedeviling how much now turned on luck. Tides and distractions, illusions and speech.

We'd tutored Moses for weeks in the ways of arrogance. "Lucy, get me a drink" or, "Lucy, get my jacket." Abraham taught him how to snap his fingers. July pretended to be a mistress and sashayed around the garden, insisting that Moses stare at her – that was the thing he had to practice the most, how to look right at a white face without flinching, hunching, or blinking. I don't know which was harder for him, imagining July white or not laughing at her antics.

"Again!" July was strict. Moses knew the rough steps of the plan, but it was possible that he didn't understand that if all went well, he'd never see his mother again. Sometimes we believe only as much as will allow for our survival.

Nobody would expect a five-year-old, even a white, slave-owning five-year-old, to write, so signed X's for the ship's manifest would be good enough, but Moses's speech hadn't traveled far enough along the road of privilege to be believable. It was Maggie who came up with the solution. Nana Lucy would wrap his chin and head in a bandage, as if he was recovering from an abscess. No clear talk possible, mumbling only. Also, if a sticky situation arose, one too hard to act his way through, he could pretend an attack of pain and faint into Nana Lucy's arms.

Nana Lucy faced grim uncertainties. Somebody could steal her at any point in the journey and sell her back into slavery. Even if she made it safely to Philadelphia, someone could kidnap her off the streets there and sell her like any other commodity. No slave catcher could legally touch her because she was free, but when had that ever stopped them?

Even if she avoided capture, she could be denied every opportunity to find work and fall into destitution. Since she could very well lead slave catchers to Moses, it was possible the two would have to separate in order to keep him safe. Keep him free. That part of the plan stayed fuzzy, because pondering it too much felt like a jinx.

This much was clear – in this adventure, Nana Lucy was risking not just her freedom, but her life. It made her heroic, Bible-level heroic. The fact that so many of us would do the same to bring about a child's freedom, even a child not our own, did not make her less of a saint. The fact that her life on the peninsula had slid into risk and danger also did not take away from her willing sacrifice. True, after someone burned down Nana Lucy's bakery, why would she stick around, especially when they might very well come after her person next? She'd felt menacing eyes watching her walk the narrow streets. She'd been forced to wonder if the ominous shadow behind her carried a razor in his jacket. She did not need to wonder just how much her success disgusted her tormentors. She knew. A white man jealous of a black woman was a dangerous man. How dare she act like a somebody, especially a somebody with property! By harassing us, the poor whites with nothing to lose had much to gain in their own pitiful self-regard. But even though staying on the peninsula was fraught with danger, her willingness to risk punishment and the loss of her own freedom was, as Saffron would say in a whisper to the night sky, "magnificent."

Mo stood on the far side of the smokehouse and waved goodbye as the boat disappeared behind an overhanging clump of dewberry bushes. I walked back into Porch House with heavy steps. With that boat, a piece of me was gone. My part in the plot was over.

On the street later, sunset washing the sky pink, for some reason I felt calm. July gave me a hug, brief but saying everything. Saffron looked distant. I didn't know what she and Maggie were cooking up yet, but it was something. I knew not to press – every secret-keeper respected the will of another secret-keeper, and anyway, slaves instinctively protected each other's privacy, such as it was.

Where language used to give Saffron peace or hope, now it hung around her throat like a noose, threatening to strangle the voice right out of her. Two syllables chipped off her tongue over and over: dow-ry, dow-ry. She wasn't able to get under them or inside them or whatever it was she used to do. Saffron near to gagged on the syllables, their echoes scorching the air. It didn't surprise me at all that poetry let Saffron down in the wedding season. We were property, plain and simple, and what poetry dwelt in that?

Later, when Miss Eliza asked where Moses was, I arranged my face and lied. "It was his day to suck water at the canal, checkin' for the brine. Mr. Tilton wanted to hire him to do the same on the morrow and Overseer, he said yes." The hope was that once they got serious about retrieving Moses, it'd be too late.

Now that the plan for Moses was underway, I could ask myself what would life on Antigua bring. I hadn't had time to worry on it before. Now I did. Mistress might be besotted by the turn of her own fortunes, but who knew what Husband in the West Indies felt or why? Maybe Master Lucas had turned into someone harder and meaner over the years – someone less likely to stare at me through pipe smoke and more likely to shove up my tunic and have his way. And what if the plot to send Moses to freedom was somehow discovered? It didn't bear thinking about.

Calico Frock
Saffron, Wappoo Plantation

This was the last day for this place. I leant on Miss Eliza's wardrobe door, the edge pressing hard into my cheek, a way to rest before beginning. July was rockin' down on the verandah – crick, crick – that was her version of idling. Indian Pete was a long way off today. He knew it was my day to go, but I didn't tell him about the dress, my final, flapping goodbye.

Some other hand would tend to Miss Eliza on wedding day. No one could do it like I do since I'm the best with comb and pins, how I tuck in flowers, but never mind. Miss Eliza was traveling from one pampering to another, born so lucky she didn't even have to see it that way. None of them did. They thought their fortunes owed or earned, comfort their due, cradle to grave.

Spite was too weak a word for why I grabbed the calico dress. More like a glow of meaning, a fit of justice. Let Miss Eliza hear how the dress was found hanging off an oak limb – just like that other calico dress so many years back. Let Miss remember how she and her mother pinned me by the elbow and forced me to feel the heat of that burning dress, forced me to witness my paper head catching fire. Their angry grip, their vicious minds. No, not this time. The same branch will do just fine.

I needed rope. I entered the dark barn with purpose, found a tack box holding rope coils. Also: a flint and a striker. A beam of setting sun slanted into the box like a blade making them tools glow. Could the message be any clearer?

Quickly now, for I still had to hang the dress off the limb, I made four small piles of dry hay. A flick of the wrist – snap, snap – and a spark turned the hay into smoldering clouds. In no time, the rafters would crackle and glow, the roof fall in, the walls collapse. Good!

I crept by the house. July sat in the rocker, mouth hanging open in sleep. Titus showed up from outta nowhere. While I stood on the chair under the live oak looping the rope over the branch, letting the calico frock dangle, he launched something at the barn. A ball? Another one. And another. Each landed with a sticky thud. Each of those lobbed balls took up fire like it was their sacred duty. They flared and shot flames upward and sideways until fire licked the entire roof. He turned to me and smiled, then walked away.

After hanging the calico, it was my turn to walk away. The dress was my curse and my goodbye. So was the destruction of the barn. I headed toward the Upper Field, ready to dodge into ditch or weeds if Overseer showed up. The fire would get him moving this way and soon.

I spoke to Daughter silently in my mind. "Baby, I'm coming. I'm coming." There was no time for last goodbyes to July – the hasty ones from supper last night would have to do. Soon it would be dark. I trotted through the alfalfa field and got to the Deep Woods just as a loud explosion took the barn. I turned and watched the glow.

The flames licked up like they wanted to consume the clouds, hot and uncontrollable, a vengeance writ clear.

On the Move

Maggie, West of Wappoo

Facing west, I put my back to Wappoo and marched on. I picked up a forked stick in case of snakes, but I haven't seen any. I touched the braid nearest my right ear and patted it – my map, my salvation. I tied one indigo ribbon after another to branches, a narrow cloth signaling hope, signaling love.

Mama's voice rose up out of my collarbones. *Go on now. Think like a fugitive, but run like you're free. After three nights, stop and wait for me.*

I was fleet of foot and pure of heart. I touched the braid above my right ear again. *Time to look for the Choctaw trail,* the map told me. Along the way, I gathered huckleberries, ate the long leaves of rocket and the lacy leaves of brake fern. Pete had said, "the tart plums of spring can keep you alive."

I looked down at my shoes, smiled at Titus's offering of Mother Soil. Mother would be here soon, wouldn't she? I was terrified that something would go wrong.

A calico frock hanging from a branch, saying remember? Why do I see this? But wait, she set fire to the barn? Won't that make them hunt her harder?

Never mind that, Mama called out of my belly. *Keep on going.* But for some reason, suddenly I wanted to go back. I was confused. I called up the rebel ghosts: "Stono Warriors. Lend me strength." *Never mind them,* Mama called out of my wrists. *You got all the strength you need. Go, brave girl. Go.*

Maybe you don't know what strength lives inside you until you gotta use it.

Four days march in all, Indian Pete had said. After three, hide and wait for Mama. *Daughter. I'm coming.*

The piny smell of the ground offered a secret. It said poetry goes heart to heart, mother to daughter. The poems Mama made out of stars and rivers, sedge and stone would flow into me. If she didn't make it, I'd keep on. Poetry would keep on. But she would make it. Mama was my art, my Milky Way, my turpentine, my fire.

And then, jogging not too fast but fast enough, a racket of wind came up. A boggy smell. Something like fear but not fear stirred a trail down my limbs. *Shelter by sunset, baby.* I dropped my head back, looked up at the slash pines, at the flappy chestnut leaves. Two crows floated up above in a wedge of light. Suddenly quiet filled me up, eerie and still. Fear chugged off. I could feel the earth turning. I could feel my feet on sacred ground, untainted by them.

Mama told me more than once that there ain't no shame in staying put or in choosing to die. None at all. But I was running. She was running. Was she?

After walking through a rivulet, I climbed a tree, hung my bag and bow off a limb. Night was coming on. I declared to my bones, tomorrow would be a new day and Mama would be closer. The two of us running away from something hard and running even harder to something new.

The Day Before the Wedding
Eliza, Cross Winds

A liveried Abraham handed me a note with a grievous air. Oh, what now? *Dear Miss Eliza, I am sorry to tell you – Saffron and Maggie are missing, possibly dead.* I dropped the note. Abraham swiftly picked it up and handed it back to me. I read on: *A calico dress was left hung on the live oak near the house. Barn burned to the ground. No saving it. Maggie's head scarf found near creek. She may have drowned running from the fire. No sign of Saffron.*

"Whose hand is this?" I asked, as if the note's author mattered more than its contents. Abraham told me that Mo wrote it, at which point Mother came into the hall, snatched the note from me, scanned it, and tossed it on to the floor. Again Abraham stooped to pick it up. Mother waved him out of the house, grabbed my arm, and drew me into the parlor.

"Listen to me, Missy. Who cares? A barn can be rebuilt. You don't live there anymore, in any case. You're on the cusp of a new life, a satisfying life." I looked at the floor but nodded. "As for the two gone missing, surely they'll be hunted and found? Not in time for Saffron to do up your buttons perhaps, but soon enough. Trust me, I can do your hair." Mother patted my shoulder. "Take heart. Even if we never recover Saffron, you'll train another. Life goes on, and soon with a husband." She smiled, satisfied. "You're not going to let a pair of slaves ruin your wedding day, are you?"

In spite of panicky dismay, my chest warmed at the word, "husband." I still could hardly believe that in very short order I would be spending most of my waking hours with Charles. And the nighttime hours, too. Something else warmed at that idea.

Mother called for Grandpapa, eager to take their morning constitutional. While waiting for him, she asked who was responsible for burning the barn, in the same tone she might have used to inquire about a neighbor's gift of a ham.

"We read the same note, Mother. It didn't say, but I'm guessing Saffron?"

Mother grunted. "I would've thought such violence out of her ken. The house is intact, I take it?"

"Presumably." Out she went with Grandpapa.

Mother's attachment to Wappoo, never strong to begin with, had loosened by the day. Honestly, she didn't seem to care at all about Saffron's vengeful destruction or the impact her status as a runaway had on the ledger. Of late, I'd found her unshakeable cheer a tad hard to endure. She seemed as implacably content now as she'd been unrelentingly miserable formerly. She performed her duties with a pep and vigor not much in evidence during the last handful of years.

In spite of my joy at being betrothed to Charles, the news from Wappoo came at me like a grim and harassing shadow. It put a stranglehold on what I was entitled to think about at this juncture, things like satin shoes, a private kiss. A gust of air came off the harbor. I pulled a couple of hairpins out and then jabbed them back in. Saffron's hands had touched those very pins – touched them more than anyone, myself included. Perhaps she would never handle them again. No, I was sure of it. She was gone. Run away or dead, but gone. I would never again see her satisfied smile after coiling my hair to perfection. I headed outside.

In the garden, a dragon fly flitted near. Iridescent, it fluttered, a denizen of light, minion of the sun. Fragility writ mobile and reflective. Perhaps the insect was Saffron? If she was dead, mightn't she have flown back along an avenue of light to offer me assurance of some kind? My insides twisted with unexpected grief. We might never know where she went. One of many curses imposed by the runaway.

That night during dinner, another messenger knocked at the door, with another note, this time reporting Indian Pete's absence.

Mother remarked, "Well, that tells me Saffron is alive, then."

Grandpapa wolfed down his meal and stormed out of the dining room. I bolted and followed. At his secretary, he scribbled out two notices, flapping the pages to dry the ink, as if its usual pace of drying was yet another affront. "Check them, would you?" I scanned the script and gave a nod of approval, but what I really thought was: what a waste of ink.

Notice: 75 Pound Reward

Runaway male, Mustee. Approximately five foot five, big head, sherry-colored skin. Wears leather boots, answers to Indian Pete. Passable English. Absconded from Wappoo Plantation, sometime in May, 1744. May have Pee Dee relatives.

Negro woman called Saffron absconded from Wappoo Plantation possibly with her daughter, Maggie, mid-May. Saffron stands five feet six, is very black and lean, about thirty years of age. Speaks passable English. Her back shows whip-scarring.

Her daughter stands five foot four or so, also very dark, about 14 years old. Left arm badly burnt. Skittish demeanor. English passable, but rarely speaks.

The above reward will be paid by the subscriber, 25 pounds per Negro, for apprehension and delivery to Wappoo Plantation or to the jail in Charles Town.

Jasmine
Eliza, Belmont

How well my rose bouquet matched the silk flowers on my pumps! And oh, how the luster of my pearls echoed the delicate Venetian lace at hem and cuff, just now catching the day's waning light! Vows said. Sealed with a kiss. Crowd fed. Crowd nearly dispersed. I've collapsed in what is to be my private sitting room upstairs, thoughtfully appointed by Charles with pink-striped damask and a matching tea set. A skull sits on my new writing table – a witty literary reference Charles knew I'd appreciate. "Alas, poor Yorick. I knew him, Horatio."

I slid to the floor in rumpled weariness, the fact of loss crowding back – a barn burnt to cinders, two females run off or dead, one male missing. And now perhaps Moses was also in the wind. It didn't escape me that "run off" and "dead" gave the same measure on inventories.

Alas, poor Saffron, I knew her.

But I didn't, did I?

They found Maggie's head rag in the spartina by the creek, suggesting death by drowning. Such catastrophic loss might send her grieving mother to suicide, but if that were the case, wouldn't at least one of their bodies have been found? Mother was right to suggest that Indian Pete's disappearance probably meant that Saffron was alive. I just don't understand why she had to burn down the barn. Of course it was her doing. If there was any doubt, my calico dress hanging from the live oak nearby banished it. That dress acted as a not-so-subtle reference to the frock burned years back after she "borrowed" it. How well I remember the sparks flying off and how we worried about the barn and how the worry nearly eclipsed any satisfaction in righteous punishment. Saffron's message was heavy-handed and suggested something other than grief.

I tossed the skull up and caught it in my palm. "'I knew him, Horatio; a fellow of infinite jest . . .'" Quite the prank, Saffron. I stood to take in the view – one of many new views here at Belmont. It was lovely. I could hear but not see Charles making arrangements out by the barn for late-leaving guests. The still-standing barn.

Secretly, I believed Maggie yet alive. I'm not sure why, but perhaps because the inaccuracy of my impressions of her and her mother had been laid so bare. For instance, I wouldn't have thought Saffron capable of such full-bodied vengeance – a loyal, poetical slave turned destructive felon. How difficult to swallow!

I needed to cast such thoughts aside, for soon Charles would ascend the stairs. I hoped he had ordered all the house slaves away – I did not wish to hear their silence or to have to interpret it. I unhitched the pearls, kicked off the pumps. Was I to let Charles remove the rest? A channel of heat thudded open in my torso. How thoroughly desire connected the heart and the belly! And below the belly. I waited in a flutter at the top of the stairs.

The front door opened and clicked shut. Wig off, jacket over one arm, Charles looked like a man in possession of himself. My husband. He tossed down the wig and coat, dashed up the stairs two at a time, and swept me into his arms. The bed in our room received us in a soft embrace. It was not the bed Elizabeth died in, naturally. It was not even the same chamber. Of course not. Charles saw to switching rooms and to boxing up his deceased wife's personal items save for a few mementos downstairs. He thoughtfully spared me and perhaps also spared himself.

Beside me: his animal warmth. Eyes open, our mouths met, the warmth of tongues. The utter surprise of it – how even the scratch of a slight stubble thrilled me and how transporting his smell. How I longed to know every part of him! His hands drifted from my back down below the waist and cupped my rear. If his touch felt this good through yards of fabric, how was it going to feel skin to skin? Suddenly impatient, I yanked up the belled skirt, then reached up to undo the collar buttons of my frock, rolling over to let him to finish. Sliding the fabric away, he kissed my bare shoulders. Up and over came the frock. In a flurry of mechanics that defied physics, we were soon both naked. Rolling on top of me, he looked at me with such tenderness and fire that I was further undone.

His fingers found the cleft of me and brought about a first ecstasy. My voice came as if from afar, calling out in pleasure. He entered me – a slight gasp and a burning, but not so much a hurting as one burning blending with another. We found a rocking rhythm as natural as riding a horse. Cantering now. Soon to gallop. Charles pushed my knees up, entering me more deeply. The sound of him calling out my name alone would've brought me round again, but there was that delicious friction too.

His loss of control, a shuddering grimace, gave me something new to love about him.

When eventually Charles stood and pulled open a window, it wasn't his form so much that impressed me – though the broad shoulders and curved behind pleased the eye well enough – but rather how comfortable he was in his own skin. The air blew in, sweet with flowering jasmine. For all the years of our marriage and beyond, the smell of jasmine would make my knees go weak. He turned and perched his naked behind on the windowsill.

"Not a bad beginning, mmm?" My throaty laugh served as answer. "I take it you met what remains of Pluto," he asked, nodding at my writing desk across the hall. Pluto? A former slave?

"I'd rather call him Yorick, if you don't mind." His turn to laugh. He craned his head to look outside. Propped on one elbow, I somberly raised the topic of the Wappoo barn. We could have it rebuilt by mid-summer, I said, and then, "I'm grateful my dear bay was spared a gruesome fate."

"Indeed. By the by, Mac's made no determination of fault." I sat up and hugged my knees. How did Charles know this in advance of my knowing it? I am married but an evening and already all authority with respect to my property (well, now his property) had fallen away. Did I mind?

I lay back down and waved him over to me. He helped me to a stand, tugged away the slightly bloodied sheet, and dispatched it to the floor. A fresh linen from the wardrobe, he snapped over our bed with deft precision. There seemed no end to his courtesies. He climbed on and offered his hand. Pulled me close. The May air floated in, redolent with sweet floral notes and the promise of summer, the promise of happiness.

We slept.

Tortoise Bisque
Melody, at Sea

The sea slapped hard, keeping time like a clock tocking with a grudge. Slap. Slap. The dainty sounds of dining – silver tinkling, ladies' laughter – clinked back, civilized, small, and pathetic. The sea ruled. Buckra's customs could not compete, no matter what beliefs they held and shined up with entitlements large and small. Dishes slid. Diners groaned.

First night out and they put tortoise bisque on the menu. Creamy, heavy seafood soup seemed a bad choice. Toast would've been better, with a dab of marmalade, maybe. If only they'd asked me. I knew that bisque'd be tasty because it came from the Poinsett Inn. I saw Ganda bring the keg aboard and drunk up the sight of him one last time.

Mistress put me behind her chair, bucket at the ready. Every cabin on the sloop, fancy and plain, was equipped with sick bags. Seasickness cared not a whit about skin color or how many coins rattled in your pocket. I was glad for my stomach of iron.

Noah was wandering about somewhere, confused about Moses. I couldn't yet tell him, holding the secret tight for now. And anyway, it was too hectic to pile grief onto the chaos of the storm – wind howling, ship tilting in heaves, biblical in scale. It didn't escape me that Mistress being sick turned an advantage. She'd be too woozy to worry about the absence of Moses. Let her make the stark tally after we'd sailed a hundred miles.

Noah won't remember this route from when he was a knee-high baby traveling in the other direction. But he's eight now, and this sail he'll remember – though what of it exactly is hard to guess. His confusion about Moses? The big sea birds, the sour smell of vomit. Certainly the fear of extinction coming with every swell would lodge itself in his mind.

I recalled how Master studied me out of the side of his face on that long-ago journey. Surely things will be different all these years later. Mistress turned out to be a nicer person with him gone. Still difficult, but nicer. I'd heard about Master's defeat in Cartagena, Colombia, years back. Was it too much to hope that the disaster had humbled him? My skin prickled in a furry fear.

The years sure had changed me. I could read now, for one thing. My furies had smudged just enough that they didn't slide across my face of their own accord, for another. I wasn't able to decide if bending toward survival tamped down my anger or if all its spark and verve shifted to my boys. Their survival.

The boat rocked hard. Chairs creaked in alarm, dishes got to sliding. Some diners held up spoons over thin air, others had two bowls competing for their laps. Men in livery tried to set things right. I pushed Mistress's chair in, but that hand went up, so I helped her stand.

"Now's as good a time as any," she chirped with that English clip-clop, but I could see sick in her face. With one hand I grabbed an elbow and with the other the bucket. I gave one last lustful look at her bowl, half full of bisque – creamy, sweet bisque, tipped up with Madeira, seasoned with nutmeg. Alas. We tottered out.

Just beyond the door she spewed three times, bisque hardly changed at all – splat, splat, splat. The bucket caught most of it. She leant on the wall, gripping her middle. The sloop slammed hard to the side again, shoving her shoulders and head back and shoving me into her. We were crushed bosom to bosom. I held that stinky bucket away as best I could.

"Quick! Get me to my cabin." I was setting the bucket down to hold her up when the sloop heaved back the other way. The bucket slid. I planted my feet into the boards and braced my mistress, scooting her along. Once the door clicked shut behind us, she moaned.

"Why did I have that soup? Why? Oh, the bucket. Bucket! Now!"

The sound of retching started coming from all round – the dining cabin, the berths. It was like a rowdy church chorus, but instead of calling down heaven, it called up the opposite.

Where was Noah? I heard waves crashing over the rails and sliding into the gunwales above. He better not be up there! A big wave slammed right above us. From far away in my mind, I remembered little Tommy peppering Master with question after question before his Atlantic journey. "How many voyages has the captain helmed? What if the mast breaks? What if we're stranded in the doldrums?" I wish I could remember the answer to that second one.

I wondered if Tommy was steadier of mood now or the opposite, more haunted? Even the life of a white person didn't necessarily go in a straight line. How would he regard his "best buddy" Noah after all the years of schooling and white society? With fondness, maybe, but something else, too – something unavoidable and ugly.

The shouts of the sailors didn't sound desperate, not yet anyway. Hoist this! Furl that! I settled Mistress in the narrow bed, shoes off, lace cap on. Fetched another bucket to leave at her side. I was about to go find Noah when Mistress grabbed my hand. "Don't leave me, Melody!" Another wave pounded the deck with terrifying violence and then washed off the sloop with a shurring sound. As if reading my mind, she asked where Noah was.

"Let me go see."

"Be quick about it." Just as I got to the door Mistress rolled over and mewled, "The bucket! Oh God." She upchucked two more times. It'd be dry retches soon.

I was patting speckles off her lips with the edge of my apron, no rag to hand, when Noah burst in.

Thank goodness! Thank goodness, too, Mistress was past caring about him bursting in. The storm stripped her of some power, acting as an equalizer.

"Huddle by," I said to Noah, whose face had gone ashy with fear.

"We'll be fine, tyke," Mistress managed to say, waving one hand, the way she do. "Just a rough patch. Better than the doldrums." She let out a little laugh, but it sounded wilted, like lettuce left out too long in the sun. Noah, I'm certain, didn't know what "doldrums" were and he didn't ask. Instead, he perched on the bunk opposite, knees up. I reached into my shoulder bag, the one that'd crossed my chest on the last journey too. I handed my Bible to Noah. "Psalm 23," I directed. A verse he'd read dozens and dozens of times. He fanned the pages to the spot and began to read, his voice clear.

"The Lord is my shepherd. I shall not want. He maketh me to lie down in green pastures. He leadeth me beside the still waters. He restoreth my soul."

Mistress echoed in a weak voice, "Still waters . . ." She knew Miss Eliza had taught me my letters, but I'm not sure she knew I'd passed my learning along. If it was news, she was too miserable to react. And maybe she needed the Good Word more than she needed to rally a nag. Seemed like the storm put her beyond worries of obedience and insurrection, what with the waves crashing, hungry for our lives, the sloop tipping in angry pitches.

Even in the middle of nature's fury, my heart split open in pride. How Noah's voice rang out, all the words finding his tongue. His tone like a church bell. "He leadeth me in the paths of righteousness for His name's sake."

The verse seemed to be settling Mistress until her eyes popped open and she called out, "The Lord wouldn't take me on my way to be reunited with Husband, would He? After all this time? After all my waiting?" She moaned. I shushed her and placed a cool hand on her forehead. Another wave slammed onto the deck, and its slurring return to the sea echoed me. "Ssh, ssh."

The Pond
Maggie, West of Wappoo

One little pool came and another, and my feet started sinking into mushy ground, telling me a swamp coming. By then I could smell it too. My fingers felt along the braid above my ear to where it turned up. Time to go to hard west. Out of my pocket, I pulled the last blue strip. I tied it on a twig at Mama-eye-height, like all the others. *She'll come, I know. She'll see it, I know.*

Late afternoon. Another lonely night on the way. After three days of walking, I hankered after company or even a fire, but it was still too soon for smoke. Wild plums soured my belly, first with gripping, then with trotting. One strip of turkey jerk left, from my own hunted bird, but it held no appeal. Thank goodness for the sweet benne wafers. Bless July!

I mostly liked the peace of no people pestering round – people with their tight shoulders, their secrets, cheeks lit up by a fire but showin' nothing, chests and backs netted with scars, stuff going on between legs. Some chittering along in noisy bubbles of cheer, like Phoebe. Others just closed up with hurt, like Abraham. But now? The slanting late-day light got me feeling wistful.

Wistful was a word my mama gave me.

I was tired. Maybe I could just sit right down in the brake ferns growing around the pond and wait. Then we could go to the Free Wilds together. *Free Wilds* – I so liked the sound of that. Even without a tallying conversation, Mama and me both rejected the word "maroons," what with it coming from Spanish, what with it sounding too much like skin color even though it wasn't that at all. It means wild, untamed. So why not say those words?

Do the Free Wilds sense me coming? What do they call themselves?

I thought about the swamp people, living free. I thought about sheltering silence and unbothered society and how they might sharpen inner eyes or change the dreamworld. I thought about having no driver, no overseer, and no line in the ledger, and how that might unshutter the soul so it can fly and hover – maybe comin' back to this pond, say, to enjoy its light-shaking beauty, or maybe just to sit and eat a bowl of food without fear. Such ordinary moments are miracles for a slave.

A crashing sound erupted across the pond. Trees here too small to climb. I unshouldered my bow, grabbed an arrow, nocked it, and sank into my knees just how Indian Pete taught. I pulled the string tight. Out of the scrub busted a wild boar. He was mostly in shadow, but I could see his grey furry body. He looked at me. He seemed uncertain. Like me. But those tusks. They caught the light. I couldn't let Mama find me with gut torn and face eaten, so I trained my eye on him.

That boar stared and I waited. My panicky breath slowed. The blue ribbon danced near my head. Hold still, blue ribbon! But he didn't much care. And then I saw why: a creaky crashing from behind. Out came four piglets – no, five –

tiny little beasts, fawn striping making them near to invisible in the dappled light. Eyes so perky at finding mama. How I felt them! How my eyes'll shine when I spy Mama. No way I was gonna kill a mama with young. I put my arrow away.

Meantime, Mama Boar decided I wasn't a bother and led her passel to the water. They tipped their heads down and drank, front feet in the pond, ringlets spreading off their snouts, catching light in curves. Somehow, this family of four-leggeds gave me hope. The light off the water aglitter with beauty.

The Map of Braids
Saffron, west of Wappoo

Tunic stunk of smoke and leftover smoke burned my throat. I ran. If patrollers pounded after me now, I was dead, Maggie motherless. I ran, ran through trees, past the hidden rope we used to tie 'cross the road to stop horses, past the fork to Hell Hole Swamp. I didn't hear Cane Creek calling to me yet, and Maggie'd gone quiet. She wasn't dead, I knew, because that knowing would lodge in my lungs and throat, an irrevocable and inescapable truth.

I had to stop from time to time, hobble a bit, but then I'd run again, cramp or no cramp. The bracken ferns snapped, shoulder bag banging on my hip. Chips of daylight fluttered through the leaves, but down where feet pounded earth, it'd gone dark already. Not velvet dark yet, but a furry, shadowed dark. It felt safe to slow.

I called out: *Daughter*. Nothing came back. Now it came sudden-dark. Sometimes night fell like that – with a slap, quick and hard. But sudden or no, the darkness hugged me, a sheltering friend to any slave on the run.

And then I saw one: an indigo ribbon. At first it seemed like a little wash of light. Scrub ghosts? But then the edges showed clear, and sure enough there it was, a blue strip tied to a branch. By Daughter's hand! Maybe I'd never find the second ribbon or the third, but I felt hope now.

My hands shook untying it. I traveled fingers to my head and read the map, the braid atop my left ear telling me to go west. The Choctaw trail coming soon. Good. Less branches snapping at my arms.

More time passed. Dark felt full, maybe it came midnight. No moon. We didn't plan that, but it was a help. I had to squat to pee, and then I moved away a bit and sat and ate four pecans. How it gave me strength knowing July'd scooped them out of the bin for me. Her steady hand and quiet giving ways. I didn't say goodbye. Once the bales in the barn flared, I had to run. *Goodbye, dear July.*

Before sleep drew down, I up and trotted. Calling out again in my mind, *Ewa, Ewa!* I checked the second turn of the braid closest to my left ear and it told me a Native trail was under my feet now. Probably won't find any ribbons for a while – but wait, I hear her now. Faint. Sweet. *Mama. You're coming!* Yes. Yes. I'm coming.

Peppered Radishes
July, Wappoo Plantation

Setting sun washed the pantry gold. After them gone, emptiness smothered every room hard, but then emptiness stepped aside for peace. It was a quiet free of fuss, the fixing of aprons, the faces of stone. No more forced courtesy, forced smiles. I leaned into the counter and sighed, and the house held me up in a way it never done before. Dust specks swirling a dance. Even they seemed glad they gone.

Three yellow mixing bowls left behind. "We're still here," they called. I picked out two of 'em and brought 'em back to the cabin. The big one, a new home for my threads. Look! They belong there! Tomorrow, I'd take a few clothes pins and wrap threads round 'em like bobbins and make order.

The small bowl was for Titus and the Ancestors. I set it down at the edge of the circle where he threw the opele. I'd fill it with chicken blood – not a gill, but a whole bowl. The dirt was swept clear now in preparation. I wondered two things, what would I learn and did I want to know?

Walking back, I pulled up a dozen radishes. Remembered the paper of pepper in my pocket. Abraham do like peppered radishes! At one of the fires, I mounded the ashes for ash cakes. Binah came round with a pile of sorrel collected on the way back from task. We'd have a dinner both common and usual, but brand new with absences.

The sky held a bit of day when I lay down. Til of late, I never done sleep in a cabin by myself. I didn't like it. Just as my eyes gone heavy, a squawk and flutter flash me to waking. A big ole crow clutched at the window sill, tipping his head one way, then the other.

"What?" He flapped off without answering, but left a glossy feather behind. Ah! It had to be a message from Maggie, the feather-collecting girl. Meaning she okay. I laid the feather in her hiding place and felt less lonely then.

Morning Three
Saffron, West of Wappoo

I came to a jewel of a pond. My heart got to racing when I saw shoe prints in the mud. She'd been here! I scrambled to the muddy rim and walked in circles round her prints as if my shoes sinking in the same mud as her shoes made for a reunion.

When my heart stilled, I pulled out the calabash ladle I'd brung, sat on my haunches, and drank. Sent my mind forward. The walking, dodging, bug-bite scratching, and hiding had narrowed my mind, forcing me to close my thoughts. Now I let 'em fly free. *Daughter! Where are you, Ewa, Beautiful One?*

I picked my way over to a sunken spot in the ferns a little way round the pond, mindful of snakes and gators. There I saw little hoofprints surrounding big hoofprints. Had Ewa seen these critters? The rummy smell of mud seemed like a potion for finding home. Close now.

Fog on the Water
Maggie, near Cane Creek

Sticky sky hanging low and bouncing sound about, scrambling direction. I paddled fast since going slow offered no gaining toward life. The paddle kerplashes so loud I worried who will hear and from how far away? Curls of mist kissed the reeds at the shore, cypress knees pokin' up like men bent in prayer, but were they praying for good or for evil? A thumping going in both temples, pulsing in time with something, but what? Whose side was this place on?

How sad if we flung off the iron of the Keepers just to be felled in the heat of escape. Mama sure is quiet, sitting behind me. How sweet our reunion was yesterday!

I'm used to the spooky oddities of a swamp because I sleep-walked to Hell Hole so many times. That giant, dank, oozing sunken place came across more like evil creature than hunk of geography, its residents clicking and plopping, rippling on the surface, crackling in the sedge. But here noises rush and echo, and I can't tell what's an inside rush, a watery twang of nerve, and what comes from outside – a chorus of reptile gods, a harping of demons. Nothing to do but keep paddling.

Mama whispers, "Ewa. Good speed!" The sounds coming from the banks smudged in fog unnerved me, so I handed her the paddles and pulled out an arrow. The feeling of being watched. Everything seemed so ghostlike, coming at us in tendrils of fog, as a disturbance of the night, a sticky hunger.

Arrow nocked, I pulled myself to my knees, scanned one way, the other. Mama sped up, a splashing commotion that might save us or speed our deaths. This was what running meant all along – salvation or death.

All of a sudden, we saw dark forms in front of us, arms waving, emerging out of the fog. A new banging, twanging commotion. Spoons? Dried calabash? Yes, they were our people, our new people, the Free Wilds, and they'd come to greet us.

I slid my arrow away. They splashed out and pulled our raft up onto mud – their raft, as I now understood. We hopped off. Six lifted the bound cypress logs and hid them in the brush, two others grabbed our hands and hurried us along. Not a time to talk. I let go and switched sides so that I could hold Mama's hand too. Some number of Free Wilds lingered at the water, blowing conches and rattling dried reeds. Others starting screeching like panthers, hooting like owls. Sounds bouncing and deceiving.

It had been them the whole time. The usual shifting menace of a swamp weren't enough to keep patrollers and ill-seekers away, so they made a creepy racket and spun a spooky confusion.

Someone would paddle the raft back for the next runaway and walk back round. For now, Mama's and my hands were locked as if for eternity. My bones went soft with relief. Mama let go my hand to touch her braids in gratitude. She went limp and the Free Wilds carried her -- celebration, not chore. I too let myself be carried. They carried us home. They carried us to freedom.

A Level Gaze
Melody, Cabbage Tree Plantation, Antigua

There were fifteen shelves in the pantry, one sugar cabinet (locked, of course), one hearth, two hogsheads – just like the other pantries. No shadow of sin here, though, at least not yet. Still, I checked on the knives and learned where I could stand and still reach them. Some memories die hard.

On the other side of the door, Mistress and Master laughed, or rather, she gurgled and he guffawed. Polly and Phoebe already run off. What had changed and what stayed the same? Noah was out back shining Master's boots. Tea was being made by others in the Summer Kitchen across the yard. I wasn't asked to help, and just as well, since I wasn't ready to be bossed about by strangers or poked with questions or ignored.

Eventually, the others would want to know what Mistress was like – did she trick and prod Master to punish, did she still have her monthlies, what soothings worked on bad days?

Noah didn't know how close we were to his birthplace, Barbados, but he could see the differences from the Lowcountry – a turquoise sea dazzling all around and cliffs and bluffs and swells instead flat marsh stretching to the horizon. I could feel the ghost of Tommy prowling around. I knew he wasn't dead, just living yet in England, but this was the place where Noah started clinging on him like he was a gift from the gods. They say he'll sail home soon enough.

Master's attentive to Mistress. When I spied him lighting his pipe, he was glancing at her, not at me. What relief! Maybe he was looking to see how stout she'd become, or looking in order to remember some old feelings of love. It really didn't matter to me as long as he kept his eyes off of me. He had a mood about him, like he'd been run into the ground and left to wither in the sun. Like he was up and about after a bath but not really revived. I didn't pretend to understand why since he had a fine military post -- lieutenant governor and all. A mahogany and porcelain life. His family back, for the most part.

They dragged me to church supposedly to look after Polly, but she needs no looking after. When the Mistress's lips formed the syllables "hallelujah," a wrench in my stomach twisted hard. Such blasphemy. A Keeper singing "hallelujah" shouldn't be allowed.

Blasphemy was a word I applied to their ledgers too. Saffron taught me the word.

All along the harbor front gulls, pelicans, and vultures went about their business, satisfying their hunger. Why couldn't buckra be more like them? Eating and consuming just enough, not straying into the unholy ways of greed. The gulls cried, the pelicans filled their gullets, and the vultures lurched along. But buckra stuffed their larders, hoarded sterling, and collected bodies.

Nana Lucy promised she would find somebody to scribe a letter from Philadelphia. The trickery was that it'd be sent to Polly and also mailed from New York instead of Pennsylvania. It would say empty things, but with a code agreed on ahead of time. Polly and Mistress would puzzle on it, for sure, but I would know the meaning. Waiting on that letter is one of the hardest things I've ever done. How was I to fill the time with anything but imagined catastrophe? Was my boy dead? Did Nana Lucy walk the streets of Philadelphia a free woman, or had she been coffled and shipped south?

Here I was, back in the West Indies, feeling used up and old, one boy at my side, one flung in a northern direction. Mistress looked younger than she did two years ago, with color in her cheeks and a ready laugh. She was glad of the move. She may never see Miss Eliza again, but at least she left her in good hands.

I was twenty-two or twenty-three years old. My apron pressed stiff, my gaze level. The bell clanged. Time to serve the afternoon sherry.

Remembering Ginger Wine
July, Wappoo Plantation

The twigs fall down into the embers, disturbing ash. Watch my cakes! Tickling wind at my neck makes me turn round to see. Could it be the Ancestors calling me home? Or maybe they's trying to hold me up.

I am left behind. I rub sore knuckles, then pull ash cakes out of the fire. I remember them high-flyin' flavors – tortoise bisque, blancmange, ginger wine, tomato jellies. Things gone by.

Even though 'twas evening and not my custom, I counted Five Blessings. Like takin' medicine, I suppose. Finger touched thumb to count the first – fire. Such a great blessing, fire. Small fires to cook on and mighty fires to burn down barns. Fires for nurturance and fires for vengeance. They still haven't raised it up. A charred badge of freedom. How I love to walk past it every morning! Blessing two: the smell of earth. Cool and wet this evening. Three – always my boys: Quaquosh, Obajani, and Ganda. Four – sleep with no dreams. Five – how morning come. The body stepping into a day even if the mind got other ideas. I'll press my apron for an empty house.

Epilogue
July 1758

Return
Eliza, Wappoo Plantation

July 12, 1758: a date forever to be tarred by grief. He went like a lamb into eternity, my Charles, with the most perfect resignation to the will of his God. Small comfort. In the days following his burial, how oft I reflected on his virtues – the clearness of his head, his sweet temper, the amiableness of his entire deportment. I did not know a virtue, in fact, that he did not possess – and now, he was gone. Forever. I'd spent the last week spilling ink in service of sharing the bad news. Never have I blotched so much paper with tears and yet it soothed me to think on his many graces.

The fever of malaria had seemed trivial at first and I didn't worry. After all, Mother had ridden the waves of the disease with a seasonal regularity that made the condition seem inconveniencing at worst. Charles's fever, however, took a deadly turn after just a few weeks, and consumed him. To think that for fourteen years I was the happiest mortal on Earth!

He'd been so glad to see his horse, Chickasaw – old now, of course, but with no less affectionate a regard. We'd gone to Belmont on our fourth afternoon back from England, but the sentimental tour had been cut short by a piercing headache, and the next day he took to bed.

For the first time since our Guinea set sail from England – a lifetime ago! – I thanked the Lord that we'd left the boys behind. It had been so difficult to say farewell to little Charles Cotesworth and our Tommy, of course, but at least they'd been spared the sight of their father's rapid decline. His hectic face. His breathy responses.

Not so, Harriott. With such tenderness, sweet Daughter had placed wet cloths upon his forehead. Murmured that God loved him. Held his hand. She turns eleven next month and I doubt there'll be an ounce of celebration between us.

And what about in years to come? The count will burden her. *If I'm fourteen, that means he's been gone for four years. If seventeen, he's been gone seven.* And so on, for the rest of her life.

The sight of the charred ground where formerly our barn stood brought back memories of a different sort. For some reason, I recalled the sweet Saffron, the one who smiled in my mirror after handing me my lace tucker. The one who tugged Polly's plaits into place. I remembered how her shadow had crossed the street one restless night so long ago, Indian Pete's soon after.

Where was she? And Maggie? Were they together? Alive? I suspected that Indian Pete went after them but would likely never know for sure.

Earlier I left jasmine on July's grave. I now understood that she'd been the beating heart of our household, a steady thrum that brought nourishment and comfort to us all, and I refer to more than her expertly prepared dishes, delivered in seasoned near-silence.

A Mouse Appears
Mo, Wappoo Plantation

It was better without them. Daughter Nanka been sayin' Mistress crying upstairs, waving a hand for tea, too done in by grief, it seem, to ask proper – not even giving up the slim voice or bell yank needed. And sharpening quills? Poor Nanka broke a few. What'd she know 'bout them?

Nanka wasn't yet born when the Lucas family first come – flush with greed for the sterling rice'd bring, all English in blustery self-regard. But I recalled. The household jealousies with Melody, the burning calico dress, the society parties.

I got my own ghosts to abide. Like Quashee, where he at now? All them years back, he done gone to the peninsula to build Mistress and Master Pinckney a palace on East Bay. Three stories. All the frills. Then Master Pinckney done freed Quash and Quash went under the waters of baptism and came up "John Williams." He'd saved coin, smart man, and got Reverend Alexander Gardner to help him buy plots of land – the very man who'd baptized him, by the by.

Quashee, I mean John, didn't need no help buying up a few slaves, including two of his three daughters. His wife he bought and then freed. But then he disappeared. Some say he went north to the Santee where he owned more land. But I suspect a hard-hearted buckra murdered him in a fit of spite. Maybe to steal his land. Maybe just to give the message: *Know your place, boy!*

Indian Pete, Saffron, and Maggie like as not still alive. Fourteen years done pass since they up and went. Melody sailed back south near to where she born. She'd be round about thirty-five today, if my adding right. Still beautiful, I reckon.

It being past conch, I wandered up the hill past Porch House. A first star pricked above the woodshed. I entered the gate into the graveyard and knelt. July had joined Benjie and James two years back, and we missed her still. She done kept herself to herself, a proud woman. Seem as how she lived by some steadying principle. If it was faith, it was a private faith. I took a pinch of dirt off the grave mound like I always did, asking the soil of her resting place to teach me something.

Crouching on my haunches, I felt the long muscles of my back curving toward remembrance, a sacred thing, but I was also tired. The sun been especial hot these past days.

A creature rustled near the woodpile. A mouse? If July gonna show herself, figured she'd come forward as a humble creature, one easy to overlook. Damn if that rodent didn't stop on the top log and turn and stare. Some magic was afoot. I breathed slow, making a big empty space between air coming in and air going out, and waited. And then I heard: "Five blessings."

I didn't understand. The mouse still staring. "What?"

And then I heard more: "Count five blessings. Every day. Trust me." The mouse disappeared into the woodpile, job done. I headed back to the street, a lightness in my step. Something passed on. Wait 'til I tell Binah. I'd count her as the first blessing each and every day.

Sabrina
Eliza, Charles Town and Belmont Plantation

Toward the end of July, Harriott and I traveled up the peninsula to attend to estate matters with my lawyer. Sweet daughter could not abide any separations right now, and I was not about to impose any, so she sat by my side as I arranged for Bills of Exchange to be sent to the boys' guardian in England, then signed this paper and that. A colossal tedium for a child, but I understood that boredom was preferable to feeling frightened and lonely. As for me, every testamentary detail reminded me that my esteemed husband, gallant friend, and the father of my children was no more.

Back on the street, Harriott and I assumed a brisk pace, as if to outrun our losses. There was a white dust coating some of the shop windows, and it puzzled me until I remembered that the Assembly had directed that a tabby wall be built just north of us as a defense against the French and Indians. A passel of slaves passed on the street's opposite side, the oddity of their black skin covered in white tabby dust making us both stare. I grabbed Harriott's hand and pulled her close.

We reached the office of the *Gazette* where I dashed in to deliver the probate notice. Moments later we were off to Belmont to visit Charles's nephew, also called Charles.

Mrs. Crokus greeted us at the door, grinning at Harriott, who I suppose reminded her of Polly. Since Charles's paralytic stroke, she'd acted as his caretaker, tending to his every need. Moving him from room to room, propping the dead arm up with pillows, rubbing his legs. Even though I'd seen him at the funeral, my breath caught to see his stroke-ravaged face again.

Mrs. Crokus seemed to want to cheer Daughter, so she took her out to the barn to see a litter of puppies. And anyway, Charles and I had business to discuss: crops, property managers, slave holdings. After a while, he gave me a look of sympathy, or at least I think he did. His losses were great too, of course, his uncle and mentor gone, his body no longer compliant.

"I am not planning to sell off our Lowcountry properties anymore," I said.

"So, you'll be . . ." Charles started.

"Staying. Yes," I learned to fill in.

"Please try Hannah's rice bread. It suits the tongue." In closing he offered up a caustic critique of city leadership. "As if a wall will keep out the natives. Has the Assembly forgotten that we hire them to sleuth runaways?" I think he meant "to track," but never mind. I had wondered about the wall too. We occupied a peninsula, after all and our pettiaugers were designed after Indian flatboats – almost all mercantile traffic coming and going by water. Why would the French or Indians come by land?

"Mark my words. The Creeks and Cherokees will join ranks against us."

A line of spittle trailed down Charles's face. When he went to lift a napkin with his good hand, he nearly toppled the teapot. I lurched to catch it. He let me take the napkin and dab off his chin. It was a tender moment, one that held his loss, my loss, and our mutual continuing.

Harriott burst into the parlor with a puppy in her arms. She'd always been a quiet child, unlike Polly and her spontaneous tumults, and since her father's death even more so, so this was a surprise. "This is Sabrina," she announced, her face aglow with adoration.

The fact that my somewhat timid, rule-abiding child was asserting a claim without first seeking my permission gave me a quotient of hope. Life had said no to Harriott by taking her father. She was to be denied his kind patience, his wisdom, his tender love. He would not be wishing her happy birthday when she turned eleven. But my daughter would adopt a puppy and name her Sabrina! A new comrade in adventure, a cuddler in chief. Perhaps it was a lot of weight for a small hound to bear, but that afternoon Sabrina served as a potent symbol for the conferral of grace in the midst of grief.

Proclamation
Moses, Philadelphia

The print shop at dawn. How it felt like home, if a runaway slave passing as a white man can ever really know home. The smell of straw and ink, shelves full of type and paper – proof of industry. A life with purpose. Every morning stretched in quiet, a quiet that I claimed – unless it was Tuesday. Delivery day.

Each week, his whistling announced his arrival. Since I was nearly always already awake, the whistling came as the morning's melody, welcome, but it was so sweet even those woken by it, I'd heard, rose with a smile. Ah, Jacob.

From the threshold, I waved. His nag perked to see me. Dobbin's eagerness likely arose from the scent of carrot in my pocket and not in response to the condition of my soul; nevertheless it was a warming appraisal.

Jacob drew a long breath. "I smell rain. After lunch, I 'spect." One suspender had slipped, and he tugged it up before hopping down and grabbing the first bale of hay off the back of the wagon. Six piled next to the door – an inventory of food for my boss's horse, but also material to scatter under the press in the evening, moisture being no friend to metal parts. Six bales made some kind of income for a free black too – how much, I wondered.

Like many vendors working the streets, Jacob was a repository of news. And like most efficient gossips, he knew to ask first, tell second. "What cheer, Moses?"

"Waiting," I said simply.

"Ah, yes. You, me, the populace," Jacob said, and then gave me a sly look, one I'd never seen on him before. "The Quakers and their silences." He shook his head.

"They should have voted by now." But I knew from the print shop's customer Anthony Benezet that the Quakers decided nothing quickly. Everything by consensus. Benezet had been making his case all week at their Yearly Meeting.

"However long it do take, it'll take," Jacob said with the wry wisdom of a man used to not getting what he wanted. That suspender slipped again. Before hopping back up on his dray, before sliding that strap atop his shoulder, he gave me that sly look again.

We were both of us eager to hear whether the Quakers would accept Benezet's proclamation against slavery. A firm and sweeping position. A proclamation which would be printed into a pamphlet and sent out for all of Philadelphia and beyond to read – the very words to be set by my fingers in the shop at my back.

"Maybe matters more –" Jacob hesitated and then nodded a quick nod as if some internal decision had been made. "Maybe matters more for your folk than for you."

I looked him square in the eye. It happened all the time. A black stranger holding my gaze a breath too long, an eyebrow raised, a nod proffered. Recognition. Though deception lived at the very center of my survival, I felt I could trust Jacob. Unlike some tellers of tales, it seemed to me that Jacob was also a keeper of secrets. A little smile tugged at my face, which he returned with a broad grin.

"It's the hair, to start," he leaned in to say, touching his own tight curls. "I don't need to tell you."

Indeed, he did not. I wore my black hair pulled back in a ponytail, but in the humidity that hugged and near to smothered Philadelphia in July, the short hairs that framed my forehead coiled, disobedient. Whites as a rule did not notice, or if they did, draw any conclusions. Not even schoolmaster Benezet with his singular focus on the betterment of the Negro race had noticed, even though the man had been teaching Negro boys in his home for eight years by then.

Up went the strap. Up hopped the man and off they went at a trot. A little salute, saying not just, "'Til next week" but also, "Your secret is safe with me, brother."

Brother, indeed. As far as I know, the Lucases never did publish any notices on me, offering a reward, triggering the slave hunter's ruthless drive. They didn't send any trackers either, else wouldn't I have been found? Captured, bound, returned to South Carolina? Like Jacob, Mama knew a thing or two about keeping secrets. The letters she received from my guardian, Nana Lucy, and later from me, went sealed to a friend in New York before being mailed to Antigua. They only spoke in code.

Jacob's knowing, very nearly tender in complexity, seemed a perfect way to begin a day when I would find out that the Quakers approved an anti-slavery proclamation. Tears of joy. Hallelujah! Hugging that kind-faced Huguenot-turned Quaker, I trembled to think that I was to be part of history. The call to end slavery and not just the trading but the owning. Right here in this small print shop with its metal press, its trays of type, the stinky inks and velvety papers, it would be my fingers spelling, condemning. Here in this year 1758, when I was nineteen about to turn twenty, freedom would be my remit.

I could conjure no greater birthday gift – except, of course, to see Mama and Noah again. The constant ache of that.

To think that at my birth on Wappoo Plantation nearly twenty years ago, the sight of me as a newborn babe, as pale as the full moon I was born under, nearly caused the Mistress to faint. So I was told. No father named. Mama mum until eventually it became clear I was fathered by a lanky sugar grower from Barbados. Whittaker. James.

Later that very day, Benezet would write out the pamphlet's title on a scrap: "Observations on the Enslaving, Importing, and Purchasing of Negroes / An Anti-Slavery Almanac." I would query him about the term "almanac," but Benezet would insist, saying Ben Franklin had popularized the term and we might as well use it.

Holding that slip in my hand, it would occur to me how good might arise out of oppression. Think on it. If the French Catholics had not harassed Benezet's family and others, the Huguenots would have remained in their villages – in Anthony's case, Antoine then, plying a linen trade. Drinking wine, perhaps of his family's own making. Burying their dead next to their ancestors. But because of the ceaseless, arbitrary, and pitiless acts of one group against another, here he was – a spokesman for the future, a beacon of light.

Perhaps to scoop up black children and invite them into his home for classes, he had to have a history like that. Acquainted with abuses of power. I didn't know. To look at his face was to see a boundless and unfeigned kindness, so maybe history had nothing to do with it.

In any case, on that fateful day I decided that no matter how tempted, I would not reveal to the abolitionist my true status, not only that I was black, but that I was a runaway slave. No matter how much I might've liked to say, "You advocate on my behalf," to see the surprise, possibly a warming pleasure. The risks could not be borne. Jacob, another black man wending his way through the streets of Philadelphia, was one thing. A white man with a following and a cause, perhaps in need of a totem, was another. I'd be a pony on a leash. Worse yet, what if Benezet, in spite of all his good deeds and his abolitionist frame of mind, found me exemplary and more suitable to be upheld to the public because of my pale skin, my ability to ape white speech, and my literacy? It would say more about Benezet than me, of course, but I was not about to give the great Huguenot-turned-Quaker a chance to so thoroughly disappoint me.

Her Lips
Ewa, Cane Creek

Brother tagged along like a shadow. Mostly I didn't mind, but this morning his sweet cheer was interfering. "My turn, my turn," he chirped. But it wasn't his turn. My bow creased Cinnamon's face. She pulled her fist back. I stood near and straightened her arm with a slight, uplifting touch. My knees went wavy. I was teaching her to shoot. Any excuse to stand close.

Every now and again, my little brother's easy ways irked me. Like now. The contrast to the hard fate I'd endured. How he padded about – a right little prince. Oh, he was afraid of snakes and thunderstorms, of the treacherous bogs that'd suck a body under, but he had no acquaintance with sea captains trading and raping flesh, overseers corralling black bodies and exercising "discipline," or with bloodthirsty hounds whose owners starved them to intensify the chase. Except for bug bites, his skin was smooth. Nobody slammed him into years of silence. If only. "My turn, my turn!"

"Pull it tighter," he piped.

Cinnamon was a little younger than me, and she could follow me all she wanted. Talking, silent, whatever she chose. Being a mustee like Indian Pete, she had rusty-red skin, and that's why she was called Cinnamon. Both Mama and she were named for exotic spices: Cinnamon and Saffron. I liked that.

Last year, the community "came by" a horse, and by "came by" I mean that Bellfast rode in on it, stolen years and years back from Silk Hope Plantation on the Edisto River. Both the horse and the man wore "TW" on their skin – Bellfast just below his collarbone, the roan on her haunch. "TW" for Thomas Wright.

When he first came, Bellfast looked about with wild eyes, wearing sticks in his hair, unaccustomed to people. He was nine when he lit out from the plantation on the Edisto some twenty years ago. He told how he headed toward Florida but not why he didn't keep on going. For some reason, the Savannah River stopped him. Maybe he couldn't find the crossing-place for horses. Maybe in his short life he'd grown fond of the Lowcountry – the egrets, bog rice, and the charge of air before a lightning storm. In any case, with only his horse for company, he camped, foraged, and stayed hidden. Eventually, something drove him west and then north, landing him here.

Bellfast had big ears and a slow manner, but he was no clown. In fact, he had layers to him, layers not everybody saw, but I did. He had both mystery and charm and a real knack for disappearing. He was generous and a little older than me. I saw Mama looking at us when we talked.

Though he and his horse were closer than most couples, he let me ride her. In exchange, after Indian Pete equipped him, I taught him how to nock the arrow, how to pull the string, how to aim. We chased down squirrels and boar together and deer when they were fat in the fall. He was like an older brother to me. Hugging close from behind on the horse, going to speed along the berm, gripping him and horse hard, I was exhilarated. But not by him. Rather it was the wind and the light flashing between trees and the rushing whisper of the name *Cinnamon*. Her name was a promise, a note, a half-dream, a tingle between the thighs.

Try as I might, I could not hear her thoughts. It seemed unfair. She was kind to all, and such wide, sweet care made her special – but what did she think of me? I could just be one among many.

That day, to show Cinnamon the proper grip, I stood behind her and grabbed the bow, pulled the string with her. Warmth spilled at my navel, my lips grew dry. Did she notice? Brother kept on like a jumping bean, begging for a turn. Twang, she let loose the arrow. It went wide, missing the practice tree and lodging into the one beside instead. I grinned and praised. She grinned and accepted praise. My brother scampered to fetch the arrow.

"Peanut." I used his pet name, partly to hide my irritation, partly to grab his attention. "Go tell Mama we'll be bringing squirrel home for dinner." He handed me the arrow and scampered off. It hurt a little to play on his gullibility, but even his innocence was interfering.

I had promised to return the horse by sundown. Now that it was just Cinnamon and me, the afternoon stretched wide, precious, and full of possibility. We would ride along the berm to where cypress and hickories ringed the bog. Squirrels galore there. I'd sit in front. She behind. She'd have to hold on tight.

Maybe she'd lean her face against my back. Maybe during a galloping stretch, she'd squeal and I'd lose my mind with imaginings.

And after we stopped, and after I helped her dismount, I might lean in to tuck her mussed up hair behind first one ear, then the other. Our faces close. Her beautiful tawny lips near mine. Oh, Cinnamon. I might lean in again, this time for a kiss.

Author's Note

When I started writing this novel, Trayvon Martin was alive, and when I finished the second draft, George Floyd was not. A lot happened in those intervening years. The nation changed. I changed. Researching slavery while also learning about redlining, mass incarceration, Jim Crow, and police brutality made me aware of what Black people everywhere in America have always known: the original sin of slavery is alive and well in our nation. This is, in fact, who we are.

I am a white woman who quilts and writes. In the spring of 2011, like many other fiber artists, I started dyeing cloth with indigo. In India Flint's book *Eco Colour*, I came across a reference to Eliza Lucas Pinckney, who pioneered the cultivation of indigo on her father's South Carolina plantation in the mid-eighteenth century. Soon after, I picked up a copy of Eliza's letters, and scenes from her point of view started materializing during my weekly writing classes. Her family's life -- their wealth, their comfort, Eliza's harpsichord lessons -- was made possible by her grandfather's money and by enslaved labor. But there is scant mention of the people her father enslaved in Eliza's letters. I wondered, What were their lives like? Answering that question prompted years of research and several trips to Charleston.

In spite of an ever-growing awareness of how my whiteness was problematic, I found that I was writing a novel set in colonial South Carolina with one white central character and three main enslaved characters.

This novel is part of an ongoing learning process. During the years of its writing, I offended more than a few with my arrogance and ignorance. Tried to do better. Failed. Tried again. Learned to shut up and listen. Sort of. More than once, I nearly gave up this project.

On the one hand, there's this old idea that every author is entitled to write about whatever they want. The supremacy of the imagination, if you will. The value of empathy. On the other hand, there's the powerful argument that white writers ought to leave Black subjects and characters alone. Good intentions are not enough (see critiques of Kathryn Bigelow's film *Detroit*). At the same time, avoiding Black characters in Southern historic work is shameful (listen to critiques of Sofia Coppola's Civil War film *The Beguiled* on the podcast *Still*

Processing, hosted by Jenna Wortham and Wesley Morris). And anyway, how dare I?

Where does imagination end and cultural appropriation begin?

Then there is the problem of white people's attachment to Black pain, a phenomenon labeled "the Black death spectacle" by Claudia Rankine (see *The White Card*). Even if Black characters are shown as resilient and with the capacity for joy and rebellion, large and small, no novel about slavery can avoid referencing the gruesome and relentless infliction of pain on Black bodies and psyches. Another problem arises if said novel earns money, for then the white author literally profits from Black subjugation.

Both Roxane Gay and Colson Whitehead have expressed the view that imaginative and empathic leaps across lines of gender and race by writers are fine so long as they're done well. Hardly encouraging to a first-time novelist, but in spite of a lot of hand-wringing and for reasons I can't quite explain, I kept at it. And as I kept at it, the Black characters who inhabit these pages gained voice, clarity, and authority. To this day, I can't say if continuing was a function of art or a stubborn refusal to put down something I'd invested so much time in. Of the many mistakes I've made in my life, I really hope this novel is not one of them.

About voice. For Eliza, the main white character, I always wrote in the first person. For the three enslaved characters, however, I started in third person and didn't switch to first person until I had been writing this story for five years or so. At the outset I thought a third person narration built in a respectful distance. While wrestling with this issue, I attended a poetry reading in Concord, Massachusetts, where I briefly met Tisa Bryant, author and educator. During a quick exchange at her book signing, she said something about how "these voices are coming through all kinds of people" and without knowing me or my work suggested that I use the first person for all my characters. I took her advice. Bryant helped me reach a point where refusing the Black women their intimate voices seemed an act, not of respect, but of cowardice.

The reader pretty much has to suspend a need for historic speech when it comes to the Black characters in this novel. To begin with, we don't really know how a field laborer or a house slave in 1738 would have sounded. Slave narratives produced by literate Black writers came later, and the WPA narratives of the 1930's, while invaluable, were collected by white people, meaning that memories of slavery were being told by former slaves or their descendants to white people with clipboards. Even though the Gullah/Geechee language is alive and well in the Lowcountry and some of its unique grammatical features are easily found online, I didn't attempt to incorporate those features in any systematic way because I lacked the skill to do so convincingly.

Given these considerations, it's clear that Melody, Saffron, and July utter words they would not have known or spoken. Melody, the only house slave born on this side of the Atlantic, has the most formal speech. Further, because I place her next to her first owner's daughter during language lessons on Barbados, she also knows some French. July's been in the Lowcountry for over a decade but is stoic and reserved and doesn't speak all that much, so of the three main Black characters, her speech is the most pared down. Saffron has recently made the Middle Passage and therefore initially her words are meant to be her native tongue in translation. After she's been in South Carolina for a while, her voice "switches" to English, but an elevated English because Saffron is a poet. She soaks up vocabulary like a sponge, even as she is conflicted about it -- English is, after all, the language of her oppressors. But the musicality of speech in all its variations wins her over and she greedily acquires words, eventually thinking in terms that reveal her poetic nature. It's a conceit that I hope the reader can accept for purposes of understanding this character's complex sensibility.

Now and then, a secondary character speaks, particularly to relate the events of the Stono Slave Rebellion. I found this departure necessary since none of my main characters were there.

I have opted not to use the n-word. Though historically correct, it wasn't going to add anything of value and as a white person I didn't think it my right. I didn't capitalize the B in Black either, though I now do so everywhere else. The word *buckra* refers to white people, and my Black characters rely on the term, even though it may have come later and may have been more generally used to describe poor white people.

About land ownership, a quick preview: during South Carolina's transition from a proprietorship to a royal colony, land was pretty much up for grabs. An aspiring planter could survey a plot, file papers at the courthouse (deemed a "memorializing"), and take possession without even paying taxes immediately. How much land a person could legally memorialize was based on "head rights." The more people in one's family or on one's ledgers, the more acreage one could memorialize. Slaves partially counted for this purpose, so it was strategic to invest first in slaves, if possible, and second in land.

As a New Englander, I was somewhat surprised at how sumptuous the lives of the elite South Carolina planters were (when they weren't smothered by heat or dying of the pox or yellow fever, that is). Historian Peter Wood called South

Carolina "a colony of a colony," referring to the fact that so many settlers to the Lowcountry had come from Barbados. The lure of the "easy wealth of rice," paired with the recognition that growing sugar required large operations, brought many small sugar plantation owners to South Carolina. During their tenure in the West Indies, these Barbadian slave owners had lived like royalty -- extravagant and decadent entertainments, Parisian fashion, antiques shipped from Europe – and they brought their lavish lifestyle with them, shaping culture for generations.

The early West Indian colonizers brought the Barbadian Slave Code as well, a particularly draconian set of rules which would be made even more restrictive and punitive after the Stono uprising in 1739.

Many events and characters in this book are based on history, but it is a work of fiction. Timelines have been compressed for dramatic purposes and some white names changed to avoid confusion (how many Sarah's, Elizabeth's, and Mary's can one novel contain?). Personalities were created out of whole cloth. It's important to note, however, that some of the most egregious examples of brutality committed by slave owners are based on primary sources. Also, many of the events in Eliza's life come from the record. For those who are interested, please find History Notes and a bibliography on my website, deemallon.com.

I am particularly indebted to the following books for context: *The River Flows On: Black Resistance, Culture, and Identity Formation in Early America* by Walter C. Rucker; *Stono: Documenting and Interpreting a Southern Slave Revolt*, edited by Mark M. Smith; *Charleston in the Age of the Pinckneys*, by George C. Rogers, Jr.; *Black Majority* by Peter Wood; *Sugar in the Blood: A Family's Story of Slavery and Empire* by Andrea Stuart; *Home by the River* by Archibald Rutledge (I based the character Indian Pete on Prince Alston, as described in the memoir); *Red, White, and Black Make Blue: Indigo in the Fabric of Colonial South Carolina Life* by Andrea Feeser (particularly for historic details about Quashee aka John Williams); *The Letterbook of Eliza Lucas Pinckney*. Also: *Cry Liberty: The Great Stono River Slave Rebellion of 1739* by Peter Charles Hoffer (though I reject his premise that the uprising was an opportunistic event); *Out of the House of Bondage* by Thavolia Glymph (especially for the historically-based cruelty imparted upon Eubeline); *Closer to Freedom: Enslaved Women & Everyday Resistance in the Plantation South* by Stephanie M.H. Camp. The story of William and Ellen Craft as told in *The Great Escapes, Four Slave Narratives* provided the basis for one of the runaway schemes at the novel's conclusion.

During my three visits to Charleston, I toured Magnolia Plantation (big house and slave cabins), Drayton Hall, Middleton Plantation, Boone Hall Plantation, McLeod Plantation, and the Aiken-Rhett House. I was lucky to visit at a time when docents were beginning to reference and honor the Black people who had lived at these sites. I also spent a weekend in a pole barn in Ravenel learning indigo-dyeing techniques from Donna Hardy of Sea Island Indigo and Kathy Hattori of Botanical Colors. Interestingly, Rebellion Farm, who hosted the weekend, was so named because it's ground that the Stono rebels may have crossed on their way south. Further, the indigo we used traced its provenance to Eliza. I can't not mention the food. We were treated to an Ossabaw pig roasted overnight by farm-owner, Tim Allen, as well as a delicious array of side dishes prepared by the now renowned Gullah Chef B.J. Dennis.

Let me finish by referring back to indigo. Dyeing with this plant is a finicky process in which a number of elements must be balanced in order to achieve a cohered batch – acidity, aeration, temperature. It's an apt metaphor for a white writer crafting a narrative with Black characters. Many elements must cohere to create a credible story – empathy grounded in historic research, avoidance of obnoxious tropes (like the kind slave owner or the over-sexualized Black woman), referencing brutality without resorting to gratuitous violence. If the elements are met, the result is gorgeous blue cloth. Or perhaps, a readable novel.

Acknowledgements

I have to first thank my husband, Ken Potochnik, without whom this book would not exist. Not only did he financially support me during all the years of its writing, he kept faith in the story even when I was ready to throw in the towel.

To editor extraordinaire, Joy Johannessen, I owe a large debt of gratitude. She separated the wheat from the chaff and helped me believe that this was a novel. Over many years, Deb Lacativa provided close edits, with important insights about character, mood, and word choices. I can't thank her enough. Same for Belinda Edwards whose careful reading afforded me critical insight. Such generosity! To the many other readers over the years – Pat Kelly, Diane Linshaw, Joan Thompson, Ginny Mallon, Josh and Lisa Eaton to name a few -- thank you!

Thank you to Kathleen Olesky for her Thursday writing workshop where most of these chapters originated. That structure and her steady support as well as the enthusiasm of the other writers in the group have meant the world to me.

Thanks go to Maureen Buchanan Jones who as a writer, workshop leader, Amherst Writers and Artists trainer, and all-round mensch inspires me no end.

To Barbara Zilber, a woman of extraordinary heart and vision, whose faith in me mattered more than I can say -- profound thanks. Tuesday Group participants as well. You know who you are. Sarah G. Cuetara gets a special shout out for her invaluable support about self-publishing.

Thanks to Donna Hardy (Sea Island Indigo) and Kathy Hattori (Botanical Colors) for a memorable indigo-dyeing weekend in 2014 and also to all the generous friends who contributed to the kickstarter campaign that partially funded my trip. Thanks to Joseph McGill, founder of The Slave Dwelling Project, and the Royall House and Slave Quarters in Medford, Mass., for hosting an eye-opening overnight. (The Royalls were contemporaries of the Lucases). Also thanks to the young man at the Avery Research Center in Charleston for making me a copy of the 1740 Slave Code and directing me to the library where I could find *The South Carolina Gazette* archive.

To Ginny Mallon and *The Fat Canary Journal*, my profound thanks for a stipend to attend a writing retreat in Assisi, Italy at the Arte Studio Ginestrelle. What a memorable experience! Marina Merli could not have been more welcoming.

To the writers in my Tuesday Workshop, what can I say -- who knew a pandemic would help create a bi-coastal writing group of such caliber? I am so grateful for Sue Harmon, Martha Thayer, Olaitan Valerie, Claire Chaffee, and Lesli Turock.

To the active readers of my blog over the years, our conversations have meant everything to me. Race, art, politics – nothing was off-limits. You were willing to learn along with me and offered ongoing and important encouragement. Thank you!

I would also like to thank just a few of the creatives whom I don't know but whose work shaped my thinking and inspired me in recent years: Tisa Bryant, Robin Coste-Lewis, James McBride, Ta-Nehisi Coates, Sue Monk Kidd, Marlon James, Lawrence Hill, Margaret Wrinkle, Claudia Rankine, Octavia Butler, Isabel Wilkerson, Annette Gordon-Reed, Sadeqa Johnson, Jamaica Kincaid, Sonya Clark, Jesmyn Ward, Maggie O'Farrell, Jabari Asim, Colum McCann, Colson Whitehead, Geraldine Brooks, Danielle Dutton, and Bryan Stevenson.

To my parents, though both long gone, their beliefs in the value of education generally and in me specifically, still hold sway. I miss them.

And last but not least, thanks go to my boys, Cary and Danny, for all the lessons on love.

About the Author

Dee Mallon is a fiber artist and writer who lives outside of Boston with her husband and dog. She has two grown sons. Former lives include: copywriter, lawyer, community gardener, and quilting instructor. Currently, she makes collages and quilts and teaches writing workshops. Her website is deemallon.com and Instagram uses her middle initial, @deeamallon. *The Weight of Cloth* is her debut novel.